Con...
of a **Red Herring**

Confessions of a Red Herring

DANA DRATCH

KENSINGTON PUBLISHING CORP.
www.kensingtonbooks.com

KENSINGTON BOOKS are published by
Kensington Publishing Corp.
119 West 40th Street
New York, NY 10018

All Kensington titles, imprints, and distributed lines are available at special quantity discounts for bulk purchases for sales promotions, premiums, fund-raising, educational, or institutional use. Special book excerpts or customized printings can also be created to fit specific needs. For details, write or phone the office of the Kensington sales manager: Kensington Publishing Corp., 119 West 40th Street, New York, NY 10018, attn: Sales Department; phone 1-800-221-2647.

This book is a work of fiction. Names, characters, businesses, organizations, places, events, and incidents either are the product of the author's imagination or are used fictitiously. Any resemblance to actual persons, living or dead, events, or locales is entirely coincidental.

ISBN-13: 978-1-4967-1656-9
ISBN-10: 1-4967-1656-6

First printing: June 2018

10 9 8 7 6 5 4 3 2 1

Printed in the United States of America

First electronic edition: June 2018

ISBN-13: 978-1-4967-1657-6
ISBN-10: 1-4967-1657-4

For my Mom, who always gives great advice.
(But only when I ask.)

Chapter 1

I felt zero guilt for calling in sick Monday. "Sick of work" would have been more accurate.

Unfortunately, they don't tolerate that at the striving, conniving, and surprisingly thriving, D.C. public relations firm of Coleman & Walters. But they allow just about everything else. From the vodka in the break-room freezer—"the only way to serve it," according to managing partner Everett P. Coleman— to expense reports with more padding than Coleman's hand-tailored Italian suits.

I'd logged twelve years as a reporter for a major metro daily and thought I'd seen enough bloodshed to last me. And that was just inside the newsroom. But the crew at Coleman & Walters took workplace warfare to a whole new level.

Case in point: Chasing a lucrative account with a certain state parks department, Coleman and several of his employees (myself included) had taken a very influential lobbyist client to dinner Friday night.

As the desserts were cleared and the brandy arrived, Coleman motioned me away from the table and slipped a hotel key card into my hand. He'd selected me for the dubious honor of being the lobbyist's post-dessert tart.

I'd responded with a few choice words of my own. And, unlike Coleman, I was none too quiet about it. I dropped the key card into his brandy and left the restaurant in a cab. Alone.

Now, sitting in my sunny kitchen, it all seemed like a bad dream.

I honestly didn't know what to do next. Part of me thought the best plan was to keep my head down and my mouth shut—and start sending out résumés. I figured that would be my practical, lawyer-brother Peter's advice.

Part of me wanted to hit Coleman with the mother of all sexual-harassment suits, which was what my best friend, Trip, suggested.

And another part of me, in a voice that sounded suspiciously like my Russian grandmother, wanted to tell old Everett P. what he should really drop into his monogrammed coffee gizmo the next time he hit the "fine grind" button.

Instead, I opted to hide at home for the day. Or so I thought.

I was halfway through a pot of coffee when the doorbell rang.

Confession time: Anyone who knows me also knows to call first. I don't open the door to faces I don't recognize. And if I'm not expecting company, half the time I don't even go to the peephole.

After pinch-hitting on the crime desk for a dozen years, I couldn't count the number of times I'd asked a victim, or a victim's family, how the "alleged perpetrator" got in. Nine times out of ten, I got the same answer: The bad guy knocked, and someone opened the door.

Is it any wonder I don't roll out the red carpet for every Avon lady, Girl Scout, or Jehovah's Witness who reaches for the bell?

On this particular morning, my friends and family believed I was laboring diligently at the office. The only people who knew otherwise worked at Coleman & Walters. And after last week, I was in no mood to talk to any of them.

The bell rang again. Followed by a firm knock. This one wasn't giving up.

Fine. Let him wear out his knuckles on my solid metal door with two deadbolts. Thank you, DIY Network.

Another, louder knock.

"Alexandra Vlodnachek, open up," a deep male voice shouted. "This is the police."

I jerked upright, spilling half my coffee. Got to be a joke. But who knew I was home?

There aren't any practical jokers at C&W. To my knowledge, no one at the firm even has a sense of humor. Because if you can't buy it at Neiman Marcus, Tiffany's, or the local BMW dealership, they aren't interested.

I peeked through the peephole. Two burly guys in what looked like polyester blazers—one navy, one burgundy—stood shoulder to shoulder on my porch.

OK, this was not good.

Speeding tickets? Parking tickets? I searched my mind. What had I done?

With a jolt of adrenaline (or, more likely, caffeine), my reporter's training kicked in.

"Let me see some ID," I said through the door. My voice sounded strained and strangely high-pitched. As I pulled my robe tighter around me, I noticed my hands were shaking.

Blue Blazer held up a shield and ID card. I'd seen enough of them to know it was real.

Damn.

I unbolted both locks and opened the door six inches. "What's this about?" I said in my new voice, clutching my bathrobe like a frightened old lady.

Three men stared back at me with grim expressions. One uniformed officer and the Blazer Brothers. There was a patrol car and an unmarked at the curb.

"I'm Detective Norris, and this is Detective Beech," Blue Blazer said. "We'd like to speak with you, if you don't mind."

"Why?" I squeaked.

"Everett Coleman died Sunday. We're talking to the people who knew him."

While Norris spoke, Beech, who had no visible neck and bore more than a passing resemblance to a bulldog, scanned me with laser-focused eyes.

"Coleman's dead?" I slipped into reporter mode. "How?" Out of habit, I almost reached into my pocket for a pad and pen.

"Actually, we'd prefer to do this at the station," Norris said smoothly. "The officer will be happy to wait while you get dressed."

That's when it finally hit me. If Coleman was dead,

and the police were asking questions, Coleman had been murdered. Double damn!

Good luck finding out who did it. C&W is a snake pit. It could have been anybody.

"I really didn't know him that well," I explained. "I only worked for him for the last three months. I honestly don't think I'd be much help."

Bulldog stepped forward. "You fought with Everett Coleman Friday night. He died on Sunday. And you called in sick this morning. Funny, but you don't look sick to me."

It was funny because a sudden jolt of nausea rivaled the only time I ever mixed hot dogs, milkshakes, and roller coasters. And despite the morning's caffeine-a-thon, my mouth was so dry I could barely form words. "Am I a suspect?"

Norris stepped between us. "We just have a few details that we have to clear up, and it will be a lot easier to do that at the station. Can you be ready in five minutes?"

My mind was on a seesaw: If they were here to arrest me, they wouldn't be giving me time to get dressed and comb my hair. They'd just read me my rights and shove me into the back of a police cruiser. Like the one parked at the curb.

Great. The neighbors were gonna love this.

But if I refused to talk, I'd look guilty. And, depending on what kind of lies that bunch at the office was spreading, the police might actually arrest me.

At this point, I knew two things: First, the only person who was going to tell them I didn't do it was me. Second, I needed a lawyer.

If I were still at the paper, a quick phone call would get me one of the dozens of attorneys they keep on retainer.

But somehow I didn't think C&W would be affording me that same privilege.

My older brother, Peter, is a partner in a New York law firm. He specializes in accounting and tax law. We haven't spoken in a couple of weeks. But, Peter being Peter, and this being his busy time of year, it's possible he hasn't noticed.

Besides, it would look really bad if his youngest sister was arrested for murder.

"Make it ten," I said.

I turned both deadbolts—old habits die hard—and lunged for the phone. I was on hold for Peter's assistant for almost two full minutes, serenaded by something classical. Heavy on the strings.

When Angela finally came on the line, she sounded short and stressed. Tax season was hell on tax attorneys, which meant it was hell on everyone in the immediate vicinity of tax attorneys.

"Angie, it's Alex. I need to talk to Peter."

She sighed. "He's not in. Can I take a message?"

"This is an emergency. I really need him. Now." Like she'd never heard that one.

But she must have caught the panic in my voice. "Alex, he's really not here. He had a client meeting across town this morning. He's not due back until after lunch. Is everything OK?"

No, I wanted to say. Everything is not OK. But I couldn't very well tell her that her straitlaced boss's little sister was in trouble with the law. For murder, no less.

"Everybody's fine. Just ask him to call my cell as soon as he gets back."

I dialed Peter's cell. No answer. This time I left a detailed message. Police. Murder. Suspect. Downtown. Interrogation. I asked him to call ASAP and left my cell number.

As I put the phone down, it hit me again. Coleman was dead. Somebody killed him. And I was a suspect.

That's when I realized my whole body was shaking.

Chapter 2

The police officer let me off at the curb, and I was never so happy to be home, sweet home. All I wanted was a long, hot shower.

When they describe a police station in books, or re-create one on a studio lot, they amp up the glamour and leave out the grime. In real life, you don't see glass walls, gleaming steel, and glossy floors. You see cracked tiles, dingy paint, and worn carpets fortified with decades of ground-in dirt.

Spotless they're not.

But then cop shops aren't looking to attract repeat customers.

Halfway up the walk, I realized someone was sitting on my front porch drinking a soda and reading the paper. My younger brother, Nick, looked up, propped his sunglasses on top of his blond head, and grinned.

That grin has gotten him into and out of more trouble than he'll ever admit.

"I thought you gave up reporting," he said, nodding toward the police cruiser receding down the block.

"Long story," I said, collapsing into a plastic lawn chair next to him. "So when'd you get into town? Do Mom and Baba know you're here? How are things in emu land?"

Nick, the youngest of the four of us, is a full partner in an Arizona emu farm. Or at least he had been when I talked to him last month.

Our perfectionist mother wants him to go back to college and become a doctor, lawyer, or pretty much anything that doesn't involve shoveling up after animals.

Baba, our Russian grandmother—our late father's mother just wants to hug him. And feed him. For a woman who came to this country when she was twelve, she's learned surprisingly little English. But she's never really needed it. It's amazing what she can say with a plate of potato pancakes and a steely stare.

Nick rolled his brown eyes. "Yeah, you're still a reporter."

"Hey, old habits."

"Uh, yeah, well," he started. "We sold the farm. It was a great first start. But I'm ready for something a little more . . . mature. A little more real-world. And no, I haven't talked to Baba yet. Or Mom. Or the rest of them. I wanted to talk to you first."

There are four of us kids. Peter's the oldest, followed a few years later by Annie. Then the trailers: me and (last, but definitely not least) Nick. While Dad has been gone for almost a decade, Mom is still a very active—and vocal—presence in all our lives.

Whether we like it or not.

What Nick clearly didn't know: She and Annie

were on a whirlwind tour of Europe. My only sister may have the looks of a supermodel (which she was), and the money of a successful businesswoman (which she is), but right now she also had my complete sympathy. I wouldn't have traded places with her for the world. Literally.

I'd been invited on their European junket. And I wasn't exactly devastated when I'd learned it was incompatible with the vacation policies at my new job.

"I've got some good news," Nick said, with a grin so wide it practically split his face.

I braced myself. The last "good news" announcement was when he bought half the emu farm from a burnout high school buddy. Before that was the time he decided he "could no longer waste his talent and potential in the sterile confines of a classroom." Something the dean called "flunking out" in the letter sent home to our mother.

"I got married."

"To who?" The last I heard, he was living a hundred miles from nowhere with a beer-guzzling slacker and fifty emus.

"Her name is Gabrielle. She's amazing. The minute I met her, I knew we were meant to be. And she's fearless. With Gabby beside me, I can tackle anything. She's incredible. We got married last week in Vegas."

I heard water draining from inside. And suddenly realized that the cola he'd been sucking down is the cheap store brand I stock for guests. And the newspaper he's reading was on my kitchen table when I was rousted from the house this morning.

"So where is the new Mrs. Vlodnachek, and when

do I get to meet her?" I had a feeling I knew exactly where she was: steeping herself in Mr. Bubble in my claw-foot tub.

"She wanted to get cleaned up before she met you," Nick said with a shy smile and an offhanded shrug. "It was a long trip. You weren't home, so we let ourselves in. I hope that's OK?"

On a typical Monday, I wouldn't be home. I have— had?—a job. One that didn't involve livestock. One with nine-to-five hours and a steady, surprisingly hefty paycheck for the first time in my life. One that I probably didn't have anymore. Damn.

I looked at my front door, which was ajar, and snapped back into the moment.

I'm not one of those harebrains who keeps a key under the mat or in one of those fake-looking rocks. There's only one key to my house. And it's on my key ring.

So apparently I'm not the only alleged felon in my family.

Just then, a tall, tanned, skinny blonde appeared at the door. In my bathrobe.

"Well, you must be the sister!" she gushed, all teeth. "Nicky won't stop talking about you!"

It would be mean to call Gabrielle a bottle blonde. But, with at least a full inch of dark roots, it would be dishonest to call her anything else.

She had what the girls in the Lifestyle section called a "fake bake." And, judging from my brother's enchanted expression, some world-class fake boobs under my bathrobe.

Almost embarrassed, I looked down, only to realize

she was also wearing my favorite pink, flowered bedroom slippers.

"Did you give her the good news?"

Nick grinned.

She held out her left hand, revealing the only thing she was wearing that didn't come from my closet: a diamond the size of a dime.

"Wow," I said. "It's stunning." I was, in fact, stunned. Numb, actually. "So when are you going to share the good news with the rest of the family?"

I couldn't wait. Baba was going to crap. The ring alone would set off a blast of Russian the likes of which hadn't been heard since Rasputin refused to die. And when Baba got a good look at the woman wearing that rock? That would be an experience the Disney World folks refer to as an "E ticket" ride. Just buckle up and hang on.

"That's part of the reason we came here first," he said, staring into the eyes of his bride, who had managed to curl herself into his lap. "This all happened so suddenly. We need a few days before we spring the news. I sold the farm, but I haven't exactly gotten settled in a new business yet. And I'd like to have that in the works before I talk to everybody. You know how they are. Gabby and I were hoping we could crash here. Just for a week or so."

Double crap. The whole reason I'd been able to afford my cute little house on a newspaper salary is because it's so damned tiny. My mother, who constantly compares my paycheck to that of my fashionista older sister, refers to it as "that darling little doll's house." As in, "when you grow up and move out of that darling little doll's house and into a real home."

And it wasn't like I could get away from them by going to work anytime soon. Come to think of it, how was I going to feed us all?

"Well, the truth is, I'm having some problems myself right now," I said, addressing myself to Nick. "I'm temporarily between jobs. And I'm not exactly sure how I'm going to make the next mortgage payment, much less groceries for the next week or so."

I was hoping at this point he'd jump in. He didn't. But she did.

"Well, that's perfect," Gabrielle squealed with a perkiness that was definitely way over the top for my out-of-work, out-of-money predicament. At this rate, if I told her I was a murder suspect, she'd probably have an orgasm.

Nick gazed into her face like a golden retriever on Valium.

"We have a little money squirreled away," she said. "We can pay rent and groceries. And you won't even know we're here."

OK, I knew that last part was a lie. But I was seriously tempted by the idea of not losing my home and being able to eat until I could find someone who would actually hire a murder suspect.

"Well, if you don't mind the guest room . . ."

Nick and Gabrielle beamed. And I hoped I hadn't just made a big mistake.

Chapter 3

The definition of a friend: someone who will help you move. The definition of a good friend: someone who will help you move the body.

Thank God for good friends.

At seven the next morning, I was sharing a pot of coffee with my very best friend, Trip Cabot, in a greasy spoon two blocks from my house. Right off the town square and across from the county courthouse, Simon's was a local institution.

Our former congressman pressed the flesh here before he got elected and took every lunch break here during his trial. Rumor has it, Simon's even catered his first meal behind bars. But none of us could confirm it.

It's also where the seventy-plus set meets every morning to talk about how they'd run the world and which way the next political wind is blowing. I love the place. But this morning, any Burger King in a storm would be just as welcome.

"Jeez, Red, you look awful," was the first thing out of Trip's mouth.

I glared at him. "Nick and his new bride got into town last night. I got about three hours' sleep."

"Late night catching up? How are the emus?"

"I wish. He sold the farm. Married some cocktail waitress from Vegas. And let's just say she's a screamer."

"No! Sweet little Nicky?"

I winced and shook my head. "At one point, I thought they were going to come through the wall. I was seriously thinking about sleeping in my car."

"What did you do?"

"Put it this way, when Mrs. Simon showed up this morning, I was outside reading the paper."

"She gets here at 5 A.M. to bake the pies," Trip said. "Why didn't you call me?"

"I opened my big mouth and promised them they could stay with me. Besides, bad luck seems to be following me lately. And Tom would kill me if I brought it to your house."

"Red, you've got to set some ground rules," he said. "Make *them* sleep in the car. Your neighbors would love that. You could tell them it's performance art and charge admission."

Across the dining room, I spotted Lydia Stewart, who owns the 250-year-old Colonial at the end of my block. As she pointed in my direction, everyone at her table turned to look.

I smiled and waved. They all turned quickly around. Odd.

Then it hit my sleep-deprived brain. News of the murder was all over town.

Despite serving as a bedroom community for D.C., Fordham, Virginia—where I'd bought my tiny, hundred-year-old bungalow—is a small town on steroids. The two D.C. metro papers are delivered daily in Fordham. There's also a local weekly and a half-dozen blogs that chronicle all the gossip and goings-on. But news still travels quickest through the town grapevine. And Lydia Stewart, whose old-money family stole their land straight from the natives, is the head sour grape.

"Who am I? Job? Which cosmic deity did I inadvertently piss off?"

"Hey, as bad as it gets, you're still doing better than your late boss," Trip said.

"They think I did it," I countered.

"Who?"

"The police. My co-workers. My neighbors. You're having breakfast with one of America's Most Wanted. You might even want to get a taster for your food."

"Nah, I heard Coleman was stabbed, not poisoned," he said, dumping sugar into his coffee. "But I could confiscate the butter knives, just to be on the safe side. Hey, if you kill the boss, can you claim it as a business expense on your taxes?"

In a newsroom where staffers are judged by their dark humor almost as much as their ability to run down a story, Chase Wentworth Cabot III, better known as "Trip," can more than hold his own.

I let out a long breath I didn't even know I'd been holding. At least one sane, rational person realized I didn't do it. And apparently the newsroom crew hadn't heard I was on the suspect list.

So I spent the next few minutes filling Trip in on what happened yesterday before I came home and found Nick on my porch.

He listened so intently he didn't even pick up a fork when Mrs. Simon slid two breakfast specials onto our table. When I finished the tale of woe that was the last twenty-four hours of my life, he exhaled one hushed syllable, stretching it into three: "Shiiii-iiii-iiit."

"That pretty much sums it up from my side," I said, reaching for the ketchup.

Suddenly, for the first time since the police knocked on my door yesterday, I was hungry. Really hungry.

"The police told Billy Bob they had a strong suspect but weren't going to release the name until they had one more thing nailed down."

"Yeah, the lid on my coffin."

Billy Bob Lopez is the paper's lead crime reporter. He's folksy, charming, and totally tenacious. A shark in sneakers.

If the police really believed I'd done it, it wouldn't be long before someone leaked that to Billy Bob.

"That's not the worst of it," I said.

"It gets worse?"

I nodded. "The cops found strands of my hair on his shirt. I mean, they haven't had time to test the DNA yet, but it's the same color, texture, and length as mine. And there aren't any other strawberry blondes in that office. At this point, even I'd bet money it's mine."

"How'd it get there?"

"No idea."

Man, was that ever true. The last time I'd seen Coleman, he was duded up in one of his Savile Row suits at the client dinner Friday night. After our little argument, I went straight home and stayed there pretty much all weekend. Except for a quick trip to the bookstore Saturday morning. But somehow, on Sunday afternoon my not-so-beloved boss died wearing golf pants and a lime green Polo shirt with my hair all over it.

"I'd be more convinced if they'd found him covered in cookie crumbs and potato chip dust," Trip said.

"Hey, it was a rough weekend," I said. "I had some major life decisions to make."

"Let me guess. Bookstore?"

"The new Spencer Quinn's out," I said.

"Red, we've got to find out who did this."

"What am I going to do? Pull an O.J. and tell everyone I'm going around looking for 'the real killers'?"

"Minus the armed robbery and multiple rounds of golf, yes," he said. "And you don't tell anyone anything. From what you've said, C&W hasn't officially fired you yet, so you could go down there and nose around. And I can help you out at the paper. Who better to prove you didn't do it? You're a reporter."

"Ex-reporter. I've spent the last three months shilling for a public relations firm."

"Not even enough time to get the ink off your sleeves. Once a reporter, always a reporter. And face it, the only one who knows you didn't do it is you. "

"There's another person who knows," I said, suddenly feeling my stomach knot up again. "The killer."

"That's why you don't tell anyone what you're up to," Trip said, stirring black pepper into his grits. "As far as everyone is concerned, you're innocent and simply waiting for the police to bring the murderer to justice. In the meantime, la-di-da, it's life as usual."

"But in reality," I said, knowing where this was going.

"But in reality, we put our heads together, figure out who did this, and clear your name."

Chapter 4

Heading down the hall, past the blue silk wallpaper, toward the elegant offices of Coleman & Walters, I felt my stomach shrink.

I stopped, took a deep breath, and pushed open the heavy oak door. At 8:35, the front office was mercifully empty. I'd timed my arrival carefully. I wanted to show up early enough that I didn't have to run the executive gauntlet, but late enough so that the doors would already be unlocked. I assumed, of course, that my key no longer worked.

The last time Coleman & Walters ejected an employee, the locksmith arrived before the ax fell. It was not pretty.

But then Mrs. Everett Coleman is the office manager-slash-comptroller. And she runs this place with the kind of efficiency a Nazi would envy.

Just under six feet tall, rawboned, and remarkably fit, she is also what my father would have kindly called "a little on the plain side." Some people carry tension in their shoulders. With Margaret, it's her jaw. While her demeanor is placid to the point of aloof, that lantern jaw seems perpetually clenched. I guess having Everett Coleman for a husband was no picnic.

Or maybe she just doesn't like me.

Margaret's most remarkable feature: her hands. From what I'd heard, mostly through office gossip, Margaret Coleman used to be a nurse. Of course, that was eons ago, before her husband's business started raking in the dough.

But those hands, while large and strong, are nimble. Skilled. Like they could beat the life back into a failing heart. Or squeeze the last breath from a lazy hen and fry it up for Sunday dinner.

I made my way down the main corridor, then turned left into another hallway that ran along the very back of the suite. Instead of empty and dark, my small office was alive with light and noise. The speakers were blaring, playing some anthem of middle-class teen angst. Even more intriguing, my computer was on.

I flipped off the music. Sitting, I noticed that the screen saver had been changed from my generic spring scene to a close-up of a buxom girl in a strappy belly shirt and Spandex short-shorts struggling up a craggy rock face. Sweat glistened on a lot of visible skin, while she tipped her backside toward the camera like a zoo ape in heat.

"Hi, Amy," I said as she powered through the door.

Clearly surprised, her eyes went wide, and for a split second she froze. I thought she might actually drop her mug.

Amy is a walking billboard for "what you see is

not necessarily what you get." With long, blond ringlets, fine features and elegant suits, she is most often described with terms like "pre-Raphaelite" and "angelic." Which, of course, she does nothing to discourage.

She also cultivates the image of a work-hard, play-hard health nut, who spends weekends rock climbing, rollerblading, hang gliding, bungee jumping and, for all I know, parachuting with Hell's Angels. Every Monday we get to hear about her high-adrenaline exploits before the big staff meeting. And the requisite photos, featuring a bare minimum of clothing, show up at regular intervals in her office.

The clear-cut message, not lost on the men in this office: Amy can play with the big boys.

Ahem.

Amy's drink of choice: chamomile tea. *"It's soooo soothing,"* she trills to anyone who would listen.

What she doesn't say: she uses it to wash down a variety of prescription meds. And while she's very specific in her choice of organic tea, she's a lot less picky when it comes to the pills. Percodan. Percocet. Vicodin. Codeine. I'm guessing that all that motocross-bungee-paragliding might have a downside.

Make friends with the cleaning crew, and you learn all kinds of interesting stuff.

Amy's green eyes narrowed. She pursed her perfect little red bow of a mouth, producing a cross between a pout and a frown, and reached for the keyboard. My keyboard.

To her credit, I've seen grown men mesmerized by

that same expression, like rats hypnotized by a cobra. But it didn't work on me.

I quickly slid the keyboard out of her reach and began to type.

"That's my work," she whined. "What are you doing here?"

"In my office? Working. What are you doing here?"

"I don't think you work here anymore. I should call the police. We know what you did."

So much for a few quiet minutes to skulk around and gather information.

"What did I do, Amy?"

"You killed Everett." The gleam in her eyes told me she didn't believe it but was getting a thrill from spreading a nasty piece of gossip. "You stabbed him. And after he was so good to you. Taking you in when the newspaper fired you."

My mouth almost dropped open. But I caught myself at the last minute and took a deep breath.

"The paper didn't fire me, Amy. Everett had been trying to hire me for months. When he finally mentioned a dollar figure high enough, I accepted his offer."

I was actually kind of proud of that. For the first time in my life, I'd negotiated a decent salary for myself. And the firm's P.R. work, while sometimes silly and often mind-numbingly dull, was easy.

But after a few weeks, I realized that the salary wasn't compensation for the job itself. It was a bribe to put up with the office politics that went with it. And it wasn't nearly enough.

American business likes to invoke the team metaphor.

Teamwork. Team player. Team mentality. But there's one big difference. If cannibalism were legal, your average athlete would go after a player on the opposing squad. The typical junior executive would be eyeing the guy in the next cubicle.

And in my case, the feeding frenzy had begun.

"You can't be here. You can't stay here. This office is mine now."

Ah, that was it. When I came onboard, I was given a sweet little office with a great big window overlooking one of the office park's green areas. It wasn't as grand or spacious as some of the executive suites. But with that oversized window, I considered it the pick of the litter. So did several of my co-workers.

In the interest of full disclosure, I have to admit that I did nothing to deserve this particular perk. The office just happened to belong to a guy who got canned on my first day. Margaret, in all her efficiency, felt it was easier to put me into his still-warm, ergonomically correct leather chair than to play musical offices. Much to the dismay of several more senior employees who had been salivating over the prospect of four-walls-with-a-view.

Sadly, the leather chair was missing when I showed up on my second day.

I looked Amy straight in the eye, speaking slowly, as if to a child. "Well, then, please call the police. I talked with them, too. They don't know who killed Everett, but I hope to God they find him. Or her."

Her mouth twitched. Uncomfortable with direct confrontation, she looked away.

Score one for my side. I'd been schooled in a

profession that used the truth as a weapon. In my case, a blunt instrument.

Now I was smiling. "But if you really do believe that I stabbed a man, you might want to get your things off my desk."

Chapter 5

I learned surprisingly little in the next few minutes.

Since Amy had logged on to my computer and never logged off, I trolled through the system as her. I hit her email box first. There was a relatively brief memo from Holly, Everett's secretary, dated Monday morning. It very plainly and primly announced her boss's demise—minus any of the juicy details, of course. It explained that the police would "be present most of the morning" and urged everyone to "take the time to speak with them, regardless of your schedules."

It hit just the right tone between somber and practical. Everett was gone, but his "partner and friend," Benjamin Walters, was "at the helm."

Yeah, and this ship is going down.

When the fearless leader is so reviled that someone plants a letter opener between his shoulder blades, how can even the slickest P.R. firm spin that?

The note finished on an upbeat "our work will

continue without pause, just as Everett Coleman would have wanted."

The king is dead. Long live the king.

Holly's name may have been on the email, but I was pretty sure Walters had dictated every word.

I half hoped for a volley of personal emails with details of the crime, police revelations, or the stories my co-workers were feeding to the cops. Nada.

Knowing this place, I wasn't really surprised. The coffeemaker and the gossip mill would be working overtime. But some things you just didn't put into writing. The place to glean that kind of information would be the break room. And if the reception I'd received in my own office was any indication, I wouldn't get much.

Amy also had a flurry of borderline dirty emails from Mr. Lascivious Lobbyist. Murder or no, neither one had wasted any time.

What *was* the proper mourning period for a dead boss, anyway?

The double entendres were flying, and they had a "dinner meeting" set up for later this week. If it were anyone but Amy, I'd feel sorry for her. The man was a toad.

Sandwiched in between the emails were memos to Walters and various C&W execs, earnestly alerting them to her progress in securing the parks department account.

Then a subject heading dated late yesterday afternoon caught my eye. Walters had scheduled an office-wide staff meeting. Purpose: to discuss updates in the Coleman investigation, announce details of the pending funeral arrangements, and alert staff to recent business developments.

That last bit, dropped in almost as an afterthought, was the real reason for the meeting. It had taken Walters and his cronies less than a day to divvy up Coleman's client roster. With time out for grieving, of course.

Compared to the minor-league squabbling over my office, this would be the World Series of blood sports. If the killing was business-related, this meeting could give me some major leads. And it was scheduled for 9:30 this morning.

I checked my watch. It was 8:40. The minute anyone with any authority arrived, which could be any time now, Amy would run and tattle. Then I'd be tossed. And my access to this place would be kaput. No meeting. No leads. No other suspects.

But not if they couldn't find me.

I decided the ladies' room was the best place to hide. I tiptoed out of my office, checking both ways before crossing the hallway. I even managed to grab a magazine off the hall table before dashing (in three-inch heels, thank you), for the ladies' bathroom twenty yards down the narrow back hall. I checked under the stalls—no feet!—and threw myself into the last one, bolting the door. My shoes were generic tan pumps. If anyone saw them, they still wouldn't know it was me.

I closed the toilet lid, sat down, and opened my mag. *Public Relations Today*. Ugh. I could've sworn I'd snagged a *People*.

The only thing worse than working in P.R. would be writing about people working in P.R. But the egos at C&W lived for a mention in this rag. Coleman was in it regularly. Ironically, his death would win him a couple more paragraphs, maybe even a full-blown feature.

Benjamin (never Ben or, God forbid, Benny) Walters would have killed to see his name in its pages more than once a year. The real question: would he have killed Everett Coleman?

I'd been in the stall only a few minutes when the restroom door banged open. I flinched. And reflexively pulled up my feet.

"Well? Are you or aren't you?"

"I don't know. I can't even take a test for a few more days. That son of a bitch! Broken condom, my ass! I know he did it on purpose. The great Everett P. Coleman marking his territory."

The first voice, I didn't recognize. The second one was Jennifer Stiles, one of the newest senior execs. A few years younger than me, she'd come on board about two weeks after I did for some special project Coleman was hatching. I didn't know any of the details, except that he'd wooed her away from a big New York firm. And, from what I'd heard, it involved mucho bucks.

My gut reaction when I first saw her at the time: "Uh-oh, here comes trouble." And that wasn't jealousy over the fact that she was petite, stylish, and sophisticated on a level I could never hope to achieve. Or even that her salary was rumored to dwarf mine. No, it was more the fact that, even on her first day, she looked way too comfortable and confident for someone starting a new job. And what I witnessed over the next few months only reinforced my first impression.

Coleman grinned like a frat boy whenever she was in the room. Which was constantly. For her part, Jennifer strutted around Coleman & Walters in a collection of pastel micro-mini suits and stilettos as if she owned the place.

But for me, it was the little things. The details that, as a reporter, I was paid to notice. When they thought no one was watching, she'd straighten his tie or pluck invisible lint from his lapel. Or he'd give her a collegial pat on the shoulder. And leave his hand there just a millisecond too long.

OK, it wasn't *Girls Gone Wild*, but anyone who's ever worked in an office could fill in the blanks.

I expected fireworks from Margaret. Instead, nothing.

Margaret was, as always, totally efficient, indifferent, and serene. I have to admit, I was disappointed. Then I started to wonder: Did she see it? Did she even care anymore? Or, like every third woman in D.C., was she dipping into her own doctor-supplied stash of happy pills?

"Son of a bitch!" Jennifer screeched.

"Are you going to keep it?" asked the second voice, whom I finally recognized as Meghan, a junior exec in events planning. From what I'd heard, these two had been sorority sisters in college. And Meghan had been the one to float Jennifer's name the last time C&W was hiring.

"How the hell should I know? Good God, what kind of market is there for a pregnant, unmarried

P.R. exec? How the hell can I make a presentation with a belly out to here? Oh God, my tits will sag."

"If he'd lived . . ."

"If he'd lived, he damn well would have married me, baby or no baby," she huffed. "Now I'm screwed."

Meghan giggled. "Well . . ."

Jennifer must have shot her a dirty look because there was dead silence.

Or had they realized they weren't alone? My heart jackhammered in my chest.

After a long moment, Jennifer finally spoke. "Look, we had plans. *Business* plans. We were going to turn this place into something. A brand name. The premier boutique P.R. firm in the country. And I'd have owned half of it."

"What about Walters?"

"Walters is a dinosaur. A relic. And Everett knew it. The only reason dorky Walters even got into P.R. is because his father handed him a dinky little firm. Everett was the one who made it a success. Walters was deadweight, holding him back. He acts like a fossil. He thinks like a fossil. He's lost his edge. If he ever had an edge.

"Everett and I were going to transform this company. We were handpicking a dream team. Young blood. Winners who aren't afraid to do what it takes. We were going to reinvent this place and take it straight to the top. Now he's dead, and I'm fucking knocked up! This is not happening!"

I didn't know whether to laugh or cry. Instead, I bit my tongue and tried not to fall over as I perched precariously on a closed toilet lid.

I couldn't believe it. This place had more drama

than *Days of Our Lives*, and the police hauled *me* in for questioning?

"Have you told anyone?"

"God, no! I've got to get my ass out of here—and fast. The only chance I've got is to sell myself to the highest bidder before anyone knows I'm looking."

"How much is Everett's estate worth?"

"What do you mean?"

"Everett's baby might be entitled to a share of his estate."

"He's already got two kids. And that Shrek of a wife."

"So the wife gets, what, half? The other half could be split three ways."

"So I get one-sixth, while Margaret and her lazy brats get the other five?"

"Do the math, and see if you could live on it. At least it would keep you going. You could start your own P.R. agency."

"And scrimp and save and suffer? I didn't come this far to become some one-woman joke firm operating out of a cheap little office in the suburbs. I can't do it. I won't do it."

"Burgoyne & Co. is looking," Meghan suggested. "I had lunch with Souci last week. She's making a bundle over there. They have all those sports contracts, so it's high profile. Good money and great perks. You'd be perfect."

"Now. In a couple of months . . ."

"A lot can happen in a couple of months. So you jump now. Then decide what you want long-term. You could always say you had artificial insemination."

"Well, doesn't that just scream desperation."

"It says that you're a maverick. You go your own way. You'd be gold with the single, working-mom clique."

"Just what I want. Fit in with a bunch of worn-out, sexless drones. I swear to God, if Everett wasn't already dead, I'd kill him."

I heard heels clicking across the floor, followed by the sound of the bathroom door swinging open and shut.

Damn.

Chapter 6

If I wanted to "attend" the staff meeting, I was going to have to employ some stealth.

Otherwise, there was a pretty good chance I'd be booted—publicly—before I heard word one. Then it hit me: the handheld digital recorder I used to keep in my purse. But was it even still in there?

I fumbled through my bag. Brush, complete with wad of hair. Lone earring. Crunched-up twenty-dollar bill—didn't know I had that. Old bank deposit slip with lipstick stain. Discarded gum wrapper, wrapped around discarded gum. Emergency purse chocolate.

In my book, being trapped in a bathroom stall qualifies as a chocolate-worthy emergency. I unwrapped the candy and popped it in my mouth.

Then I plunged my hand into the bottom of the purse and groped around. That's when I felt it. Still there, after more than three months.

Take that, clean freaks.

The batteries would still be fresh enough. And with

fifteen hours of recording time, it should catch what I needed and then some.

I just hoped it worked. It was a gift from my sister. And Annie always bought the best.

But I'd never used it. My track record with recorders was mixed. Probably because I always picked up the cheapest model I could find. Half the time, I'd get back from an interview, discover that the machine hadn't recorded a word, and be grateful I'd never stopped taking notes.

One time, though, one of those cheap gadgets had saved my life. My career, actually.

Put it this way, sometimes a source had a memory lapse once he saw his name above the fold. But it was hard for him to deny talking to a reporter when the reporter had his voice on tape. Saying exactly what she quoted him saying. Followed by ten minutes of him grumbling about what a "tightwad schmuck" his boss was.

The real reason newspaper reporters almost never use recorders: we're lazy. (Yeah, who knew?)

Every minute of conversation takes at least two minutes to transcribe. Who has that kind of time? Especially when you have an editor with onion breath barking at you to finish a story so you can get out to the fairgrounds to cover the heartwarming tale of a tyke who raised a 1,200-pound steer from a calf, then sold his blue-ribbon best friend to a meatpacking company for a buck five a pound.

Give me a pad and pen any day.

Now all I had to do was plant the recorder. The meeting was being held in the main conference room—the only space large enough to accommodate the entire staff. Designed to impress both clients and employees alike, the room gave new meaning to the word "opulent."

Jennifer could say what she liked about Benjamin Walters and his "dinky" firm. For good or bad, C&W has always had a reputation for old money. Old-money décor. Old-money connections. Old-money values.

And that was pure Walters.

Jennifer described the company Walters had inherited as "little." I'd have said "select." With a client roster of D.C. insiders who were loyal as hell. The kind of people who didn't hire a P.R. firm to get their names into the papers so much as to keep them out. Or to put a good spin on things when, despite their best efforts, they couldn't avoid publicity.

Walters knows where a lot of bodies are buried. In this town, that counts.

I only had a few minutes before people would start flooding into the office. Mentally, I pictured the scene. Walters would lead the meeting. From the head of the table, no doubt. And just behind that chair was a huge antique bookcase, which housed a matching pair of large Wedgwood vases. Perfect.

I checked both ways before leaving the restroom and fast-walked to the side door of the conference room. I passed only one secretary. And she was on the phone, with her back to me.

The recorder was ready to go, and I popped it into the vase directly behind the chair where Walters would likely sit. Since the device was voice-activated,

I was hoping it would ignore the background noise and start recording when he started talking. But, as it hit the bottom, I heard a distinct "click." Was it still on?

Somewhere, Richard Nixon was laughing.

I was reaching a hand in to check, when I heard a woman's voice right outside.

"Yeah, in a sec," she said.

I quickly crouched low beside an oversized antique cabinet, just as she popped into the room.

It was Elizabeth, C&W's receptionist. If she came around to the head of the table—where Walters would be later—I was dead meat.

I held my breath.

Elizabeth called to someone just outside the door. A muffled male voice said something in response.

"OK," she replied. "Powdered or glazed?"

Another muffled answer. Followed by a rustling in the conference room.

"I snagged three, including a jelly donut—that should hold us 'til lunch," Elizabeth called as she walked out, shutting the door behind her.

I stood up, clutching my purse, and beat it out the side door. The same secretary was still on the phone, still facing the other way. But now she was doing leg lifts with her shoes off. I bolted for the restroom again.

Empty.

I quickly ducked into "my" stall. So much for trading the stress of deadlines and twelve-hour days for the boring, nine-to-five grind.

I checked my watch: forty minutes to showtime.

I'd go late and hover outside with the overflow crowd. By that time, and with any luck, the others would be too absorbed in the meeting to even notice me. And I could catch most of what was said.

Hopefully, I'd never need the damned digital recorder.

Chapter 7

By the time I sidled up to the conference room door, the meeting had been going on a good ten minutes. They would have already dispensed with the sad preamble.

And the donuts.

If past meetings were any indication, I had a pretty good idea of who was sitting where. In the corporate world, just like real estate, it's all "location, location, location." The most important people, or those who wanted to seem important, would be sitting closest to Benjamin Walters. Lesser gods would be farther down the table. And wannabes would ring the room, most of them standing.

Once in a while, especially in the newspaper biz, you'd get a late arrival standing near the door, arms crossed, as if to say "I'm too valuable to spare more than a few minutes of my time for this bullshit." Somehow, I didn't think that would happen here.

Out in the hall—unseen—would be the interns

and a gaggle of secretaries to the lower-level execs. And, hopefully, me.

When I approached, Walters was talking about Coleman's funeral. The tentative date, "absent any unexpected developments" (translation: if the police release the body), was Friday afternoon.

"Margaret and the children will be accepting condolences at their home on Thursday evening," Walters intoned soberly. "I trust that everyone in the Coleman & Walters family will stop by and offer their sympathies."

Walters cleared his throat. "Friday evening, after the interment, this firm, in conjunction with the Washington chapter of the International Institute of Public Relations Professionals, will host a wake in Everett Coleman's honor at The Barclay."

OK, for those of you outside the beltway, The Barclay is one of D.C.'s most elegant watering holes. Situated on the ground floor of the stately Standard Hotel, it's a favorite of the P.R. crowd.

I'd been there exactly twice, on business both times. The cheapest glass of wine was twenty dollars. And if I'd wanted a mixed drink, I'd have had to hock my hubcaps.

Still, the wronged wife, the possibly pregnant mistress, and the sole surviving partner together in the same room with booze flowing? Love to be a fly on that wall.

"What are you doing here?"

I recognized the voice even before I turned to see Margaret Coleman, hands on hips, glaring at me. Taller than my five ten, and clad in a shapeless black dress with her trademark blond braids wrapped around her head, she looked even more formidable than I remembered. Like an angry Valkyrie.

For some reason, I felt like a child caught listening at the door. Like I really didn't belong here anymore. My face went hot.

"You get out," she practically spat at me, raising the volume as she carefully pronounced each word. "Now."

"Margaret, I'm very sorry for your loss . . ."

"How dare you!" she screeched, the muscles and sinews in her jaw working overtime. And I smelled something on her breath that definitely wasn't Scope. Vodka?

"You killed my husband! And you have the gall to show up here? How dare you!"

"Margaret," I said softly, hoping to appeal to reason. "I didn't lay a hand on him. You must know that."

At that moment, Benjamin Walters appeared in the doorway. He glanced back and forth between Margaret and me, then stepped out into the hallway and shut the conference room door behind him. The interns and secretaries scattered.

"Is everything all right, Margaret?" he asked gravely.

"The woman responsible for my husband's death decided to just waltz right in here this morning," she said, jerking her chin in my direction.

Walters straightened his tie and squared his shoulders. With his short-cropped salt-and-pepper hair, charcoal suit, and drawn complexion, he was literally a study in gray. "I think it's best for everyone if you leave now," he said quietly.

Part of me wanted to run. I hated this place. Now more than ever. And that was saying something. But a small, increasingly vocal, part of my brain was screaming, "This isn't fair." OK, it's a five-year-old's argument. But in my case, it was true.

I matched Walters' even tone. "I work here. I haven't done anything wrong. If I had, I'd have been arrested. You can't fire me for something I didn't do. And, for the record, I was trying to offer my condolences."

Walters shook his head. "I'm afraid that's not going to cut it, Miss Vlodnachek. Everett had been concerned about your work performance for some time. He had decided, after your little outburst on Friday, that your services were no longer required here. I'm afraid I have no choice but to honor his wishes."

Was he kidding? Trying to pass the buck to a *dead* man? Even for C&W, that was a new low.

"The only thing I did Friday night was tell Everett Coleman that I would not sleep with one of his clients."

The hand cracked against my cheek so fast I never saw it coming. If Margaret Coleman ever decided to give up being a comptroller, she could make a bundle on the MMA circuit. I couldn't feel the left half of my face.

I took a step back and kept her in my line of sight. She wasn't going to catch me off guard again.

Walters just shook his head sadly. "I'm very sorry you feel the need to make up stories, especially about a good man who isn't even here to defend himself."

"Margaret's doing a pretty good job in the defending department," I said, rubbing my cheek. How much would it hurt when the feeling came back?

Walters put his hands behind his back and bent forward slightly, using a conspiratorial tone. "Whatever else you may have done, you clearly have no respect for this firm, our clients, or even the truth. You are no longer welcome here, and you need to leave immediately."

Now I was pissed. And sorry that there was a closed conference room door between me and that digital recorder. There's no way it would pick up this little conversation. I shot a glance at Margaret to make sure I was still out of arm range before I let fly.

"Let me get this straight. You're firing me for not sleeping with a client? Are you aware of a little thing called the Equal Employment Opportunity Commission? It maintains that I can expect to keep my job without turning myself into a whore. And if my employer should try to turn me into a whore, then I can sue and take every nickel, every dime, and every stick of furniture in his overpriced office. And just so we're clear, I've already told the police everything that went on at that client dinner Friday night. Every. Single. Thing."

Walters pushed the owlish black frames up onto the bridge of his nose and acted as if he hadn't heard me. "You have shown a total lack of regard for this woman, your boss's widow. You are unqualified. You have been completely unwilling to even attempt to learn this business. You obviously don't understand your role here. And, frankly, you haven't gelled with the team."

He paused to nudge his glasses again. "I've also heard some very disturbing reports that you have, to put it mildly, conflicting loyalties."

I glanced over at Margaret. She was serene again, listening intently.

"Conflicting loyalties? I told Everett Coleman there was no way in hell I was going to sleep with a client. There's absolutely nothing conflicted about that."

Walters shook his head. "My partner wanted you to move on because, aside from being incapable of doing your job, he had also learned that you hadn't left your former employer."

OK, at this point, Margaret could have hauled off and hit me again, and I wouldn't have felt a thing.

"We can't prove that you did what the police believe you did," he said evenly. "Though they seem to be making excellent progress on the case. Regardless, since you never truly worked for us, you may want to think long and hard before you apply for unemployment. Fraud is something that we, and the government, take very seriously.

"I should also let you know that I'm having the firm's attorneys look into possible sanctions against you. If you persist in spreading this malicious gossip, we'll have to add slander, and possibly libel, to our list of grievances."

"You're suing me?" Un-freaking-believable.

He nodded. "We're in the process of documenting the fact that you never left the employ of that newspaper. An exposé on the public relations industry, indeed. At the very least, we'll expect you to return the salary we've paid you. Depending on what sorts of irregularities our people uncover, we may also have to contact some friends of mine at the IRS.

"Of course, if you or some minor editor made a mistake, I'm sure the leadership at your newspaper will do the right thing once we bring this to their attention. But if they continue to keep you on, they'll be liable for much harsher reprisals. Ones which we'll have no choice but to pursue."

Son of a bitch! He wasn't just firing me. He was making sure that the editors at my old paper could never rehire me. If they did, they'd give credence to his inane story. And open themselves up to a huge lawsuit.

The chunk of chocolate in my stomach had turned to lead. There was no truth to any of this. But once the rumors started, my career would be over. I'd be radioactive. No paper would touch me. Ditto any public relations firm.

In the cutthroat world of P.R., killing the boss could be overlooked if you brought in the bucks. But penning an insider exposé was a definite no-no.

"I suspect, since my partner was a very smart man, he may have had even more documentation than we currently possess. That may very well be why you killed him."

Margaret, playing the moment for all it was worth, clamped her hands to her face and staggered away.

I was tempted to blurt out that each of them had a better motive. Along with a few of the juicy details.

But the reporter in me wanted solid evidence—real proof—before I revealed what I knew.

"That's a lie. And you both know it."

"There is a security guard waiting in your office," Walters said, reaching for the conference room doorknob. "Please gather your things and leave."

Chapter 8

After a rough week, or particularly bad day, the gang at the newspaper would usually go out for a beer. So what do you do when you've had the worst day in recent memory, you're totally alone, and it's not even 11 A.M.?

After a night of no sleep, I decided to go home. To bed. And, depending on how things looked in twenty-four hours, I might get up then.

Someone must have taken pity on me because when I got home, the house was empty. Quiet. Peaceful.

I headed straight for my bedroom and locked the door. I didn't want to deal with Nick. Or Gabrielle. And definitely not the two of them together. I just wanted sleep.

I changed into a plaid flannel nightie (and I use the term loosely), that Baba gave me for Christmas five years ago. "Keep you warm 'til you get man," she had said with a wink.

It hung like a sack, covering me from neck to ankles. Lest anyone forget I was a girl, there was a ruffle around each wrist and another around the hem. "Good, sturdy cloth. Last long time. Won't shrink," Baba had said proudly.

God forbid it should shrink. Someone might actually be able to find me in it.

But I loved it. It was soft. Comfortable and comforting, like a hug from Baba. And right now, I needed it.

I flipped on the TV to some generic talk show, just for background noise, curled up in a ball, and pulled the coverlet up over my shoulders. I fell asleep almost instantly.

But even my dreams were tortured. First, I was back in college, taking a test for a class I'd never attended. Later, thin, ugly gray monsters with owlish glasses were chasing me. The faster I ran, the closer they got. At one point, I was at Everett Coleman's funeral. Except they had him laid out on the bar at The Barclay. He sat up in his coffin, pointed at me, and announced that I had killed him. I dropped my martini glass, and it shattered into a hundred pieces.

Somehow, I sensed that the sound of breaking glass had come from outside my dream. Outside my door. I sat bolt upright in bed, heart pounding.

"Nick? Gabrielle?" Dead silence.

I called again, thinking they must not have heard me. "Nick? Is that you?" No answer, but a definite scuffling sound. And something that sounded like heavy breathing.

Oh, shit.

Had whoever killed Coleman come for me?

Normally, I'd phone the cops. But after yesterday,

I was half afraid that if I called attention to myself, they'd find a reason to lock me up for good.

I also didn't want to be murdered in my bed. I grabbed the phone off the table. Who could I call? Everyone I knew was at work, hours from here. Nick was God-knows-where. We didn't have Neighborhood Watch. And all my neighbors thought I was Jackie the Ripper.

I reached under the bed and pulled out my father's old Louisville Slugger, picking off dust bunnies. Dad didn't believe in guns, especially with a house full of kids. But he did believe that the sight of a six-foot-two-inch, former college lacrosse star swinging a league-approved bat would deter most potential perpetrators. And he'd been right.

So I wasn't six two, and I'd never played lacrosse. I could still do some damage. Besides, it made me feel a little less alone.

The house was still. The scuffling had ceased.

Click. Click. Click. Click. Like someone drumming fingernails on my hardwood floors. And it was getting closer. Then it stopped.

Silence. I clutched the bat tighter and dialed 9-1 on the phone.

Scratching. Someone was actually scratching at my bedroom door. Half of me wanted to throw it open and let whoever-it-was have it with the baseball bat. The other half wanted to dive out the bedroom window.

Rowr! Rowr! Rowr! Rowwwwwrrr?

I went to the door, opening it a crack. It was snowing. In my house.

Something small and furry ran past, dragging something bigger, as it rained down white fluff outside my door.

A second glance revealed that the larger mystery object was actually one of my couch cushions. The pricey ones that came with the couch. And the smaller something was a dog. A little, fawn-colored puppy who was tugging, gnawing, and jumping on said cushion. Making it snow all the harder.

I sagged against the doorjamb, leaned the bat against the wall, and forced myself to start breathing again.

"Hey," I said, addressing myself to my furry intruder. "Do you mind?

I think I'd have been less surprised to confront a space alien. "And where did you come from, anyway?"

Really, where? The neighbor's yard? The chimney? FedEx? To paraphrase the old rap song, "Who let the dog *in?*"

He paused and considered me for a split second. Then he trotted down the hall, turned and ran pell-mell toward the cushion. At the last second, he pounced—sending another wave of stuffing into the air.

"Ruff! Rowr? Rrrrr!" With his teeth, he tugged at a piece of stuffing still stubbornly attached to the pillow. The devil dog had oversized white ears that seemed to move independently, like fuzzy satellite dishes. Along with a single-minded hatred of my sofa.

Sporting a green cloth collar with two tags, he had to belong to somebody. I bent down and fingered the tags. The first one stated that his name was "Lucy."

OK, *her* name.

The second proclaimed that Lucy had been vaccinated for rabies. Well, good for her. But what was she doing in my house?

Lucy pulled away, sniffed at the baseboard, then squatted and peed. Finished, she glanced over at me and bounded off.

"Damn!"

Heading to the kitchen for paper towels, I surveyed the wreck that had been my living room. The breaking glass I'd heard? A crystal vase that had been in my mother's family for generations.

My sofa cushions were scattered across the floor—an amazing feat considering that they were three times the size of the dog. A second one had been gnawed so badly that there was a trail of stuffing across the living room.

And right smack dab under the middle of my oak and glass coffee table, nestled on a peach-colored throw rug, was a small pile of poo. A little hostess gift from my uninvited guest.

Pretty much the only thing she hadn't vandalized: a tower of mailing boxes in the corner that hadn't been there earlier this morning. I examined the one on top. Still sealed, it was addressed to a name I didn't recognize. Odd.

There was no sign of Lucy the Destroyer as I slammed around the house cleaning up various messes—literal and figurative. Not a bark, not a whine, not a growl. Not even the "click, click, click" of her malicious little nails on my polished hardwood floors. Which was a good thing because I was royally pissed and making no secret of it.

I shoved the bigger pieces of stuffing and foam back into the cushions, and followed the trail of foam crumbs with the vacuum cleaner. But I had to shut it off to move one overstuffed chair away from the wall. That's when I found her.

Wedged between the chair and the wall, she'd made a nest with the blue cotton blanket I'd left on the sofa when I fled the house this morning. She was curled into a ball, head to tail, quivering. Next to her were a few of the treasures she'd pilfered during her stay. One of my running shoes. An empty pie plate that hadn't been totally empty when I tossed it in the trash last night. An old gym sock—Nick's?— with a hole in it. And the stuffed toy I kept in my home office to squeeze or throw in times of angst. One plush ear was damp and ragged from chewing but, other than that, Stress Bunny was remarkably unscathed.

Lucy raised her head, looked at me, heaved a big sigh, and set her head down on her paws again.

I stroked the back of her head. One ear rotated. I gave it a scratch. She sighed again. A little less dejected this time?

I patted her soft, silky back. Her fur was the color and texture of a young doe. Reddish golden brown. Velvety.

"Look, I don't know where you came from, although I have a pretty good idea. But I'm sorry I was so grumpy. I've had a very bad day, and that's not your fault. You're really very sweet. When you're not trashing my home and all."

She nibbled my fingers, then rolled over, exposing a round white tummy replete with swirls of puppy fluff.

"Do you want a belly rub?" The tail started to wag. Lucy might be the puppy, but up to then, I'd been the one in the doghouse.

I gently scratched the fuzzy tummy, and she thumped her leg in bliss. All was forgiven.

Chapter 9

I hated to admit it, but Walters had rattled me.

If the man did what he promised—which was basically what he did for a living—I was toast. I'd never work again. Pay back my last three months' salary? I'd be lucky to make the mortgage next month.

But sitting on the floor with the pup curled in my lap, something clicked. I decided it was time to, in the words of the philosopher Dr. Phil, "take back my life." And after a light lunch of reheated sweet-and-sour chicken with rice for Lucy and me, I got down to business.

I figured I'd attack my current problem the same way I went after a story: talk to everyone I could, gather the facts, and take plenty of notes. Besides, reducing the details to keystrokes (file name: "Who Killed Coleman"), made it seem a lot less personal.

My trip to the office hadn't been a total waste. I'd come up with a few really good suspects. By my clock, it was time to let the world know that I had been the least of Everett P. Coleman's worries.

I called Trip's cell but got voice mail. Since anything

connected to the newspaper office was subject to prying eyes and ears, we'd decided that I would phone his cell to leave the highlights of whatever I discovered. He'd dig for more details, too—and leak some of the juicier bits to our intrepid crime reporter, Billy Bob Lopez.

That's when I noticed the red light on my landline was blinking. Fast. Three messages.

I hit *98.

"Hey, Alex, it's Billy Bob from the newsroom. Man, it sounds like you're having a rough week. Call me."

I hit "7" and erased it. If it wasn't still on the phone, it never happened.

The second message started.

"Alex, it's Billy Bob. Give me a buzz. We need to chat."

Delete.

"Alex, it's Billy Bob. Don't mean to be a pest, but the cops are calling you 'a person of interest.' I know there's more to it than that. Call me."

When this first happened, there was no way I'd have talked to him.

News is like sausage. Once you see how it's made, it's a lot harder to swallow.

To be fair, a lot depends on who's doing the reporting—and the editing. I know Billy Bob is a decent guy as well as a first-rate reporter.

And after this morning, I wondered if it might be a good idea to at least get my side of the story out there.

Second step to reclaiming my life: I dialed Richard Holloman, my new attorney.

The guy is a legend in D.C. I'd read about him a

couple of years ago, when he represented some high-profile defendants. Crime reporters hate him. Unlike some lawyers who crave media attention, Holloman shuns it. And them. Even more galling, he's smart enough to do it in such a way that gives them absolutely nothing to quote. Not even a "no comment."

That he was willing to take my case was a miracle. And Peter's doing.

My big brother might be three states away and in the middle of his busiest season of the year, but he came through for me. Two phone calls and he got me a one-man dream team. If he hadn't, I'd probably still be sitting in that bleak little room with the peeling paint and the one-way glass, drinking bitter, luke-warm coffee out of a Styrofoam cup.

When Holloman rolled into the station yesterday, it was a toss-up who was more shocked, me or the cops. Peter had already briefed him on the case—such as it was—and agreed to pick up the tab.

Of course, I promised Peter that I'd repay him. But knowing I might be out of work soon, I'd felt like a total fraud.

Through the whole thing, Holloman's attitude had been totally reassuring. Basically, we were in "wait and see" mode. If the police came up with some-thing and actually charged me, then he'd swing into action. If not, I was to keep my mouth shut and go on with my life.

It was still technically the lunch hour, so Hollo-man answered his own phone. "Kill anybody new today?" he said in a deep Virginia drawl. Like a lot of the politicians and attorneys I'd run across, I noticed he could layer on the accent, as thick as he wanted, at will.

"Not yet, but it's still early," I countered with a bravado I definitely did not feel.

Quickly, I briefed him about Billy Bob's phone calls, and my continued status as a suspect despite several much more promising candidates.

So what did he think of the possibility of my giving an interview?

Holloman cut me off before I even finished. "Hell, no."

"But this is what I do for a living. This is one part of the process I do know. And these people are my co-workers. I understand how to talk to them, and I know how they think."

"No." It came out clipped, and I could tell he was genuinely horrified. "You might know the process, but you're not a co-worker. Not anymore. You're a suspect. A story. Because they do know you and don't want to come off as biased, they'll print any and all of the dirt they can dig up. Ever rip up a parking ticket? Make a smart-assed comment during a staff meeting? Bounce a check? Have words with the boss? Drink too much at the office Christmas party? Get ready to read all about it. And it's going to look ten times worse in print. Absolutely not," he said with all the finality of someone who had, on one occasion, told a sitting U.S. Senator to "piss off."

There was dead silence. I felt stupid. How could I have even considered it?

"If anybody talks, it'll be me," he said finally.

"What would you say?"

"Same thing I always say: my client is innocent,

the charges are scurrilous, and in time, the truth will prevail."

"You left out the part about it being a travesty of justice," I said.

"See? It can't be that bad if you can still make a joke. Get some rest, kid. This is all going to come out in the wash."

"And if it doesn't fit, they must acquit?"

"Right. And since you're paying me $1,000 an hour for this witty repartee, I'm going to do you a favor and hang up now."

"There's one other thing," I stumbled. I felt like a death-row inmate trying to buy a little time before that final long walk. "My job. My former job . . ."

In what felt like a rambling, robotic monotone I detailed the blow-by-blow of almost everything that had happened in the office that morning. The big meeting. The not-so-merry widow. The confrontation. The slap. The firing. The story they were spinning about my still being with the paper. The demand to repay three months' salary. The IRS threat. Being escorted out of the building with a security guard under each arm. I left out only the part about planting a (possibly illegal) recording device in the conference room, and the dignity-scorching visual of me cowering-slash-eavesdropping in a bathroom stall.

When I finished and stopped to breathe, there was about five seconds of silence. I braced myself. I was prepared for almost anything. Except what he actually said.

"Don't sweat it."

"What?" I expected he'd be a little more upset that

my ability to pay him, or pay back my brother, had been severely compromised. I even thought he might suggest switching attorneys.

To my absolute horror, I began to cry.

I tried to stifle it. But the more I tried to control myself, the worse it got. Holloman didn't even seem to notice.

"To be expected," he said, almost blithely. "You had to go in and at least go through the motions. Termination? Not totally unforeseen, given their prior behavior. They have the right to fire you for any reason. Or no reason. But using the threat of a lawsuit? Big mistake. You've got a better hand for a lawsuit than they do. Scapegoating you publicly? Assailing your reputation? Spreading untruths and affecting your ability to obtain other employment?" I could almost see him ticking off the points on his fingers.

"Actionable. Depending on how they disseminated the information, they're looking at defamation of character, slander, and possibly libel. I'll phone their counsel this afternoon. That should put an end to the worst of it. Then, we wait for the police to do their job. When it's over, who knows? You might decide you want to sue them."

"That's it?" I said, gulping down air like a guppy.

"That's it."

I had to hand it to Peter. He couldn't have found me a better lawyer. I never talked to Holloman without feeling at least a little bit better about being a suspect in a murder investigation. And the possible target of a frivolous civil suit. Not to mention broke and unemployed. But a little better, none the less.

I hung up with Holloman and took a couple of deep breaths. Now, as I saw it, I needed two things. Money. And, if I wanted to retrieve that recorder, access to the conference room. Three phone calls later, I knew exactly how I was going to get both.

Chapter 10

Later that afternoon, as I sat in a ratty blue leatherette chair, wearing a pilfered blond wig and five pounds of makeup, I tried to remind myself that this was actually a step up.

Technically, I was about to commit a crime. Not dognapping. Although Lucy was, on this crisp and breezy day, happily ensconced in the back of my aged, airy Chevy wagon (windows at half-mast), alternating her attentions between a new tennis ball and one of my old running shoes, sans laces.

No, I was going for a major felony: impersonating a cocktail waitress.

The only way I was going to get past the security guards and into my old office was in some sort of disguise. The rent-a-cops wouldn't know what to do with a real criminal, but they probably had my photo posted at every entrance. Emblazoned with a red circle and a line through it.

But there's one group of people who moved in and out of any office virtually unnoticed: the cleaning crew. And I knew from talking with some of the ladies who clean—not to be confused with the ladies who lunch—that there was a pretty regular turnover. As soon as somebody got a better offer—or any offer— they left.

Turns out that the cleaning ladies weren't the only ones with short expiration dates. The office park had changed janitorial companies a week ago. Something it did pretty regularly, according to a very surly assistant property manager I'd phoned earlier that morning.

"So, would you say you'd recommend their services?" I asked, playing the part of a prospective customer checking references.

"They're cheap and, after a week, they're still showing up. If you wanna count that as a gold star, knock yourself out," he said, slamming down the phone.

Given that the whole purpose of getting this job was to relieve my former employer of my own property, it might be problematic to apply in my own name. Luckily, I didn't have to look very far for an alter ego. If Gabrielle could appropriate my bathrobe, my slippers, and half the food in my fridge, I figured I could borrow her driver's license and Social Security card. Besides, I bargained with my conscience, if I actually make any money at this gig, it's going to restock one very empty cupboard.

Imagine my surprise when my fishing expedition into my brother's new wife's purse yielded not one but five different driver's licenses under five different names. And an equal array of coordinating Social Security cards.

Exactly how do you broach that subject at dinner? "Excuse me, while I was rifling through your purse to steal your identity, I happened to discover that you may be guilty of crimes that make mine look like jaywalking."

There was also a picture. One of those photo-booth strips you can get at special events and carnivals. A man and a woman. She sat in his lap, his arms wrapped protectively around her waist. They were both grinning, kissing, and mugging for the camera. The woman was definitely Gabby. And the guy was definitely not Nick.

I pocketed the only pair of cards with "Gabrielle" on them. If, indeed, that was her real name.

To make myself look more like the driver's-license photo, I shoveled on the makeup with a trowel. A thick layer of concealer and foundation, some green eye shadow left over from Halloween, false eyelashes (ninety-nine cents in the drugstore bargain bin), and five coats of inky black mascara. I even fished a long-forgotten eyeliner out of the bottom of my makeup drawer and rimmed the top of each eye with a wide, black half-moon.

As Trip would say, "Tacky, tacky, tacky."

I also liberated a wig from my new sister-in-law's collection. And I learned that blondes definitely do not have more fun. The platinum pageboy made my scalp sweat. That, in turn, made my head itch. So I'd been scratching like a maniac for the last hour.

And in the short time I'd been wearing the eye-lashes, the glue had turned my eyes red and watery, while my lids were itchy, puffy, and swollen. With the oversized clothes I'd chosen to disguise my lack of silicone frontage (in case anyone checked with

Gabrielle's former employer), I could have easily passed for a clown.

If my mother had been here, she'd have blamed my reaction on guilt. I contend it was cheap eyelash glue.

What did I have to feel guilty about? A crime isn't really a crime if it's for a good cause, right?

I snuck a quick fingernail under the wig and gave the back of my head a good, hard scratch.

Little did I realize, I could have shown up with my real name and a murder warrant pinned to my sweater. Turns out the only thing Mr. Gravois cared about was if I had a pulse and a willingness to work nights. And the pulse was probably optional.

Mr. Gravois (he never offered a first name), was presumably the president, founder, and CEO of Gravois & Co. International. He was also the only person sitting in the dingy, sparsely lit, one-desk office.

Short and stocky, he managed to be both balding and hairy. He barely glanced at the driver's license and ID before checking his watch.

"You work tonight?" he asked in a thick French accent that carried a hint of something else. Morocco? The Middle East?

"Tonight would be great," I said brightly. The quicker I got in, got that recorder, and got this over with, the better. Plus, my head was really starting to itch.

"Here at 6 P.M.," he said. "We take the crew in bus. We give supplies. We give you apron. We come back at midnight. No breaks, no talk. We clean. End of each week, you do good job, you get cash money. One hundred eighty bucks."

OK, so Mr. Gravois wasn't versed in the finer points of minimum-wage law. Or tax law. Or employee relations. All I wanted was access to that office. And a sharp fork to scratch my head. Or a Brillo pad.

"OK," I said earnestly, feeling sweat trickle down my inflamed scalp. "I'll be here at 6."

"Don't be late. Bus leave at six. You miss it—no work, no cash money."

"I will be here ready to work," I said through clenched teeth. Just. Want. To. Scratch. Now.

"And thank you for the opportunity," I said, standing and sticking out my hand. Hey, did my momma raise me right, or what?

Gravois looked at me blankly and turned away, toward a file cabinet beside the desk. "Bus leave at six," he said over his shoulder.

Chapter 11

The evening ride over to the office park was like a third-grade field trip. Minus the singing, talking, and fun.

We paired up and piled into the van. Mr. Gravois drove, and his wife sat beside him. They spoke French to each other, but every once in a while, she'd turn around and shoot us a dirty look.

Behind them sat Olga and Maria, who chatted away the whole time in rapid-fire Russian. From the evil looks Mrs. Gravois was giving them, it was obvious that, while she didn't speak the language, she suspected she was the butt of every joke.

More like half. Sixty percent, tops. Not that I'd ever let on.

I sat two seats behind them with my assigned cleaning partner, a sad-faced, dark-skinned African girl whose English seemed limited to "yes," "no" and "thank you."

When the bus turned into the entrance of the office park, my stomach clenched. What was it about this place?

By the time we arrived at the back-door loading dock, I was shaking. What had I been thinking? What if someone saw me? What if they recognized me?

Then I got a look at myself in the reflection of the gleaming steel service elevator. I had done another quick change since this afternoon's job interview. No way I could maintain my "Gabrielle" look all night. So I'd opted for "unrecognizable." And succeeded.

My hair was skinned back into a tight bun, concealed beneath a large, blue handkerchief. Awkward, black square-rimmed glasses—another drugstore purchase—obscured half my face. And I'd completed the look with an oversize blue sweatshirt, baggy jeans, and my $6 Payless sneakers.

My own mother wouldn't recognize me. OK, knowing my mom—who has a penchant for designer labels—she'd recognize me but pretend not to.

Mr. Gravois motioned for us all to gather and started barking out orders. "Tonight, floors one, two and three," he shouted in an accent so heavy he sounded like Pepé Le Pew.

What? Coleman & Walters was on ten. I *needed* to be on ten!

"Madame Gravois and I vacuum. Maria, you and Olga empty trash, dust, and polish furniture. Gabrielle," he said, addressing me by my new stage name, "you and Elia clean bathrooms."

No! No, no, no, no, no, no, no! screamed the two-year-old inside my head. Six hours of cleaning bathrooms, and I wasn't going to get anywhere near the tenth floor? *No!*

"We go now. Start on three." And with that, everyone rolled their trolleys into the service elevator.

OK, I resolved, taking deep breaths, I can handle this. I'll just wait for the right moment and sneak up to ten when no one's looking.

Five hours and as many escape attempts later, I'd learned three things about Madame Gravois. First, she did have a given name: Capucine. Which suited her for reasons that had nothing to do with the famous French model. Second, she kept an iron grip on the crew. And third, she had a nicotine habit like no other human I'd ever met. Every time I managed to slip away, there she was, with a scowl on her face and a cigarette in her claw. "No breaks—back to work!" was all she said to me all night.

By 11:55, my back ached, and my giant yellow rubber gloves had become permanently sweat-glued to my arms. I was so tired I could barely keep my eyes open. Or I might have been passing out from the toxic effects of the industrial strength, lime-scented cleaner we used on the bathrooms. Where did they get this stuff?

I now understood why Olga and Maria seemed so perky on the ride over. Clearly, toilet duty was reserved for the new girls—the lowest women on the totem pole. Compared to a night of mucking out bathroom stalls, a few hours of giggling, gossiping, and polishing seemed like a vacation.

Elia seemed to take it all with grim resignation. I'm guessing that, wherever she hailed from, cleaning toilets in a suburban Virginia office park was an improvement.

As we exited the men's room, Elia closed the bathroom door behind us, and we collapsed into cubicle chairs to catch our breath before the whole group migrated back to the loading dock.

Elia hadn't said more than two or three words all night, so I didn't know how much English she spoke.

"Are you as tired as I am?" I ventured.

She glanced over, then away, and nodded.

"So, how long have you been doing this?"

"This is my second week," she said, never taking her eyes off the floor. Her English seemed fluent, her accent almost musical.

"Where are you from?" I asked.

"Congo."

"Family here?"

"Some," she said, halting. "My aunt and my cousins. I live with them. I am in college, but it is very expensive. I work."

"Cleaning toilets?"

She smiled, still studying the floor. "It leaves the days free for my classes. And Mr. Gravois pays in cash—off the books. I have scholarships, but they do not cover textbooks and supplies. And my family needs the money."

"Where do you go to school?"

Her chin came up and for the first time she looked me straight in the eyes. "Georgetown. Pre-med."

"Damn."

Elia shot me the same look my mother used when, as a kid, I said something dumb in front of company. Not an infrequent occurrence.

"So how did *you* come to be here?" she asked.

I made a snap decision, based on nothing but pure gut instinct. "I was accused of a crime I didn't commit. I'm trying to clear my name."

Elia laughed. Then stopped when she realized I wasn't kidding. "What do you mean?"

For a split second, I wondered if my gut instinct, like everything else in my life at that moment, had gone completely haywire.

"I used to work in this building. On the tenth floor, at a public relations firm. One of the men who runs it was murdered. I had nothing to do with it, but some of the people who work there are telling the police that I did it. I took this job to get back into the building and get something of mine. Something that I hope will clear my name."

She stared at me, wide eyed. And, having said the whole thing out loud for the first time, I felt like an idiot. It was a lousy idea. And, one way or another, I was probably going to jail. Soon.

"There is evidence there that will prove you did not do this murder?"

"I hope so."

"We will not be cleaning floor ten until Thursday. This evidence, it will still be there then?"

Now I'm the one looking at the floor. "If no one else finds it first."

"The evidence, is it in the toilet?"

"Uh, no. Why?"

"Then on Thursday," she said, smiling, "we have to make sure we are not cleaning the toilets."

Chapter 12

When I opened my eyes the next morning, I ached. Everywhere.

Worse, I felt a strange pressure in the vicinity of my rib cage.

I blinked a couple of times. A blurry, doe-colored shape shifted, sighed, and rolled off my chest, taking most of the covers. Lucy.

"Coffee," I said aloud. "Need. Coffee."

Lucy yawned and moved into the warm spot I'd vacated. So much for constant companionship. I grabbed my robe and padded out to the kitchen. A sharp rap on the front door made me jump.

"Come on! We're going to be late!"

Trip.

I threw open the door, and my best friend gave me the once-over. "Love the hair. You trade the blow-dryer for an eggbeater? Oh my God, what the hell happened in here? It looks like a frat house exploded."

I looked around the living room. He was right. Pizza boxes littered the floor, with two congealed slices on the coffee table. Sofa cushions and crumpled soda cans were scattered around the room. There was an empty cake box, on its side, in front of one chair. The stack of mailing cartons in the corner had morphed into a small mountain. And the place reeked of cigarettes.

Somehow, I didn't think I could blame this one on Lucy. Not unless she'd learned how to dial Dominos and started chain-smoking Salems.

"Someone throw a party?" Trip asked, eyeing the wreckage.

"Nick and Gabrielle were burning the midnight oil when I got back last night. Apparently, she runs some kind of online business, and she's a night owl. So they were up late working."

Retrieving a gold pen from the inside jacket pocket of his pristine light gray, chalk-stripe suit, Trip gingerly picked up a purple lace thong from the back of a chair. "Hate to break it to you, Red, but that's not all they were doing."

I rolled my eyes. "What are you doing here? What are we going to be late for?"

"Your dental appointment, remember?"

I smacked myself on the forehead. "With everything else going on, I totally blanked."

"Big surprise," he said skeptically. "You're still not getting out of it."

When it comes to visiting the dentist, I am a total wuss. So Trip and I have an agreement. He comes to the dentist with me. And I help run interference every year when his Great-Aunt Camille comes to town. Not a perfect system, but it works for us.

"What did you mean 'when I got back,'" he said. "Where were you last night? Hot date? New job?"

"Long story."

"That's OK, we can still make this work," Trip said, shooing me toward my bathroom. "You go get ready. I'll tidy up a little, and we'll get you to Dr. Drill-and-Fill fashionably late."

"Did you get a dog?" he called after me.

I looked over my shoulder and saw Lucy sitting in front of him, staring up.

"She belongs to Nick and Gabrielle. She loves shoes, and she pees on things."

"Gabrielle or the dog?"

When I glanced in the bathroom mirror, I understood Trip's crack about my hair. I'd been so tired when I got home, all I could think about was a shower and sleep. I fell into bed without even combing my wet hair. Now I looked like *The Bride of Frankenstein*.

All of us kids have Dad's brown eyes. But when it comes to hair color, we're a box of Crayolas. Peter's hair is dark, like Dad's. Annie and Nick—thanks to some trick of recessive genes—are blond. And I'm what's politely referred to as "strawberry blond." Heavy on the strawberry.

No time for vanity. I smoothed my fright wig back with a little water and a lot of mousse and pulled it into a ponytail. Then I gave my teeth a thorough brushing and followed up with mouthwash and floss.

Hey, I don't want Dr. Braddock to think I'm a total heathen.

I threw on a sweater and jeans, grabbed my mascara and lipstick from the bathroom counter, and jammed them into my purse.

When I skidded to a stop in the living room, Trip was closing a trash bag and chatting with Lucy, who was looking up at him lovingly. The pillows were all back in place. And the cans, pizza, and food boxes were gone. I was hoping the purple thong had gone with them, but I didn't want to ask.

"I gave the beast a potty break, so we're all set," he said.

"If you drive, I can put on my makeup in the car."

"Works for me." Turning to Lucy, he added, "Now, you be a good girl and remember what I said."

"What did you say?"

He narrowed his blue eyes. "Never you mind. That's between me and the little beast."

Lucy gazed at him, besotted. I gave her a quick pat, and we bolted for the door.

"So, it looks like you're getting new neighbors," Trip said, as he angled his shiny red Corvette convertible out of my narrow driveway, maneuvering it around the huge moving truck parked on the other side of the street.

"Huh. That's weird. The only house up for sale is that old Victorian place across the street. And it's been on the market for years. I don't think they're ever going to unload it."

"Why not? It looks OK from here."

"Yeah, and this is as close as you'd ever want to get," I said without looking up. "The inside's a hot mess. A bad seventies remodel with lots of hideous shag carpet and dark paneling. And it hasn't been cleaned in decades. I don't know how structurally sound it is, either, because they've had crews out here working on it off and on for the last couple of months. Plus, for reasons that make absolutely zero sense, the owner wants a pile of money for it."

"Well, then give the local real estate industry a gold star, because some poor schmuck bought it."

With that, he gunned the engine, then hit the brakes and rolled lightly over an all-but-hidden speed bump at the end of my street. I turned to him with mascara smeared across my forehead.

"Interesting look for you. Very Frida Kahlo."

I stuck out my tongue.

Chapter 13

With two new fillings and one less wisdom tooth, I bounded from the dentist's chair. I hit the cashier's desk feeling what I always did at the end of an appointment: like I'd cheated death.

Unfortunately, my mouth was full of more drugs than a rock star.

"Hiiiuh!" I greeted Sherrie, the dental assistant.

"Hi yourself," she said with a giggle. "Here, sign this."

"Okuuh!"

"Now, that'll be $758," she said, checking the chart.

"Whuuuah! I haa inthurah. Inthurah!"

"No, I checked with the company an hour ago. They said you don't have coverage. So we need to get payment from you this morning."

"Whuh? No coothath? Hoooww?" At this point, Curious George would have been easier to understand. But Sherrie was used to people talking under the influence. She didn't miss a word.

"They didn't say. Just that you didn't have a policy with them anymore. Maybe there's been a mistake.

You can call them later. In the meantime, we can take cash, check, or a credit card—whatever's easiest."

I did some quick math. I didn't even have thirty dollars in my checking account. But I did have two credit cards. It would be the most I'd ever charged in my life. But hopefully it was only temporary. Just until I straightened things out with the insurance company.

I handed her my Mastercard. A minute later, Sherrie handed it back, shaking her head. "I'm sorry, but this one was declined. Do you want to try another one?"

"Dekiin! Theah muth be thum mithaa. Hoow caah I be dekiin?" I waved the card, motioning for her to try it again.

But she just shook her head. "I already tried it twice," she whispered. "The code indicated I should confiscate it, but that's just mean."

I fished my Visa out of my purse and handed it to her. It had a $450 balance and a $4,000 limit. But I was getting a funny feeling about this, and it had nothing to do with the Novocain.

A minute later, she was back again with the card. "A no-go on this one, too," she said softly. "You want to write a check? We take checks."

With two declined cards and no insurance, even I wouldn't have taken my check.

"Thaa wooh be fii. Hoow muth?"

"Seven hundred and fifty-eight dollars. You don't have to make it out. Just fill in the amount and sign it. We have a stamp."

I handed her the check, realizing that the payment would put a sizable dent in the savings I was planning to use for frivolous impulse purchases, like food and mortgage payments.

"Remember, if you start having any pain, just give us a call. Your next appointment is on July sixth at 8 A.M. for a cleaning." She handed me an appointment card.

"Thaaann-ooou."

"Sooo, how'd it go?" Trip asked when I walked into the waiting room.

"I'b bruuukh."

"Huh?"

"I'b brokh. I haa no inthurah, and I'b brokh."

He fumbled in the jacket pocket of his suit and produced a small pad, a pen, and a handkerchief. He handed me the handkerchief first.

"Whaaauh?"

"You're drooling."

"Oh." I mopped my chin and held the linen square out to him.

"You keep that, Rainman. Something tells me you're going to need it for a while."

After he handed me the pad and pen, I scribbled furiously for two minutes and handed back the pad.

"Drool!" he barked.

I blotted my mouth again. "Thannnth!"

"Don't mention it. Really. To anyone. Damn, your handwriting is awful. You really should have gone to medical school."

"Twibbb!"

"All right, all right. OK, something's definitely screwed up. In the meantime, I'll loan you the money. Then you straighten things out with the insurance company and the credit cards, and everything's back to normal."

"Noooh!"

"I said *loan*. You can pay me back."

"Noooh!"

"Oh, all right. Don't bite my head off. Oh gross, drool again."

"Kwabb!" I said, resolving to keep my mouth covered with the limp rag that had been Trip's starched linen handkerchief. For the rest of the day, if necessary.

"Can I interpret that to mean you want to go home now? Bark once for yes, twice for no. Better yet, stamp your hoof."

I pulled the rag away from my chin just long enough to stick out my tongue.

When Trip pulled into my driveway, there was definitely something going on across the street. The moving van was parked at the end of the block. Trucks from the phone company and the cable company were in the driveway of the Victorian, along with a few expensive cars I didn't recognize. And one I did: Lydia Stewart's little white Mercedes.

She was backing out as we climbed out of the car. I turned to wave, and she hit the gas.

"Wow, she really is warming up to you."

"Bii me!"

"Drool. And I'm going to assume you're trying to tell me that Timmy fell down a well."

"Wuh!"

The minute I opened the front door, Lucy bounded

out, tripped, rolled down the steps, leapt up and ran around my light pole like a drunken, demented squirrel. Then she squatted and peed at the base of the pole and ran back to us.

Trip reached down and scratched her behind one fuzzy ear. "Looks like somebody's getting house-broken," he said to her.

Exhausted from her labors, Lucy threw herself on the ground and rolled onto her back, wiggling her legs in the air.

"What a lovely little dog—what breed is she?" inquired a clipped British accent behind us. I turned to see a tall, dark-haired man in jeans and a navy blue Windbreaker at the foot of my driveway, holding what looked like a stack of envelopes.

"Mixed-breed," Trip said quickly. "A rescue." To me, he hissed, "Drool!"

"I'm Ian Sterling," the stranger said, walking toward us. "I'm afraid I just bought the monstrosity across the street. We're going to be neighbors."

I'd have put Sterling's age somewhere between thirty-five and forty. He was taller than me—over six feet—with wide shoulders, a tanned face, and high cheekbones. Handsome, but not in a Hollywood pretty-boy kind of way.

When he looked directly at me, I noticed blue-gray eyes rimmed with dark lashes. I swear I felt my heart flutter. But it could have been the dental meds.

I attempted my best neighborly smile and realized that, with no control of my lips, I couldn't smile without drooling. I also couldn't form recognizable words. So that just left me staring at the guy without smiling. Which would probably ensure he was never coming back to borrow a cup of sugar.

"I'm Trip Cabot. This is Alex Vlodnachek. Alex lives here; I'm just visiting. So, you must have plans for the old place."

"A B&B, actually," Ian said. He stepped forward and held out the stack of envelopes. No wedding ring. Why did I notice that?

"I think I received some of your mail in error," he said.

Five bills and a postcard with a Monet on the front. Reflexively, I flipped it over. Annie.

"Uh," I started. Trip shook his head almost imperceptibly.

"You'll have to forgive Alex. She's just back from the dentist. And the anesthetic hasn't quite worn off." Between clenched teeth, he hissed, "Drool!"

"Oh, well, I should go and let you recuperate. Nice meeting you both," he said, shaking Trip's hand and then mine. "Feel free to pop over any time."

"Oo, too!" I called after him, as he headed down the driveway.

"I'm sorry?" Ian said, turning.

"She says, 'You, too,'" Trip hollered after him. To me he whispered, "Drool!"

Chapter 14

The next morning, I stumbled out to my kitchen with one thought: caffeine.

I had just poured my first cup when Nick walked into the room yawning. Sporting a gray Arizona State T-shirt, jeans, and a serious case of bed-head, he looked all of sixteen.

"Hey," he nodded, eyes barely open as he poured himself a mug.

"Hey," I returned, raising my cup.

We Vlodnacheks have never been mistaken for "morning people."

After a few minutes of silent contemplation, he set his cup on the table. "Soooo, what's new with you?"

"Oh, the usual. Giant dental bill. No credit. Found out some weasel canceled my health coverage. I'm broke. And I've got a night job cleaning toilets."

"That explains the smell," he said.

"Really? Oh my God, I wasn't imagining it. Do I reek?"

"Only when you first get home. After you wash up, not at all."

"You're probably getting used to it," I said.

"Yeah, no. Trust me, that's not gonna happen."

To my shock and horror, I started to cry. I dropped my head on the table, put my hands over my eyes, and tried to rein it in. But the more I tried to smother it, the harder my body shook.

I never cried. What was wrong with me, lately?

"Hey, come on, it's not that bad," Nick said, patting the top of my head. "Besides, you really don't smell now. If you did, I'd tell you."

He would, too.

"It's not that," I squeaked through my hands. "It's everything. I really am broke. I've got a college degree and more than a decade of experience, and I'm cleaning public toilets for a living. I've lost my job. And I'm going to lose my house. Oh yeah, and I'm probably going to jail."

"Well, if you go to jail, that takes care of the housing situation."

I looked up. He was smiling.

I took a deep breath, wiped my face on my sleeve and hiccuped. "Not funny."

"Oh, come on, it's a little funny," Nick said. "Of all of us kids, I never thought you'd be the one facing prison time."

"So who did you think it would be?" I asked.

"Peter. Hands down."

"Peter? Mr. Straight Arrow? He of the starched collars and cuffs?"

"Sure, that's what he wants you to think," Nick said. "That's his cover. But in reality, it's a little embezzling here. A little insider trading there. An offshore bank account for his casino winnings . . ."

The idea of our straitlaced, order-obsessed older brother doing anything even remotely questionable made me giggle.

"Seriously, what's with the toilets?" Nick asked. "I mean, aren't there other jobs you're qualified for? Flipping burgers? Greeter at Walmart? What made you wake up one morning and say, 'Hey, there's something I've never tried. Toilets!'"

I wiped my nose with my sleeve. "I didn't really take the job for the job."

"Good benefits? Sex with the boss?"

Unbidden, a picture of hairy-knuckled Mr. Gravois popped into my head. "God, no."

I took another deep breath and was relieved when my voice sounded almost normal. "I needed a way to get back into my old office building. Right before I left work the last time, I planted a listening device—a sound-activated digital recorder. Now I need to retrieve it."

"OK, so this isn't about an addiction to lime cleaner?" Nick said. "We don't need to stage an intervention?"

"Is it really that bad? Can you smell it now?" I had been in the shower last night for over an hour. At this rate, $180 a week wasn't going to cover my hot-water bills.

"No, only when you first get home. I was just ragging you."

"Thanks."

"As for the broke part, I wasn't kidding about Gabby and me paying rent. I already have some of the money from my share of the farm. And Gabby's doing great with the online boutique."

Dear God, I forgot about "the boutique."

"It's not that," I started. "It's just that I always knew who I was. Alex Vlodnachek, reporter. And I was kind of good at it. Now I've been fired. I'm being framed for murder. Half the people I run into think I did it, and the other half seem to want to make my life miserable for no reason at all."

"Well, to be fair, you didn't get fired from being a reporter," he said. "You quit. Did you like being a flack?"

"I hated it."

He smiled.

"OK, not cleaning-bathroom-stalls hated," I said. "But almost. It just seemed dishonest. Manipulative. With reporting, you lay out all the facts, everything you can find at that moment, and let the reader sort it out. With P.R., you decide in advance what you want the other person to think. Then you give out only the information that leads in that direction. It's like a sleight-of-hand trick: look over here, don't look over there. I ended up despising it. Oh, and my boss tried to pimp me out to a client."

"Man, talk about burying the lede," Nick said. "No wonder somebody killed the guy. He sounds like a giant ass-hat."

"No argument there."

"You loved newspapers. I never understood why you left."

"Money," I said. "Ironic, right? The P.R. agency actually offered me a salary I could live on. They seemed to value my skills. And I was tired of fighting the same newsroom battles I'd been fighting for twelve years. To get the beats I wanted. To cover the stories I wanted. To keep the copy desk from screwing up my stories. All while making juuussst enough money to stay afloat.

"At first, I didn't mind an entry job that paid virtually nil. I was thrilled to be working for a big metro daily. I figured I'd get my foot in the door, show them what I could do, then renegotiate. Only it never worked out that way. Every year when review time rolled around, it was the same old song and dance. Circulation is down. The price of newsprint is up. All raises are capped at three percent—no exceptions. But I discovered there were exceptions. Plenty of them. And I learned from the newsroom vets that the time to haggle over salary is before they hire you. You have the most leverage before you commit."

"Like dating," Nick said.

"Exactly," I said. "Anyway, by the time they offered me a little more money to stay, I was already walking out the door."

"Yeah, that's pretty much what happened with me and the emus."

"What did happen with you and the emus?"

"I got sick of living in the middle of nowhere, trying to launch a business with a guy who was stoned most of the time. I mean, the emus were cool, but they're a lot of hard work. And I was doing all the heavy lifting. You know how you feel about cleaning toilets?"

I nodded.

"Same thing, but with feet and feathers," he said. "I was spending ten, twelve hours a day shoveling emu crap. It got to the point where I was giving them names. That's when I knew it was time to get out."

"You named them?"

"Hey, emus are very good listeners," Nick said. "And they all had very distinct personalities. Besides, I had no cable, crappy cell reception, and every time I got an iPod, it disappeared."

"Brandon?"

"Him or the emus. In the beginning, I think he was trading my stuff for grass."

"In the *beginning*?" I asked.

"Long story," he said. "Anyway, look at the bright side."

"There's a bright side?"

"At least with Annie and Peter, the 'rents are batting .500."

I drank what was left of my coffee. No longer scalding hot, it was still comfortingly warm.

"So how exactly was your boss killed, anyway?" Nick asked.

"Stabbed in the back with a sterling silver letter opener."

"'Cause otherwise he'd come back as a werewolf?"

"Because anything other than sterling was unacceptable," I said. "Too bad I can't say the same for his character."

"So who do you think did it?" he asked.

"No idea. But I'd sure like to find out."

"Where'd it happen?" Nick asked.

"In his office on Sunday afternoon."

"Who had a motive?"

"Everybody."

Nick rolled his eyes.

"Well, let's see," I said, beginning to tick them off on my fingers. "There was his pregnant girlfriend, who he had hired a few months ago. His grieving widow, who worked at the company and may have known about his pregnant girlfriend. His business partner, who he was pushing out of the agency—an agency that said partner's father founded. And those are just the ones who have offices within fifty feet of the crime scene. No telling who else he's screwed over in his business or personal life in the last six months."

"Wow. A regular *How to Win Friends and Influence People.*"

"Pretty much," I said.

"So who do you think did it?" he asked.

"No idea."

"If you had to choose right now," Nick said, pointing his finger at me like a gun. "Gut instinct."

"I don't know. My gut's so messed up at this point, I don't think we're on speaking terms."

"Well, it wasn't his girlfriend," Nick said.

"What makes you say that? Because if she's a mistress, she has to be pretty?"

"If she's hot, she did it not."

"Thank you, Nicky Cochran."

"No, because she needs him alive. Think about it. Her best hope is if he marries her. Or gives her a big payoff. He can't do either if he's dead. And his wife sure as hell isn't gonna."

"That makes sense," I said. "But what if he decided to do neither? She could have flown into a rage."

"How many times was he stabbed?" Nick asked.

"Just the once."

"Sounds too controlled for rage. Stabbed a bunch of times, maybe. But one cut that kills? Sounds almost too . . ." he hesitated. "Precise."

"From what I managed to learn from the cops, there wasn't much blood, either," I added. "I mean, there was some. He was stabbed, after all. But not nearly what you'd think. Definitely not slasher-flick time."

"So that leaves the wife, the partner, or one of your boss's many admirers."

"Where'd you learn so much about homicide?" I asked, impressed.

"Without cable at the ranch, we could only pull in one channel with a tabletop antenna," Nick said. "And whoever did the programming was a *Law & Order* freak. It was on, like, two or three times a night. All three versions. *Special Victims Unit. Criminal Intent.* And *Law & Order* classic—frankly, my favorite of the trilogy. Maximum drama, minimum character backstory. I mean, who cares if Stabler's marriage is on the rocks, or that Benson can't maintain a relationship outside of work?"

"OK, I think you got out of that desert just in time," I said.

"Amen," he said. "So we rule out the girlfriend?"

"Sounds about right."

And suddenly, like that, it was back. That tingling in the pit of my stomach that signaled I was onto something. Now if I could just figure out what it was trying to tell me.

Chapter 15

Later that morning as I was loading the dishwasher, the phone rang. I flinched.

Billy Bob was now calling three or four times a day. He'd open with bits of newsroom gossip, commiserate about my "situation," and ask me to call him. The lead crime reporter at the *Sentinel* phoned just as often, but he was a lot less friendly.

And the credit card companies must have had me on speed dial. The reps would reference my joblessness, eagerly offering "assistance." Then they'd probe to find out what I was doing to get work and when I planned to pay off my balances.

I hated the sound of my own phone. And checking caller ID had become a reflex.

I snuck a peek. Mom.

Where's a bill collector when you really need one?

"Hey, Mom, how's Paris?"

"That's a question you shouldn't even have to ask," she said. "Honestly, I don't understand you. Those people ran that company for years without you. Do you really think they couldn't spare you for two weeks?"

"Seen any nice paintings?"

"Don't try to change the subject. Your poor sister is simply devastated."

That I believed.

"Sorry, Ma."

No lie.

"And it's not like you get this kind of opportunity every day . . ." she started.

Even my best interview skills were no match for her. I waited until she took a breath and cut in. It was like jumping in front of a verbal locomotive.

"I'm sorry, Mom. You have no idea how sorry. If I had it to do all over again, I would have totally come. But I want to hear all about your trip."

Dead silence. For about ten seconds.

"Are you joshing me, Alexandra?"

"No, Mom, I really mean it."

Unfortunately, I did. And I could feel another crying jag coming on. I seriously needed a good night's sleep.

"Are you all right? Is something wrong?" she said.

"No, Mom, it's just been a long week. But tell Annie I got her postcard. It's beautiful, and it's up on my fridge. So what have you guys been up to?"

No surprise, Paris was wonderful. But, according to my mother, it was less wonderful for my not being there. So there was that.

Still, if I couldn't catch a nap, I needed to get out of my head and out of the house. After Nick fed Lucy—and while Gabrielle was locked in the bathroom with her cell phone—I decided to take the pup on a quick tour of the neighborhood. I grabbed the leash and opened the front door.

She sprang off the porch, rounded the corner of the house, and darted behind a big azalea bush. When I peeked over, she shot me a dirty look, and turned her back.

I did an about-face. Who knew dogs had a sense of modesty?

Presumably refreshed, Lucy came bounding out and raced around the lawn in wide circles. For a puppy, she was fast. No way I was taking her out of the yard without a leash. I snapped it on, and she trotted over to the daffodils that were blooming around the mailbox. I'd put an extra blanket of pine straw over them two weeks ago. It was the last normal, home improvement thing I'd done before my life blew up.

She approached them slowly, staring. She bent and sniffed one. Ditto a second one. The third one she also licked. Then she cocked her head and sniffed the air.

What a weird little dog.

"You want to go for a walk? Lots of flowers for you to see."

She looked up at me and blinked. I swear those liquid brown eyes looked hopeful.

I led her down the sidewalk. "OK," I said softly, "this is where we live. Our yard. Now, we're going to go past some other yards. But we have to be on our best behavior. No pooping or piddling. Flower sniffing is OK, though."

What was I, nuts? After umpteen calls, I couldn't even make my insurance company understand I'd never canceled my coverage. Did I really think I could talk to a dog?

But Lucy appeared to think this over. Then she trotted down the sidewalk.

Two doors down, in front of Mr. and Mrs. Clancy's giant pine, she stopped. Uh-oh, I thought. Now we're in for it.

Stock-still, she stared up, mesmerized. I followed her gaze to see what she saw. Branches, blowing in the light breeze, and fluffy white clouds in the sky. She was entranced.

"Say, what have you got there?"

I looked over and saw Mr. Clancy coming around the yard with a bag of mulch. "Oh, hi! This is Lucy. She's visiting for a few weeks with my brother and his wife."

Somehow, I hadn't yet made the transition between "his wife" to "my sister-in-law."

Maybe it was because of all the "honey," "baby," and "sugar" I heard on my way past the bathroom this morning.

Not that I was eavesdropping.

So was she talking about the boutique? Or was she chatting with Mr. Photo Strip? Then again, Gabby pretty much called everyone "sugar."

"Well, hello there, Miss Lucy," Mr. Clancy said, setting down the bag.

Hearing her name, Lucy turned, decided he was worth liking, and began wagging her tail vigorously.

"Well, isn't she a cutie," he said. Lucy looked up demurely and allowed herself to be admired.

He took off a gardening glove and scratched her behind one ear.

"I thought I'd give her a quick walk around the block," I explained.

"Perfect day for it," Mr. Clancy said, wiping his forehead with one sleeve. "The missus loves dogs. If you ever need someone to look after Miss Lucy here, you just let us know."

Two years I've lived in this neighborhood, and that was the longest conversation I'd ever had with either Clancy. Mostly, our relationship consisted of waving from the mailbox, waving from the car, or waving from the driveway after dragging the garbage out or the bins in. Never anything out of the ordinary. No screaming. No 7 A.M. leaf blowing. No loud parties. And—most important for me—no requests to borrow, watch, water, or collect anything.

In short, perfect neighbors.

Two houses down, Lucy spotted something across the street. She raced to the curb, pulling at the leash.

"No, no, no! No street for little puppies. The street is bad. Cars are bad."

She looked at me like I'd lost my mind, then continued her assault on the curb.

"Just what is over there that's so fascinating?"

I cautiously looked both ways and told her to heel. She kind of obeyed. Almost. The tension in the leash was so tight, she was practically dragging me across the street.

Once on the other side, I gave her some slack and she went running pell-mell for a patch of daffodils at the corner of one driveway. When she got within a couple of feet, she suddenly stopped. She crouched, frozen in space and time. She shifted slightly to one side. Then the other. The crazy pup was stalking something.

Then I saw it.

"That's a butterfly, you nutty little dog."

She inched closer, watching it intently. Unaware it had an audience, the butterfly danced from flower to flower. Lucy followed its every move with her eyes. Apparently, this was the puppy equivalent of March Madness.

"Oh, hello again," said a deep British voice behind me.

Startled, I jumped. Of course, it was Ian Sterling. Why did I always run into this guy when me and mine were at our weirdest? Then again, my life was fresh out of normal at the moment.

"Uh, hi," I managed.

"How's the little dog this morning?" He cast a curious glance at my obviously crazy canine.

"Enjoying a nature walk," I said brightly. "And right now, she's doing a little butterfly watching." Hell, give me a walking stick and a solid pair of brogues, and I could be a character straight out of an Agatha Christie novel.

"Fancy that, she really is. How charming."

Is "charming" British for "odd"? I wondered.

Wearing a spotless white oxford-cloth shirt with the sleeves casually rolled up to reveal strong, tanned forearms, Sterling looked more like a polo-playing aristocrat than the owner of a decrepit B&B. Up close, he smelled like a blend of exotic spices and sawdust. And when he pushed a lock of dark hair out of his eyes, my stomach actually did a little flip.

Oh, please, I chided myself.

Lucy's butterfly fluttered off, and she flopped dejectedly on the grass.

"Lost a friend, eh?" he said, scratching her head. Her tail began to wag slowly.

"I've got some biscuits that might cheer you up," he said, as the wagging tail gained speed.

Lucy may not know "heel," but "biscuit" she gets.

"And some tea for you, if you've got time," he added, looking up at me. I couldn't have been more surprised if he'd struck me with a shovel. Really.

"That would be nice, thanks." Wow. My first sentence that hadn't begun with "uh." Trip would be so proud.

Then it hit me. Having tea at Ian's home would necessitate actually entering Ian's home. I'd been in there—for all of three minutes—a little more than two years ago. And I was none too eager to repeat the experience.

Before I'd made an offer on my own little house, the real estate agent, salivating at the prospect of selling something hideously expensive to my supermodel sister, talked Annie and me into a "quick look-see" of the Victorian across the street.

To this day, we refer to it as "the time we ran screaming from the ogre's castle."

In broad daylight, the interior had been pitch black. What we could see was covered in dust and cobwebs, with some kind of matted shag carpet that looked like dead grass. Annie never got more than three steps inside the front door, her hand clamped firmly over her mouth. I ventured farther and got to see the back walls coated in pea-green slime.

"On the bright side, no rats or roaches," Annie said later.

"Yeah, even they have standards," I'd replied.

So, cute as Ian was, I really didn't want to go back to that house. Ever.

As we approached, I noticed that the place looked different than I remembered. It had been painted a faint golden color that seemed to catch the light and almost glow. The gingerbread trim was dazzling white. The lawn, which had been pretty scraggly, was a short, thick carpet of green. Even the sidewalk gleamed.

"Wow."

"Looks a bit better, eh?"

"It looks fantastic. How did you get all of this done so fast? This is amazing."

"Money," he replied. He smiled, and I swear those gray-blue eyes twinkled. My heart was doing that flippy, fluttery thing again.

"Seriously, there isn't anything you can't get done quickly if you throw enough dosh at the problem," he added. "And at this rate, we should be printing the stuff in the basement. Come on in, and I'll show you the rest. But I warn you, it's moving a lot more slowly inside."

My stomach lurched. Would it be rude to take my tea on the porch? I really didn't want to revisit the pea-green slime palace.

What sane person would buy this place? I asked myself. *Who says he's sane?* was the reply.

"So the painters finished the outside yesterday. And I've hired a master gardener and his crew to tackle the initial yard work and draw up a plan for flowers, plantings, and trees. We're also putting in a kitchen herb garden, and we'll have a gazebo out back."

We? Oh well, it figures. You don't buy an old B&B to renovate and run by yourself. So not only have I allowed myself to be lured back to the ogre's castle, but if I'm lucky I'll get to meet Mrs. Ogre. And have tea. Great. Just great.

I gave myself a mental slap. The man was trying to be neighborly. In spite of the fact that when we'd first met I was—literally—a drooling idiot. And my life has been rolling rapidly downhill ever since. My online dating profile, if I had one, might as well read: "Broke murder suspect, cleans toilets for a living, seeks worldly sophisticate for court appearances, jailhouse romance. Turn-ons should include: rubber gloves and industrial cleaning solvents. Experience with nail files in cakes a plus. Must love dogs."

Lucy looked up at me suddenly, puzzled. I swear she could read my mind.

After fiddling with the key for what seemed like forever, he swung open the ancient oak front door. Lucy trotted right in.

Great, now I had to follow. Thanks, dog.

Just how long would I have to stay to maintain my "good neighbor" status?

I braced myself, stepped inside, and gasped. "Damn!"

Ian grinned. "Not bad, eh?"

"Did I say that out loud? I mean, wow!" I took another step, then another.

It didn't look like the same house. For one thing, it was flooded with light, which seemed to come from every direction. And for another, it was clean. Really,

really clean. I had to hand it to Mrs. Ogre. She was a wiz with a scrub brush.

The dead-grass carpet was gone, replaced with rich, wide-plank hardwood floors. I moved farther into the room, drawn by the light. The pea-soup walls were sparkling glass.

"Glass?" I said, pointing like a little kid.

"Yup. It's a sunroom. Didn't even know it was there until we started cleaning. I had plans to add one. Now I don't have to. Turns out all I needed was a few dozen liters of something called 'Windex.'"

"This is amazing."

Ian was clearly pleased. "That's where we'll serve breakfast and a nice afternoon tea."

"How did you get so much light in here? I mean, it used to be so . . ."

"Grim and grimy?" he laughed. "I know. It was awful. I'm glad you saw the 'before.' Makes the 'after' that much more of a magic trick. First, I hired a team to clean the place, top to bottom. They're the ones who discovered the sunroom, actually. Then I worked with a general contractor on the windows. Keep a secret?"

I nodded.

"We added that bank up there," he said, gesturing to a row of clerestories that sat above the regular windows. "We also installed a couple of bay windows, in keeping with the home's original character. But the real no-no," Ian said, dropping his voice to a conspiratorial tone, "is that we replaced the windows in the back of the house with slightly larger versions. It's not discernible to the casual observer, but the difference it makes in the light levels is marvelous.

"Can't say how your historic-preservation people would take it, though," he said, grinning. "So we have to keep it—how do you Yanks say—'on the down-low.'"

A B&B owner with a touch of larceny? I was really beginning to like this guy. "How did you pull it off?"

"We confined the changes to the back and sides of the house. And we used a lot of screening to block the view from the roads and the neighbors. The building inspector's fine with it, as long as it meets code, which it does. And since the house is eligible for, but not actually on, the historic register, that's all we need. Not only will the increased light save us scads on electricity bills, but it also gives us the option of adding some solar features later—which I definitely want to do. After we're up and running, of course."

"This is unbelievable. It's beautiful."

"I knew the place had possibilities," he said. "But it was touch and go for a while. Still have a lot to do, of course. Eventually, we'll have eight guest rooms. But we'll open with four. As I finish the others, we'll add them to the roster. To meet our burgeoning demand, I trust."

"How long before you open?"

"Oh, another three weeks should do it. But I'm having a little party for the neighbors, a few travel writers, and some visitors'-bureau types the Sunday after this one. I'd love it if you could drop by. Nothing formal. If the weather's good, we'll have it on the back lawn. Victorian garden party. Tea, sandwiches, fairy cakes, that sort of thing. Bring friends. And definitely bring the pup."

Lucy-the-self-aware looked up at him adoringly.

"By the by, I'm afraid I received more of your mail this morning," he said. "Let me just get it from my office."

A cream-colored drop cloth covered something large and rectangular leaning against the wall near my feet. I lifted it and took a quick peek. Two paintings. The one in front—with pastel colors and a gauzy style—looked familiar. I had something similar on my refrigerator. Only mine was a postcard.

I peered closer at the signature. Monet.

I gently tilted it forward and recognized the one behind it from a museum trip with my parents decades ago. Simple, colorful lines rendered a minotaur playing the flute with happy creatures and a beautiful, naked woman dancing joyfully on a beach. Picasso.

The paintings smelled musty. The frames held a thin film of dust. If they were copies, they were old copies.

So what exactly was going on here? Was Ian a wealthy collector? An art thief? A forger? Or were these just reproductions he picked up to decorate his new hotel?

I glanced at Lucy, and she looked up at me.

A door closed off in the distance. We both jumped.

I dropped the cloth back into place and quickly stepped over to one of the windows and pretended to study the backyard. Lucy followed.

From the hallway, I heard Ian.

"It was actually out in the street this time," he called. "But I managed to gather it up before the wind took it."

He walked in and proffered a stack of envelopes.

"Thanks," I said, hoping I'd cloaked the paintings completely—whatever they were. "I've got to have a talk with our mailman."

"Now, if you ladies want to make yourselves at home in the so-lar-i-um," Ian added, giving a mock bow, "I will go and see about that tea."

Chapter 16

When I got home, Nick was in the shower. Either that, or a bad Harry Connick Jr. impersonator had invaded my bathroom. Gabby was back in bed.

But I was relieved to see that the pile of boxes had shrunk. Shrank? Hey, there were fewer of them.

I flipped through the mail I'd gotten from Ian. Mostly bills. At this point, I figured he was getting more of my mail than I was. What was with our mailman all of a sudden?

And what was with the mysterious artwork?

If Ian really had something to hide, he probably wouldn't be inviting people into his house. But our tea was a spur-of-the-moment thing, so maybe he forgot. Or he just figured no one would see the paintings and recognize them.

More likely: After C&W, I was just paranoid.

Between the bills, I discovered another postcard. I studied the watercolor on the front—a sidewalk café set against an Eiffel Tower backdrop—and felt a little pang. What would it be like to be there right now?

Carelessly sipping café au lait, nibbling pastries, and chatting with Mom and Annie?

I flipped it over.

My older sister's beautiful, flowing script, and seven words: "Not too late to change your mind."

I sighed. I was relieved that she and Mom had no idea what was going on in my life. At the same time, if I had accepted her (very generous) offer of a free ticket to Paris (first class, of course), I wouldn't even be a suspect right now. They'd have had to pin Coleman's murder on some poor sap who was actually in the country.

I felt like crying all over again.

I flipped through the remaining mail. One business-size envelope stood out from the stack of bills I could no longer afford to pay. I recognized the creamy paper and the precise, almost mechanical handwriting. Peter.

That's odd, I thought. He could have called. And, other than a quick conversation when I first got home from the station house—to say "thank you" for Holloman and share the news that Nick was in town—I hadn't heard from him. I ripped it open.

Alex,

> *Thought you might be able to use this to tide you over. Rest and recoup.*

Peter

Enclosed was a check for $5,000. Damn! My big brother was a man of few words. But his actions put him right up there with Superman, in my book.

My first thought: "We're saved! I can pay my bills. I

can buy food. And, if I ever get my hands on that recorder, I can stop cleaning toilets."

My next thought—blame it on my mother's guilt genes—was that I should return the check. Before I was tempted to cash it.

So I did what I always do when faced with a tough choice. I put it off.

Say one thing for my sibs: every single one of them had come through for me.

Almost ten years ago, when we lost Dad, the tightly bonded atom that had been our nuclear family blew apart.

Already in New York, Peter buried himself in work and made partner in record time. Then he and Zara—whom I'd always teasingly called "my favorite sister-in-law" (because she was my only sister-in-law)—moved out to Fairfield, Connecticut.

Annie, already famous and successful, was seldom in the same city three nights in a row. After Dad was gone, there was even less incentive to stay put. She launched her agency and collected a string of homes around the world. And a string of fiancés and ex-fiancés. While she's hardly ever there, home base is an airy Manhattan penthouse. (My favorite: her sunny Miami Beach condo.)

I think it hit Nick the hardest. He flunked out of college, floated for a bit, and finally bought into the emu ranch when one of the pair of high school buds who owned it wanted to bail.

We all stayed in touch regularly via phone and Skype. And we gathered at Mom's place or Baba's for the requisite holidays. But even after a decade, there was still something—someone—missing.

Dad and Mom balanced each other out. He was easygoing, affable, a great listener—and deep.

Mom's the perfectionist—quick, dry, and acerbic. Nothing escapes her gaze.

Both bright, they shared a great sense of humor. And they made each other laugh. A lot.

Their bond held us all together. But, until it shattered, I don't think any of us realized it.

At least, I didn't.

Somehow, I didn't think anyone would be feeling Coleman's absence that intensely ten years from now. My ex-boss had been dead for four days, and I was still learning just how much of a thoroughly rotten human being he really was.

As for who'd murdered him, I had zilch. Part of me wanted to say "good riddance to a rotten boss." But whoever killed him also royally screwed up my life.

How's that for self-centered?

I flipped open my laptop and pulled up the "Who Killed Coleman" file. Five minutes later, I was still staring at the blinking cursor, hypnotized.

It wasn't writer's block. In a noisy newsroom on deadline, I could bang out a story no matter what was going on in the background: ringing phones, screaming co-workers, the occasional fistfight.

When the flow of words dried up, it always came back to the same thing: not enough information.

Tonight, Margaret would be receiving condolence visits, and the funeral was tomorrow afternoon. I needed eyes and ears in both places. Even though the funeral was public, after the scene at the office Tuesday, I had my doubts about getting in. And

Margaret's house was a definite no-go. Besides, about the time Margaret would be dressing to admit her well-heeled guests, I'd be pulling on my yellow rubber gloves to go clean toilets for the evening.

But even though I couldn't attend, I knew someone who could.

I grabbed the phone and got Trip's voice mail. My message was short and sweet: "Don't make plans for tonight. Have I got a gig for you. Call me."

Lime cleaner or no, I think he was getting the fuzzy end of the lollipop.

I Googled Coleman. Glowing accolades about his business and four days' worth of news stories about his murder, plus the obit and a funeral announcement. The news stories featured lots of quotes about the police being "tight-lipped" and stating that "sources close to the investigation" (which, depending on the ethics of the reporter, could be anyone from a police department higher-up to the sandwich delivery guy), claimed that "an arrest was imminent."

My read: the police didn't know squat and weren't talking.

I Googled Walters and got almost nothing. The C&W website, complete with bio and photo. Ivy League college. Wharton B-school. Nothing new there.

I hit my old newspaper's online archive and pumped in his name. If he'd gotten married, had a kid or buried a parent, there would be a record.

Two items from 1987. A short obit for his father, Benjamin Walters Sr., who "died following a long illness." Survivors listed a wife, Enid, and a son, Benjamin Jr.

It ran the same day as a longer feature story on Walters Sr., full of quotes from D.C. movers and shakers of the day. Thirty-one years later, I still recognized a lot of the names. Senators, congressmen, developers, and business tycoons. Senior definitely played in the big leagues, and it looked like he'd groomed his son to follow in those footsteps.

Junior had done just that. But where was the personal life? No mention of a daughter-in-law or grandkids in Senior's obit. No wedding or birth announcements for Junior in the intervening thirty-one years. No professional accolades, club memberships, or charity efforts chronicled in the society pages. It was as if, when he exited the elegant oak doors of C&W each night, Benjamin Walters Jr. ceased to exist.

I Googled Margaret Coleman. A string of stories popped up, mostly from the lifestyle pages.

Secretary of the Fordham Garden Club. OK, that explained how she knew Lydia Stewart. Typically, Old Money types ran those clubs. But once in a while, they'd toss a bone to the nouveau riche. Especially if they were really, really riche.

Margaret had also done a lot of work for the local heart foundation. Apparently, you didn't actually need a heart to raise money for them.

I clicked on an early article, circa 1995. Margaret had hosted a costume party that raised mucho bucks for the cause. I scanned the story. ". . . a former ICU nurse, Mrs. Coleman is a longtime supporter of preventive care efforts . . ."

Bingo. So Margaret really had been a nurse. And in the ICU, at that. Maybe those powerful hands really had beaten life back into a failing body. I wondered where she'd worked, and why she'd given it up. Traded the career for marriage and kids? Or had it been something else?

I switched back to my "Who Killed Coleman" file and typed what I'd learned. It didn't take long.

The phone rang, and my stomach dropped. I quickly checked caller ID.

Trip.

"So what nefarious plan have you got for me tonight?"

"More like a secret mission," I said.

"If it involves dumping your sister-in-law at a bus station, it'll have to wait. I'm putting the paper to bed."

"Any mention of me in the pages?" I asked, mentally crossing my fingers.

"Not so far," Trip said.

Thank God. "Actually, it's a condolence call."

"The scary widow?" he asked.

"She's accepting visitors between six and eight P.M. at their home."

"And you want to see if my reporting skills are still sharp?"

"Exactly. Plus if I show up, Margaret will have me arrested or shot. Probably shot."

"And that would make a great metro front," Trip said. "Because I gotta tell you, right now we've got zippo."

"Metro front" is the front page of the local section. Short of the actual front page, it's the most prized real estate in the paper. Some writers believe that their bylines alone merit at least the metro front. As an editor, it's Trip's job to disabuse them of that notion. He'd run wire copy or photos before he'd run crap.

"So the page is going to be blank tomorrow?" I asked skeptically.

"Right now I'm looking at a supersized photo of a very small tot eating a very large ice cream cone at the Cherry Blossom Festival. So cute you wanna puke. But I could swing by on my dinner break. Say a few hellos. See what I can glean."

"That would be great. Now all I have to do is figure out how I can get into the wake."

"Where is it?" he asked.

"The Barclay. Tomorrow night."

Silence. I could hear the synapses firing. "I might be able to help," Trip said finally. "Tom knows a manager over there. Let me make a few calls."

Tom, Trip's partner, is the chef at Polaris, one of the area's hottest restaurants. When it comes to food and drink in D.C. and surrounding environs, Tom knows everyone who's anyone.

"I've got to go," he said quickly. "Billy Bob just walked in, and he's got a shit-eating grin on his face. I'll call you later. We'll reconnoiter."

So why did I suspect my life was about to get a whole lot worse?

Chapter 17

When my alarm clock went off at 4:50, I felt like I'd slept for a week instead of just three hours.

Lucy, who had been curled at my feet, tumbled off the bed, righted herself, and dashed around the house like a maniac. I opened the back door, and she raced behind a bush. I closed the screen, leaving the door open, so that I'd see her the minute she reappeared.

That's when I spotted the envelope. On the kitchen table, with my name on it. I recognized the scrawly handwriting. Nick.

I reached in and pulled out the note. And a wad of cash. The note was pure Nick. Short and to the point. No extraneous details. Or details, period.

Alex,

Thanks for letting us stay with you. Here's a little of my "emu money" to help out.

Gabby and I are running errands. Back around 6. Let Lucy out for a quick "break" before you leave. I'll feed her when I get back.

Nick

At the bottom, in big loopy writing, there was a postscript.

> *P.S. And thanks again, Sis!*
>
> *Love,*
> *Gabby*

Sis?

The bills were all wrinkled twenties. I did a quick count: $300.

I was curious. What kind of "errands"? Newlyweds getting settled in? Or was this about the ever-changing mountain of mailing boxes in my living room? Or the multiple IDs in her purse?

Dear God, what if Nick had a similar set lurking in his wallet? Who was she really, and what had she gotten him into?

I opened the screen door for Lucy, and she bounced into the kitchen.

"Better?"

"Rowr," Lucy replied, loping past me and over to her water bowl. She lapped delicately for a minute or so. Then nosed the food bowl, which was empty. She looked up at me, pointedly. Without breaking eye contact, she put an oversized paw in the food dish.

"Nick says you have to wait 'til he gets back."

She reached down with her nose and pushed the bowl toward me. Then she looked up expectantly.

"An hour, tops."

She ducked again, this time sliding the bowl right into my feet. Then she sat back on her haunches and stared up at me.

I looked away. Then back. I swear I heard her stomach rumble.

"Oh, all right. But if anyone asks, this was just a snack."

I opened the fridge. Precious little.

First thing tomorrow, I was taking Nick's rent money and buying some groceries. But tonight we'd have to get creative.

I found four eggs, a couple of slices of bread, and—hiding way in the back—a half-jar of salsa. I didn't remember buying the bread, but it was mold-free. Sold!

I pulled half a package of turkey bacon out of the freezer and threw it on the counter with a *thunk*. Lucy's ears shot up.

"It's bacon. You'll love it."

While Lucy was a shorthaired dog, she still had her puppy fat and her puppy fuzz, which gave her a fluffy look. And her velvety ears seemed to have come from a much larger dog. On the outside, they were the same reddish-brown as the rest of Lucy. Inside, they matched the creamy color of her belly.

One oversized ear rotated to the side, while the other stood at attention. And she must have believed me, because her eyes never left that bacon.

I threw half the bacon into a pan, glanced at Lucy, and tossed in the rest of it. As it heated up and sizzled, she watched, fascinated.

I dumped two slices of bread into the toaster and cracked the eggs into a second pan. Minutes later, when the toast popped up, Lucy jumped. "Wuff! Rowr!"

"It's OK. It's toast. Food. Good stuff."

She looked dubious. The smell of bacon and eggs had obviously attracted the evil toast-monster, a clear and present danger. And I was clueless.

I turned off the stove, pulled two paper plates from the cupboard, and put exactly half of the eggs on each. I dropped three slices of bacon onto my plate, along with a slice of toast.

I crumbled the remaining three pieces of bacon onto Lucy's eggs. I put the plate next to her food bowl, and she stepped up immediately. She tasted a little mouthful, and followed it with a bigger mouthful. Pretty soon the plate was empty.

When she came sniffing around the table, I bent down and put half a slice of buttered toast in her mouth. She trotted across the kitchen, dropped it onto her plate, and spent the next few minutes gnawing on it.

As I shoveled in my last bite of eggs, I glanced at the stove clock: 5:25.

Luckily, getting ready for work these days took little to no effort. I pulled on an extra-large pink sweatshirt from the Walmart sale rack, and a ten-dollar pair of mom jeans that gave new meaning to the word "roomy." Most important, I pulled my reddish blond hair into a tight bun and hid it beneath a giant blue calico scarf. I skipped makeup, put on the glasses, and topped off my ensemble with a big black cardigan.

It was amazing how different I looked with no makeup, no hair care, and an outfit that was god-awful.

Not only didn't I look like myself, but whoever this person was, she'd been seriously ill for months. My disguise swam on me, which was intentional. What I hadn't anticipated: long hours, stress, and worry had gifted me with deep, dark circles under my eyes. Another week and they'd be joined by bags big enough to pack all the groceries I couldn't afford.

My landline rang again. I was tempted to ignore it. Then I remembered Trip's comment about Billy Bob. Was this the end of the line for me?

I checked caller ID. Annie's cell.

It wasn't her fault my life had turned to sand. She'd tried to take me on a sweet European getaway.

"Hey, Annie, I'm on my way out the door. What's up?"

"Ooh, business or pleasure?"

Thank goodness we weren't Skyping. If she could have seen the getup I was wearing, I'd have never lived it down.

"Business. Strictly business."

"Damn, Alex, you really are working too hard. I understand not being able to take a two-week break. But you owe yourself a little fun."

"Look who I'm talking to. How many days off have you had lately? And don't tell me traveling with Mom qualifies as a vacation."

"You got that right. But I always find ways of having fun, too. Like tonight. We're going to a party at a gallery. One of the guys we're meeting is the director. Super cute, too. Anyway, he's giving a small group of us a special tour of a modern art exhibit that won't open to the public until next week."

"That sounds great," I said.

It did. The closest I was going to get to modern art tonight was scrubbing gunk out of a toilet bowl.

"So is Mom naming your artistically inclined children yet?" I asked.

"Chloe and Jean-Louis," Annie said, deadpan.

"No!"

"Hey, you know Mom. She wants grandkids."

Peter and Zara would have been her best bet. They'd been married for years. But neither one of them ever mentioned the subject. And for Mom, that was a special kind of slow torture. It was almost enough to make me feel sorry for her.

If I didn't actually know her.

"You know what she gave me for my last birthday?" Annie said.

"No, what?" I asked.

"Six pastel onesies and a bottle of folic acid," she replied. "In a pretty pink and blue gift bag."

"No!"

"Honest!" Annie's giggle was contagious. She was undoubtedly decked out in a designer outfit curled up on the sofa of a five-star Paris hotel room, getting ready for a party. I was wearing cheap clothes that stank of cleaning chemicals, sitting on the floor of my bungalow (so that I didn't get that smell on my sofa), gearing up to go clean bathrooms.

And still she made me feel better.

"Thank you," I said finally, when we both stopped laughing. "You have no idea how badly I needed this."

"Take it easy, Cissy."

"Have a good night, Anna Banana."

I gave Lucy five minutes in the backyard, then carried her to the living room and settled her into her new doggie bed. God bless Gabby for that one. Where it had come from, I didn't want to know.

I stroked the top of Lucy's downy head. "Nick's going to be back inside of an hour. Be a good girl."

She looked intently into my face and blinked her liquid brown eyes. To say I felt a stab of guilt for leaving such a small, defenseless creature alone would be an understatement. More like a raging, romping case of remorse.

My mother was going to love this dog.

Chapter 18

This is finally it, I thought as we rode up in the service elevator. *My last night cleaning!*

I'd managed to convince Mr. Gravois that, due to a flare-up of my asthma (nonexistent), I needed to avoid the bathroom disinfectant for twenty-four hours.

When he announced the night's duties, and passed out the aprons that served as our uniforms, Madame Gravois narrowed her eyes, which darted back and forth from her husband to me.

Oh, please.

Maria and Olga shot me dirty looks and traded stage-whispered insults in Russian.

"Spaciba!" I replied. *Thank you!*

Both of them looked startled, then twisted their surprised expressions into matching glares.

Didn't matter. I. Did. Not. Care. After tonight, I was never going to see these people again.

Unless Madame Gravois popped up in my nightmares.

This evening's lineup was my favorite double feature:

kissing off Coleman & Walters and Gravois & Co. in one fell swoop.

No more mops, pails, or industrial-sized scrub brushes. No more lime-scented bathroom cleaner. And no more elbow-length yellow gloves and stupid, black canvas smock "uniforms" with "Gravois & Company International" stamped across the chest in rubberized, white cursive script. I don't know if that last touch was Gravois's idea of advertising, or if he really was afraid one of us might filch one.

Elia looked as placid as always. But when we got off on ten, she gave me a small, encouraging smile.

Everybody at C&W was at Margaret's, expressing their sympathy. Whether they felt any or not. Since visiting the grieving widow was mandatory, this place would be emptier than a looted tomb. So to speak.

I wasn't wasting time on the appetizers. I went right for the main course, wheeling my trolley straight to the conference room. The sooner I got my hands on that digital recorder, the better.

But the conference room wasn't empty.

Huddled on one side of the table, deep in conversation, was Everett Coleman's right-hand monkey: a short, slick twentysomething who went by the name of "Chaz."

If Chaz hadn't gravitated to public relations, he'd have been selling high-end used cars. And you'd have been smart to count your fingers after shaking hands.

Next to Chaz, seemingly captivated by his every word, was Mira Myles.

Mira was bad news. Literally. She wrote a gossipy news (or newsy gossip) column for the *Washington Sentinel*, my former paper's competition. Her stories were short on facts, long on innuendo. And a lot of her best "sources" didn't exist.

OK, that last part was just my opinion. But we'd worked a couple of the same stories, and there was definitely something weird there.

Sporting a brunette Anna Wintour bob-with-bangs, she was the boogeyman a lot of the editors used to scare young and not-so-young reporters. "Mira got an interview with someone who saw the Senator stumbling drunk before the accident. How come it's not in your story?"

Never mind that Mira's "witnesses" evaporated like smoke, never to be heard from again. Then it was on to the next story.

So why was Mira here? And why wasn't Chaz being Chaz and brown-nosing at Margaret's house?

Neither of them even looked up when I pushed my cleaning cart into the room. That's when I realized: I wasn't just part of the furniture, I was invisible. I didn't rate being noticed at all.

Straining to listen, I grabbed a feather duster, making what I hoped were the appropriate motions. Not that these two would know the difference.

"You realize," Chaz said, dropping his voice, "that I could be fired for even talking to you. This has to be off the record."

My bullshit meter was going haywire. Chaz didn't move his lips without getting Coleman's permission. So who was pulling his strings now?

"Not 'off the record,'" Mira corrected. "We'll say, 'not for attribution.' That means I'll quote you, but I won't use your name."

"I don't know. I've never done anything like this

before," Chaz said, with all the sincerity of a hooker on her wedding night.

"You're doing the right thing," Mira coaxed. "You want the truth to get out. You don't want a murderer going free, do you?"

What? If Chaz knew the killer's identity, Chaz would either be living off his blackmail money in Rio or decorating the inside of a pine box. The only "right thing" Chaz cared about was opposite his left thing.

"This is really difficult," he said, pausing to gather himself. "I mean, we were really close."

True. If Chaz could have gotten any closer to Coleman, the killer would have had to drive that letter opener through both of them.

"I understand," Mira said, tapping her navy frames with her pen. "Just take your time. And for the purposes of identification, we'll just say you're 'a company insider.'"

"Could we say 'industry insider' and 'close friend of the suspect'?"

Huh?

"This is so hard. We dated almost four months. I'm the one who got her the job here in the first place."

Say what?

Mirrored in the glass I was repeatedly dusting, I saw Mira nod consolingly. "So you probably feel more than a little responsible."

"She just started acting so weird lately. Distant. I mean, we kept it quiet at work, anyway. No one knew we were dating. But still, something was different. I could tell."

Mira's pen flew across the page. "How did you come to suspect she was still working for the paper?"

Oh, hell no.

"Little things. I wanted to meet her friends, but she always made excuses. I never met her family. We'd go to her place or mine. Or some out-of-the-way dive. I thought she was ashamed of me."

I looked over my shoulder. Mira shook her head sympathetically and placed her hand on his.

"She was using you?"

"Yeah."

I felt like one of those patients you read about who wakes up during surgery. I was the center of attention, but no one noticed me. And I was frozen to the spot.

"She always had a lot more money than she should have. I mean, the pay here is great, but she was just throwing it around. She always picked up the tab for drinks and dinners. Always paid cash. And she always had plenty of coke, too."

I hadn't laid a finger on Coleman. But at that moment, it took every ounce of restraint I had not to grab my carpet rake and beat Chaz like a piñata.

I'd never done drugs. Annie told me so many stories about stoned model has-beens who lost their looks and careers to drugs that I steered clear of the stuff. Never even took the customary toke in college.

Chaz, on the other hand, was rumored to have a big-time love of the white powder.

"Anyway, one of the times she was high, she said something about having a second income," he said. "I thought she was dealing. I told her, no matter how much money she was making, it wasn't worth it—that she had to get clean. She just laughed. That's when she said that, at a time when lots of people were having trouble getting one full-time job, she had two. Along with two supersized salaries."

I moved to another picture, attacking it vigorously with the duster. In the glass, I could see Mira's pen poised over her notepad. "Two jobs. Did she say what she meant by that?"

"She said she was still working for the newspaper. She was writing an insider's account of the P.R. industry. And she was going to keep the gig going for as long as she could. Because the money was—I'm sorry, these are her words—'un-fucking believable.'"

Yeah, that's why I'm broke and taking handouts from my brothers.

"Did you tell your boss?"

This was going to be tricky. If he said, "yes," and the police found out, the D.A. could haul him in and ask him to repeat that juicy little tidbit under oath. Spreading lies was one thing. Committing perjury was another. And Chaz would not do well in prison.

He shook his head. "I should have. If I had, maybe Everett would still be alive. Maybe I could have prevented all of this."

"You can't blame yourself."

"Everett found out anyway."

"How?" Mira asked.

Yeah, Chaz, how? I mean, as long as you're spinning this fairy tale.

"Everett was plugged in. I mean, when it came to networking, there was none better. Word got back to him."

"Did he ever say how he found out?"

"No," Chaz said. "Although I think one of his friends at the paper might have tipped him."

Good answer, Chaz. Scintillating, but vague. Untraceable. And it doesn't put you in the hot seat. Very smart. Which means that you're just reading the script. No way you wrote the play.

I glanced over my shoulder. Mira had the pen tip to her lips. She was practically salivating.

"Did you know that Everett was going to fire her?"

"He'd all but made up his mind. Friday night capped it. After she made that scene at the restaurant, he had to let her go."

"Go back to when he discovered she was still working for the paper. What did he say?"

"Everett kept saying, 'She's troubled, Chaz. That one is troubled.' I remember him shaking his head when he said it. He looked sad."

Oh, come on. The Everett Coleman I knew could mow down a flock of nuns on his way to lunch and still put away a three-course meal, plus cocktails.

"Everett didn't know you were seeing her?"

"I'd broken it off by that point. When I found out she had two jobs, that she was using me—using the agency—I had to make a clean break of it. When Everett found out, he told me he'd have to let her go. Friday night—her blowup in the restaurant—that was just the last straw. But even after what happened, Everett didn't want there to be bad blood. He arranged for her to come in on Sunday afternoon, so they could talk. Really talk."

Chaz paused for dramatic effect and pushed a lock of "sun-streaked" hair from his face.

I could almost see the stage direction in his script: "pause for dramatic effect." And the Oscar for Best Performance by a Lying Corporate Toady goes to . . .

"Well," Chaz said, sighing heavily. "You know the rest."

Son of a bitch. Well, at least this little dramatic recitation explained why he wasn't paying court at Margaret's. Someone had given him a hall pass to be here instead. My money's on Walters. Although I'm guessing the part about the coke was Chaz improvising. No matter how much Walters wanted to blacken my name, he'd have never sanctioned a drug reference in relation to his precious firm. Even so, it had been a bravura performance. I'd give it three-and a-half stars.

With my back to them, I rolled the cleaning cart out the door and closed it behind me. As I did, Mira said, "Now, tell me what Alex is really like."

I didn't know whether to scream or cry.

Chapter 19

The hell with Pilates or spin class. I was going to make a fortune with the Scrubwoman's Workout. Rubber gloves optional.

I never did get my hands on that recorder. Every time I got near the room, I could hear Mira and Chaz inside, going over the shocking details of "my" life.

After I hauled my aching body into my old Chevy, locked the doors, and cranked the engine to get the heat going, I checked my cell. A message from Trip, ten minutes ago. I hit speed dial. "You rang? How was Margaret's?"

"I got a few things. I'm almost done here, but I'm starving. Thanks to you, I missed dinner. The grieving drink, but they do not eat."

"Just like vampires. Waffle Barn?"

"Definitely Waffle Barn. I should be there in about twenty minutes."

"I'll be the one who smells like limes."

When I walked in, Trip was already working on the "bottomless cup" of coffee that's made Waffle Barn a favorite among long-haul truckers, third-shift workers, and college students.

The pressroom guys—the ones still left after pagination—love the place and pack the booths after the final run, ordering artery-clogging platters of waffles, eggs, bacon, and hash browns.

No reporters, though. Waffle Barn doesn't serve booze.

I'd stripped off the baggy cardigan and added a little mascara and lipstick. So now I was only moderately schleppy.

At almost 1 A.M., Trip looked the way he always did: like he'd just stepped out of a *GQ* shoot. He'd removed his charcoal suit jacket, revealing suspenders and the wide, white French cuffs of his lavender shirt—along with a pair of gold cuff links I'd given him for his last birthday. Even after a sixteen-hour day, there wasn't a blond hair out of place.

"How's my favorite cleaning lady?"

"Don't even start," I said. "And for the record, I didn't clean toilets tonight. Just dusting, polishing, and vacuuming."

"Virtually a promotion."

"You laugh, but I've spent the last two nights on latrine duty. Do you have any idea what it's like to scour a public toilet?"

"Honey, until I moved into my own place after college, I thought toilets were self-cleaning."

"I forgot who I was talking to."

Trip's family has money. Piles of it. His childhood home is a three-hundred-year-old mansion surrounded by five hundred acres of prime Virginia horse country. Anyone else would call it an estate. His family refers to it simply as "the Farm."

"Think about it," Trip said. "You flush them all the time, and they're always sparkling."

"You didn't know about the midnight elves with scrub brushes?" I asked.

"Not a clue," he replied. "I was too busy super-gluing sequins to my Keds. And, for what it's worth, your name wasn't mentioned much tonight at Margaret's."

"So they don't think I did it?"

"Oh, they think you did it," Trip said. "They've just taken to calling you 'that redheaded she-devil.' As in 'that redheaded she-devil who killed our beloved Everett.'"

"Great. Just great."

Trip wrinkled his nose. "What's that smell?"

"Welcome to my new lime-scented life."

"It's not exactly limes," he said. "More like petro-chemicals with a citrus chaser."

"The latest designer fragrance: Poverty."

"Can't say I care for it," Trip said. "I thought you didn't do toilets tonight."

"I didn't. But they make us wear black smocks that smell like they've been marinated in the stuff."

"Did you at least get the recorder?" he asked.

"No. Walters—at least, I suspect it was Walters—left one of his little flying monkeys behind," I said. "He was using the conference room to give Mira Myles an exclusive. Apparently, I'm a coke-snorting slut who was sent by the paper to write an exposé on the P.R. industry. I was collecting two salaries and spending the excess on men, drugs, and fast living."

"That explains tonight's fashion statement," Trip said, pointing to my bubble-gum-pink "World's Greatest Grandma" sweatshirt.

"Hey, this was on sale for $3.99," I protested.

"You were overcharged."

"You know Mira," I said. "She'll use the stuff with just enough 'sources believe' and 'rumors persist,' that her paper's covered. How does she get away with it?"

"She's essentially a gossip columnist, and gossip sells papers," Trip said. "That buys her a lot of latitude. Plus, she claims she has corroboration but needs to protect her sources. So her editors allow her to keep those sources private."

"Private, as in imaginary," I said.

"Just like her childhood friends," he added.

Mira had been jailed at least three times for "protecting" her sources. It made her the darling of the local media. The hard-charging reporter challenging the system.

I'd been a big fan, too. Until she was behind bars the second time. I was working the same story, and something about Mira's information didn't sit right.

When it was challenged by the subject of her story, a local political aide, she stonewalled, claiming an ironclad duty to her source. A judge tossed her in jail, and the local media—plus several national outlets— went nuts.

Reluctant to keep such a popular D.C. celeb behind bars too long, the judge gave her a severe finger wagging and released her.

A few sparsely attended hearings over the next year resulted in a finding that, while the "facts" in her story were technically wrong, she hadn't purposely printed lies. Mira and her paper were off the hook. And on to another story.

"Any idea when it will run?" Trip asked.

We were now talking in terms of "when," not "if."

I shook my head.

"Ideally, it would be the morning of the funeral," he said. "But that's today. So she probably didn't make the deadline."

We could both see the page in our heads. My photo, looking like a deer in the headlights. Headline: Killer Employee? (The question mark would give them some deniability.) Or, for those who liked alliteration: Supermodel's Sister Suspected Slayer.

"It's got to be soon," I reasoned. "This murder isn't getting any fresher. So what did you hear at Margaret's?"

"Nothing that'll improve your appetite. Some interesting gossip, though. Any idea how Coleman and Walters got together?"

I shook my head. "Through work, I assumed."

"Margaret."

"Margaret?"

"She nursed Walters Sr. through his illness," Trip said.

"Not too successfully. He died."

"Well, apparently, Junior doesn't hold a grudge. Shortly thereafter, Everett P. Coleman married Margaret, became business partners and best buds with Walters and acquired half the agency."

"That's odd," I said.

"Yeah, I thought it smelled, too," he admitted. "I've got some ideas, but I want to do a little checking first."

"Want to give me a clue, Scooby-Doo?"

"Nah, it's probably nothing," he said. "And it might not even be relevant. But in the interest of running down every possible lead . . ."

"Before they run me over with a steamroller."

"Eggs-actly," Trip said. "And speaking of eggs . . ."

The waitress appeared, and we both ordered the same thing: the Barn Burner. Two eggs with cheese, onions, and peppers. A side of hash browns. Three slices of bacon. And a giant waffle slathered with butter. They should call it "Heart Attack on a Plate." But that probably wouldn't move the merchandise.

When she left, Trip wrinkled his nose again.

"That bad?" I asked.

"We've got to get you out of there," he said. "Which reminds me, you've got to call in sick tomorrow. You're working the wake."

"What?"

"Coleman's wake. Tom made a few phone calls. He knows the guy who runs catering at The Barclay, and he needs a few extra hands to work the event. You're in."

"I can't just pop up there," I said. "Hell, at this point, if those people could get their hands on me, they'd burn me at the stake."

"That's the best part," Trip said. "You'll be in disguise. And at The Barclay, the servers are practically invisible anyway. Throw in the dim lighting, a little creative makeup, plus massive quantities of alcohol, and you're good to go. The real problem is that Tom promised the guy three waiters."

"The bunch at C&W has already seen you," I said.

"Yeah. Besides, I want to show up as a guest."

"You're going to the wake?" I was truly touched.

"You think I'm going to send you into that shark tank alone?" he said. "Of course I'm going. And if we're going to learn anything, we need all the eyes and ears we can get."

"Where are we going to get two more servers to work a wake?" I asked, thinking out loud.

"How many cocktail waitresses do you know?"

"No."

"Look, I know Nick will help you out," Trip said. "And Gabby's got actual experience. Of some sort."

"I don't want him mixed up in this," I said. "Besides, there's something about her that's a little off."

"As opposed to your life, which is running like a Swiss watch at the moment?"

"Point taken," I said. "But she's packing five different Social Security cards and matching driver's licenses. All with different names. All with her photo."

"And you learned this how, exactly?" he asked.

"Rifling through her purse. But that's beside the point. She's also carrying snaps of a boyfriend. And she spends hours in the bathroom with her phone."

"You're afraid what she's really carrying is a torch?" Trip said.

"Why else do you keep a guy's picture in your wallet?" I said.

"Maybe she's a hit man, and he's her next target."

"Better than what I'm thinking," I said. "What if she got into some kind of scrape—the mail-order business, the boyfriend, whatever—and needed to book it out of Vegas fast?"

"So she hops on the first Nick out of town?" Trip countered. "Seems a little extreme. I mean, there are plenty of other ways to leave Las Vegas. I believe they even made a movie about it."

"Yeah, but this would also change her name at the same time. Legally. And it's not like they took a plane, or a train, or even a bus. Nick drove here in a little used car he picked up in Vegas. So she wouldn't show up on any travel records. Plus, they've been spending nothing but cash. Which means no telltale credit-card receipts. Hell, if Nick checked into the highway motels along the way, she wouldn't even have had to show a credit card or driver's license."

"Sounds like she's got the driver's license thing covered," Trip said. "Have you talked to Nick about any of this?"

"You mean Nick-the-happy-honeymooner who's convinced he can do anything as long as they're together?" I said.

"So I'm guessing she's better looking than an emu?"

"Much. She also sleeps 'til noon, stays up all hours, and moves mountains of mailing boxes in and out of my house. And when she's not on her laptop, she's on her phone. I tried to talk with him a couple of times, but things keep coming up."

"You don't think the mail-order business is drug-related, do you?" Trip asked, leaning forward.

"Nah, Nick would never get mixed up in that," I said almost blithely.

"We're not talking about Nick. We're talking about a strange woman you don't know who's staying at your home." He paused, studying me. "What did you do?"

"OK, I may have peeked a little."

"Annnnnnddd?"

"Designer bags. iPods. Smartphones. Jewelry. Exactly the kind of stuff Nick said she was selling."

"So she's up to something, but it's not drugs," Trip concluded.

"Pretty much."

"No offense, but we could use a little larceny on our side for a change," he said.

"So you want me to offer an olive branch?"

He flashed a devilish grin. "What's the worst that could happen?"

Chapter 20

By the time I got home, it was almost 3 A.M. All the lights were blazing, so I knew Nick and Gabby were up. I just hoped they weren't up to something.

As I hit the front porch, the door opened and something shot past my legs. Lucy.

"Hey, you're out late," Nick called from the doorway.

"I met Trip for an early breakfast."

Lucy ran back and scampered around my legs, sniffing furiously. The canine equivalent of "What'd you bring me? What'd you bring me?"

I reached down and scratched her head. "Nutty little dog."

"She is that," Nick said, holding the door open for Lucy and me. "By the time we got home, she was so hungry, she'd actually eaten one of her chew sticks. I think she's part goat."

I glanced down at Lucy. She looked away.

On the sofa, Gabby was typing madly on her laptop. I also noticed that the stack of boxes in the corner had changed. Grown. Pretty soon the pile was going to need its own room. Maybe it could pay rent, too.

Suddenly, I was exhausted. Physically tired, and tired of the way my life was going. I wanted to take a shower and sleep for a week. Instead, I cleared my throat.

"Guys, I could really use your help with something," I started.

The next ten minutes were a blur. I remember a lot of squealing and hugging (Gabby), and a solid slap on the back (Nick). Bottom line: they were happy to help.

Gabby even volunteered to help me with my disguise. Or "makeover," as she called it.

"Honey, you're cute, but you don't wear nearly enough makeup," she said. "Lucky for you, I can fix that."

Later that same morning, Nick was in the backyard with Lucy, who seemed genuinely intrigued by the idea of peeing and pooping outside. Being a small dog with an even smaller bladder, she was hitting the mark about fifty percent of the time.

But she was getting better. The puddles were closer to the doors. And I noticed she'd started avoiding the carpets, in favor of the hardwood floors or the vinyl in the kitchen. At least if she wasn't completely housebroken, she was getting easier to clean up after.

It was only a little past 8 A.M. when the phone rang. Say what you want about the bill collectors, none of them ever called before nine. So what kind of bad news gets up this early?

I decided this was a job for voice mail.

Five minutes later, I got up the nerve to check the messages. "Alex, this is Linda in Dr. Braddock's office," said a crisp female voice. "The check you wrote for your last visit was returned by the bank. We're going to need you to come in this morning and pay your bill."

What?! How? I knew the money was in my account because I'd transferred it from savings right after I wrote the check. I'd moved just enough to cover the dentist and buy some groceries—leaving a hefty twenty-eight-dollar cushion in my checking account. Look out, Vegas, here I come.

Lucy bounded in the kitchen door, tripped over nothing, and rolled. She righted herself, plopped down at my feet, and flipped over, offering her belly for a rub. Of course, she got it.

Why couldn't my life be that simple?

I walked into the dining room that I'd turned into my home office. What did I need with a formal dining room? The meals I didn't eat at my cozy kitchen table, I ate on the couch in my living room. Or stretched out in front of the TV in my bedroom.

When I logged into my checking account, I got nasty surprise No. 2. The balance was $476 and change. It should have been either $786 or twenty-eight dollars, depending on whether Dr. Braddock had cashed his check.

I scrolled down to "recent transactions" and saw a bunch of charges for various bank services, plus six overdraft fees at thirty-five dollars each. Yikes! And more important, how?

I grabbed the phone and started dialing.

"Helicon National Bank. This is Allie. How can I provide great service today?"

I supplied Allie with two pin numbers (for security), and the short version of my story. Unpaid dentist. Twelve mystery charges. No checks outstanding except the one to said dentist. Who still hadn't gotten his money.

"Let me place you on a short hold while I check your account," she said.

Three minutes later, Allie was back and a lot less friendly.

"I'm sorry, but the check was returned due to insufficient funds. That's why you incurred the fees."

"I had $786 in my account. The check was for $758. How is that not enough?"

"Your balance wasn't $786 at the time the check was presented. It was $28.32. You made a deposit after 2 p.m. So it didn't go into your account until this morning, just after midnight."

"I transferred cash from one account to another. That's supposed to go in immediately."

"That was under our old policy. Under the new policy, which went into effect on the first of the month, all deposits made from a foreign ATM before 2 p.m. are processed that evening after midnight. Transactions made after 2 p.m. won't be processed until the next business day. Since you didn't have enough money in your account to cover the check, you incurred the NSF fees."

"That explains one of the charges. What about the other eleven?"

"Actually, six of these are NSF charges. Let's see, you transferred money through a foreign ATM. So there's a ten-dollar foreign ATM fee. Then you withdrew one hundred dollars from a foreign ATM. That's a second foreign ATM fee. Since there were insufficient funds in your account, that also triggered the second NSF fee. You were assessed your monthly account maintenance fee, which is twenty dollars. Since you didn't have enough to cover that, there was a third NSF fee. Then, there was an excessive savings withdrawal fee, since this is the third time this month you've removed money from the savings account. That's fifteen dollars, plus another NSF fee. And a twenty-dollar charge for printing checks. You did order checks?"

"Ten days ago. But . . ."

"Well, since you had a negative balance, there was an NSF fee for that, too. Oh, and there was a twenty-five-dollar penalty fee for dropping below your required one-thousand-dollar minimum balance."

"Let me guess, that also came with an NSF fee?"

"Yes, it did. "

"I don't need to keep a minimum balance. I have free checking. No monthly fees, and I get free check printing, too."

The only time I ever had more than a thousand in my checking account was when it was time to pay the mortgage. And that lasted three days, tops.

"I'm sorry, but you're no longer eligible for our employer-sponsored Platinum Free Checking. As of"—and there was a pause while Allie clicked some computer keys—"Monday, that privilege was revoked. You'll be getting a notice in the mail. You've been switched to our Premium Checking product."

Man, C&W wasted no time sharing the good news.

Was there anyone in greater D.C. who didn't know I'd been fired?

"Since I was switched without my knowledge or permission, can you at least erase the current fees? As a courtesy?"

"I'm sorry, we can't do that. Notification was mailed promptly. It's up to you to keep up with your account."

I have to say, she didn't sound sorry. She sounded like she was eating ice cream and enjoying it. The bank wasn't stealing money from my account, I was "incurring fees." It was my fault they were draining me dry.

"Yes, but I signed up for free checking with no minimum balance. Your bank switched me. Without telling me."

"There's nothing we can do. The Platinum accounts are only for employees of client businesses. Once you're no longer with a participating employer, you're no longer eligible for the program. Is there anything else I can do for you today?"

"Else? What exactly have you done so far?"

"Good-bye, Ms. Vlodnachek. Have a nice day."

Chapter 21

That afternoon, my living room took on the air of a 1960s Vegas caper movie.

Gabby had me in a kitchen chair with an apron around my neck and was applying makeup with the swift, sure strokes of a true artiste. My shoulder-length hair was wrapped tightly around my head, held in place with dozens of bobby pins and a few globs of hair gel. The polish on my fake crimson nails was still drying, and I'd been instructed not to move.

I felt like a mummy undergoing the embalming process.

"You look kind of like a drag queen," Nick said, as Gabby added a few dabs of scarlet lip gloss.

"Honey, I've got news for you," she drawled. "All beautiful women are drag queens at heart. Real glamour doesn't just happen. It takes work."

I slid my eyes over to Trip, who was struggling not to laugh. And losing the battle.

Gabby slipped a dark brown wig onto my head, tugged twice, and clipped a couple of fasteners into place. Then she stepped back, looked me up and down, and broke into a big smile. "Gorgeous. Ab-so-lute-ly gorgeous."

"She does look different," Nick said.

"I wouldn't recognize you," Trip said, studying me from all angles.

I reached for the mirror, but Gabby blocked my hands.

"Un-uh," she warned. "Not 'til that polish dries. I don't want you to touch anything for another ten minutes." Instead, she held up the hand mirror.

My wavy, red-gold hair had been replaced by a brunette Julia Roberts halo that fell to my shoulders. And false eyelashes made my brown eyes look huge and cat-like. Even the shape of my face looked different. And somehow, with Gabby's experienced hand wielding the glue, my eyes didn't itch. Come to think of it, neither did my scalp.

Good lord, this might actually work.

"OK, kiddies, gather 'round," Trip said, clapping his hands. "Time to get to know the players in our little drama."

He tossed photos from a stack onto my coffee table like cards from a deck. "These are pix of the crew from Coleman & Walters. Obviously, you have to wait on everyone tonight. But you want to pay special attention to these folks. Stay near them as much as you can. Try and listen in on their conversations. And remember any interesting morsels."

"Where'd you get those?" I asked, pointing at the candid shots.

"Snapped them last night with my cell phone. Surreptitiously, of course." He held up the first one.

"This is the grieving widow, Margaret Coleman. Former nurse. Currently the office manager-slash-power-behind-the-throne at the firm."

"There's a woman who could definitely use a makeover," Gabby said, shaking her head. "Not much to work with, though. Maybe one of those TV extreme thingies?"

"Say what you will, she can hold her booze," Trip said. "I saw her knock back three scotches in an hour last night, and she didn't even wobble.

"And these are the kids," he added picking up a photo in each hand. "A boy and a girl. Twins. Pat and Patti. Both were supposedly away at college when it happened. But the time of death on Sunday gives them plenty of leeway. Plus, they could spill some interesting stories, especially if they're drinking."

"Ooooh, they look just like Momma," Gabby said, shaking her head.

"Yeah, pretty unfortunate," Trip said. "And this is the mistress, Jennifer Stiles."

"Hey, now she's cute," Gabby said. "I like the hair. Very Angelina Jolie."

Nick gave me a thumbs-up.

"I can't believe she showed up at Margaret's," I said.

"She had to," Trip said. "Think about it. It would have looked funny if she hadn't."

"She might be pregnant, so she may or may not be drinking tonight," I added. "And I'm curious to know, either way."

"This is the business partner," Trip said, holding up an image of Benjamin Walters. Even in a color photo, Walters looked gray. "We think he was getting cut out of the company. What would help is to know a few of the details."

"Who else will be there?" Gabby asked.

"Chaz, the office weasel," I chimed in.

Trip gave me a pat on the back. "One of Alex's co-workers, who's spreading some pretty nasty lies to the press. Don't have a picture of him because he wasn't there last night."

"Just look for a short, stocky guy with bleached blond streaks who's oozing slime," I added. "That's Chaz."

Trip grinned. "For the most part, you'll be serving senators, congressmen, aides, lobbyists, corporate honchos, media and P.R. types," Trip said. "It'll be a regular 'Who's Who' of D.C."

Gabby threw back her shoulders and grinned. "This is sooooo exciting. Anything else we need to know?"

"Yeah," I said. "Odds are, one of the people in that room tonight is a killer."

When Trip left for the funeral, Nick took Lucy over to the Clancys', where she would spend a well-supervised evening. Gabby retreated to the guest room to finish getting ready.

Hand it to The Barclay, the uniforms were a lot better than what I usually wore to work these days. A white long-sleeved blouse with a simple black skirt (for the girls), or a white dress shirt with black dress slacks (for the guys). Men wore ties. Women: a gold chain and earrings.

It was nice to dress up for a change. Even if I was still the hired help. Best of all, we'd get to bring home the leftovers.

Which reminded me.

I grabbed my cell, tried to dial, and—thanks to my new nails—fumbled. It was like having chopsticks glued to my fingertips. How did Annie manage this stuff?

I retrieved the phone from the sofa, where it had landed. Gripping it in my left palm, I clutched a pen in my right fist and poked out the call-block code, followed by the number to Gravois & Co. I swear I'd seen apes do the same thing on the Discovery Channel.

"Allô."

I coughed into the phone. "Mr. Gravois," I wheezed, using my best raspy voice.

"Oui, this is Gravois."

"Mr. Gravois, this is Al . . . uh . . . Gabrielle. I'm afraid I'm not feeling well. Bronchitis. And it's aggravating my asthma. I won't be able to work tonight." I punctuated that last statement with a couple of coughs for good measure.

"Is fine. No work, no cash money."

That's when I remembered: today was payday. And Gravois, high-flying financier that he was, paid cash.

"I can collect my pay when I come in on Monday," I said, scraping my throat with a few more coughs.

"No cash on Monday. Cash on Friday."

"But you can hold my cash and pay me Monday."

"No work on Friday, no cash money."

"I've scrubbed toilets and cleaned offices all week. You have to pay me."

"You say you not work. No work, no cash money," he said, his accent suddenly getting a lot thicker. His English might be sketchy, but his grasp of capitalism was first-rate.

"What if you gave my money to Elia? She can hang on to it for me."

"No substitutions!" he barked. "No come to work, no cash money."

The guy was a broken record.

"I'll be in on Monday," I said. Fortunately for my new fingernails, you couldn't slam a cell.

Like it or not, I needed access to that building. Even if it meant cleaning toilets for free.

Chapter 22

The events manager at The Barclay kept his instructions short and sweet. "Keep your trays loaded, and don't stop moving."

Nick, Gabby, and I were clustered around a booth in The Barclay's special-events room, along with a regular waiter named Travis, and the restaurant's ancient maître d', Ralph. The five of us, plus a bartender who hadn't shown up yet, would be staffing the wake.

Gianni (who was a friend of Tom's), had already presented the three of us with the black, pearl-button vests that completed our "uniforms." We looked like waiters, but I was dubious. Any minute now, I was certain I'd be discovered and tossed out.

Which pretty much described my life at the moment.

The room itself was impressive. Definitely not the usual four-walls-and-a-banquet-table-jammed-into-a-claustrophobic-backroom that most restaurants offered. Think small hotel ballroom. Fitted out with a full bar, recessed lighting, and lots of polished oak and brass, it was more like a slightly smaller version of The Barclay itself.

"Don't worry about smiling, this is a wake," Gianni stressed. "Be omnipresent and invisible."

My new motto.

"At the end of the night, the event gratuity will be split seven ways," he continued. "Two shares for Ralph, one for everyone else."

Ralph, as well-known in D.C. as the Washington Monument and twice as old, nodded gravely.

With an open bar and a room full of heavy drinkers, that math could still net me more than $300 at the end of the night. Take that, Gravois.

Since Coleman had been buried earlier this afternoon, this wasn't a wake in the traditional sense. This event was strictly for the living.

And two hours later, the room was packed.

I quickly discovered that Gianni's advice was easier in theory than in practice. Keeping the trays moving meant either pushing people aside (not great wake etiquette), or trying to find an open space where virtually none existed. I'd said "excuse me" so many times I was beginning to sound robotic.

Gabby, on the other hand, made it look effortless. She waltzed through the crowd with her tray like she was on *Dancing with the Stars*. She didn't even seem out of breath.

Whatever else my new sister-in-law was into—or up to—she was a first-rate waitress. I didn't know whether to feel relieved or guilty. So I settled for vaguely uneasy.

Nick received a field promotion to bartender when the regular guy didn't show. He was ensconced behind the massive oak bar pouring twenty-year-old scotch—the liquid of choice for this crowd—along with a fair amount of wine and imported beer.

I'd heard Ralph tell him that if any of the guests "requested anything more complicated than scotch and soda," he'd shuttle it over from The Barclay's main bar. But from what I could see of the empty glasses, that hadn't been necessary.

I was a wreck. Lifting trays apparently used a whole different set of muscles than cleaning toilets. My legs throbbed. My back ached. My arms felt like they were going to fall off. And, since I hadn't eaten all day, I was starving.

Margaret was holding court in a corner booth, with Walters at her elbow. Gabby was covering that area.

"Your boss's wife is a witch," she confided in the kitchen, as we restocked our trays.

"No argument here. What'd she do this time?"

I reached for a mini-quiche, and a cook slapped my hand. "No tasting!" he said. "At The Barclay, the waitstaff serves the food. The waitstaff does not eat the food."

I glared at him.

But Gabby flashed a big smile and—I swear I am not making this up—batted her lashes. "We just wanted a liiiitle nibble. It all smells so goooooood."

"OK, just a bite," he said, winking. "And don't let anyone catch you," he called over his shoulder as he headed back to the main kitchen.

"How do you do that?" I asked.

"Sugar, it's all in the attitude. Besides, that's why

we're here tonight, right? Charm the socks off these nice folks and get some information?"

Some reporter I am.

"Charm's good," I said, grabbing a quiche. "So what'd you learn about Margaret?"

"She's more worried about the insurance money than she is about losing her man. The insurance company hasn't paid yet, and she is teed off."

That was weird. The company should have mailed a check by now. Or be preparing one.

"Did she say what the holdup was?"

"The pale guy told her that the company was just dotting the i's and crossing the t's before writing a couple of checks that big. He kept saying it was 'completely routine.' Those were his exact words."

"What did she say to that?"

"You don't want to know."

I raised my eyebrows.

"OK, sugar, she said, 'Everybody knows the red-headed bitch is responsible. I want my money.'"

"Did either of them happen to mention how much money we're talking about?" I was curious. What did a slightly used Everett P. Coleman go for these days?

"Thirty million for the business policy," Gabby said. "Another fifteen million for the family policy."

Ka-CHING! The not-so-merry widow has another motive. And this one's impossible to hide.

"Bland guy told her he could buy her half of the company with part of the business insurance," Gabby said. "Something called a 'key-man policy?' Honestly, that part didn't make a lot of sense."

I'd learned about key-man policies from Peter. They were a fairly common business tool, and his

firm used them. You took out life insurance on all
the principals in a company, both to cover what it
would cost the business to replace them and—in the
case of the actual business owners—to compensate
the spouse and kids for the deceased's share of the
company.

It gave high-strung corporate types some assurance
that they wouldn't wake up one morning to discover
their new partner was an eighteen-year-old demanding
his late father's corner office and a company Ferrari.

"What did she say to that?"

"She said, 'That's not going to happen, Benjamin.'
Super cold. Then a bunch of folks came up, and she
went back to being the tearful wife. At that point, my
tray was empty, so I had to shake my tail feathers back
to the kitchen."

I started to tell her she'd make a great spy. Then I
remembered the multiple IDs and bit my lip.

"You did great," I finally said.

Gabby beamed.

"Cheddar popover, sir?"

Trip put one hand to his chin and pretended to
study the tray. "These people would give the newsroom bunch a run for their money in the drinkers'
Olympics," he said softly.

"Hey, it takes real effort to drown your soul and
keep it dead," I replied. "Any front-runners?"

"I wouldn't rule out Pat and Patti."

"Any reason? Besides the fact that their parents
named them Pat and Patti?"

"I know. Sounds like a bad lounge act. Now playing

at the Oxnard Airport Hilton, the smooth, soulful stylings of . . . Pat & Patti. I'll tell you one thing, Pat can't hold his liquor. Two beers, and he was facedown on the bar. Nick had to walk him into the kitchen for some coffee."

"Then he doesn't take after his dad," I said. "That man was a gold-medal lush."

"So's his wife. By Nick's count, she's had five scotches already. Good thing she's got Walters for a designated driver."

"Is that what he's telling people? Walters never drinks. At least, not that I've seen."

"Oh, and here's a newsflash: Ralph's already thrown Mira out twice."

"She's here?"

"With pad and pen at the ready. All she needs is a little badge that says 'press.'"

"I'm surprised Walters didn't whisk her to the head table. It's his fiction she's ghosting."

"She doesn't know that. Besides, plausible deniability dictates that he has to be 'highly offended' by all the dirt she's digging up. Oh, yummy!" he said, finally plucking a flaky pastry from the tray. "Thank you, serving wench."

"My fazer waza sunovabish."

I slammed into the kitchen to find Nick propping up a seated Pat Coleman.

"Two beers," Nick said, holding up two fingers in a "V." Pat's head hit the table with a thud.

"Look, I've got to get back out there," he added.

"If we cut off the booze flow, it's going to get ugly. Can you handle him?"

Pat was now snoring softly. How tough could it be?

"I've got him," I said. "But where's the other one? I thought twins were supposed to share some mystical, psychic bond that alerts one when the other's in trouble."

"Apparently getting blotto and passing out at your dad's wake doesn't trip the alarm. She's locked in the staff bathroom with a fifth of vodka and one of the busboys."

"That's Daddy's little girl."

Nick gave a mock salute and dashed through the kitchen's swinging doors.

"OK," I said to the snuffling blob at the table. "We're going to get you some coffee."

I'd just figured out how to work the industrial-size coffeepot and gotten it brewing when Ralph came through the doors.

"We need you out front," he said, jerking a thumb so wrinkled it looked like an overboiled hot dog.

"I'm on babysitting duty," I said, nodding at Pat.

Ralph put his hand on Pat's neck and felt for a pulse. "He's just sleeping it off. He'll be fine. But we need to get some food out there pronto. Or the rest of them are going to look just like this."

I grabbed a tray of prawns and hustled out the door, just missing Gabby.

"Watch it out there, hon," she said with a wink. "They're getting a little handsy."

Why was I even surprised?

I'd made it halfway across the room when a voice sent ice down my spine. "Hey, I know you!"

I froze. But my accuser kept coming. A pudgy, middle-aged guy, he was a higher-up in the local P.R. association. Named Phil? Bill?

Will! I'd met him all of twice. How the hell did he recognize me? My heart was pounding double time.

"I'd know that pretty face anywhere!"

Pretty face?

"You're the cheese puff girl. Hey, Troy, this is that pretty little thing I was telling you about. The one with the great big . . . cheese puffs." At that, the two of them dissolved into raucous laughter.

The prawns and I scooted to the other side of the room. I crashed into another body. And froze.

Chaz.

"Hey, watch where you're going with that thing," he slurred.

"Sorry," I said, raising the tray again in self-defense. "Prawn?"

"What the hell, free food," he said, grabbing a giant shrimp with his free hand, and thumping his chest with his lowball glass. "It's good to be Chaz!"

Right behind him, Gabby paused momentarily, then changed direction.

I made for the bar and set down the tray, pretending to rearrange the prawns. Nick was nowhere to be seen. But Trip and Jennifer were deep in conversation at the end of the bar. She was sipping what looked like seltzer water. Or it could have been gin and tonic.

From what I'd noticed, she'd been on her own most of the night. As comfortable as she'd appeared on her first day at C&W, that's how miserable and out of place she looked tonight. It wasn't that she was being overtly excluded. More like someone had put her behind an electric fence and erected a flashing "keep out" sign. And, hand it to the folks at my old office, they were great at reading the signs.

I saw Trip pat her shoulder as they talked. Well, good. Now that she'd found a friend, I hoped she was spilling her guts.

I went back to working the room, pausing only long enough to present my tray and eavesdrop. Not necessarily in that order.

"I heard it was his bookie," said a trim, dark-haired guy I didn't recognize. "Coleman liked the ponies, but he couldn't pick 'em."

"Couldn't pick 'em is right," added one of the suits from C&W. "It was some redhead he was banging at the office."

Swell.

"I heard there hasn't been any vodka in the freezer since he died," said a shellacked, forty-something blonde.

"Yeah," said her brunette companion, stumbling slightly as she lurched to retrieve a prawn. "And . . . they're . . . using . . . grocery . . . store . . . coffee."

"No!" said the blonde.

Wow. How will those kids survive the week?

At my elbow, I heard a voice I recognized. Paul, one of Walters' favorites, was talking to another guy I didn't know. "I'm not kidding," he said, turning to grab a shrimp. "An IRS audit. They notified the office three days before he died."

"Then maybe it was suicide," the second guy said. They both laughed.

Interesting. Maybe Benny's "friends" at the IRS weren't so friendly after all.

"I heard Burgoyne & Co. put out a contract on him," a reedy female voice whined behind me.

Yeah, 'cause a letter opener is a hit man's weapon of choice.

"Let's put it this way," a man's voice drawled from another direction, "it was a lot easier to snake that account with the old man gone."

"Quite a coup," said his female companion.

I whipped my head around, but neither looked familiar.

"The old guy would have taken it for himself, if he'd had a pulse. Now it's all mine. And let me tell you, that baby's going to mint some serious coin."

The woman giggled and rubbed his sleeve.

Unbelievable.

"Ya gotta love it," roared a baritone behind me. "He was scared shitless of his wife. And then it's his girlfriend who goes and kills him! Never trust a redhead."

You can trust this one to spit in your drink. And why is everyone so convinced that I was his girlfriend?

"The old bastard actually had the nerve to threaten to make me pay for it," another male voice boomed. "He actually pretended to be indignant. Red in the face. Shouting. Slamming his fist on the desk. The works."

Oh, goody.

"Acted like he hadn't planned the whole campaign. Of course, it was my signature on all the paperwork. So when the clients started to squawk, he cut me loose. And threatened to sue me. Me! After all the shit I cleaned up for him over the years. I say the old bastard got what he deserved."

"Karma's a bitch."

"Yeah, but tonight she's my bitch."

I glanced over my shoulder. The guy with the grudge was Bingham, one of C&W's former account execs. I didn't know the other one.

As the night wore on, the tone of the room went from collegial to college frat house. My ass had been pinched so many times it felt like a pincushion. And one would-be Romeo actually took my hand and offered to trade me a shrimp for "an extra large."

Gabby was getting the same treatment. She just laughed it off.

"The trick," she told me one of the many times we were restocking our trays in the kitchen, "is to wink at 'em and keep moving. Like it's a big joke, and you're in on it."

"So I can't kick 'em in the nuts?"

"Not if you want tips. And, honey, in the waitressing game, we live on tips."

Over the next few hours I learned a few things. First, even though everyone seemed to have a good motive for killing Coleman themselves, I was the sentimental favorite for having dispatched him to The Great P.R. Agency in the Sky. Or wherever he was currently residing.

Although a few wacky souls were at least considering the mob-hit scenario.

And second, extreme grief was giving these people

an appetite. Or maybe it was just the booze. Either way, they were picking the trays clean in record time.

I slammed through the kitchen doors, only to find Mira, bottle in hand, pouring something into Pat's coffee. And it wasn't creamer.

She glanced up, then back at him.

"An' zhats when he tol' me I had to come home," Pat pronounced. "Jus' like zhat. Jus' come home. Jus' cuz I wanted to change majorzzz. Basss-tarddd!" he said, spitting the last word as he nestled his head on the table.

"What about the girl in your father's office? The redhead?"

"I like blondzzzzz," he said sleepily.

"Here, drink your coffee. Now, tell me about your father's girlfriend. The redhead. When did you know they were sleeping together?"

"Mmmmmm. Sllleeeep," he said, closing his eyes.

I barreled back into the crowd and found Ralph right outside the kitchen doors. "Mira's back. She's got Pat," I said, pointing frantically.

Ralph might be ancient, but that man could move. When I walked back into the kitchen a minute later, there was no sign of Mira. She'd disappeared. Poof.

My eyes slid involuntarily back to the big meat locker in the corner. He wouldn't. Would he?

"Uh, where is she?" I asked, not sure I wanted to know.

"Alley," Ralph said, jerking a hot-dog thumb toward the kitchen's back door. "That's probably how she got in. Damned reporters are like roaches. I locked it, but she'll probably be back, so keep an eye peeled. Nice work, by the way."

"Uh, thanks." As a former roach, I didn't know what to say. But the label fit Mira. I pictured her scuttling back and forth across the alley, sniffing for an opening. Ick.

By the end of the night, I had sore feet, aching arms, a dozen crackpot murder theories, a handful of realistic motives, and a new appreciation for waiters and waitresses.

I'd pushed myself past exhaustion, but at least this time I'd have some cash to show for it. And, after getting stiffed by Gravois & Spouse, I really needed it. Except for a half-eaten jar of salsa, the only thing left in my fridge was the lightbulb.

When I'd swung by the bank that morning to straighten out the mess that was my checking account, I'd learned that—because of all my recent "infractions"—I'd been put on some sort of a bad-customer watch list. Not only did they refuse to cash Peter's check, but I practically had to arm-wrestle the bank manager just to withdraw my own money. End result: except for twenty dollars each to keep my checking and savings accounts open, the remainder of my worldly wealth now resided in a coffee can in my bedroom closet.

And I had just about enough left for a couple of mortgage payments. Provided I didn't eat or pay bills.

As the last of the mourners trickled out, Gianni and Walters put their heads together at the bar. Tip time!

I grabbed my tray and made for the kitchen. Travis had collapsed into one chair, vest open, tie at half-mast, rubbing his eyes. Gabby was in another chair, downing a can of Coke while Nick massaged her shoulders.

Margaret had already collected Pat, whom I assumed was going to be carried home and tucked into bed. I kind of felt sorry for him.

Patti had finally returned the busboy but not the vodka, and Ralph put her in a cab. She'd nicked a bottle of scotch on her way out.

Now we just had to settle up, and we could go home and get some rest ourselves. Ralph came through the doors looking dour. But that was pretty much his usual expression. He was clutching a handful of bills.

"Our tip," he said, laying six twenties on the table.

"A hundred and twenty dollars?" I said. "For all of us?"

"For the whole night?" Gabby exclaimed.

"Wait a minute, the bar tab alone would have gone five figures," Nick said. "At least."

"That's why the regular staff never wants to work these things," Ralph said, handing each of us a Jackson, and pocketing two for himself. "The Barclay is one of the few establishments that still does not impose an automatic gratuity for events. And when these people aren't spending someone else's money, they're skinflints."

Chapter 23

By midnight, we'd gathered again in my living room to share what we'd learned. Three nearly empty pizza boxes decorated my coffee table.

"I thought you said higher heels equaled higher tips," I said, rubbing my ankles.

"Sugar, in Vegas it does. These Washington folks are a bunch of cheapskates."

"D.C. may be budget-conscious, but I think C&W is taking it to extremes," I said, reaching for my third slice.

"Sounds like that office of yours is going through a radical shift," Trip said, pulling out a slice and placing it carefully on Lucy's plate on the floor.

She trembled with excitement, but held herself back until he was clear of the plate. Then she pounced.

"Can dogs eat pizza?" I asked. "That's her second piece."

"Can she? Sure. Should she? We'll find out in about twenty minutes," Nick said. "Fifteen if it's greasy."

Trip winked at me. "I gave her the Meat Monster,"

he said. "No onions, no garlic. She should be fine. No guarantees on the effects of the grease, though."

Lucy devoured the pizza like she was the queen of the pack and it was an unwary wildebeest.

Soon she was parked at my feet, looking up at me with those deep brown eyes.

"No more. First we've got to see how those two settle out."

She cocked her head to one side and continued to stare. I felt my forehead grow hot. I looked over at Trip, Nick, and Gabby, who were chowing down totally free of canine panhandling.

"Why me?"

"Soft touch," said Trip.

"Soft head," said Nick.

"Heyy!" I punched him in the shoulder.

Lucy, ever hopeful, had backed off to a respectful distance. And stretched out with her head on her paws. But she was keeping a drowsy eye on the pizza boxes. Just in case.

"OK, kiddies," Trip said. "What did we learn tonight? Other than dogs like pizza."

"Well, I learned that Coleman's son isn't much of a drinker," I said. "And that he had some kind of beef with his father."

"Daddy had him majoring in public relations," Trip said. "He switched to archaeology. Daddy pulled the plug on college."

"Damn," said Nick. "That's cold."

"It's also a motive," I said. "But somehow, I can't see him doing it."

"So we put him in the 'maybe' pile," said Trip. "What about the sister?"

"Also had issues with Daddy, but worked them out a little differently," I said.

"I'll say," said Nick. "I saw the busboy afterward, and he looked like hell."

"Motive?" I prompted.

"Just the usual teenage, upper-middle-class crap," Nick said. "Her parents love her. New car at sixteen. Free ride to college. So she gets even by torturing them. Except instead of singing about how much she hates them and how they don't understand her, she bags busboys."

Trip looked at me with a question in his eyes. I shook my head infinitesimally.

One of Nick's college girlfriends was a trust-fund baby and a huge Avril Lavigne fan. In the year they dated, she dragged him to nine concerts, and he's never quite forgiven her.

"OK, so we know that Patti had issues with Daddy," I summarized. "And that Nick's not buying Avril Lavigne tickets anytime soon."

"Hey, I'm just saying that's the vibe I got."

"So we put her in the 'maybe' pile?"

"Long-shot maybe," said Nick. "She's almost too self-centered to think about anyone else, much less kill them."

"Interesting take," said Trip.

Nick shrugged. "What about the widow?"

"She'd be my pick," Gabby said. "That woman is cold."

"And a stone-cold drunk," Nick said. "She was tossing back drinks all night and never missed a step or slurred a word."

"She reminds me of a lizard one of my roommates

had," Gabby said. "Sat there with those bulging eyes, just watching everything and everybody. But you never knew what was going on inside that flat head."

"The lizard or Margaret?" I asked, deadpan.

"Both, sugar. Both. Burrr!" she said, shivering.

"Gabby heard something interesting between Margaret and Walters," I added. "About the insurance policies. Not only have they not paid, but apparently, the insurance company is doing some kind of investigation."

"That is interesting," Trip said. "I wonder if that's typical."

"Might be worth finding out," I said. "If the insurance carrier is dragging its feet, how much of the delay is because they don't want to part with the money until they absolutely have to . . ."

"And how much is because they don't want to reward a murderer?" Trip finished.

"So if one of them did it, the insurance company doesn't have to pay?" Nick asked.

"Depends on how the policy was set up," said Trip. "With the average life insurance policy, you just skip over the murderer and the money goes to the next beneficiary on the list. Or, failing that, an heir. But with a business policy, if the only beneficiary is also the killer, I don't know how it would work."

"What if there was another partner?" I asked suddenly. "Or what if Coleman added a beneficiary and didn't tell Walters?"

"What do you mean?" Trip asked.

"When I heard Jennifer talking in the bathroom after Coleman was killed, she was going on and on about the two of them taking over the agency and being full partners with Coleman. What if he'd already changed the insurance to reflect that? That might slow things down a little, come payoff time. Especially if the others weren't expecting it."

"Sugar, that would give her a pretty big motive, too."

Trip shook his head. "I talked to her for a long time tonight. She seemed pretty honestly devastated."

"Then she was one of the few," I said. "I've never seen a more upbeat group of mourners."

"Even if she's up for a chunk of the insurance, I don't think she killed Coleman for it," Nick said. "From what you said, he was just going to hand her half the company. Now she's got to arm-wrestle Walters to get even a piece of it."

I noticed Lucy's heavy eyelids had finally closed. Her soft chest gently rose and fell. Did she dream of pizza-flavored wildebeests?

"Do you know an Alan Piper?" Nick asked.

"The name rings a bell. Wait a minute, I think he worked at C&W. Left a few months before I started. Heard he had some sort of breakdown. Was he at the wake?"

Nick nodded. "Drinking like a fish. Said he went to the funeral, too. Quote, 'Just wanted to make sure the old bastard was really dead' unquote."

"Ouch!" said Trip. "Did you ever hear what happened with Piper?"

I shook my head. "Supposedly embarrassed himself and nearly cost the firm an account. Once in a while the name would come up, but no one ever said much. It was like he had a contagious disease."

"Yeah, " said Trip. "Unemployment."

"Well, he didn't stay long at the wake," said Nick.

"But he spent most of that time at the bar. I kept pouring, and he kept talking."

"That's my man," Gabby said, giving him a pat on the shoulder.

"Piper reeled in a big client. Something called the Tryon Alliance. They wanted C&W to mastermind a big push to raise their profile. It was Piper's client, so technically, he was in charge of it. But really Coleman was running things behind the scenes, crafting the strategy and the client pitch."

"That tracks. From what I saw in my three months, Coleman was a total control freak. Whenever he put anyone 'in charge' of anything, that just meant they did the grunt work."

"That's pretty much what Piper said. And it really pissed him off. Anyway, about six months ago, there was a big meeting with the Tryon guys. Lots of pomp and ceremony. But at the end of the presentation— dead silence. The Tryon guys hated the plan. Too young. Too edgy. Which was what Piper had been telling Coleman all along.

"And when the presentation bombed, Coleman acted surprised that Piper had recommended such a radical approach. He assured the Tryon guys that he'd take over their account personally, create a traditional, conservative campaign, and manage it himself."

"Thereby earning a reputation as the guy who can step in and fix anything," I said. "And the next day he canned Alan Piper?"

"Leave no witnesses," Nick replied.

"Six months is a long time to wait to settle a score," Trip said.

"Piper has a sick kid, and his wife's working a job at Starbucks to cover their health insurance," Nick said. "And they just lost the house."

"That would make the hurt fresh again," Trip said.

I could relate. Coleman had been dead and gone for a week now. But he was still finding new and creative ways to screw up my life.

Nick nodded. "I think what bothered him the most was the way Coleman was having him blackballed in the industry. Forget getting a job, he couldn't even get an interview."

Trip's eyes met mine. "Lot of that going around," I said.

"Coleman spread the word that the campaign had been Piper's baby," Nick said. "And that it was so bad, so inappropriate, it almost cost C&W a big client. Never mind that it was Piper's client in the first place. Or that it was Coleman who screwed up the campaign. Coleman claimed he had to fire Piper because the guy made a fool of himself—and the firm—in front of the clients."

"I don't get it," said Gabby. "Was Coleman setting the guy up to fail? Did he want to get rid of him?"

"Nothing that personal," I said. "It's a typical CEO strategy. You want to try something new—in this case, a new strategy for a P.R. campaign. But you don't know for sure if it'll fly. So you set it up as someone else's idea. If it fails, you cut 'em loose. If it succeeds, you step in and take the credit."

For half a minute, we were silent. Business gains and losses were one thing. But it was chilling to realize that there were some walking among us who could name the livestock and eat them anyway. Without a trace of remorse.

"Piper says Coleman even fought him on unemployment," Nick said quietly. "Lawyers. Hearings. Appeals. The whole deal. And, somehow, potential employers were getting all the juicy details."

That sounded like vintage Coleman. In his mind, it wasn't enough to win. You had to "obliterate the enemy."

Fair enough, if you were up against a business rival. Not so much if you were going to war with some poor schmuck who was just doing the job you hired him to do.

"Was he mad enough to kill?" I asked.

"They just moved in with his wife's parents. And his wife is scrambling to pick up enough shifts so they can keep up with the medical bills."

"So you're saying yes."

"Not just yes," Nick said. "Hell yes."

"What about Walters?" I ventured.

"That man sure doesn't talk much," Gabby said.

"That's what he's famous for," I said.

"I thought public relations was about glitz and glamour and making a splash," she said.

"That's advertising. Public relations is about getting people to believe your side of the story without even considering the alternatives. It's advertising that the public doesn't recognize as advertising."

"Stealth advertising?" Nick said.

"Exactly. And while Coleman was the master of promotion, Walters was the one you went to if you didn't want the information to leak out in the first place."

"They have guys like that in Vegas," said Gabby.

"I don't think it's quite the same thing," I countered.

"You've got a dead body, girls pimped out to clients, and people lying to the police," Nick said. "How is it different?"

"Well, when you put it that way . . ."

An hour later, Nick and Gabby had retired to the guest room. Quietly, I was relieved to hear.

Trip and I were sitting on the front porch, sipping beer. It was one of those perfect, balmy spring nights. The kind we usually don't see until May or June. Even so, I was wrapped in two sweaters. I couldn't seem to get warm. Maybe it was all the talk of death and disaster.

"I didn't want to say anything in front of the newlyweds, but I got you a lead on a freelance job," Trip said.

"Really? You're kidding! What is it?"

"It's only a one-shot thing. And it's not your usual cup of tea. But it's a first-rate publication, and the pay's good—three thousand."

Three thousand dollars! Hot damn! Up to now, I couldn't even get the local ad rag to return my calls. OK, I hadn't really called them. I had my standards. Plus if they had said "no," it would have killed me.

"What's the assignment? What's the publication? Do they know about my little situation?"

I didn't want to get my hopes up only to lose the gig when the editor discovered their new freelancer was the Lizzie Borden of Washington, D.C.

"Know? Yes. Care? Not if you can make the deadline. Hence the three thousand dollars."

"What's the deadline?"

"Two and a half weeks from today."

Tight. But doable. "What's the story?"

Trip cleared his throat. "A first-person account of how to create a wedding gift registry."

"What?"

"It's for *D.C. Bride.* They want to know what a bride goes through when she drafts a gift registry, along with some tips on how to really do it up right. Apparently, you don't just sit down and make a list anymore. It's all computerized, and you take actual classes."

"They do know I'm not getting married?"

"They do. And as long as you're willing to pose as a bride when you do the reporting, you can come clean in the article. They're even open to your writing it as a humor piece. As long as you leave out the Bridezilla references."

"So now I'm flacking for brides?"

"Yup."

"OK, it's a step up."

We sipped in silence for a few minutes.

"Piper's probably not the only one, you know," Trip said quietly.

"I know. I heard another guy at the wake with a similar story. Charlie Bingham. I'd be willing to bet

Coleman's probably got a few Pipers and Binghams for every year he's been in business."

"And if a few of them came to that wake . . ."

"That means they had motive and proximity," I said.

"But whoever it was, Coleman had to let them into the office. There was no forced entry."

"Coleman wouldn't have thought twice about meeting Piper in his office. The victor hosting the vanquished. It never would have occurred to him that it could turn physical. Or that he'd lose if it did. But there's another possibility."

"What's that?" Trip asked.

"That whoever it was had help," I said. "From the inside. Someone to let him in. Someone who may well have realized that it would get ugly. And someone who didn't stick around to be a witness."

"Who?"

"Someone who knew about Piper," I said. "And who didn't want to be the next Piper."

"In other words," Trip started.

"Someone who out Coleman'd Coleman," I said.

We sat in silence, both of us letting this new possibility sink in.

"Did you see Gabby in action tonight?" Trip said finally.

"Yeah, she really knows her way around a tray," I said.

"She also knows her way around a wallet."

I sat forward suddenly. "What?"

"She was picking pockets all night," he said.

"Nooo! Are you sure? Why didn't you say anything?"

"To who? The manager Tom approached to get

you guys in there? Or the cops, who—if they checked—would discover that she was the only real waitress in the room?"

"OK, good point," I said.

"She did put everything back."

"What do you mean?"

"She'd take a wallet," Trip said. "Five minutes later, she'd return it."

"Robin Hood? Doing it for the thrill?"

"More like doing it for the credit card numbers," he said. "If the card's missing, people tend to notice and report it. But if they still have the card, they don't realize something's up until the bill comes. If then."

"The online boutique," I said, feeling suddenly sick. "She's funding it with stolen credit cards."

Trip nodded. "That would be my guess. Do you think Nick knows?"

"Normally, I'd say 'no.' I mean, he's no saint, but trafficking in stolen goods isn't like him. But he's so in love with her, who knows? I've never seen him like this around a woman. Damn, I was really beginning to like her."

"Con men have to be likable," Trip said. "Otherwise the cons don't work."

Which was worse: that she might be conning my brother? Or that he might be in on it?

"Who'd she hit?" I asked, finally.

"A few guys whose suits and body language screamed 'Centurion card,'" Trip said. "No one I recognized. Except for Chaz."

"She got Chaz?"

"Why do I think she might have been doing that one just for fun?" he said.

"Well, the girl is family," I said. "We shouldn't judge her too harshly, until we have all the facts."

"Sounds fair," Trip said.

We clinked cans.

Chapter 24

No matter how old you are, Saturday morning is still Saturday morning.

When I was a kid, it meant instead of eating oatmeal at the kitchen table and going to school, I could eat Cocoa Puffs in front of the TV, watching cartoons.

And when I woke up on this sunny Saturday, that's exactly how I felt.

No Coleman. No cops. No lawyers. No cleaning toilets. And, ID theft or not, my new sister-in-law was beginning to grow on me.

But I still wasn't signing for her packages.

Since I'd drained my checking account and part of my savings to pay my dentist yesterday—in cash, thank you very much—I had just enough savings left for a couple of mortgage payments. And I still had to cover bills, groceries and anything else that came up before I got the check for my bridal story.

Granted, I had Peter's check. But how could I accept his money when he was already picking up the tab for Holloman?

So I made an executive decision. With three people

and a dog to feed, and nothing but some very iffy salsa in the fridge, I was going to take some of Nick and Gabby's rent money and visit the farmers' market.

I padded out to the kitchen, hit the switch on the coffeemaker, and opened the back door for Lucy. She made a mad dash, tumbling down the steps.

I dialed Trip. "I'm thinking of hitting the farmers' market this morning. You wanna come?"

Dead silence.

"Trip? Is everything OK?"

"You seem awfully perky this morning, considering."

"Well, why not? You can't let the bastards get you down. It's a warm, clear, beautiful Saturday morning The sky is blue. The sun is shining. And Lucy's chasing butterflies in the backyard."

I looked out through the screen. Actually, what she was chasing looked more like a cricket. Or a grasshopper. Possibly a roach. Nutty dog.

"Oh my God, you haven't seen the *Sentinel* yet, have you?"

That happy, fluttery Saturday-morning feeling suddenly gave way to a fist-sized rock in my gut. "What's in the *Sentinel*?"

"It's not as bad as it looks."

"How bad does it look? And what exactly are we talking about?"

In my heart, I knew. My mind went blank. I felt numb. I almost didn't want to see it. But I was now moving toward my front door, as if pulled.

The *Washington Tribune*, my former paper, was—as always—in the center of my driveway. My "delivery boy" was a sixty-eight-year-old woman trying to keep up the payments on her Audi. And she had an arm like a Cy Young winner.

The *Washington Sentinel*, on the other hand, was never in the same place twice.

Today, it was wedged in an azalea bush. At various times, I'd retrieved it from mud puddles, trees, and even the top of my car. Last spring, a Sunday edition took out a dozen tulips along the walkway. And the time it landed on the roof, it stayed there until the guy came to clean the gutters six months later.

I didn't know who delivered the *Sentinel*, but I suspected he drank. Heavily.

I scraped leaves off the bag, slipped it out, and unfurled the front page. Nada. So far, so good. I flipped to the metro front. And saw my own face staring back at me. Above the fold.

"Vlod the Impaler?" screamed the giant headline above my giant headshot.

No!

"Red? Honey, are you OK? Alex?" I heard Trip's distant voice from the phone in my hand.

I rolled up the paper and ran back inside. At this rate, the mobs with burning torches would arrive any minute.

"Alex? Alex!"

"I'm here. I'm fine. What the hell?"

"Mira's column. It's a doozy."

"You've read it?" I couldn't get past my enormous head on the section front. Where did they get that photo? It actually looked like I was smirking. "How bad is it?"

"Not great."

Which was the same thing he said after a fifteen-dollar haircut left me with bangs so short I looked like Mr. Spock.

"How 'not great'?"

"Well, the upside is your mom and sister are still out of the country. And Baba's grasp of English isn't all that good."

I covered the photo with one hand, and forced myself to read the story. And what a story it was. Her lede:

> "Sometimes pretty girls do ugly things."
>
> That's what one source said, confirming that a celebrity's sister is a prime suspect in a grisly, local murder. Alexandra Vlodnachek, sister of supermodel Anastasia, is reputedly "a person of interest" in the stabbing death of her former boss, Washington public relations executive Everett P. Coleman.
>
> Coleman, the managing partner of the prestigious, boutique P.R. firm of Coleman & Walters, was found dead in his office one week ago—stabbed in the back with his own silver letter opener.
>
> Vlodnachek had recently been fired from the company. And one industry insider, who knew Vlodnachek well, confirmed that she was scheduled to meet with Coleman at his office the very afternoon he was killed.

Thanks, Chaz.

> Soon-to-be-released DNA test results are also expected to confirm that the

strands of red hair found on Coleman's body are Vlodnachek's.

Police questioned Vlodnachek, who immediately retained powerhouse D.C. celebrity defense attorney, Richard C. Holloman. And she hasn't said a word to authorities since.

Yeah, because they haven't called me.

One possible motive: it's rumored that Vlodnachek, who didn't possess the requisite knockout looks to follow in her stunning sister's footsteps, was writing an insider tell-all about the public relations industry. And, as one industry insider revealed, Coleman—a major player in local circles who was known for his networking acumen—discovered her plan.

Vlodnachek's actions—and her silence—have angered many in the tight-knit public relations community. But some refused to comment, for fear of angering the redhead, who has been called "volatile," "vengeful," and downright "dangerous."

No one spoke on the record because no one wanted to get sued. Come to think of it, could I sue Mira?

Former co-workers are murderously angry themselves.

"It's outrageous," exclaimed one beautiful, pre-Raphaelite blonde, speaking only on the condition of anonymity. "Everett Coleman was a good man. A family man. He gave her a chance—a shot at a real career with an elite agency. The idea that she abused his trust and used him like that—it's monstrous."

And it went on from there. Nameless quotes. Groundless supposition. Plus a hundred and one words for "floozy." I had, sources breathlessly "disclosed," perhaps even seduced the victim himself. Before he came to his senses and repented, of course.

In any event, I was a brazen siren using my average looks and loose morals to lure unsuspecting men to their dooms.

Mira's article was chock-full of phrases like "some believe," "sources say," and, at least twice, "one theory is." Followed, of course, by one of Mira's crackpot theories.

In other words, enough wiggle room for Mira and the *Sentinel*, if I phoned Holloman. Which I was considering.

Trip's anxious voice broke my fog. "Alex? AL-EX!"

"Son of a bitch."

"Ah, that's my girl. Welcome back."

"I'm going to kill her."

"Can we at least clear you of the other murder first?"

"What am I going to do? This is my life. She just shredded my life. Publicly. With photos. I can't even show my face around town. And I've got no food in the house. I'm gonna have to eat Domino's for the rest of my life."

"You can come stay with me."

"Tom would hate seeing me at the breakfast table."

"Tom's never here. Tom works 'til after midnight, and he's up just after dawn. Hell, *I* never see Tom at the breakfast table."

"No. Thanks. Besides, I can't just abandon Bonnie and Clyde."

"You could all stay at the Farm."

"That doesn't keep everybody from reading Mira's little nasty-gram. My friends. My family. People I'd hoped to work for someday. And some of them will actually believe her load of crap. I want my life back. My life. In my house."

I felt my eyes well up. Again.

"Are you going to blubber like a big, ol' girl?"

"No," I said sniffing. "Maybe."

"Look, do nothing for the time being. See what happens. Hell, they say nobody reads newspapers anymore, anyway. Worse comes to worst, we parcel you and the Fresh Air Fund kids out to my place or the Farm. We'll even bring your Baba and make it a party to remember."

Chapter 25

By 4:30 that afternoon, the sidewalk in front of my house looked like a movie set, with klieg lights, camera guys, and cables running God-knows-where. Satellite trucks lined the street, one from as far away as Manhattan. I blamed Annie for that one.

If one crack dealer stabs another fighting over a street corner, nobody cares except their mothers and the cops. Move it to the 'burbs and make the victim a CEO, and it gets a few more inches in the papers. Link one of the suspects to someone even remotely famous, and you have every anchor wanna-be for 250 miles trampling my lawn.

That's also when I realized I had to do some damage control. I decided to give Annie a heads-up first. Even though she was a continent away, it was possible some enterprising reporter would call her New York office for a comment.

I'd have shown up in person, but that's just me.

Hand it to my protective big sister, she was more worried about me than her own rep.

"Alex, that's awful," she said softly. "Are you OK?

Do you want us to fly home?" I could hear a strange echo as she spoke.

"I'm not on speaker, am I?"

"I'm in the bathroom. It's the only place I could get a break from you-know-who."

"Wanna trade places? Right now I've got an entire press corps just outside my door."

"Believe me, if I could snap my fingers and switch, I would. And I wouldn't be doing you any favors. Seriously, do you want us to come home? Present a united front?"

"No, it's actually a good thing you guys aren't here. Fewer targets for them to go after."

We sat silently, both of us thinking hard. I could practically smell the smoke.

"But there is one thing," I said tentatively.

"Yes?"

"Any chance you could keep Mom from finding out?"

Next, I called Baba. She lived ninety minutes away in Baltimore—and was more likely to watch *Family Feud* or the Weather Channel than local news. But I didn't want to take any chances.

It rang ten times. No answer. Baba didn't have voice mail or even an answering machine. Despite our many attempts to change her mind.

"But what happens if I call and you're not home?" Peter asked her last Thanksgiving.

Her dark eyes went wide with disbelief and hurt. "You will not call me again?"

Baba: one. Technology: zip.

* * *

None of the neighbors would have anything to do with the reporters. Well, almost none.

Mr. Rasmussen, who lives behind me, went on for a full minute about how "my" gopher was destroying his yard and lowering property values.

The reporter asked him straight out if he believed I'd stabbed my boss.

"Well, if she did, I don't see why she couldn't do the same thing to that gopher. My home's a custom job. Hardwood, granite—all the upgrades. And it's priced to move. But it's just sitting there. You know why? Curb appeal. My agent says it all comes down to curb appeal."

At which point, the strained-looking reporter stepped in smoothly. "And that's the latest on the woman some are calling 'Vlod the Impaler.' Back to you, Frank."

Behind her, I could see Rasmussen, still angling for the camera. "Hey, if anyone's interested, it's listed at $499,900. That's $50,000 below appraisal value. And I'm having an open house next Saturday!" he shouted, cupping his hands.

With the constant media calls, I'd turned off my cell and even unplugged the landline. If anybody wanted me, they could leave a message. Or just turn on their TV.

I swiped Nick's cell and tried Baba two more times. Still no luck.

"She's probably at the grocery store," Nick reasoned. "Or visiting friends."

"I just hope they don't have a TV," I said.

A little before five, I flipped my cell on to check voicemail. That's when my heart stopped. There was a message. From Holloman.

"This is Richard Holloman. Call me as soon as you get this: (703) 555-0100, extension 111."

I played it again, listening for details I might have missed. Like instructions on what to pack for prison. Or how many hours until my imminent arrest. Nada. I played it a third time, trying to read the tone of his voice. Totally businesslike. Of course, he wasn't the one going off to the Big House.

My hands were shaking as I dialed his number. Would they maybe allow me house arrest? If they did, I could finish my freelance story and keep the bills paid. Or was it straight to the slammer? If that happened, I was going to lose my home and everything I owned.

"Glad you called," he said matter-of-factly. "Quick question: when did you start using a glaze on your hair? And do you do it yourself or get it done professionally?"

"Huh?" Of all the things I'd expected, trading hair tips with my lawyer was definitely not on the list.

"Glaze. The lab tests on the fresh hair sample the police took from you at the station show some kind of residue. A hair product used fairly recently. My paralegal informs me it's called 'a glaze.' She says it's supposed to make the hair thick and shiny. Got to say, that's a new one on me. So do you do it yourself or get it done professionally?"

I was struggling to turn my brain back on. "Uh, professionally. I got my hair cut two days before the client dinner. The stylist recommended it."

"Ever had it done before?"

"Um, no. Why?"

"Can you get me the name and phone number of your stylist?"

I couldn't hold it in anymore. "Am I going to jail?" I blurted.

"No, but next time you get your hair cut, you might want to leave a very large tip."

Since I'd never made it to the farmers' market, we ordered a stack of pizzas and spent the evening flipping from channel to channel, catching various versions of the story—complete with live feeds of my house.

My favorite: the one from the local Spanish-language station. Apparently "Vlod the Impaler" is pronounced virtually the same way in Spanish.

Nick liked that one, too. But I think it was more because the reporter's dress fit like Saran wrap.

Gabby preferred the guy from the Reston affiliate, who was decked out in a suit she pegged as Hugo Boss. "Totally dishy," she proclaimed.

Later, when the news was over and Gabby was on a bathroom break, I dashed to the kitchen to help myself to a piece of the cake we'd ordered with the pies. What we lacked in food quality, we were making up for in quantity. And carbs.

Nick wandered in carrying an empty plate. "Which one is the old guy who's worried about the gopher?"

"Rasmussen. He lives behind me."

"Great! Just want to know which way to lob the flaming poo."

"No! No flaming! No lobbing! Look, I know he's acting like an idiot. But I live here. And I want to keep living here. That means I get along. I trim my trees. I mow my lawn. I rake my leaves. And I buy Girl Scout cookies from three different families. In equal amounts. Because, believe me, those little fascists compare notes."

"Well, you probably won't have to fight off the cookie pushers this year. If the gory crime stories don't scare them away, the news crews on the sidewalk will. Too bad it's not Halloween. Gather 'round children, while I tell you the tale of Vlod the Impaler and her ferocious, man-eating gopher."

"And her brother, Nick the Smart Ass, and his flaming bag of crap."

"Speaking of crap bags, we really ought to move your car."

At 11:35, I checked my cell. I'd just missed Trip, so I dialed him back.

"Your house looks smaller on TV," he said.

"Try it from the inside with three people and a dog. Poor Lucy doesn't know what to make of it. Nick let her out into the backyard, and three cameras tried to film her taking a poop."

"Offer still stands for you guys to come to my place. Or the Farm."

"If they're still here Monday, I might take you up on it. Has Billy Bob heard anything?"

"That's the good news," Trip said. "According to his police sources, you're no longer a person of interest."

"Tell that to the army camped out on my lawn."

"It'll be in our follow-up tomorrow morning."

"Can't be too soon for me. It looks like they're filming an episode of *Cops* out there. All I need is some dude in a wifebeater hanging off my porch yelling, 'Don't take her away—I looove her!'"

"Speaking of which, how are Bonnie and Clyde holding up?" he asked.

"Gabby wanted to send out a pizza laced with laxatives."

"Poison's not a great way to beat a murder rap. At least you've got Nick on your side."

"Yeah, he wanted to start lobbing flaming bags of dog poop at my neighbors."

"Dog poop is flammable?"

"So he claims."

"Anybody suggested the banana-in-the-tailpipe routine?" Trip asked, lightly.

"Yes, until I pointed out that we actually *want* the news crews to leave."

"On the bright side, this should put a dent in your sister-in-law's side business."

"Don't remind me. I'm afraid to let either of them

out of my sight. I feel like I'm running a sleepaway camp for juvenile delinquents."

I told him about my earlier conversation with Holloman.

"Love to ask you more about that one, but given where I am . . ."

"I know, I know, red hair for the red herring, right?"

"You took the pun right out of my mouth. So what did he say about the reporters?"

"Quote, 'don't talk to 'em, don't feed 'em. Either one just encourages 'em.'"

"Sounds about right. What about suing you-know-who?"

"We can, but he doesn't like the odds. Basically, as long as Mira can show she wrote what people told her, absent malice, she's bulletproof. And we all know where the story really came from. But Holloman said that if the TV crews were still here Monday, he could work some legal mumbo jumbo to at least get them off my sidewalk."

"See if he can get the police to issue a formal statement that you're no longer a suspect," Trip suggested.

"Did the cops say who they're looking at?"

"Not so far. Billy Bob's playing this one close to the vest. But my read is he suspects the cops were just using you as a decoy. And he thinks the killer is someone with a big-time grudge."

"Piper?"

"He wouldn't say. Only that Mira and the news crews are way off track. And it turns out you were right: Piper has a lot of company. Coleman pulled that build-em-up-and-cut-'em-down routine at least half a dozen times in the past few years alone."

"Will that be in tomorrow's story?" I asked.

"No such luck. Later this week, if we really push. And we are. A lot of these guys want to talk. But no one wants to have his name attached."

And unlike Mira's column full of innuendo, half-truths, and no-truths, the nameless sources weren't going to cut it in a real news story. Especially if Trip was editing.

"Did Billy Bob get them talking?"

"He can't get them to shut up. These people are calling him at all hours, blathering on like they're in some kind of support group. But when he says he needs to go on the record, they clam up."

Typical. When a reporter shows up, everyone wants to be Deep Throat. They'll share stories you don't want to hear, with details you wish you could forget. Like how it took twenty-five hours for Aunt Millie to deliver Cousin Clem because the kid wrapped his hands around her colon on the way out. Or how PawPaw had his grapefruit-sized goiter bronzed and turned into a Christmas tree ornament.

But ask someone something useful—like how to spell his name—and he suddenly gets amnesia.

"OK, so despite the fact that I'm the D.C. poster child for homicidal maniacs, and my lawn looks like a Hollywood back lot, my life is actually getting better?"

"Pretty much."

Chapter 26

Since the "early morning rise and shine" routine netted me nothing but grief on Saturday, I adopted a more Gabby-like approach on Sunday: I slept 'til noon.

And it paid off.

The news crews had vanished. Except for dead grass, candy wrappers, and a couple of Styrofoam cups, it was as if they'd never existed.

As promised, the story proclaiming my innocence—or at least the fact that the police had dropped me in favor of more promising suspects—made the metro front of my paper. OK, my *former* paper.

No photo this time. Fine by me. I still felt like having the article framed. Or printed on T-shirts.

While the cops leaked to Billy Bob that I was not a suspect, they didn't tell him why: Preliminary tests had revealed that red hairs found on Coleman were mine. But they weren't coated with the chemicals my stylist had applied three days before the murder. Chemicals that were still on my hair when I went to the police station after the murder. Which meant those "incriminating" strands had been taken earlier and planted on Coleman's body.

Holloman told me, and I told Trip. But the three of us—and the cops—weren't sharing those styling secrets with anyone.

As late as it was, I was still the first one up. I found a large puddle on the vinyl by the kitchen door. And a small pile on the parquet by the front door.

The puppy pads were, as usual, spotless.

My theory: Lucy had noticed that when she used one, we threw it out. And she didn't want to ruin them.

I let Lucy out, cleaned up after her, and scrubbed like I was prepping for surgery. Then I made coffee. As I filled the pot, I glanced at the newest postcards on my fridge. And, from the absence of frantic phone calls from Mom, I was pretty sure Annie had been successful in her secret mission.

So far.

I pictured them sitting at that same little outdoor café with the Eiffel Tower backdrop, dashing off notes home after indulging in plates of crepes stuffed with coq au vin and coquilles St. Jacques.

My sister may be an ex-model, but she's never believed in starving herself. I swear it's one of the reasons why she's still jaw-droppingly beautiful.

That and the fact that she won the genetic lottery.

The front of Mom's card was a watercolor of a Paris street scene. The back was a window into my mother's mind:

Alex,
  You really should have come. You'd have picked up a few skills for that new job—particularly how

*to dress. The Parisians—so chic! And the art!
Three galleries just this morning. Exquisite. Of
course, costs are terribly inflated. I suspect when
they hear an American accent, the price doubles.
Still, would have been nice to have "the girls"
together one last time. Who knows if we'll ever
have the chance again?*

*Love,
Mom*

She hit the guilt button, praised the French, in-
sulted the French, and took a shot at my wardrobe.
All in less than seventy-five perfectly formed, perfectly
aligned words. No blops, smears, or cross-throughs.
My mother would have made a great reporter. Or
hit man.

From the postmark, I could tell she'd sent it before
her phone call earlier this week. Before I had a
chance to apologize for blowing off the trip. So,
hopefully, we had reached some sort of détente.

Annie's missive, on the back of a replica of "Starry
Night," was a little more succinct.

*Alex,
    Paris is great. Even with Mom.
    Really wish you were here.*

*Love,
Annie*

I'm guessing they didn't compare notes before
hitting the mailbox.

I'd hung all the postcards on the fridge with magnets. It might not be a Paris art gallery, but it was as close as I was going to get for a while.

I'd just settled in with the papers when I heard a knock at the front door. I knew it wasn't good news. Lately, it was never good news.

I looked out the peephole. Rasmussen.

What did it mean when your day started with a steaming pile and went downhill from there? For me, it meant I wasn't opening the door.

Five minutes of intermittent bell-ringing and hard-knuckled rapping later, I switched tactics.

"Hello, Mr. Rasmussen."

"You need to do something about your gopher. He's vicious, and he's ruining my lawn. I have an open house next Saturday. And I need him gone by then."

"It's not exactly my gopher. I don't know what you expect me to do."

"You can kill it, can't you? The TV and the news-papers say you're Jack the Ripper."

"That was a mistake. And it was Vlod the Impaler."

"What's the difference?"

"My former boss's body was pierced once, with a letter opener that was left in him. Technically, im-paled. If he'd been stabbed multiple times, cut up, slashed, or eviscerated, that would be a ripper."

Rasmussen scratched his ear and backed up a step. "Well, uh, thanks for clearing that up."

"Hey, no sweat. It's important to get the details right."

As I closed the door, the house phone rang. Trip.

"You're not using your Hotmail account to confess to murder, are you?"

"Not today. I'm too busy defending my gopher."

"Is that slang for your lady parts?"

"No, a real gopher. With fur and fangs."

"Gophers have fangs?"

"I don't know. I've never actually seen one. But my neighbor says it's vicious. And for my money, vicious means fangs."

In the next room, I could see Nick stretched out on the couch, flipping channels with the remote. He hit a basketball game and stopped.

"Is that the idiot who was on the news last night?" Trip said.

"Yeah, Rasmussen. The news crews were gone when I got up. But he's been banging on my door carping about the gopher. Did someone really sign my name to an email confession?"

"'Fraid so. To us and the cops."

"Are they following up?"

"Nah, they're not taking it seriously, either."

Suddenly, there was a loud pounding on my door.

"Shit. That'll be Rasmussen. Again."

Nick got up and checked the peephole. "Not this time," he hissed. "It looks like a kid. All I can see is the top of his head."

"Oh please. Nobody's going to let their kids within a half-mile of this nuthouse. And the only neighbor who's still speaking to me wants to put out a hit on a gopher."

Bang! Bang! Bang! "Alexandra Edwardovna!"

Nick and I looked at each other and froze.

"It's Baba," I whispered into the phone.

"On the other line?" Trip asked.

"On the front porch."

"Forget the Farm," he said. "You need witness protection."

Chapter 27

Oh God, how could I have forgotten Baba?

Baba is a tornado packaged in a deceptively small, deceptively sweet-looking human form. But the minute you lower your guard, you're finished.

If scientists were studying her, they'd call that "the Baba effect."

Seriously, if Allied forces had come to their senses and air-dropped Baba behind enemy lines, World War II would have been over in an hour. Baba would have strangled Hitler with a wooden spoon and used it to cook lunch for the liberating armies.

She's the toughest woman I've ever met. Half of me wants to be exactly like her when I reach her age—whatever that is. The other half is just glad she's on my side. Most of the time.

She is, in the words of my father, "very Old World."

According to family lore, Dad didn't take Mom home to meet her until just before the wedding. And it did not go well.

My mother, who's been known to airbrush a few uncomfortable truths, claims that's total hogwash.

But I've seen the wedding album. Baba's the only one wearing black. Head to toe.

I opened the door. Baba looked up at me with wide, worried eyes. "What they mean, this 'Vlod the Impaler'? How can they say these things? Lies! All lies!"

Trip was wrong about one thing: Baba understood English as well as any native. But when she got emotional, her normally thick accent got even thicker. At this point, I practically needed subtitles.

I folded my arms around her. She was such a force of nature, I forgot how small she was—not quite five feet tall. The top of her head, covered with a black watch cap that matched her sweater, smelled like violets.

"*Nichevo,*" I murmured in Russian. "*Nichevo.* It's fine. I'm fine. It's all just a big misunderstanding. It's gonna be OK."

"*Da, da,*" she said, hugging me.

When we parted, I noticed Baba had on her traveling clothes: a brightly flowered housedress that came well below her knees, stockings, socks, black sweater and watch cap set, and a new pair of Asics running shoes that Annie and I had helped her pick out.

Behind her on the porch I also spied two very large suitcases.

Uh-oh.

"Here, let me," I said, reaching for both bags.

I hefted one easily enough. The other felt like it was weighted with rocks. Or bricks. Or a body.

"Uh, what's in here?"

"Pots. Pans. Potatoes. Carrots. Onions. I cook. You need good meal. Good food."

Double uh-oh.

Baba's cooking is in a class by itself. She starts with the finest ingredients. Then she scrubs, peels, pounds, and boils them beyond all recognition.

My father used to joke that he actually gained five pounds in the army because mess hall chow had more flavor.

But Baba had packed her pots and pans (and potatoes), and left her home in Baltimore to come and cook for me. Because she loved me.

So I guess I could stand to lose five pounds.

"How did you get here?" I asked.

"Dog bus."

I had a momentary vision of Baba driving a dog-sled through the streets of urban D.C.

"Greyhound bus?" The station was at least five miles from my house.

"Da!"

I set the lighter bag inside the door and went back for the other one. I threw my back into it and managed to lift it ankle-high. I'm guessing Baba brought the cast-iron stuff.

"Vheels!"

"What?"

Baba motored over, took the bag from my hand, dropped it, and yanked it up quick. Four black rubber wheels popped out of the bottom.

"Vheels!" she said triumphantly.

"Cool."

Wheeling her suitcase into the kitchen, I realized that the house was quiet. Too quiet.

Then I heard Nick's car engine in the driveway. I

beat it to the front porch just in time to see taillights and a cloud of exhaust.

Baba was already unpacking the first bag in the kitchen, so I grabbed the second one and headed for my bedroom.

"Hey, Baba, Nick's in town. He's set up in the guest room, so I'll just put you in with me."

"I can sleep on sofa. Is closer to kitchen."

My house is the size of a shoebox. Everything is close to the kitchen.

"My bed's plenty big enough for two. And it's a lot more comfortable than the sofa. I'll clear space in the closet, too. We'll be roomies."

She said something that I couldn't hear over the clanking of heavy metal kitchenware. But I know Baba. It sounded like happy clanking.

I opened my bedroom door. There was a crash and a jet-propelled, doe-colored streak.

Lucy.

She shot into the living room and ran circles around my coffee table as if she was chasing an invisible rabbit. Panting, she bounded over to the sofa and pounced on an unsuspecting throw pillow. Once she had it subdued, she began to gnaw on it.

"Oh no, you don't, you little goofball," I said, lifting her to the floor and patting her back. "Pillows are not on your diet. Let's go get a cookie."

Here's what Lucy heard: "COOKIE!"

I know this, because at the C-word, the oversized ears went straight up over her head. She puppy danced all the way into the kitchen.

You gotta love anyone who gets that excited over a

dog biscuit. I've tasted them. Hard-baked crud with a meaty coating. But Lucy loves them.

The minute she crossed the threshold into the kitchen, Baba whirled around and fixed Lucy with a gaze. I swore the pup froze, mid-wag.

"You have dog?"

"She's Nick's. Her name is Lucy. She's just a puppy. She was abandoned. Gab . . . uh, a friend of Nick's found her eating out of a garbage can and took her hom . . . um, over to his place."

Baba's face softened slightly, and she wrinkled her nose. "Humf! Dogs in house. Foolishness." She turned back to wiping down my stove.

Lucy stood stock-still, her eyes glued to the back of Baba's head. Slowly, her tail started to wag.

I slipped her a dog treat from the big mason jar on the counter. "You're not out of the woods yet," I whispered. "You've got to be a good doggie."

She looked at me hopefully.

Baba spent the rest of the afternoon wiping, sponging, polishing, and scrubbing every surface in my kitchen, with Lucy nestled under the table. She even took down the curtains and threw them in the washing machine.

She was miffed when she discovered I didn't have a big bucket and scrub brush for the floor. She eyed my snazzy, purple Swiffer with suspicion and distrust.

Both times I tried to help, I was shooed from the room like a single guy at a baby shower. I exiled myself to my desk and decided to update my "Who Killed Coleman" file.

My suspect list was a lot longer since the wake. So how come I was the only one who made the metro front?

Piper had a good motive. But if I'd been on his jury, I'd have voted for justifiable homicide and taken an early lunch.

Margaret had at least fifteen million reasons to kill her husband. And she was very anxious to get her hands on that insurance check. I didn't know anything about their personal finances. But, Coleman being Coleman, if he really had been planning to split from the marriage, he would've moved a lot of their money out of her grasp. Serene or not, that would not have gone over well.

I needed to learn more about those insurance policies. And why they hadn't paid.

When the phone rang, I wasn't surprised to see Nick's cell number on caller ID.

"Vlodnachek Hotel. Felons welcome."

"Hey, it's me."

"Hey, Houdini. How's the Invisible Woman?"

"Baba still there?"

"That's a big 'yessir!'"

"Any idea when she's leaving?"

"Judging from the amount of cleaning and luggage, I'd say sometime next month. Where the hell are you?"

"The mall. Gabby needed to do some work for the store."

"Yeah, we gotta talk about that."

"Later. Look, what are we gonna do?"

"We? I wasn't the one burning rubber out of the driveway."

"You know what I mean!"

"Have you got any money on you?"

"I don't want to stay in a hotel. Gabby needs her clothes and laptop and stuff. Plus she's got more deliveries coming."

More deliveries?

"I'm not talking about a hotel. Listen. Here's what you do. You come home. And you face Baba like a man. But before you do, you stop off at the store and pick up some groceries. I've got a list. I can pay you back in cash. Oh, and I'm sure Baba's got a few ingredients she needs, too."

"Oh God, she's cooking?"

"When it rains, it pours. Welcome to my monsoon."

"What am I gonna do?"

"Time to face the consequences, Romeo."

"It's not the consequences I'm worried about. It's the firing squad."

"Hey, she might take to Gabby and love her as much as you do."

"You think so?" He actually sounded hopeful.

"Hell, no. But at least your secret wedding will distract her from the wreck I've made of my life."

"You'd throw me under the bus?"

"Have you seen my life lately?"

"Good point. So what do you want from the store?

Chapter 28

As Baba was finishing up in the kitchen, there was another knock at the door. Ever the optimist, I was hoping it was Trip with a pizza. Or Nick and Gabby with a pizza. Or the neighborhood flasher with a pizza.

Instead, it was a man I'd never seen before, wearing what looked like an old-fashioned gray chauffeur's uniform, complete with cap. He was carrying a large wicker basket wrapped with cellophane and topped with a giant gold bow.

OK, definitely not a pizza delivery boy. But he also didn't look like a UPS driver or a member of the Gopher Death Brigade. And even if he was a process server, at least he'd brought something resembling food.

Cautiously, I opened the door.

"Good afternoon, Miss," he said, in the plummy tones usually reserved for the British upper crust—or employees of the British upper crust. "Sir Ian wanted you to have this basket of scones, with his compliments. They are just out of the oven."

Sir Ian?

"Oh, wow," I said, accepting his offering. "That's so nice of him! Please tell him thank you very much, Mr. . . . ?"

"I'm Harkins, Miss. The master was very sorry he wasn't able to offer you any scones the day you came for tea. But he hopes that this will make up for it."

The way the news crews descended Saturday, I should be the one buying gift baskets for the whole block. I can't believe Ian is still speaking to me. Much less sending over a present.

"More than. They smell wonderful. Please thank him for me."

Harkins tipped his cap. "I will be happy to do so, Miss."

With that, he was gone.

I walked into the kitchen with my parcel, and what I'm sure was a goofy grin on my face. I felt like I'd just won Miss America. Or at least first runner-up.

Baba had a Swiffer pad pasted to her palm and was going at my kitchen floor like it was a terrorist withholding information. Lucy was stretched out under the table, watching from a safe distance.

"Schtow eta?" she asked, pointing at the basket.

"It's a gift from the new neighbor across the street. Scones. Kinda like biscuits. He bakes them himself."

"Could be poison?" she asked. Given where she grew up, it was a perfectly legitimate question.

"No, no, just his way of being kind. He's turning his place into a bed-and-breakfast. They're going to serve tea and all kinds of pastries. He's just making nice with the neighbors."

"What is bed-and-breakfast?"

"Kind of like a place where people come to stay, just for a few days."

"Humpf! Boardinghouse!" With that, she went back to punishing my floor.

I looked around amazed. I'd always thought my kitchen was clean. But now it positively gleamed.

"Hey, Lizzie Borden, open up! Your groceries are here!"

Lucy shot out from under the table. By the time I made it to the front door, she was clawing at it frantically.

"Yeah, yeah, your favorite guy is home," I said to her. "At least try to play it a little cool."

I should talk. I still had that silly grin on my face. I scooped her up and threw open the door.

"About damned time," Nick said. "I thought my arms were gonna break. We got everything."

I looked out and saw the backseat of Nick's sporty black Hyundai stuffed with grocery bags. It looked like they'd cleaned out the store.

"Lots of snack food and stuff that doesn't have to be cooked," he said, barely above a whisper.

"Awesome."

Lucy, freed from the prison of my arms, hopped at his feet. I'd never seen anyone so happy. Then Baba emerged from the kitchen, her face beaming.

"Nicholas! Let me see you! My little Nicholas!"

Nick had at least fifteen inches and a hundred pounds on her. But to Baba, he would always be "little Nicholas."

He dropped the groceries in a chair and wrapped her in a bear hug.

"Hey, you look great," he said. "Have you grown? Somebody's getting taller!"

"Bah, Mr. Smart Mouth," she said, hugging him back. And in that moment, I swear I saw a tear trickle down her cheek. She hadn't seen her "baby" grandson in a year. And in Baba-time, that was way too long.

"Good news," Nick said, his arm around her shoulders. "I've sold the emu farm. I'm moving back to D.C."

At that point, her tears really started to flow. And I was crying watching her crying. Even Nick's eyes were moist. Lucy, the maniac, was dancing around on her hind legs, trying to get in on the hugging.

"Don't stop there, sugar! Tell 'em the rest!"

Not only hadn't I heard Gabby come in, but—in that fleeting moment of pure joy—I'd forgotten she even existed.

I looked at Baba, whose eyes darted back and forth between Nick and Gabby. From the sobering expression on her face, I'd say no one had to tell her anything. Baba was nobody's fool.

"Baba, I want you to meet Gabrielle. Gabby. At some time in the not-too-distant future, we're getting married."

Say what?

Baba took in all of Gabby—from the peroxide locks to the platform pumps—in one long up-and-down glance. Then she did something that seriously scared the crap out of me.

She smiled.

If I'd had a basement, I'd have been checking for

pods. As it was, I was afraid someone or something had taken over her brain. Or maybe she'd had a stroke.

Baba reached out and took one of Gabby's slim, well-manicured hands gently in her two strong, gnarled ones, looking deeply into her eyes. For a split second, time stopped. "I am very happy to meet you," she said slowly, in carefully enunciated English. "Nicholas is a good man. He deserves a good woman."

When she let go of the hand, Gabby sagged and grabbed the back of the sofa.

"Now," said Baba with a sprightly twinkle, "I make us all a good dinner."

When she was safely out of earshot in the kitchen, I lit into Nick. "What the hell? *Getting* married? At some time in the not-too-distant future? Are you married or not?"

"I'll get the rest of the stuff from the car," Gabby said, disappearing out the front door.

"I'll help you," Nick chimed in.

I blocked his path. "Oh, no, you don't. Married or not? Did you lie to me, or did you lie to Baba?"

"I can't lie to Baba!"

"Why did you lie to me? I've shared everything with you. OK, admittedly nothing great, lately. But everything I've got at the moment."

"I know, I know," he said. "And I'm sorry. It's just that the whole family still treats me like a kid. I was afraid if I showed up with Gabby and no job, you'd never take us seriously. But this time, it really is different."

"So if I'm such a judgmental jerk, why didn't you just go to a hotel?"

"I damn well would have if I'd had the cash."

"What about the money from the sale of the farm?"

"We were up to our eyeballs in debt. Most of it went to some very serious people who were threatening some very serious things if we didn't cough it up pronto."

"The mob?"

"The IRS. Turned out Brandon had been using our tax payments for pot. By the time I found out, we were so far in the hole, the only way out was to sell everything."

"Oh jeez. I'm sorry."

He looked at the floor and shook his head. "It's OK."

"So you're totally broke?"

"Just temporarily. The buyer is paying us in three installments. Taxes and my stopover in Vegas wiped out most of the first one. But I'll get to keep some of the second, and most of the third."

"You were broke, and you went to Vegas?"

"I had a little money, and I needed a lot of money. Seemed like a plan."

"So who paid for the groceries?"

"Gabby. Like I said, she's doing really well with her store."

Damn. Was there some sort of law about profiting from the proceeds of a crime? If I ate Mint Milanos bought with ill-gotten gains, would that make me an accessory?

"The buyer couldn't pay you all at once?" I asked.

"Didn't have the money. But they were the ones who offered the most. And they were willing to meet all of my conditions."

"Conditions?"

"Not to kill the emus. Or sell them for oil or meat."

"Not to be mean, but what else are emus good for?" I asked.

"Guano."

"What?"

"Shit. Scat. Excrement. Feces. They drop a ton of it. And thanks to Brandon-the-Burnout, I discovered the stuff's worth its weight in gold as fertilizer."

"Really?"

"In the middle of the Arizona desert, Brandon had a green space that would make an Iowa farmer weep," Nick said. "Unfortunately, he was using it to grow pot. Apparently, when he finally ran out of money to buy the stuff, he decided to raise his own."

Three cheers for American ingenuity. And they say this country isn't producing anything anymore.

"Why emu dung?"

"Hey, you use what you got. When I discovered his garden, I realized two things. One, I had to sell the ranch. And two, there was definitely a way out of the mess I was in."

"I can appreciate that."

"Thought you might. Anyway, I destroyed the pot and planted some, um, more pedestrian crops. And when they started to come in, I contacted the folks at the Arizona State University. They're turning the place into a green research station. Sort of an incubator for bio-friendly farming techniques. And they're studying the value of emu dung as a soil additive."

"What about Brandon?"

"Fell in love with a teaching assistant from the

university and enrolled. I don't think it's going to last, but . . ."

"But you and Gabby aren't really married?"

"Not yet."

"Then congratulations on your upcoming nuptials."

"Thank you!"

"Don't thank me yet. Baba's here now, so you're sleeping on the couch."

We trudged back and forth unloading groceries from Nick's car like a line of carpenter ants. During one trip, I detoured to my coffee-can bank just long enough to grab a wad of bills.

"So how much do I owe you?" I asked Gabby, as she hoisted two bags from the car.

"Sugar, save your money."

"No, really. That's the deal I had with Nick. I was supposed to go to the farmers' market yesterday, and I never made it."

"It was $336," Nick said.

I peeled off seventeen twenties and proffered them to Gabby.

"Sugar, your money's no good here."

I turned to Nick. He took it and—in one smooth motion—slipped it into Gabby's jeans pocket, grabbed the two grocery bags from her arms, and leaned in for a lingering kiss. Then he turned and started for the house, leaving Gabby grinning and shaking her head.

I decided to strike while the iron was hot. So to speak.

"Look," I started. "Baba's being here changes things a little. The boxes—the deliveries for the store? I can't have that stuff coming to the house anymore. I mean, you can get a post office box or a mail drop. But not the house directly.

"Sugar, I've got to make a living."

"I know. Believe me, I understand that. And I'm grateful for the money you guys are kicking in. But I've got to keep a roof over all our heads. And, as you witnessed last night, I'm under a lot of scrutiny. Legal scrutiny. Plus, someone is still trying to pin a murder on me. And the mail keeps getting misdelivered. I mean, it's one thing if it's just a couple of bills and some bulk mail coupons. But it's a lot more serious if your business stuff gets hijacked."

"OK, sugar, that makes sense."

Well, what do you know? Being framed for murder actually has an upside.

By the time we unloaded the last of the groceries, Baba had mysteriously absented herself to my bedroom. After her odd reaction to Gabby, I wanted to give her a little time.

"Hey, what's this?" Nick said, pointing to the basket on the counter.

"Scones. A present from the bed-and-breakfast guy across the street. He baked them himself."

"The English stud muffin?" Gabby chimed in. "Ooooh, honey, he likes you."

"Nah, he's just buttering up the neighbors. That way, when his guests park all up and down the block and trample the grass, we won't call the cops."

"After last night, you should be giving him scones,"

Nick said. "Your news trucks were blocking the whole street."

"Hey, those were not 'my' news trucks. Just like it's not 'my' gopher. But those are my scones. Sir Ian's chauffeur said so."

"Sir Ian?" Nick asked.

"Chauffeur?" Gabby gasped.

"Let's try these suckers," Nick said, pulling off the cellophane. He offered the basket to each of us, then grabbed a scone for himself.

Lucy circled Nick's legs.

"Oh, jeez!"

"Blah!"

"Sugar, did he say 'scones' or 'stones'?"

"OK," I said, "so they're a little hard. Maybe they're better under some butter?"

"They'd be better under six feet of dirt," Nick said. "We gotta bury these things deep so the animals can't get at them."

"Hey, maybe if we dunked them in coffee or . . . Oh crap, what is this? Does this look like a raisin? Please tell me this is a raisin."

"Hey, don't give that to her!" Nick barked.

I looked up to see Gabby innocently offering what was left of her scone to Lucy, who took a sniff and bolted.

"Man, food so bad even a dog won't try it," Nick said, wiping his hands on his jeans.

I pitched my scone into the trash. It made a hard *thunk*. "There's the slogan for their brochure."

* * *

Dinner was uneventful.

The main course, something Baba concocted and poured over bread, was gray and runny, with lumps. It could have been anything. Chicken. Potatoes. Lettuce.

We all scarfed it down and asked for seconds. Baba beamed.

Hours later, as we each headed off to bed, I brought sheets and blankets out to Nick.

"Schtow eta?" Baba asked, glaring at me.

"Gabby's staying in the guest room, so Nick's sleeping on the couch," I explained.

"No," she said, shaking her head vigorously.

"You," she said, pointing at Nick and gesturing toward the bedroom door Gabby had just closed. "You both in guest room." With that, she grabbed the linens and marched them back to my room.

When I came in, she was packing them into the chest that served as my linen closet.

"Baba, you're sure you're going to be OK with Nick and Gabby staying in the same room?"

"Da."

If she'd suddenly sprouted rocket skates and announced she was taking up professional roller derby, I couldn't have been more surprised.

"What about all that stuff you told me growing up? 'He won't buy the cow if he can get the milk for free'?"

"Oh, Alexandra," she said with a strained smile. "This cow we don't want him to buy."

Chapter 29

Even though I was unemployed, Monday still felt like Monday.

The good news: I had a freelance assignment, thanks to Trip. And a kitchen full of groceries, thanks to Nick and Gabby.

The bad news: my article was due in less than two weeks. I was no closer to discovering who killed Coleman. And I hadn't told Baba about my night job.

Plus, unless I wanted to keep blowing through my rainy-day mortgage fund, I had to get some money. And that meant cashing Peter's check.

When I walked into the kitchen, Nick was sitting at the table drinking coffee and reading the paper. He looked freshly shaved and showered. And he was, for Nick at least, fully dressed—decked out in jeans and an Arizona State Sun Devils sweatshirt. Lucy was curled at his feet, dozing.

"How long have you been up?"

"This is my second pot," he said, raising his cup.

"Good God, why?"

"I've discovered a new form of birth control."

"What?" I asked.

"Baba in the next room."

"Hey, she's fine with it. It was her idea. Besides, she sleeps like the dead."

If the dead could snore.

"Doesn't matter. She knows stuff. It's spooky. So at this point, I might as well be sleeping in the bathtub. Ain't gonna happen."

Well, what do you know?

"Hey, by any chance, do you have a local bank account?" I ventured.

"Not yet. I was gonna open one in the next few weeks. I'm not due to get the second installment on the ranch 'til later next month. Until then, it's all about the Benjamins. Why do you ask?"

I left Peter's name out of it, but explained I had a large check I needed to cash, and gave him the short version of my now-strained relationship with the bank.

"Why don't you just go to a check-cashing place?"

"I never thought of that," I said. "Would they do it?"

"They'd take a hefty fee, but yeah, they'd do it. It's where you go when you don't have an account. Brandon used them all the time."

"Brandon was a drug dealer."

"Exactly. So you know they don't set the bar too high. Told Baba about your night job yet?"

"Why do I get the feeling you're enjoying this?"

"Hey, I've done my time in the hole. It's your turn."

"I'll tell her tonight, before I leave," I said, pouring coffee into my favorite mug, which happened to be the size of a bongo drum.

"I'm guessing right before you leave?" Nick said, handing me the Nesquik.

"What are you? My conscience, Jiminy Cricket?" I popped the top on the Nesquik, dumped in three heaping spoonfuls, gave it a stir, and took a long, happy sip.

He grinned. "Can I at least be there when you tell her?"

I spent the morning working on my bridal story. By noon, I realized that if I had to listen to one more bride blather on about her "perfect wedding," "perfect day," or "perfect dress," I was going to go perfectly mad.

I grabbed the phone and dialed Trip. "I need a fiancé."

"Admitting your problem is the first step toward recovery."

"There's a bridal registry clinic Thursday evening. I have to go for the magazine story. And it's couples only."

"That's the part that makes zero sense to me," he said. "What kind of clinic do you need? You find something you like, you zap it with a price gun and—bam!—it goes on your gift list."

"I know," I said. "It's stupid. But I'm supposed to be writing an insider's account, so I've got to go and drink the Kool-Aid."

"Will there be actual Kool-Aid?"

"Punch of some sort. And little sandwiches. Then they teach you how to set up a proper household with shrimp forks and silver napkin rings."

"Sounds like one of Sweetie's garden parties," Trip said.

"See? That's why you'd be perfect for this."

"I'd have flashbacks," he said. "I'll never forget the time I spiked her punch with grape vodka. You haven't seen funny until you've seen an entire DAR chapter skinny-dipping in a duck pond. With gloves and hats."

"Did she ever figure out who did it?"

"Of course," he said. "And the best part was, I never had to attend another garden party."

"So the message here is?" I asked.

"Don't drink the Kool-Aid. Spike the punch."

"Words to live by. I still need a groom."

"What about Lord Sir Bed-and-Breakfast?" Trip asked.

"Let's see, should I actually be wearing the wedding dress when I invite him? Or save that for Thursday?"

"Too forward?" he asked.

"Too forward."

"Would make a great first-date story to tell the kids."

"Yeah, but it pretty much guarantees they'd be someone else's kids. What does it say about me that my only options for a fake groom are you, my brother, and a neighbor I just met?"

"It says you definitely need to get out more," he agreed. "Look, nobody in their right mind is going to buy me as your fiancé."

Trip jokes that he "came out" at birth.

Which initially confused the hell out of his family. They'd been expecting little Chase Wentworth Cabot III, scion of the family and future Virginia gentleman farmer, to be a rough-and-tumble little boy. Which he was. But he also liked eyelet curtains, high-fashion Barbies, and the color pink. So his family did the only thing they could think of: they loved Trip for Trip.

Consequently, despite the Southern Gothic pre-requisite assortment of kooky aunts, crazy uncles, and oddball cousins, Trip is one of the most well-adjusted, down-to-earth people I've ever met.

Not that he'd ever admit it.

"I was such a shock that after the birth, my mother had her ya-ya sewn shut," he announced during tea at my first visit to the Farm.

I nearly dropped the ancient bone china cup I was balancing on my lap, as I tried not to choke on a cucumber sandwich.

"Ah most cuh-tainly did naht," drawled Trip's mother, a gently worn, fifty-plus blonde who claimed to be forty-five, acted fifteen, and went by the improbable name of Sweetie.

"It was a little tightening procedure." She pronounced it pro-SEE-jah. "Strictly restorative."

"Restorative?" I croaked, once I'd settled the cup in my lap.

"Ah was a young bride, and he had a head like a wah-ta-melon. Would anyone like more tea?" she added brightly.

Was it any wonder that if I had to venture into the land of fine china, pressed linens, and silver place settings, I wanted Trip riding shotgun?

"Take Nick," Trip said finally. "He actually is en-gaged, so it's not a total lie. Oh, and don't forget the rock."

"The wrestler?"

"The ring," he said. "You want to run with the brides and be accepted as a member of the pack, you need a diamond. Preferably a big one."

"Why big?"

"You put ten brides in a room, they're going to start comparing engagement rings," Trip said. "And size matters. You need to represent."

"I was just going to say that mine was at the jeweler's."

"Lame. Any chance Gabby will loan you her boulder?"

"The engagement's kind of a touchy subject around here," I said. "I don't want to ask. Besides, she never goes anywhere without it. Not even the shower."

"See? If you're going to be a bride, you need a ring," Trip said. "What about Annie?"

As anyone who reads *People* knows, my sister's been engaged. Five times. And each ring was bigger than the last.

When she invariably broke it off, her exes always insisted that she keep the bling. My theory: each of the poor slobs was hoping she'd change her mind and take him back. Which just proved how little they understood my sister.

"I'll ask the next time she calls," I promised.

"Failing that, I might be able to borrow something from Sweetie that could pass for an engagement ring."

"Failing that, I can hit the costume jewelry counter at Penney's," I said.

"Tacky, tacky, tacky," Trip chided. "A fake fiancé is

one thing. But a fake rock? You'll never make pack leader with that attitude."

Nick and Gabby were off at some mall in Towson. More "reconnaissance."

I grabbed a quick lunch with Baba. I made us each a sandwich, and she heated up some gray soup that tasted suspiciously like an even waterier version of last night's main course.

After lunch, I decided to do a little reconnaissance of my own. I'd found the Starbucks where Piper's wife was working and figured this might be a good time for a latte break.

I ducked into the kitchen to tell Baba I was on my way out, just in time to catch her ladling several cups of warm soup over Lucy's kibble. The pup was vibrating with excitement.

Baba shrugged. "Get rid of leftovers," she said.

Chapter 30

Way out in the Virginia 'burbs, the Starbucks took up one end of a strip mall that included a pizza place, a Thai restaurant, a nail salon, and a karate studio. A drive-through cleaner occupied the other corner.

I cruised through the parking lot, curious whether I'd be able to spot which was Ellen Piper's car.

My pick: a blue Corolla so old that the paint was fading in patches. Two worn bumper stickers were plastered to the back fender: "Lafayette Elementary School PTA Boosters" and "The American Lung Association: It's a matter of life and breath."

From the look of it, the Pipers had been barely scraping by for a long time. How desperate were they now? Could Alan Piper have visited Coleman to try to win back his old job? Or in a last-ditch effort to stop the blackballing?

What would Piper have done if Coleman refused? Or, more likely, if Coleman just laughed off the whole thing as a good joke?

I could have walked through that door blindfolded,

and still known exactly where I was. It smelled like every Starbucks everywhere. Delicious.

The lunch rush was over, so the place was nearly empty.

The heavyset barista—who went about six feet, and sported blue bangs, a gold brow piercing, and a sparse soul patch—didn't look like an "Ellen."

In the back, a small, thin, harried-looking woman with close-cropped, mousy brown hair was wiping down tables. Bingo.

"I'll have two medium mocha lattes," I said.

I love the coffee. But memo to HQ: that "tall," "grande," "venti" stuff isn't fooling anybody.

"Whipped cream?" the barista asked.

"Definitely."

If I was splurging five dollars for a cup of chocolate coffee, I wanted my money's worth.

I paid and stuffed another fiver into the tip box. The gold piercing went up an inch.

Two minutes later, I grabbed my coffees and headed for a table in the back.

"Ellen?"

The woman whipped around, surprised. She wore little makeup. But professional stage pancake couldn't have camouflaged the deep, dark circles under her eyes.

"Do I know you?"

"I used to work for the same company as your husband. I was wondering if we could talk for a minute." I held out one of the coffees.

She just stared at me.

"Mocha latte," I said. I've heard there are women who don't like chocolate. But I've never met any.

"You work at Coleman & Walters?" she asked, eyes narrowing.

"Fired. Last week."

"Justin, I'm taking my break now," she shouted to the barista, finally taking the cup from my hand.

From the register, Justin waved.

She sank into one of the chairs and took a sip of coffee. I popped the lid off mine and proceeded to eat the whipped cream.

"Have you got a lawyer?" she asked.

"Yeah."

"We tried that. But we had to let him go. He said we had a good case, but we couldn't afford him. And even if we could have gone the contingency route, Alan's heart wasn't in it."

"My brother's paying for mine. I couldn't have swung it, otherwise."

She nodded.

"We had a little money in savings, at first. Too much to qualify for legal aid. But Bobby's medical expenses are enormous, even with the insurance. He's autistic, and he has epilepsy and asthma. This job just barely covers our COBRA premiums, these days. And I was lucky to get on here."

I nodded and felt like a schmuck. What was one dental bill compared to what this family had been through? What they were still going through?

"They canceled my insurance," I said. "C&W. Told the insurance company that I'd dropped it when I hadn't."

"They're bastards. Total bastards. Alan gave that son of a bitch everything he had, every spare minute, every brilliant strategy, for the last seven years. You know why? Everett Coleman kept dangling the promise of a vice presidency. Giving Alan his own group within the firm. Creative control. When it still hadn't materialized after a few years, I told Alan he was crazy to stay. That was when I realized that Everett Coleman was never going to give anyone else an ounce of autonomy in that company. His company."

So how would Alan have reacted if he'd learned about Coleman's plan to rebuild the agency with a bunch of young turks? If Alan discovered he'd not only been fired, black-balled, and bankrupted—but played for a chump for seven long years? Could that have been the final insult that drove him to kill?

I decided to prime the pump. "They're black-balling me. I can't even get a job interview."

"Standard C&W procedure. Right out of the Everett Coleman playbook."

"Destroy the enemy."

"And if you're not Everett Coleman, you're the enemy." Ellen shook her head. "I know business is business. Heaven knows, I'm not young and naïve. But I think he enjoyed playing God. Using people as pawns and tossing them away. It gave him a thrill. It sounds simplistic, but the man was evil. Pure evil."

"Any idea who'd want to kill him?"

"I did. But I'm not sure I could have stabbed him only once," she said with a rueful snort. "If I'd gotten started, he'd have had a few more holes in him."

There was no easy way to ask what I had to ask. I opted for the Band-Aid approach. "Could Alan have done it?"

You'd have thought I'd asked her if Alan could drive a stick shift.

"You know, I really wish he could. After Coleman fired him, he just lost heart. Retreated into himself. The only time he even left the house this month was to go to the funeral.

"Most days, he doesn't even change out of his sweats. But he's terrific with the boys. And they're crazy about him. When the kids are home, the three of them have a great time. When they're not around, he never leaves the sofa. Of course, that sofa is now at my mom's house. That doesn't help. But at least it's a roof over our heads."

"He wouldn't have gone down to C&W last Sunday to try and get his job back? Or talk Coleman into letting up on the blackballing?"

"No. As bad as things are, he doesn't want to go back. And Everett Coleman wouldn't have backed off even if Alan had asked him to. Just the opposite. Coleman would have seen it as a sign of weakness. And Coleman hated weakness. It was like waving a red flag in front of a bull."

Or a white flag in front of a bully.

"He even blamed us for Bobby's condition. Told Alan more than once that the problem was we coddled the boy. That we needed to toughen him up. Can you imagine saying something so cruel about a sick child?"

Unfortunately, knowing the man who said it, I could. I shook my head.

"So you never believed it might have been Alan there last Sunday?"

"I know it wasn't. My parents were away for the weekend, and I pulled a double shot—sorry, coffee-speak—a double shift here. Alan was with the kids all day. He wouldn't have left them alone. And with Bobby's medical problems, we can't trust sitters."

I nodded.

"Any idea who might have done it? Or wanted to do it?"

"Wait a minute! I remember you! You're the one from the newspaper story. The impaler!"

I sighed. Explaining my connection to a murder was becoming routine. How weird was that?

"I've talked with the police. They're satisfied I wasn't involved. But someone at C&W started a rumor campaign. Walters, I suspect. Even though they keep pointing the police in my direction, I've been officially cleared. That was in the papers this weekend."

When the police flack admitted on-air Sunday morning that I was "not a person of interest," even Mira's paper had to print it. On the second-to-last page of the metro section. Next to an ad for a three-day tire sale at Big Jimmy's Oil-N-Lube.

"You're trying to find out who did it!"

I nodded.

"And you think it was Alan?"

"No, but I think Alan might know things that could shed some light on who did. I only lasted three months at C&W. Your husband survived seven years. He's seen things. He knows the players. And if Coleman was trying that hard to destroy him, Coleman must have been afraid of what he could reveal."

"They're trying to destroy you, too."

"I was a convenient scapegoat. I'd had a falling-out with Coleman the Friday before he was killed."

"What kind of falling-out?"

All in, as my father used to say. "He tried to give me to a client for the evening."

"That man was scum. Why do you even care who killed him? Hell, give 'em a medal."

I had to admit, she had a point. I paused.

"Even though the cops have cleared me, the C&W crowd is still trying to keep my name in it. They're telling everyone who'll listen—and in this town, that's everybody—that I killed Coleman because I was working undercover for my old newspaper, and he found out about it. It's a lie. But it means the paper can't hire me back. And no one else will even talk to me. If I ever want to work again, I need to make sure the real story comes out. And, between you and me, I think it was one of them."

Ellen considered the information and shrugged.

"Did Alan get anything when he left? Any severance at all?"

"Are you kidding? They even kept us from getting unemployment. Claimed it was 'termination for cause due to substandard work performance.' That's a laugh. It was Everett Coleman's plan the clients hated. But Coleman made sure that Alan was the one who led the meetings and signed off on everything. Coleman had a paper trail a mile long to back him up. Lawyers out the wazoo. Mountains of files. Hearings. Depositions. You name it. He cleaned us out.

"We went from a $150,000-a-year job with benefits to nothing. Overnight. Alan made a big chunk of his money in bonuses. But they pulled some legal maneuver and C&W got to keep that. Threatened to come after us for the last one, too. Claimed they had evidence of 'long-standing breach of contractual obligations.' It was all bullshit. But between the out-of-pocket for Bobby's medical bills, the insurance premiums to keep the coverage we did have, two mortgages, and the lawyers' bills, we were wiped out. In less than six months."

"Seven years with a top firm, and no job nibbles at all?"

"Coleman was the face of the firm. Any good thing that happened, he soaked up all the limelight. When I finally realized that, I started urging Alan to jump ship. But, thanks to Coleman, no one else recognized his real worth. So the money wasn't there. And Alan was happy at C&W. He may not have liked Everett Coleman, but he loved his job. I didn't want to be some dissatisfied harpy. So I backed off."

I nodded.

"A few weeks after Alan left, we heard that Coleman was putting the word out that Alan had stolen money from the firm."

"Embezzling? That's a pretty serious charge. I'm surprised that one didn't make the papers."

"It was all whispering behind the scenes. Nothing official. Nothing he even hinted at to the authorities or the unemployment people."

"Because then he'd have had to prove it."

She nodded. "He just made a few phone calls. Said he wasn't going to bother reporting it, of course. That it wasn't that large an amount. But that money was definitely missing, and Alan was the one with access. Claimed Alan made a habit of padding his expenses in a big way, too. From what we heard, Coleman trumpeted that he was sympathetic because he knew we needed the cash for Bobby. Said he'd personally repaid all of the money out of his own pocket and wasn't going to prosecute."

"Coleman the hero again. And once word got around . . ."

"The smaller companies already couldn't afford to have Bobby on their insurance. The bigger ones believed Alan was either incompetent or a thief."

I patted her hand. "I'm so sorry."

"About a month later, Alan found out that the new industry slang for publicly embarrassing yourself and getting canned was 'pulling a Piper.' I think that's when he just gave up." She sighed. "How in the world do you bounce back from something like that?"

Good question. And it definitely put my situation into perspective.

"Look, I understand what you're trying to do," she said finally. "And I hope you come out of this OK. Hell, if it's one of them, I hope the bastard gets the chair. But if someone took out every single one of them tomorrow, it still wouldn't make life one bit better for my family."

Chapter 31

It's a lot harder to sell something when you're not that convinced yourself.

Later that afternoon, I finally told Baba about my night job. She was not pleased.

That made two of us.

When I came out to the living room at 5:30, she was sitting on the sofa waiting for me, her purse in her lap.

"I come," she announced, standing.

"I can't do that. There's no place for you to wait."

"I clean," she said.

"OK, why do you want to come with me?"

"Is not safe. Is night. Murderers in office. Thieves in street."

I sat down on the sofa. "It's a lousy job with bad hours. And I'm going to come home stinking of toilet cleaner."

Forget the thieves and murderers. The biggest danger I'm facing is lung damage from the petrochemicals.

"And my boss, who pays in cash, under the table, will use any excuse not to pay us. But it's safe. We all go to the office together in a van. We stick together while we're there. "

Too much, frankly. I could use a little more alone time to nose around.

"And the van drops us right back at our cars. I keep my doors locked and come straight home."

Except for the night I met Trip for breakfast. No need to mention that.

"And Nick always waits up for me."

Nick's a night owl and would be up anyway. No need to mention that, either.

"Besides, it's just for a couple of nights, tops. Once I retrieve that recorder, I'm gone. Nick, help me out here."

"She's right," Nick said. "Compared to some of the stuff she did as a reporter, this is nothing. Tell her about that double murder at the milk plant. Man, I will never look at a carton of chocolate milk the same way again."

Baba glared at me. I glared at Nick. He grinned.

"Not helping?"

"Not helping. What Nick is trying to say is that this is a safe job."

Grinding and soul sucking, but safe.

"Yeah, when you think about it, you were in more danger when you actually worked for the public relations firm," he said. "I mean, you were probably sharing an office with a potential murderer."

"So not helping."

"Hey, I'm just saying."

But something he said sparked an idea. "Why don't you give us a minute," I said to Nick.

"OK, I'm taking Lucy for a walk."

Once they left, I took Baba's hand. For her part, she'd fixed her gaze on the living room wall. From her expression, I was expecting the wall to give way any minute.

"No one at my former job knows I'm cleaning their offices. By the time I get there, they've all gone home. It's just the cleaning crew. If one of my ex-coworkers wanted to hurt me, they'd come here. I need you here. To help me protect everybody."

"Humf!"

"Not buying it?"

"Don't kid a kidder." My father's words in Baba's voice. Who said she had a limited grasp of English?

"They really don't know I'm there. That's the point. I am careful. And I will come straight home. But I can't take you with me."

"What Nicholas said is true? About reporter job?"

"Uh, yeah. Although usually we show up after something bad happens, not during. The milk plant thing was kind of an exception. Rare. Very rare."

"Humf!"

A half hour later, after I parked at Gravois & Co., I phoned Nick.

"How's she doing?"

"Hard to tell. She's been locked in the bathroom since you left."

"Crying?"

"Cleaning. If she doesn't come out soon, I'm gonna be knocking on your neighbor's door."

"Good luck with that. Oh, and Nick?"

"Yeah?"

"Keep Thursday evening open. I need your help with a little errand."

I swung out of the car and made myself a promise. After this night was over, Coleman murder or no Coleman murder, I was going to sleep for twelve hours straight.

It hadn't exactly been a restful weekend. And a houseful of people made afternoon naps a thing of the past.

Well, as soon as I snagged that digital recorder, I was out of here. I could live off Peter's check until my freelance money started coming in and keep normal, non-vampire hours again.

Gravois was a riddle wrapped in a hairy enigma. First, he handed me an envelope. Inside, I found two fifties—most of my pay from last week. Even eight dollars light, it was a hundred dollars more than I was expecting.

Then he announced we were cleaning floors eight, nine, and ten—and put me and Elia on toilet duty. I pleaded lingering bronchitis. He was unmoved. Maria and Olga giggled. I'm guessing I know who had toilet patrol on Friday.

I pulled them aside. "Look, I'm still feeling lousy, and I need a break from the fumes tonight. If you volunteer to clean the toilets, he won't care. He just wants someone to do it." I held up a fifty.

Maria looked over at Olga and snatched the bill. Then Olga put out her hand. I placed the other fifty in her palm.

Easy come, easy go.

Elia had been watching the transaction warily from a distance. "We're on dusting duty," I told her.

"You are funny," she said, shaking her head.

"Yeah, that's me. A little ray of sunshine. Let's hit that conference room first."

Since leaving C&W last week, I'd worked harder and longer than I ever had in my life. I'd earned a grand total of $120—less than half of what my bank had charged me in penalty fees.

And I'd just given away most of it.

When I turned the knob on the conference room door, it didn't budge.

Stubbornly, I tried again.

"*Ocupado!*" an irritated male voice yelled from within. Walters.

What was he doing here? Didn't any of these people have homes?

"*Excúseme, por favor,*" I replied, doing what I thought was a halfway decent accent.

Elia rolled her eyes.

"Hey, one of my college roommates was from Mexico City," I stage whispered.

"So you can speak Spanish?"

"Not with native speakers—they talk too fast. But I can sing the Macarena, count to ten, and flirt with slow-speaking gringos."

"Skills that will serve you for life, clearly."

"Hey, we can't all be doctors. Let's start at the other end of the suite. We can double back to this room right before we leave. He'll be long gone by then."

"So what is in there?" she said, pointing to the door.

"Right now, my ex-boss," I whispered, as we rolled our trolleys down the darkened corridor. "And a small digital recorder my sister gave me. Voice activated. It's in one of the two vases on the giant bookcase in the back. There was a big meeting in there last week. I'm just hoping the recorder picked up something that will help me."

Even if all they talked about was the ongoing plan to frame me.

When we got to the very back of the office, I hit the lights.

"Holy crap!" I said.

Elia looked at me. I pointed to a desk with something taped to the side of the computer monitor.

"That's me," I said. "From an article that ran in one of the papers this weekend."

My photo—the smirky one that accompanied Mira Myles' column—had been decorated with devil horns and a nose wart.

The next desk had one, too. Only the artist had gone for a pirate theme. Eye patch with a scar on the cheek. We scanned the room.

"They're everywhere," Elia breathed.

For the next five minutes, we held our own version of an Easter egg hunt. Or "Where's Waldo?" Only it was my head, and it was *everywhere*.

I found them taped to walls, mugs, desks and file cabinets. All sporting a selection of black eyes, over-size ears, mustaches, goatees, eye patches, scars, horns, witch hats, and tattooed epithets.

Someone even put one on the dartboard in the back of the office.

And one techno-savvy individual had turned it into a screen saver. The head inflated like a balloon until it exploded. That one freaked me out a little.

"What did you do to these people?"

"Ever read *The Lottery*? Shirley Jackson?"

Elia shook her head.

"Scapegoat thing. They've been told I killed their boss. Doesn't matter that it's not true. This gives them a safe outlet and a common target for their rage."

"Because they loved him?"

"Because they hate this place and everyone connected to it."

"America is so strange."

"Tell me about it."

If I couldn't get into the conference room, I was going for the next best thing: C&W's sanctum sanctorum. Otherwise known as Margaret's office.

There weren't any pictures of me, I'll give her that. Of course, she'd vented her rage on the real thing.

Immediately, I noticed two changes. First, three large floral arrangements, each set off with a wide black velvet ribbon around the vase. Condolence flowers.

Second, the candid shot of her and Everett, which had occupied the heavy, silver frame on her desk, was gone. Replaced with a studio portrait of Pat and Patti.

Grief? Guilt? Refocusing her energies? Or just redecorating?

As I pulled on a pair of yellow rubber gloves, I took a minute to study the neat-as-a-pin desk. Because, after I rifled through it, I wanted to put everything back perfectly. If I didn't, Margaret would notice. And that would not be good.

I opened one of the file-sized drawers. Neat, orderly

rows of files. Unfortunately, none of them labeled "redheaded she-devil." I was gonna have to wing it.

I flipped through until I found one labeled "Founding Fathers Life Insurance."

Hmmmm.

The first page was a letter from the company, addressed to Margaret. It offered "our sincerest condolences on your recent loss," and apologized for the delay in payment, explaining that its investigation was "still ongoing" and "would be concluded in the near future and with the utmost possible haste."

Interesting. What, exactly, was the insurance company investigating?

There was a policy number at the top of the page. I copied it into the small notebook I'd stashed in the pocket of my oversized jeans.

I flipped through the file and found a copy of the policy itself. Fifteen million dollars. All to Margaret. Taken out ten years ago. It made sense—that was about the time C&W moved into this office.

I kept flipping. Another letter from the company. This one, a Xerox, had been addressed to Walters. It skipped the condolences and simply informed him that the payout of C&W's business policy would be delayed, pending the conclusion of the insurance company's investigation.

Love to share a mocha latte with that investigator.

I scrawled down the policy number and the name of the executive who'd signed the letter.

And I kept shuffling. Near the bottom of the file was another policy. "The insured: Everett P. Coleman and Benjamin H. Walters."

"Beneficiaries: The last surviving of the above-named insured. Amount: thirty million dollars."

Bingo!

I checked my notepad again. The policy number matched the one on the letter to Walters.

Damn! Of that thirty mil, I'm guessing a good portion would go to Margaret to buy out Everett Coleman's half of the business. Then again, if she went to jail, I bet Pat and Patti would sell cheap.

That's when inspiration struck. Or maybe it was just the memory of Margaret's open hand.

I grabbed the policies and the letters and hit the copy room. Five minutes later, I fed the copies into C&W's fax machine, and punched in a familiar number. As I watched the high-speed fax inhale the pages, I dialed Trip.

"Billy Bob's getting a fax."

"You're his psychic secretary now?"

"Yes, and I predict twenty-two pages. Just make sure he sees it."

"You OK?"

"Yeah, but babysit the fax tonight. He might get more stuff."

"Where are you?"

"Belly of the beast."

After I replaced the originals, I divided the stack of copies, wrapped half around each ankle, and yanked up my socks.

I went back to the drawer and spotted another file, intriguingly labeled "IRS." I pulled it out and flipped it open.

Wow. Thank you, Santa.

Not only was C&W being audited, but the Feds were less than impressed with Margaret's bookkeeping. And there was some money missing. To the tune of nearly ten million.

I ducked outside the office. "Any sign of him?" I called to Elia.

"Locked in that room still."

"If anyone comes, give me a heads-up."

She looked puzzled.

"Signal me. Or come and get me."

"What are you doing?"

"You don't know, and you don't want to know."

I kept the copy machine warm for the next few minutes, then fed the fax again, and dialed Trip. "Second batch, coming through. Fifteen pages."

At this rate, I was really thankful C&W had shelled out for the lightning-fast model. The one at the paper, a relic from the '90s, crawled along at one page per minute. And with Walters still in residence, I didn't have that kind of time.

"This one's from the IRS," I hissed into the phone.

"That should definitely get Billy Bob's attention," Trip said. There was silence for a half a beat, and I heard a door close on his end. "Hot damn, millions in insurance. This is dynamite. Literally. Are you sure you want to do this?"

"Am I sure I want to? Yeah. Is it a good idea? Probably not. But I'm tired of running from the monsters. I want to do the chasing for a while."

"Hey, look out for yourself," he said. "I mean it."

"Yes, Mom. Gotta go. Look, I'll call you when I get back to my car."

I had one more mission. And this one was strictly personal.

The name I was looking for this time: my own. And it was hiding at the very back of her drawer, behind some blank, empty files.

It was pitifully thin. Just a copy of my résumé, my insurance application (complete with my Social Security number), and a canceled check stapled to a form authorizing direct deposit, which I'd supplied on my first day.

There was also a form I'd never laid eyes on: the one canceling my health insurance.

The guy from Selecta HealthCare was half-right. Someone had checked the box dropping my coverage. But the signature was not mine. Someone—Margaret?—had tried to catch the flavor of it with the slant and lack of loops. But it was a good thing Margaret was already a rich woman. She was a lousy forger.

"My" insurance form was clipped to a typed note on C&W letterhead. One sentence stating that "Alexandra Vlodnachek is exiting the group health insurance plan, both medical and dental, effective immediately." It was dated last Monday, and signed by Margaret's assistant.

I wanted the originals. But eventually Margaret would realize they were missing—back of the file drawer or not. And that would be like signing my name to the information leak.

As it was, the phone number and time-and-date stamps on the faxed pages would show that they came from someone inside C&W. Let 'em chew on that.

I made two quick copies and tucked the originals back into place. Then I rolled the copies—the IRS letters together with my insurance pages—into a tight tube and shoved it down the front of my bra. I emptied the trash, sprayed air freshener and furniture polish into the air, flipped off the lights, and closed the door.

At this point, I had so many sheets of copy paper stuffed in my socks, I was limping. But for once I was actually grateful for the apron and my baggy sweatshirt. They helped obscure the mobile file cabinet that was my bra.

So much for the glamour of espionage.

I gave ten more offices the "dump-the-trash-and-spray-the-air" treatment.

When Gravois came to collect us, Walters was still locked in the conference room. Alone, apparently, because he wasn't talking to anyone. There was just the occasional shuffle and thump.

I wondered if the long hours had anything to do with the impending audit or the missing millions. Or maybe it was just the murder.

Life wasn't easy for the new head of Coleman & Walters.

And I planned to make it a lot harder.

Chapter 32

The next morning, I slept late. When I finally dragged myself out of bed, the sun was shining, the birds were singing, and there was a lovely cinnamony smell in the air.

Either I was still dreaming, or I was in the wrong house.

When I shuffled into the kitchen, Nick was taking a pan out of the oven. Several more pans were cooling on the table. And covered cake tins filled with God-knows-what had sprouted up on my counters.

"This place smells like Cinnabon."

"Yeah, I just finished a batch of sticky buns. But they have to cool. I want you to try a scone."

"No way. I'm never eating one of those things again. Ever."

"That's not what they're really like. Those were evil scones."

He set a steaming cup of coffee in front of me, along with something that looked suspiciously like one of the English rocks we'd thrown out Sunday.

"Just try it. Trust me."

"You do know I don't have dental insurance, right?"

"One bite."

I broke off a piece and sniffed it. What can I say? Living with Lucy has rubbed off on me.

Still warm, it had a rich, buttery aroma. I took a bite. And another.

"Oh my God, Nick, this is wonderful! It's light! It's yummy! It's actually delicious!"

"That's what they're supposed to taste like. That other thing was a mutant. Here, put some butter on it."

"I want another one."

"Just one, for now. I'm saving the rest."

"What for?" God forbid we were getting more houseguests. We'd have to sleep them on the roof.

"I invited your nice British neighbor over for tea."

"Ian? You invited Ian over? Why?"

"I figured after the other night we should do a little fence mending. And he seemed like the logical place to start. Plus, he was so cool about sending over that food basket, even after all the news trucks and everything."

Mr. Flaming Bag of Poo was making nice with the neighbors? Something definitely smelled here, and it wasn't cinnamon buns.

"Did you invite Mrs. Sterling?"

"I don't think he's married," Nick said. "But you might want to change. He's gonna be here in about twenty minutes."

"What? Today? You invited him today? And come to think of it, when did you learn how to bake?"

"At the ranch. In the middle of the desert, if you want bread, you make it yourself. And Brandon loved the baked goods."

"Brandon *was* baked goods."

"I had to play around with the recipes a little, to account for the difference in humidity and altitude. But I really think that last batch is some of my best work."

"Who are you, and what have you done with my brother? And where's Baba?"

"She took Lucy for a nice, long walk," he said. "But only after she had two of my chocolate croissants and told me they 'melt in mouth.'"

"Chocolate croissants?"

"Not until you go get ready. And a little mascara wouldn't hurt."

Thanks to Baba, my bathroom smelled of lemons and lavender. And it had never looked better.

But I couldn't say the same for me. The night hours were taking a toll. My eyes looked like two fried eggs. And my hair just looked fried. I was Ronald McDonald's younger, scarier sister.

Well, the heck with it. I didn't invite Ian. And I'd be damned if I was going to get all glammed up. This wasn't a date. This was just having a neighbor over for coffee. Or tea.

I brushed my teeth and pulled out an outfit that was casual but cute: a long-sleeved, forest green T-shirt and dark jeans. Then I attacked my hair. With a lot of brushing and a little water and mousse, I managed to make a loose, presentable ponytail.

I kept the makeup light: liner, mascara, a little concealer, a touch of blush, and some tinted lip gloss.

No push-up bra. No perfume. No way I could compete with the smell of cinnamon buns, anyway.

I blew into the kitchen with one thing on my mind. "I want a chocolate croissant!"

There was a firm knock on the front door.

"Go greet your guest," Nick said.

"He's your guest. You invited him."

"I have to finish here—go," he said, pointing to the front door. "Nice work with the makeup, by the way. You look almost human."

I stuck out my tongue.

"Your face will freeze," he called out behind me. "But in your case, it'll be an improvement."

I checked the peephole and opened the door.

Ian stood there holding a plant in a clay pot, wrapped with a purple bow. He was wearing jeans and a perfectly pressed oxford-cloth shirt with the sleeves rolled up—blue this time. And there was clearly some muscle under that refined exterior.

So what had he done before he bought the B&B?

"Hullo there," he said, smiling. The breeze carried in a waft of his cologne—subtle, spicy, and masculine.

I felt butterflies in my stomach again. And I regretted not wearing my push-up bra.

"Hey, come on in. Nick's finishing up in the kitchen."

For the first time, I noticed that my living room was almost as clean as my bathroom. And the stockpile of mystery boxes was gone. Oh yeah, something was definitely up.

"This is for you," Ian said, presenting the plant.

"It's beautiful, thank you."

"Gardenia," he said. "In a few weeks, it should do very well outside. And I noticed from your yard that you have a very green thumb."

"Yeah, I went a little crazy when I moved in two

years ago. I finally had a place where I could dig in the dirt."

I decided to take a stab at solving at least one mystery. "I thought you both were coming," I said.

"Oh, I'm afraid my father is spending the morning at something called 'NAPA Auto Parts.' He needs a few odds and ends to get the Bentley in fighting trim."

"Is Harkins his first name or his last?"

"Last. Don't tell me, let me guess. He played the old family retainer when he dropped off the basket?"

"Even managed to doff his cap. Are you really Sir Ian?"

Ian grinned, and my heart beat a little faster. "I'm afraid not. But my father believes it adds a little class to the place. So where's the little pup?"

"Out for a walk with my grandmother. She's staying with us for a few days."

"Wow, you've really got a houseful."

"Yeah, whoever said misery loves company wasn't sharing one bathroom with three people and a dog."

"Your dog uses the bathroom?"

"She likes to unravel the toilet paper," I said. "And she actually fell into the toilet once. I still can't figure out how she managed that one."

"Poor little thing."

"Yeah, she was pretty freaked out. For the next few hours, every time someone went in, she sat outside the door and howled."

"I've been reworking the bathrooms in our old place," Ian said. "I must say, I've felt like howling a few times myself."

"Demon plumbing?"

"Precisely. But we're leaving that off the website."

"So what did you do before you bought the B&B?"

"Oh, a little of this, a little of that," he said casually. "Nothing terribly interesting. But this has always been my dream. When I finally got the chance, I leapt at it."

Could he be more vague? As a reporter this was when I'd press for more information. And ask about those paintings. But at a neighborly tea, that would probably be considered rude.

"So you have a Bentley? Is that for the business, too?"

"Yup. That's Dad's bailiwick. Thanks to him, we can ferry guests to and fro in a vintage Bentley. Of course, 'vintage' means he's had to practically rebuild the thing from scratch. For a while, I believe it was using more oil than petrol. But now it's a real beauty, and he's got it running like a top."

"Anybody up for tea?" Nick said, bearing a tray with an elegant china teapot, along with matching cups, saucers, and pastry plates. He even had tiny little silver teaspoons and powder blue cloth napkins.

Since I didn't have a single matching mug, didn't own any saucers—or teapots—and the only silver I had was in my jewelry box, I was more than a little curious. Was I going to be drinking hot tea out of hot china?

"I hope you don't mind, I dragged out your good stuff," Nick said pointedly.

"That's what it's for," I replied, feeling like an understudy who'd wandered onto the stage without reading the play.

"Why don't you pour, while I get the rest of it?"

Alex in Wonderland, here I come.

"Your home is lovely," Ian said in a hushed voice. "Did you have to do much work on it?"

Finally, a familiar topic.

"No, I was lucky. The couple who lived here before me did all the heavy lifting. Not that there was much to do. To hear them tell it, the place was in great shape. But they put in a whole new kitchen, and a couple of walk-in closets. I just painted the inside and put a fresh coat of wax on the floors."

Nick reappeared with a second tray, this one featuring a multi-tiered cake plate loaded down with baked goods and a silver butter salver with three matching butter knives.

"Oh, lovely," Ian said, his face lighting up. "Did you enjoy the scones I sent over?"

"They sure went fast," Nick said smoothly. "I had to bake up some more. Along with a few other things."

"You bake?"

"It's a hobby I picked up living on a ranch out West. We were in kind of a remote area. It was either make your own or do without."

After Ian helped himself to a scone, I snagged a chocolate croissant.

"Good lord, man, this is wonderful! How do you get them so light?"

Nick grinned.

I took a bite and warm, melted chocolate filled my mouth.

"Mmmmm. Nick, this is seriously fantastic."

The next few minutes were a sugar-fueled blur. I polished off the croissant and a warm sticky bun with butter. Then Ian and I split something Nick dubbed a lemon tartlet: a flaky pastry crust filled with lemon-flavored custard and topped off with whipped cream and strips of candied lemon rind.

All the while, Nick played host and kept filling our cups with tea.

"This is seriously one of the best things I've ever eaten," I told him. "Forget the guest room. From now on, you live in the kitchen."

"Hey, I love doing it. And now that I've sold the ranch, I've got a little more time on my hands."

"So you don't live out West anymore?" Ian asked.

"No, my fiancée and I are moving back here. We're just bunking with Alex until we find a house."

News to me. But with a mouth full of tartlet, I wasn't going to object.

"Might you do this professionally?" Ian said. "I don't know if your sister has told you, but I'm opening a bed-and-breakfast across the street."

Nick looked at me and raised a surprised eyebrow.

"A big part of the business will be offering a traditional British afternoon tea," Ian explained. "Not just for our guests, but for locals and community groups, too. I'm a pretty fair cook. But I'm afraid I haven't quite caught on to the baking end of it quickly enough. So I've been looking into purchasing some of the necessities. Frankly, this is far superior to anything I've sampled. If you were willing to do it, I could make it worth your while financially."

I looked back at Nick. I felt like I was watching a tennis match. Or a slow-motion mugging.

"Wow. I love doing it, but I never thought of going pro. And it's not like we need the money."

Oh, please.

"Think about it. You've got a gift. The estimates I've been getting are quite pricey. And the food is nowhere near this quality."

We need the money. We need the money.

I looked back at Nick.

"Well, it would be fun. Of course, it would have to be OK with Alex. It is her kitchen."

Since when? Lately, everybody in the house is spending more time in my kitchen than I am. Even Lucy.

"Fine with me," I said, reaching for another croissant.

"It's a deal then. Drop by tomorrow and we can talk menus and prices. By the by, I'm having an event Sunday afternoon. A garden party with tea and sandwiches. I'd love to have a selection of pastries to offer. But I understand if that is too little notice."

"I'll pull out the books. I think I have a couple of go-to recipes that I could put together fairly quickly."

"Fantastic! This is beautiful." He glanced at his watch. "Oh, I've got to dash. I've got the landscaping crew coming in just a few minutes."

Nick started to clear the dishes, and I walked Ian to the door.

"Please feel free to pop over again," he said quietly. "I'd love to show you the new herb garden. And I'll let you have some clippings, if you want to give it a go."

I looked up into his blue-gray eyes. My mind went momentarily blank.

"Uh, that would be great, thanks. And thank you for the gardenia. I can't wait to put it in the yard."

When the door closed, I turned and followed Nick to the kitchen. "Mascara? I can't believe you were pimping me out to sell pastries!"

"A bit of crumpet to move a bit of crumpet," he replied in a bad British accent.

I punched him in the arm. "You could have at least warned me. And where did the tea service come from?"

"I got it at Macy's yesterday," he said. "And it wasn't cheap, lemme tell you. The pot and cups cost more than I ever made in a week."

"You can't take them back," I said.

"I'll never use them again!"

"You've already used them," I said. "Think of it as an investment in your new business. If you ever need to give another demo tea, you're all set."

"Yeah, that did go well," Nick said.

"And come to think of it, where's Gabby? How come she wasn't part of your little drama? You could have had her dressed as a French maid."

"She's sleeping in. Forget playing a maid, she was the real deal last night. She was cleaning, while I was baking. We were damned near up 'til dawn."

"Yeah, I noticed the box pile is gone," I said.

"Not gone, just relocated."

"I can dream, can't I? Hey, how long has Baba been out?"

"She took Lucy a few hours before you got up," Nick said. "Said something about 'good long walk.'"

"Good God, hours?" I said. "Shouldn't she be back by now?"

"It's Baba. Nobody's gonna mess with her. Besides, it's broad daylight, and this is a safe neighborhood."

I watched as he prepped a tray complete with tea, two croissants, a fresh blue napkin, and the lifestyle section of the paper. For Gabby, I assumed.

"I know," I said. "It's just that she's new here. She came to take care of me, and I feel responsible for her."

"Well, cut it out," Nick said. "She's an adult. She can take care of herself. If she's not back after lunch, we'll mount a search party."

Gabby strolled into the kitchen in a short, black silk robe, looking none the worse for her nighttime travails. "How'd it go, sugar?"

"He wants to buy my stuff," he said. "I'm supposed to go over tomorrow to finalize the details."

"Stick to your guns," she said. "You've got something he wants. You deserve to get top dollar."

While Lord and Lady Macbeth honed their closing skills, I decided to take a long walk of my own. And if I just happened to run into Baba, so much the better.

But when I walked into the living room, she was standing by the front door. She had Lucy's leash in one hand and a brown paper grocery bag cradled in her other arm.

"Baba!" I grabbed the bag and gave her a squeeze. "Where were you?"

"Store. We need food."

Last I checked, we had a kitchen full of food. "What about the groceries Nick bought?"

"Not that food. Real food. Food to cook. I go this morning," she said, freeing Lucy from her leash and giving her a little pat on the rump.

I put the bag on the sofa and glanced inside. Ten pounds of potatoes. Five pounds of carrots. And something large wrapped in butcher's paper.

"Did you carry this the whole way?" The nearest grocery store was at least three miles from here.

"No. I get cart," she said, reappearing from the porch with another large bag.

"You bought a cart at the store?"

"Not bought. I use cart they give for food."

"A grocery cart? You stole a grocery cart?"

"Not steal," she said indignantly, pulling herself up to her full height of almost five feet. "Cart for food. I use for food. When I go back to store, I bring." She stomped into the kitchen with her bag and mine.

I walked out to the porch to find a Giant Food cart with two more bags. I hoisted them up, balancing one on each hip, slammed the front door shut with my foot, and headed for the kitchen.

Baba was safe. My house smelled like a bakery. And, despite the fact that half my relatives were living here, the place had never looked better. I had a writing job, and Nick was launching a new endeavor of his own.

OK, so we were having a small problem in the sticky fingers department. All in all, life was good.

Chapter 33

I'd lied to Baba.

Since I hadn't gotten my hands on the digital recorder yesterday, it looked like I'd be spending quite a few more nights cleaning. I was beginning to wonder if I'd ever get to quit.

Worst of all, Gravois seemed to have Elia and me on permanent latrine duty. Silly me, I thought maybe once he saw my skills with a duster, I'd at least get to spend a few nights outside the stalls. No such luck.

The Tuesday session was particularly rough. One of the engineering firms had hosted some kind of booze bash with hors d'oeuvres. Deviled eggs and Vienna sausages. I'll never touch either one again.

Wednesday the weather turned foul. Cold, wet, and gray. Typical D.C. spring.

Icy rain pelted my windshield as I drove home. Luckily, there weren't many cars on the road after midnight. I was relieved to finally make the turn onto my street. But when I pulled into the driveway, the house was dark.

Odd.

Nick opened the door with a flashlight in his hand. "Come on, don't you have to go out?" he asked Lucy.

She didn't budge.

"Hey, is this what they mean by 'a night not fit for man nor beast'?" he asked me.

"I don't blame her," I said. "I wouldn't be out voluntarily. It's pretty nasty."

"Yeah, well, your floor's not so hot, either. So far tonight, she's left three puddles and a pile of poop by the front door. But when I try to get her to go out, she looks at me like I'm nuts."

"Smart dog."

"P.U.! Let me guess, toilets again."

"No, it's my new cologne. It's called 'Desperation.' Yes, toilets again. Toilets yesterday. Toilets tomorrow. And always toilets today. But enough about me. Why's the house so dark? Did you guys turn in early?"

Even in the muted glow of the flashlight, I could see Nick was giving me a weird look.

"Why didn't you tell us?"

"Tell you what?"

We stepped into the house. It was warm and toasty, but dark. And quiet. No TV. No rumbling heater in the background. A couple of flashlights, up-ended on tables, served as makeshift lamps. A fire crackled in the fireplace.

Gabby was clicking away on her laptop. Baba was dozing in a chair near the fire, and Lucy ambled over and curled up at her feet.

"What the hell? How long has the power been out?"

"It went out right after you left. When the temperature dropped, Baba and I got a fire going. Why didn't you tell us things were this tight? I mean, we knew it was bad, but we didn't know it was this bad. Gabby and I can spot you some cash."

"I paid the bill."

"Not according to the power company."

"That's impossible. I paid it two weeks ago, right before I got canned. The check's already cleared. You called? What did they say?"

"Not much. I didn't know your Social Security number, so they just kept saying, 'The owner of the account is apprised of all the developments pertaining to this account.' I figured that was drone-speak for 'no money, no honey.'"

Most of the houses in the area were gas and electric. Mine was the rare, all-electric exception. It was one of the many things I loved about my cozy little home. But tonight, it meant I'd be taking a long, cold shower since I wouldn't have any hot water, either.

"No, it sounds like my friends at C&W have been at it again."

"Again?"

"They've made an all-out assault on my finances. Talking to my bank. Canceling my credit cards. And my health insurance. Margaret's the one who did the health insurance. I found the paperwork earlier this week, when I was cleaning her office."

"Cleaning?" Nick asked.

"Cleaning. Snooping. Rifling through her desk drawers."

"Po-tay-to. Po-tah-to," he said. "So you think this is her, too?"

"Could be," I said. "Or it could just be that the feeding frenzy has begun."

"How's that work?"

"Sort of one-upsmanship, corporate style," I said. "Everybody takes a swing at the designated piñata."

"And you're the piñata?" Nick asked.

"*Si, señor*," I said. "What did you guys do for dinner?"

"Pizza. Gabby suggested firing up the grill, but the weather was lousy. Baba wanted to cook in the fireplace. Of course, I pointed out that we needed to keep all the cold air inside the fridge, so we should order out."

"Quick thinking."

"I'm at my best under pressure," he said. "Besides, I was jonesing for a pie. Oh, and your phone's out, too. I had to use my cell to call the power company and the pizza place. On the bright side, at least the bill collectors stopped calling."

I pulled the cell from my pocket. It had been strangely silent all night. Now I knew why. It was on the same plan as my home phone. I hit the power button and got the "no signal" message.

Tired as I felt, I was racing the clock to save the rapidly warming food in my fridge.

"I need your cell," I said to Nick.

He wrinkled his nose and took a step back.

"That bad?" I asked.

"Kinda."

I grabbed a flashlight from the table and headed to my desk, where I rooted around and finally found my utility bills. "C'mon, I really need your phone."

"You'll get stank on it," Nick said.

"You want heat and light and a working oven? I need your cell."

"Fine," he said.

Remembering the melting fridge full of food, I called the power company first. After almost a full minute, I got an actual human.

"Powhatan Power and Light. What's your emergency?"

"My power's off." I gave the guy my account number, name and address, along with the last four digits of my social. Then there was dead silence for almost two minutes.

"You had the service disconnected. Says here you moved from that address yesterday."

"There must be a mistake. I never called."

"Yup. Called Monday. Would have had to verify your identity, too."

"Look, someone's gotten hold of my personal information. And they've been playing hacky sack with my life. I didn't cancel my service. And I'm living in the same house I've been in for two years. If you look at my records, you'll see that my account is current, and that the last payment, which I made two weeks ago, was for $110.74. Check number 1284. What it won't show you is that I have a house full of very cold relatives and a refrigerator full of very warm food. Is there anything you can do?"

"Well, I can switch the power back on. But it can take up to two hours before it's restored at your location."

"That would be great. Can you put a rush on it?"

"That is a rush. In the meantime, you might want to add a security code to your account."

"What will that do?"

"It's a special four-digit number. You make it up and register it with us. But it won't be listed on your bill. Anyone wants to make changes to your account, they have to know the code."

"Perfect."

My call to the phone company was pretty much a slow-mo instant replay. I now had two new "security codes" and a sneaking suspicion that I was going to have to start playing a better game of defense if I didn't want to end up cold, hungry, and living on the street.

After forty minutes in an icy shower, I was curled up in my flannel nightgown, robe, and a sweater, with a towel wrapped around my head and a hot slice of pizza in my hand. Nick had ordered another pie while I was in the shower. And this one was piping hot.

"Had to get soda," he said. "They don't do hot coffee."

"I don't care. This is great." I tried to ignore Lucy, who was giving me her sad, hungry puppy look.

"Don't even think about it," Nick said. "She's already had two pieces of the first one."

"She's a growing dog," I said.

"The olives looked exactly the same coming out as they did going in," he reported. "It was freaky."

"I'm guessing that was the pile in the front hall?" I asked.

"Yeah. Gabby held the flashlight, while I cleaned it up."

"Sounds fair."

Baba was snoring softly. When the lights suddenly popped on, she sat straight up and blinked.

"Power's back," I said.

"Bah, I go to bed." She looked at Nick. "You put out fire?"

He nodded, kissed her on the forehead, and gave a mock salute. "Aye-aye, captain."

She reached over and patted my arm. "You eat. Get warm." And with that, she trundled off toward my bedroom.

Once the door closed, we all sprang into action. "I'm turning up the heat," I said, running for the thermostat.

"I'm checking the fridge," Nick called, heading for the kitchen. "Hey, this is in good shape," he shouted. "The Fudgsicles are still like rocks!"

"Cranking it up to eighty-two!" I yelled from the hall.

"How about some hot chocolate?" he called.

"Oh, sugar, I could use some of that," Gabby chirped.

Five minutes later, we were clustered around the kitchen table as Nick ladled out frothy cups of steaming chocolate.

"So you really didn't bounce a check to the power company?" Gabby asked, dropping a handful of mini-marshmallows into her cup.

"I'm playing it a lot closer to the line than I'd like. But this month's bills are paid, and I have enough squirreled away for the next couple of mortgage payments. And I'm working now. Plus, Peter sent me a check to tide me over."

"How much?" Nick asked.

"Nicky! That's none of our business," Gabby said.

"Hey, he's my brother, too," Nick said, reaching for the can of whipped cream. "I'm just curious."

"Five thousand," I said. "But I haven't been able to cash it because the bank has me on some sort of watch list."

"You just need to find the right check-cashing place," Gabby said.

"That's what I told her!" Nick said. "Does she listen to me? Nooooo."

Gabby patted my hand. "Don't you worry, sugar. I'll find you a place, and we can go there together."

Oh, goody.

Chapter 34

My new hobby: sleeping late.

When I opened my eyes, a wonderful smell pulled me into the kitchen.

Baba was tending a boiling pot on the back of the stove, as Nick slid a tray from the oven.

"Just in time," he said. "I need a taster. Strawberry tartlets."

"First, boiled egg," Baba said. "Make you strong."

"She already smells strong," Nick said. "Does that count?"

Baba waved a spoon at him.

I hit the cupboard for a coffee mug. "That reminds me. Nick, don't plan anything for this evening. You're going to help me with an errand."

"Is that cleaning job?" Baba asked, clearly worried.

"No, I'm not going tonight. I'm calling in sick."

"Sick of the stench of lime cleaner?" Nick said.

"No lie," I said, spooning horseradish on my plate for the egg. "We can leave here around six thirty, and I promise to have you home by nine thirty."

"That'll work," he said. "I need to spend tonight trying out a few new cookie recipes."

"Sounds like I picked the right night to skip work."

"Good girl. Eat egg," Baba said, dumping a brown egg onto my plate.

Two eggs and three tartlets later, I decided that—if C&W was attacking my finances—it was high time to fortify my defenses.

First, I called the post office and put my mail on hold. From now on, if I wanted my junk mail, bills, and flyers for pressure washing and discount car repair, I was going to have to wait in line and show ID. At least, until I could afford a curbside mailbox with a lock.

Then I checked the calendar and realized the letter scheduling my unemployment hearing was way overdue. I had a nasty feeling there might be a reason for that. I dialed the state's automated helpline and punched in my Social Security number.

"Thank you for calling the Virginia Employment Commission. The status of your claim is . . . pending. Your hearing is set for April first at eleven a.m."

Say what? That's today! In forty minutes!

I hit "0," and prayed for a real, live human being.

"Employment Commission, can I help you?"

"I have a hearing. Today. In forty minutes. I never got the notice in the mail. Is there any way to postpone it?"

"Ma'am, slow down and give me your name and Social Security number."

I held my breath as she entered my information into the computer. "No, I'm sorry. This is a contested matter. There will be other parties in attendance.

Less than an hour prior is too late to reschedule. And I have to advise you, it's never a good idea to miss a hearing. That could result in a default judgment."

"What's a default judgment?"

"In a contested claim, the matter could automatically be decided in favor of the attending party."

"Can you at least tell them that I might be a few minutes late? I never got the letter. Someone's been taking the mail from my box. I even reported it to the post office." I was babbling.

"I'll inform the officer that you're coming. But you need to get here as soon as possible." She lowered her voice. "They really don't like to be kept waiting."

I got directions to the office and hung up the phone. "Nick! Put the tartlets on hold! I need a ride! My unemployment hearing's today. In thirty-five minutes."

I didn't wait for his response. I bailed into the bathroom, ran a brush over my teeth, then locked myself in my room. In my closet, I shoved my body into my last good pair of pantyhose, a conservative white blouse, and my nicest suit. I slapped the makeup mirror onto my dresser, brushed my hair, shaped it into a businesslike twist, and fixed it in place with a little hairspray.

Perfect corporate drone.

I snatched up a lipstick, eyeliner, foundation and mascara from my makeup box, and jammed them into my purse with a wad of Kleenex. I glanced in the mirror, considered the dark circles, and grabbed the concealer, too.

"Come on, Nick, we've got to leave now!" I hollered toward the kitchen.

"Can't! I've got an oven full of brioche rolls. Gabby's gonna take you."

I ducked into the kitchen in time to see him give her a long, passionate kiss then hand her a thermos, car keys, and a brown lunch bag.

My soon-to-be sister-in-law was decked out in snug-fitting jeans that tapered off into snakeskin boots, and a long-sleeve, leopard-print T-shirt that covered her like a second skin. She topped it off with an orange ski vest that, in the event of a water landing, could be used as a floatation device. Her hair—or today's wig—was big, blond, and poufy. Harkins, she wasn't.

But beggars can't be choosers.

I checked Baba. She had her back to the scene, vigorously stirring something on the stove.

I handed Gabby the directions. "Thanks for doing this," I said. "The mail's still going missing, and I just found out my unemployment hearing's in thirty minutes."

"No sweat, sugar. I'll get you there in plenty of time. Grab your check, too. I think I found you a check-cashing place. We can swing by after. This will be fun. We'll be like Thelma and Louise."

"Uh, didn't Thelma and Louise die in the end? In a fiery car crash?"

"Did they? I never saw it. That's probably why there wasn't a sequel."

She gave me a closer look and squinted. "You're going to do your makeup in the car, right?"

"Um, yeah. That's why you're driving."

"Oh good. I was afraid you were going out like that."

I actually made it to my hearing five minutes early.

If Thelma and Louise ever need a driver to take them over that cliff in the sequel, Gabby will have no problem getting the job.

I'd been worried about going up against one of C&W's silk-stocking lawyers. But after facing down death multiple times on the ride over, I was fresh out of fear.

When we arrived, Gabby elected to wait in the car and eat her brown-bag breakfast. Which seemed like a good idea to me.

So did walking home.

I gave my name to the receptionist, who consulted a clipboard, then escorted me to the back of the office. She pointed to a desk in the corner, where a middle-aged African-American woman was typing notes into a desktop computer.

A plaque on her desk read "Irene Jenkins, Supervisor." She was wearing a short-sleeved beige silk blouse and had a celery green suit jacket hung on the back of her chair.

"Uh, hi, I'm Alex Vlodnachek," I said, approaching.

"Irene Jenkins," she said without looking up. "Have a seat."

A half-minute of silence later, she finished typing, made some notes on a legal pad, then set it aside.

"All right, do you understand how this works?"

"Not really."

"Never applied for unemployment before?"

"No." I looked at the floor. For some reason, the fact that I was applying at all was embarrassing. Shameful.

She gave me the visual once-over. I couldn't tell if I'd passed or failed.

"Your former employer's opposing your claim. You'll give me your side of the story. The employer's rep will give theirs. I'll make a decision. If anybody doesn't like my decision, they can appeal."

"While that's going on, what happens with payments?"

"If I decide in your favor, you will receive benefits. But if your employer wins on appeal, you'll have to give that money back. Likewise, if I deny your claim, but you win the appeal, you'd get any back payments you were due."

"Seems fair."

"Any other questions?"

I shook my head.

"OK, why did you leave your employer?" she asked, turning to the computer screen. "Coleman & Walters?"

"I was fired."

"When?"

"Tuesday, March twenty-third."

"Who fired you?"

"Benjamin Walters."

"Did he explain why he fired you?"

"That's kind of a long story."

Irene Jenkins put both forearms on her cluttered desk and leaned forward. "Well, your friends aren't here yet, and I've got nothing but time."

I could tell she was sizing me up.

I took a deep breath. "Friday night, Everett Coleman,

Walters' partner, tried to send me to a hotel with a client. I refused. Coleman was killed in his office Sunday afternoon. Tuesday, Walters fired me. He contends that Coleman had fired me earlier, and that I killed him."

"Did you?"

"No. And the police will back me up. I've been cleared."

She nodded.

"Walters also alleges that I was still working for the newspaper—that's where I worked before Coleman & Walters—and that I was doing some kind of exposé on the public relations industry."

"Were you?"

"No. But I am beginning to wish I'd never switched careers."

"I can see why. Is that the reason he gave for your firing? That you killed your boss?"

"That and the double-job thing. He also said I didn't do my job well. And that I wasn't a team player. I took that for code that I wouldn't sleep with a client."

"Have you secured other employment?"

My stomach lurched. I didn't want to lie to her. I also didn't want the C&W crowd to know about my cleaning job. For so many reasons.

"Yes. But I'd rather not tell the folks from Coleman & Walters, if that's OK."

"That's fine. It's none of their concern. What are you doing?"

"Cleaning."

"Cleaning?"

"I took a job with a janitorial service. I clean offices at night."

I swear she winced.

"During the day, I'm trying to get freelance writing jobs."

"OK, what are you earning at the cleaning service?"

"A hundred and eighty dollars a week."

She checked the computer and shook her head. "It doesn't show up on your records."

"They pay in cash."

One of her eyebrows went up. "When did you start?"

"The same day I got fired. That night."

"So you've gotten at least one check?"

"Cash. But, yeah. I got a hundred dollars for the first week. But I had to give it to Maria and Olga."

"'Scuse me?"

"I only worked three nights that week, so I only got a hundred dollars. And the industrial bathroom cleaner we use is pretty toxic, so I traded the money with two other workers to let me dust and vacuum for a night. Otherwise, the new workers always have to scrub the toilets."

She gave me a hard look. I could practically read the words "Am I being punked?" on her face.

"OK, here's how it works," she said. "Any money you take home—you have to declare that, cash or not. It'll be deducted from your benefits for that week. At this point, based on your previous salary and work history, it looks like you're eligible for about two hundred and fifty dollars a week."

"I'm not going to be staying at the cleaning service much longer," I said. "I already got a freelance assignment, and I'm hoping to pick up more."

"What does that pay?" she asked.

"Anywhere from a few hundred dollars to several thousand, depending on the job," I explained. "The one I'm working on now will pay three thousand dollars, but I won't see the money for four to six weeks."

"Still better than cleaning toilets. So why did you take the custodial job?"

Fudge time. "My younger brother and his fiancée moved in the day before I got fired. Nobody's working. And Walters is telling everyone in town that I'm a murderer who was doing an undercover exposé for the paper. Other public relations agencies won't even take my calls."

"Fair enough," she said. "Keep a written record of your job search. And be sure to declare every dollar you bring home, the week you earn it. It will be deducted from your weekly benefits, less fifty dollars. And if your earnings are higher than your weekly benefits, you just won't get an unemployment check that week."

"You mean I can still get unemployment?" I was so relieved, I felt tears in my eyes.

"Yup."

I swallowed a couple of times, took a few deep breaths, and tried to maintain control.

She pulled out a Kleenex box and handed it across the desk.

"I'm sorry. I never cry. I swear," I said, welling up.

"Losing a job is traumatic. I've seen grown men cry. Truckers, welders, dockworkers. It's nothing to be ashamed of. It gets better. And it looks like you've got some prospects. Clearly, you're not afraid of hard work. Any other sources of income?"

"My older brother sent me some money. A check.

I haven't cashed it yet. Five thousand dollars." I was babbling again.

"Nice. I wouldn't mind having a brother like that. Instead, I've got a brother-in-law sleeping on my couch. Been there six weeks. If I didn't love my sister's kids, I'd have killed him by now."

"Do I declare my brother's check now, or when I cash it?"

"Neither," she said. "Honey, you only declare income. What you work to earn. Somebody wants to hand you a bag of money, that's their business. Doesn't have anything to do with the Employment Commission."

She glanced down at her notes and back at the computer screen. "Let's see. Murder. Working two jobs simultaneously. Not a team player. Anything else your employer is going to tell me?"

I shook my head.

"All right, barring anything totally unexpected, I'll green-light your payments," she said. "They begin one week after your official separation. That first week is unpaid. So they should cut you a check tomorrow for about two hundred dollars, and you'll probably receive it next week. You can also elect to have direct deposit, if you prefer. Call in once a week and report how much money you've brought home in wages. And keep detailed, written records of your job search. You'll be eligible for regular payments for up to six months. But it doesn't sound like you'll be needing it anywhere near that long. Any other questions?"

I shook my head again, and used the wad of tissue to blot my eyes and wipe my nose.

She glanced over at her computer. "Good, because it looks like your former employer's people are here."

I don't know what I was expecting. One of the firm's attorneys. Someone from HR. Or some flunky of Margaret's.

But not Walters himself. In living gray and white. Flanked by a lawyer on each side.

He descended into the only available chair, while the attorneys hovered over him like avenging angels in camel-hair coats. Or muscle in a bad mob film.

Irene Jenkins didn't bat an eye. She jabbed an intercom button. "Jessie, we're gonna need a few more chairs back here."

Walters, ramrod straight and decked out in a charcoal gray banker's suit and conservative rep tie, handed off his London Fog to one of the attorneys, took in his surroundings, and leaned forward.

"Ms. Jenkins, I'm Benjamin Walters, head of Coleman & Walters. For obvious reasons, I will not be addressing the suspect directly. Instead, I'll confine any and all comments—those that my legal team will allow me to make—to you."

He sat back in the chair and pursed his lips.

"Mr. Walters, this is an unemployment-benefits hearing. I'm asking the questions. You're answering them. Anything you don't want to answer"—she looked back and forth at the two attorneys—"for whatever reason, I'll note in the records. And, just to be clear, Ms. Vlodnachek is a claimant, not a suspect."

I swear he blanched. But since he was pretty pasty already, it was hard to tell.

"Now, is it true you fired Ms. Vlodnachek on Tuesday, March twenty-third?"

"No. Absolutely not."

"How was her employment with your company terminated?

"My partner—my late partner, Everett Coleman—fired her the previous Friday. That would have been"—he gestured to one of the attorneys, who leaned in and whispered something—"the nineteenth of March."

"Why?"

"I'm afraid that is an ongoing employment issue and quite possibly the basis of a lawsuit. We cannot discuss it at present." He gave a thin-lipped half smile.

"Mr. Walters, this is an unemployment office. Ms. Vlodnachek applied for unemployment compensation because she was fired from your company. You requested this hearing to fight her claim. Either surrender your opposition to the claim—permanently—or tell me why she was fired."

Walters stopped smiling. He leaned over and whispered something into the other attorney's ear. The lawyer shook his head.

Walters sat back and crossed his hands in his lap as the attorney started to speak. "Mr. Walters feels that . . ."

"I don't give a flying damn *what* Mr. Walters feels. Tell him to save his feelings for his therapist." She leaned forward and looked straight at Walters. "What I *asked* you was 'Why was she fired?'"

Walters narrowed his eyes, leaned to his left, and whispered to the other attorney. More head shaking. He sat back and sighed.

"She was confrontational, contrary, and completely unwilling to do the work assigned to her.

She was totally unqualified for the job. Which was something that my business partner—my late business partner—discovered within days of hiring her. He gave her the benefit of the doubt and tried to make it work. But recently, he had discovered that she was still in the employ of that newspaper. Engaging in some type of nefarious corporate espionage. And since we were not her true employer, we owe her no unemployment. As to why she left her real employer, if indeed she has, you'll have to ask them."

OK, game over. At least with the freelance gig, I'm not gonna starve, right?

But apparently, Ms. Jenkins wasn't done yet.

"You got proof of that?" she asked.

Walters drummed his long, tapered fingers on the wooden arm of the cheap office chair. "Which part?"

"Start with the firing on Friday. Were you there?"

"No."

"How do you know she was fired?"

"I discussed it with my partner."

"Before or after she was fired?"

"After. By phone."

"When was she fired?"

"I've already told you. Friday."

"What time?"

"Approximately 11 p.m."

"Awfully late hour for work."

"There was a company function. For a client. Ms. Vlodnachek made a scene and nearly cost us a very lucrative account. It was the last straw. Everett called me later, and I agreed with his decision. You should also know that Ms. Vlodnachek is the prime suspect in the murder of my business partner, which took place two days later."

I noticed Walters' semi-smile was back.

"Have you got paperwork on that?"

"The murder?"

"The termination. An exit interview? A performance review? Anything in writing?"

"No. However, we can supply the performance reviews at a later date, if you require them. There were several, and they were all unsatisfactory. Very unsatisfactory. There wasn't an exit interview, for obvious reasons."

"I never had a performance review," I said evenly. "Coleman told me I'd get one only after I'd been there six months. And another after a year."

Ms. Jenkins' eyebrows went up.

"Ms. Vlodnachek is mistaken," Walters said, pointedly addressing himself to her and not me.

"OK, so no paperwork for now," she replied. "But you can confirm terminating the claimant on Tuesday?"

"I merely reiterated my partner's earlier statement, when Ms. Vlodnachek had the audacity to show up at my offices to harass my late partner's widow. But all of this is moot. She was never our employee. She was working for that rag of a newspaper. And she very likely killed my partner."

"See the sign up there? 'Virginia Employment Commission.' Does it say anything about homicide? It does not. You got a murder? You take it up with the police. As your legal dream team here undoubtedly told you, this is a hearing to figure out whether Ms. Vlodnachek's termination allows her to receive unemployment benefits."

"Well, it doesn't. She never worked for us. She was spying on us for that newspaper. Therefore she doesn't get benefits."

One of the lawyers placed a hand on Walters' arm, leaned over, and whispered into his ear.

"You done?" Irene Jenkins asked after the attorney pulled back.

The lawyer nodded.

"Good. This is how this works. Who gets—or doesn't get—benefits is my decision. Not yours. There's no proof that Ms. Vlodnachek was working for anyone other than your company. And I should know—I've got the same filings as the tax office right here," she said, tapping her computer.

"Then they paid her under the table," Walters insisted. "If we have to, we can subpoena her bank records, and comb through her finances. She was not, and never has been, our employee!"

"You don't have to subpoena my bank records," I said quietly. "I have a total of twenty dollars in my savings account, and another twenty in my checking account because Coleman & Walters went behind my back and canceled my health insurance after they fired me."

Ms. Jenkins' eyes narrowed. "They canceled your health coverage? That's a definite no-no, Mr. Walters."

To me she said, "When was it canceled?"

"Tuesday, March twenty-third. The insurance company received a fax the day before, from Coleman & Walters, on company stationery. Along with a form declining coverage, with what's reputed to be a very bad imitation of my signature. I walked into an expensive dentist's appointment Wednesday, thinking I had coverage, and had to clean out my checking account—and part of my savings—just to pay for it."

Irene Jenkins shook her head.

"My company did no such thing," Walters protested. "If this woman elected to cancel her health insurance, that has nothing to do with my firm. And I resent the implication. My family spent decades building a company with a reputation for honesty, integrity, and trust. How dare she resort to cheap theatrics and lies to tarnish our reputation?"

"According to the insurance company, the cancelation form was signed and dated Monday," I said. "But I didn't go to work on Monday. I was at the police station for a good part of the day. And when I went in Tuesday, I was escorted from the building by security around ten that morning."

"She could have signed it last week. Who knows why she canceled her health insurance. Maybe she was still getting it through her newspaper."

Jenkins gave Walters the once-over and shook her head again. Then she looked over at me.

"You're eligible for COBRA. That means you can stay on your former employer's group health plan if you pay thirty-five percent of the premium every month. After six months, you have to pay one hundred percent, but you can remain on the policy for up to eighteen months after your exit date with the company. And, Mr. Walters, you'll be happy to know I'm going to side with you. Since you have given your statement, in front of your two attorneys and me, that Ms. Vlodnachek was fired on Friday, that will be the official termination date."

Walters almost smiled as he sat up even straighter in his chair.

She looked across the desk at me. "That means anything the plan administrator did regarding your health insurance after that date is invalid. I'll give you a form to send to the insurance company and you'll be reinstated, with no lapse in coverage. And given the"—she paused and looked at Walters—"*confusion* regarding your policy status, I'd recommend sending those premiums directly to the insurance company each month, rather than through your former employer. Furthermore, I'm granting your request for unemployment compensation, effective the very Friday Mr. Walters has stated that you were fired. That will put two more days' worth of compensation into your first check, Ms. Vlodnachek."

Walters pursed his lips tighter and tighter until he couldn't contain himself. The words exploded from his mouth. "Will she be able to collect those checks when she's behind bars?"

"Of course not. If she were incarcerated she would be unavailable for work, and therefore ineligible for benefits."

"But you're telling me she can murder her boss, and then turn around and collect a weekly check from the state?"

"Precisely, Mr. Walters. Although I'm guessing you may not want to spread that bit of good news to the troops back at your office."

One of the lawyers stifled a laugh, covered his mouth with his hand and tried to turn it into a cough.

"Mr. Walters, in case you haven't noticed, Ms. Vlodnachek hasn't been accused, arrested, or charged by the authorities, much less convicted of anything. And the Commonwealth of Virginia doesn't put a lot of stock in finger-pointing, no matter how many lawyers you have sitting next to you."

Walters was turning pink before my eyes. It was the first time I'd ever seen color in his face. Or evidence that he had actual blood.

"You know what I find curious?" Irene Jenkins put her elbows on her desk and leaned forward. "According to my records, which go back ten years so far, your company has filed objections every single time one of your former employees put in for unemployment compensation. Every single time."

"I fail to see how that's relevant here," Walters countered.

"Here's how it's relevant, Mr. Walters. When an employee is terminated, they are—barring extreme circumstances—entitled to collect benefits until such time as they are reemployed. In exchange for that, they promise to diligently look for work. It's a safety net for the hard-working citizens of Virginia. And your company is supposed to assist in providing that compensation, as part of its duty to the commonwealth. But in the last ten years, despite dozens of claims, your company has not paid one dime in unemployment compensation. Not one dime. No employee has ever collected benefits. Do you know what the odds of that are?"

"Again, Ms. Jenkins, I fail to see the relevance of . . ."

She cut him off. "The relevance, Mr. Walters, is that based on what I've seen and heard here today, combined with past records, it appears as if your company has been deliberately and intentionally abusing the system. I say 'appears' because, of course, we won't know anything until we investigate. Which this office will do immediately. I'm flagging your company's file. It will go to our audit department, and you'll be notified shortly regarding further actions. It's a good thing you brought these two," Irene Jenkins said, waving a hand side to side to indicate the attorneys, "because you're going to need them. Regarding Ms. Vlodnachek's application for benefits, which I am granting immediately, you can appeal, but that hearing will be conducted under oath. Your testimony will be sworn under penalty of perjury, and the threshold for evidence will be much higher than in this"—she cleared her throat—"informal setting. And, confidentially, the evidence you've presented so far has not impressed me. Ms. Vlodnachek, I'd love to see the letter and cancellation form that your insurance company received."

"No problem," I said. "I'll get your fax number and have them send it over today."

Irene Jenkins looked back at Walters, who was now so pale he looked as if he'd spent a week at Dracula's castle. As the main course.

"Excellent," she said.

I flew to the car, riding a high that was better than champagne. Or at least better than the cheap stuff I bought every New Year's Eve. Gabby was on her cell, but clicked off quickly when she saw me and slipped it in her purse.

"We won!" I cheered.

"We won?" she asked.

"Game, set, and match. Not only am I getting unemployment benefits, but they're helping me get my health insurance back. So I'll recoup most of the money I paid my dentist. And the firm's getting audited by the employment commission for suspected abuse of the unemployment-benefits system."

"Oh sugar, that's not all," she said. "More good news."

My stomach constricted. The past two weeks had taught me that "good news" often translated to "impending disaster" in my Gabby-to-English dictionary.

She grabbed something out of the backseat and shoved it at me. It was my former paper. Today's edition.

"You solved the Jumble?"

"Not that," Gabby said. "The other section." She rummaged through, and held up a page triumphantly. "These two mugs look familiar?"

Separate pictures of both Coleman and Walters. On the metro front. With Billy Bob's byline. I grabbed the page and scanned it.

It was official.

"C&W's being audited by the IRS," I said. "And the state's Bureau of Criminal Investigation is sniffing around? Oh, man."

Gabby giggled.

"Sus-pec-ted im-pro-pri-et-ies," she pronounced, reading from the page. "Sounds like somebody's been caught with his hand in the till. But at least those IRS guys let you keep your thumbs. If that happens in Vegas, you have to blow town and change your name."

Hmmmm.

Oh, the hell with it. I wasn't letting Gabby's possible

flight from justice—or whatever—get me down. I was reclaiming my life. Here and now.

I did some quick math in my head. The insurance company would drag its feet on repaying me. And the check for my bridal story was at least a month away. In the meantime, I still needed to eat and pay bills.

That's when I said twelve words I'd later come to regret. "You know what? I think I'm ready to cash Peter's check now."

Chapter 35

The check-cashing place was a pawnshop. It sat at the far end of a run-down strip mall that also boasted a liquor store and a tattoo parlor.

The pawnshop's front window sported burglar bars, an impressive coating of grime, and flashing neon signs hawking check cashing, payday loans, title loans, money orders, and money-by-wire.

At 1 P.M. on a Thursday, it was virtually deserted. A homeless guy was going through the trash can in front of the liquor store. And three thugs in matching hoodies were having an animated discussion outside the tattoo parlor.

On the bright side: the gangbangers had their hoods down—a sure sign that spring was finally here to stay.

"Uh, I don't know about this," I said to Gabby.

"Sugar, there aren't that many places in this neck of the woods willing to handle a big check like that. Most of them cap it at two thousand dollars. That's why we had to drive all the way to Maryland."

"That's great, but unless we get an armed escort back to the car, there's no way we're leaving this neighborhood with five thousand in cash. Or alive."

"You worry too much," she said, shoving her purse under the seat. "It's a pawnshop. We'll buy a little something, come out with a bag, and no one will be the wiser."

Unless that bag was shaped like a rifle, I still wasn't giving us good odds.

"Am I dressed right for this?" Fresh from my unemployment hearing, I was wearing my best "interview suit" and heels.

"Lose the jacket and pull your blouse outside the skirt," she instructed. "Can you run in heels?"

"Sure."

"Then, honey, you're good to go."

It was almost enough to make me miss Allie and the gang at Helicon National.

But it turned out Gabby was right. I had no reason to worry. The minute we hit the curb and the gang-bangers spotted her, I could have been dressed as the Easter Bunny and no one would have noticed.

"Whoa! Babbbyyyy!"

"Hiiiyah! Hiiiiyah! Hiiiyah!"

"Mmmmm, baby! My, oh my! Can I get some fries to go with that shake?"

I had a flashback of a trip to Rome I'd taken with Annie and my mom the summer before I started college. We'd been followed and heckled by a couple of local guys who'd recognized Annie. Specifically, one of her recent swimsuit spreads. My mother's voice couldn't have been clearer if she'd been standing right next to me: "Keep walking, hang on to your purse, and try not to look dim-witted."

"Pick up the pace!" I hissed to Gabby. I swear, if anything, she'd slowed down and was exaggerating the swagger.

The doorway of the check-cashing place reeked of cigarette smoke and urine. In equal parts. But I was grateful when that door closed behind us.

"Can I help you?" a man's voice called through the haze of cigarette smoke.

"Uh, yeah. I need to cash a check."

The guy disappeared into a small booth enclosed behind thick glass. Bulletproof?

"Endorse the check. Put it through the slot, along with your ID. Fee is ten percent." He puffed while he spoke, never even taking the butt out of his mouth. Thanks to the cloud, the glass was nearly opaque.

"I thought it was illegal to smoke indoors," I said.

"You the tobacco police?"

Gabby elbowed me in the ribs. "Sorry," I said. "But aren't you worried about secondhand smoke? And fire?"

"'Round here, be a hell of a lot more dangerous if I stepped out back," he said, almost smiling.

"That fee," I asked, trying not to cough. "Ten percent of what?"

An ear-piercing scream ripped the air. I looked at Gabby. Gabby looked at me.

Joe Camel didn't even bat a rheumy eye. "Ten percent of the face value of the check. That's if it's good. If it's not, we take collection action, too. And we report it to the CheckBlox network."

Another scream. This one lasted almost a half-minute.

"Ah, should we call the cops or something?" I asked, after it finally stopped.

"No need. It's just the tattoo parlor next door," he said shrugging. "Even the tough guys aren't so tough the first couple of times the needle goes in."

"Don't they use anesthetic?" I asked.

"They numb you up. They don't knock you out. It still hurts." He slapped his arm and pushed up the sleeve of his T-shirt, revealing a saucy-looking mermaid on his bicep. "Got this on my way home from 'Nam. When I flex, she flaps her tail."

"That's pretty work," Gabby said, contemplating the image as if it were a Picasso in the Louvre.

Through the wall, we could hear loud moaning, sort of a cross between a whine and a shout.

"Forty-five years, and the color's barely faded. That's quality." He jerked a thumb at the wall next door. "Not like these guys today."

The moaning had stopped. It was eerily quiet.

"Ten percent?" I asked, when my brain kicked in again. *Five hundred bucks?*

"Yup."

"Uh, hang on a sec. Gabby?" My partner in crime had disappeared into the smog. But I found her at the jewelry case, studying bright, sparkly things.

"Gabby," I said under my breath, "he wants five hundred dollars to cash this. That's a lot of money just to cash a check I could cash at the bank for nothing. Peter will kill me if he finds out I spent that much of his money just to cash his check."

"It's a buyer's market," she said. "When you can't use a bank, you don't have a lot of options."

"So I've got to pay through the nose?"

"That's the point, sugar. You might be able to cash

it at your brother's bank. Do they have any branches around here?"

"Nothing south of Manhattan."

"Can you drive to New York for less than five hundred dollars?" she asked. "We could make it a road trip. You're allowed to leave the state, right?"

"Yes, I'm allowed to leave the state! I'm not a suspect. At least, not anymore. But I can't go to New York now. I'm working two jobs."

And trying to catch a murderer. And trying to help the authorities nail C&W for the illegal crap they've been pulling. And trying to keep my future sister-in-law from turning my house into a fencing operation. And trying to keep my brother from firebombing the neighbors. And trying to help Lucy learn to poop outside.

"Look sugar, either you make up with your bank or you pay Mr. Merman ten percent, and we walk out of here with forty-four hundred in cash."

"Uh, wouldn't that be forty-five hundred?"

"Yes, but you haven't seen this sweet little sapphire and platinum bracelet. Art Deco, by the looks of it. Sugar, it was made for you."

My Aunt Martha always said that Satan wears many forms. At that moment, I was convinced one of them was my soon-to-be sister-in-law.

I'd walked into this place with five thousand dollars of my business-savvy brother's money. And the most I was walking out with was forty-five hundred. Not counting what I was going to have to give up in the parking lot. Or at the jewelry counter. And I was reasonably certain that most of the five-hundred-dollar check-cashing fee was going to Big Tobacco. Something in me snapped.

"No deal," I said finally.

"You sure, sugar?"

"Yeah. Let's bounce." I waved to the booth, just as the screaming started again. The guy had a set of lungs, I'll give him that.

"We're gonna take a pass!" I yelled over the din. "Thanks anyway!"

Our friend behind the glass gave us a full-armed wave, still puffing away. We dashed from the shop to the car. The thug trio was nowhere in sight. The homeless guy was sitting on the curb next to the trash can, eating a sandwich.

"Hang on a sec," I said, fishing through my wallet and pulling out a tenner. "It's been a good day. Might as well share the wealth."

"Damn straight," Gabby said, handing me another Hamilton. She threw the car into reverse and did a wide J turn, bringing us parallel with the liquor store.

I hopped out and handed off the money to the man on the curb. "Just a little something for a snack later," I explained.

He stopped eating, looked into my eyes, and took the bills. "Thanks," he said, smiling.

As we pulled away, I could still hear screaming coming from inside the tattoo parlor. It wasn't as loud, but it had gone up half an octave. I couldn't help but wonder which part of his body was getting inked.

Chapter 36

Nick's brioche rolls were heaven. Even with a layer of Baba's molten stew poured over the top.

After lunch I called Trip. "You rat!"

"You rang?" he said.

"You didn't tell me Billy Bob's story was going to run this morning," I said.

"I was planning to show up at your door with donuts and the paper. But then I had to be back in here at eight."

"Ugh, forget that. I actually slept in this morning."

"So how's the life of leisure coming?" Trip asked. "Add any new relatives to your menagerie?"

"Don't ask. And no. Although, the way Annie was going on about Mom yesterday, I wouldn't be surprised if she showed up requesting sanctuary."

"Nah, she'd go to one of those high-priced spas with luxury amenities, like real food and individual beds."

"Maybe she'd take me with her," I said. "Hey, I've got a news tip for you."

"We newshounds don't take tips from just anybody," he said. "You got cred?"

"I've got crud. But it's in my kitchen."

"That's no way to talk about your grandmother's cooking. What's up?"

"C&W's now facing a probe by the commonwealth's unemployment office," I told him. "Possible ongoing, pernicious abuse of the system. It was referred for investigation this morning."

"Oh my God, that's wonderful," Trip said. "What did you do?"

"I'd love to take credit, but this was all the hearing supervisor. She'd really done her homework. Plus Walters was a total ass."

"Walters came to your hearing?"

"Sporting a matching pair of attorneys," I said. "For all the good it did him. The supervisor had pulled up old records and noticed a pattern of habitually fighting claims. Do you know that bunch hasn't paid unemployment in at least ten years?"

"Until now, he said hopefully?"

"Until now. Not only will I get benefits, but I'm going to get my health insurance back. Along with reimbursement for the money I spent at the dentist."

"Yeee-haaa!"

"You said it, cowboy."

"This calls for a celebration," Trip said.

"You wanna come for dinner?"

"Only if I can bring my own dinner."

"Tom has spoiled you," I said.

"Edible food has spoiled me. I can't believe it. You're bringing C&W to its knees."

"If Billy Bob can get his support group to go on the record, he'll have a hell of a story," I said.

We both went silent.

"I want you on this story, too," Trip said, finally. "None of this would have even been possible if you hadn't been working it from your end. This whole thing is gonna be over soon. Come back to the paper."

"I don't know. My goal was to find out who killed Coleman. That's the story I'm working. And I still haven't cracked it."

"Yeah, but you put Walters in hot water," he said. "Political juice or no, he'll have a hell of a time wriggling out of this."

"Your mouth to God's ear. Now if I could just figure out who killed the other weasel."

"Speaking of weasels, have you heard the latest on Mira?" Trip asked.

"She's moving? She's in jail? She's moving to jail?"

"No such luck," he said. "She's getting hitched."

"Someone wants to marry that?"

"Apparently."

I remembered her batting her eyes at Chaz. Nah, couldn't be. Could it?

"Who's the schmuck?" I asked.

"Her publisher's son. Lenny? Denny? Donny? It's a family newspaper group, so the kid stands to inherit the whole shebang some day."

"Figures," I said. "Marriage as a career move sounds like Mira."

"Yeah, it's almost enough to make me feel sorry for a billionaire's son."

"I think Margaret has a new hobby," I said.

"Torturing small animals? Setting fires?"

"Impersonating me."

"Good lord," Trip said. "Why would anyone want to be you?"

"My very thought every time I look in the mirror. Someone claiming to be me, with my Social Security number, called the phone company and the power company and had them disconnect service last night."

"You think this is health insurance scam, part two?" he asked.

"Sounds like. She's got all the information. And she definitely hates me, although I don't know why."

"Mira's column did imply you might have been sleeping with her husband."

"Yeah, but like everything else in her story, that was a total fabrication," I said. "And since C&W did the fabricating, they know it's not true. Besides, I've seen her around Coleman's real mistress, and Margaret was always totally placid."

"I don't know, Red. Struck me as a little tightly wound."

"Struck me across the face, so I'd have to agree with you. Here's the weird part: more of the mail's gone AWOL. I nearly missed my hearing this morning because I never got the notice. And when I realized my latest mortgage statement hadn't arrived, I phoned the mortgage company this afternoon. You know what they told me? Someone had already called them to make arrangements to surrender the house. Told them she was me, and that I was out of work and couldn't make the payments.

"Oh, jeez . . ."

"I straightened it out," I said. "And I'd already put my mail on hold indefinitely."

"Red, if she's taking your mail, that means she's been coming by the house. Recently."

"Yeah, I know. Scares the crap out of me. Nick says she's escalating."

"He studied crime in Arizona?"

"With an intensive course of *Law & Order* reruns," I said.

"Problem is, he's right."

"Problem is, Nick and I are going to be out of the house tonight at a bridal registry seminar."

"I'm only working until six or so," Trip said. "I could swing by and protect the womenfolk."

"Who'd protect you?"

"Hey, your Baba loves me."

"She does. Which means she'll want to feed you."

"Are you *trying* to scare me off?" he asked.

"Gotta run. I gotta pick up my engagement ring."

"From a cereal box?"

"From the post office."

"Next time," Trip said, "get a mail-order groom to go with it."

Chapter 37

I decided not to tell Nick where we were going until we were already en route. Less chance of him jumping ship.

"You gotta be kidding," he said, when I finally informed him of our plans for the evening.

"Hey, if I can finish this story inside of ten days, I get three thousand dollars."

"How much do I get?"

"How about a roof over your head and a working kitchen?"

"With power and heat?" he asked.

"That was not my fault," I said.

"Yeah, that's what they all say. So I'm pretty much being kidnapped and forced to go to this thing?"

"Unless you want to jump out of a moving car."

"Right now that does seem like my best option," Nick said.

"Oh, relax. You'll drink some punch and eat a few sandwiches, while I get a handle on what it's like to create a bridal registry. Then we're outta there. Besides, it'll be good practice for you."

"What do you mean?" he asked.

"You're engaged. You guys might want to do a registry yourselves."

"Yeah, I don't think Gabby's the wedding registry type. I know I'm not. Besides, at this point, I'm not exactly sure we're even getting married."

"Really?" I asked. "What happened?"

He sighed. "Nothing happened. I just don't know if she's over her last boyfriend. They were together for years. I think he's been calling, and I think he wants her back. Hell, I know he wants her back. Why wouldn't he?"

Mr. Photo Strip. I wish I'd been wrong.

Nick turned and looked out the window. We rode in silence for a couple of miles.

"Hey," I said suddenly, "we need names."

"You mean like secret identities?"

"We have our secret identities. I'm Reporter Girl, and you're Baker Boy."

"Baker Man."

"Whatever," I said. "What we need are alter egos."

"Or Baker Dude. Or Super Baker."

"Names," I said. "We need names. We're spies, and we're being dropped behind enemy lines into Bridezillaland. It's a police state where fascist fiancées rule with iron fists. Perfectly manicured, of course."

"Sounds grim."

"You have no idea," I said. "Try listening to a week of nonstop bridal bitching."

"Nick and Nora?" he asked.

"Big stretch for you."

"Peter and Mary Jane?"

I shook my head. "Sorry, Spidey."

"Clark and Lois?"

"Why don't we just call ourselves Woodward and Bernstein?"

"Works for me," Nick said. "I wanna be Bernstein."

"Names!"

"George and Martha?" he offered.

"No."

"Fred and Wilma?"

"No."

"Fred and Daphne?"

"No!"

"Fred and Ginger?"

"OK, that one I kinda like," I said. "But no."

"There's just no pleasing you brides," he said.

"Tell me about it."

"Boris and Natasha?" he suggested.

"No!"

"Darren and Samantha?"

"No!" I said. "No Brad and Angelina. No Brad and Jennifer."

"How about Brad and Gwyneth?"

"We're supposed to be typical," I said. "Forgettable. You ever meet a Gwyneth?"

"Tom and Jerry?" Nick asked. "We could spell Gerry with a 'G,' like it's short for Geraldine."

"Again, think invisible," I said. "Like, 'blends into the background.' You know, normal. How about Kay and Bill?"

"I don't feel like a Bill," Nick said. "I'm feeling more like a Jim this evening."

"Fine. Kay and *Jim*, then," I said." Now what about last names? And don't say 'Stabler and Benson.'"

"Brandon."

"OK, you're Jim Brandon. How about Kay Wood-ville?"

"Man," Nick said, "when we go white bread, we really go bleached white bread."

"Hey, not everyone is blessed with a last name no one can pronounce," I said.

"Or spell."

"We're spies," I said. "Remember, bland. Forget-table."

"So no food fights?"

"If you're going to throw food, start with that road tar Baba made for lunch," I said. "She's got plenty of leftovers."

"No thanks," he said. "The only thing worse than that stew would be a weaponized version of that stew."

The store hosting the registry seminar had closed to the public for tonight's "special event." As we walked in, couples were milling around a table of sandwiches and a big crystal punch bowl set up in the middle of the store.

I glanced down at the ring Annie's assistant had overnighted me. It was one of the smaller ones. From her second engagement. "Only two carats," Annie promised.

I felt like I had a paperweight tied to my finger.

I didn't want to be too obvious with a reporter's notebook, so I'd brought a small, red spiral to take notes. With my lousy handwriting, no one would know the difference. They'd just assume I was doing research for "my special day."

Nick made a beeline for the food table. When I

caught up with him, he had a mini-napoleon in one hand and some kind of puff pastry in the other.

"You can use a plate," I said.

"Hey, you're lucky I'm using napkins. Man, these really suck. The crust is tough, and the filling tastes like snot."

"You oughta know. Where's your name tag?" I had "Kay" dutifully written on a pink, heart-shaped sticker pasted under my left clavicle.

"I don' need no stinkin' name tag," he said.

"I hear that, man," said a burly guy next to Nick. "I'm Mike."

"Jim."

"So how'd she get you here?" Mike asked.

"I was kidnapped," Nick-Jim said. "You?"

"Told me we were going to the auto show," Mike said.

"That's cold."

"Tell me about it," Mike said. "I didn't even have a chance to pack supplies."

"Hey, I'm Kay," I said. "Supplies?"

"The strongest stuff in that punch is ginger ale," Mike said. "And this gig is supposed to go at least two hours."

"Gotcha," Nick said. "So which one is yours?"

Mike pointed to a tall, slim brunette chatting animatedly with two other brides over a display of formal place settings. "Sophie," he said.

"Very nice," Nick observed. "Wanna trade?"

"Right now, I'd swap her for a bus pass and a ticket to the auto show."

"Ain't that the truth," Nick said. "Have an éclair, my man."

Fifteen minutes later, it was like a junior high

dance: all the girls on one side of the room, all the guys clustered around the food.

Unfortunately, no one had spiked the punch.

Nick-Jim was in the center of a knot of men. Knowing Nick, if they didn't start this thing soon, there were going to be a few less grooms to work with.

"So what do you want to get out of this?" I asked a bubbly blonde whose tag read "Christy."

"Loot," she said with a giggle.

"Really?"

"Look, we're spending sixty thousand dollars. And we've got three hundred people coming. If we don't clear gifts worth at least two hundred dollars each, we're losing money."

"You don't have to tell me," said a pretty Asian bride, whose name tag read "Molly." "My sister spent fifty thousand on her wedding last year. And some of the guests sent cheap stuff that wasn't even on the registry. The other half picked the least expensive thing on the list. She ended up with thirty salad forks. Can you imagine? Salad forks!"

"That's not going to happen to me," Sophie said. "I'm not putting anything on my registry that's less than two hundred and fifty bucks."

"Can you do that?" the blonde asked.

"Of course! At least that way if we get the same thing twenty times we can trade it for a decent amount of cash."

"At least the people who go off-list don't dare come to the reception," said another brunette whose name tag read "Tricia."

"Really?" I asked.

"Oh, yeah. Nobody who does that is going to have

the nerve to actually show up. But sometimes the ones who can't come will send really nice gifts to make up for it."

"Guilt gifts!" Christy squealed. "I love those!"

"I'm hitting up every really long-distance relative I have with the first batch of invites," said Tricia. "Then I'm following up with a phone call telling them how much Sam and I are *really* looking forward to seeing them."

"What if they actually come?" I asked.

"Win-win. If they come, they pretty much have to buy something nice."

"Saving-face gifts!" another bride said.

"Nice ring," said Molly. "Two carats?"

"Yeah," I said. "But I'm beginning to regret it. It's too big for my hand."

"Mine's three," she said, presenting her left hand. "And there's no such thing as too big."

"Like penises," Christy said with a giggle.

Sophie shot her a dirty look. "Mine's three and a half. Mike tried to get away with two, but I took it back."

My jaw dropped, and I had to force myself to act nonchalant. I was a visitor in a strange land, where none of the normal rules applied.

"Can you do that?" I asked.

"Oh yeah," she said. "Of course, you don't tell him that."

"So how does it work?" I asked.

"First off, you say 'yes,' and tell him you love the ring," Sophie said. "A week or so later, you drop a few hints that the cut isn't exactly right for your hand.

Do that for a few days, and he'll be begging you to exchange the stone for the shape you really want. After all, a diamond is forever."

"Yeah, and once you get back to the jewelry store, the staff will take care of the rest," said a blonde named Sandy.

"What do you mean?"

"When you walk in there with your guy, they're not going to show you smaller rocks—only bigger," Sandy said. "You just pick the one you want."

Diabolical. I'd interviewed con men with more scruples.

"So which one is yours?" asked a redhead named Emma.

I looked over at the gaggle of guys. "The one balancing a stack of plastic cups on his head."

"He's cute!"

"Yeah. Adorable."

"How did you meet?" Sophie asked, scoping out Nick-Jim with a none-too-detached eye.

"Our parents introduced us," I said.

"Nice," said Sandy. "My parents would never introduce me to someone that hot. I met Phil at work."

"Have you set the date?" Sophie asked her.

"It was supposed to be July, but his stupid wife keeps dragging out the divorce."

"Bummer," I said.

A petite woman with spiky orange hair and a lemon-colored pantsuit stepped to a spot halfway between the two groups and cleared her throat.

"Please let me be the first to welcome you to our little event," she said, smiling widely. "We're very happy you all made the time to come out and join us this evening. And congratulations on your upcoming nuptials! Tonight is just a first step in your exciting, new lives together. I'm Cherry Arsenian. I'm a stylist and lifestyle consultant, and I'm going to help you each assemble the perfect wedding registry to launch your new lives together. Now, if you can find your partners and take your seats, we'll get started."

Once we'd all paired off, there was one guy left over. His name tag said "Dennis."

Cherry gave him the once-over, sniffed, and scanned her electronic tablet.

"Dennis," she said, pausing. "Of course, we're happy to have you here, but this is really a couples experience. Do you think your fiancée will be arriving soon?"

Dennis shifted uncomfortably in his chair and ran his fingers through thinning brown hair. In a rumpled button-down shirt, dun-colored suit pants, and a gold tie, I pegged him for an accountant, or maybe a mid-level manager.

"I just called her," he explained, reddening slightly under Cherry's scrutiny. "She has to work late. But she wants me to take notes."

"That's fine," Cherry said, tightly. "But you'll have to come back with her later to create your gift registry. That's definitely something a couple needs to do together."

She sighed audibly. "All right, let's take a five-minute break to use the restrooms, and then we'll get started."

I waved to Dennis. "You can sit with us," I said.

The guy actually looked grateful. "Thanks."

"Kay and Jim," I said pointing to myself and Nick.

"Hey," Nick-Jim waved. "I'm going to hit the rest-room."

"There's no back door, and I've got the car keys."

Nick mimed putting a gun to his head and pulling the trigger.

"I'm sure your fiancée is really sorry she's missing this," I said to Dennis.

"I don't know," he said. "Between work and wedding planning, I think she's forgotten I exist. And I can't seem to do anything right anymore, anyway. A couple of days ago, she loved the ring. But now, it's the wrong cut."

Uh-oh.

"Like tonight. When she said she couldn't make it to this thing, I wanted to pick up dinner, take it to her office and spend some time together."

"That sounds great," I said. "I'd love it if some-one . . . uh, if Jim brought me dinner."

"Well, it just pissed her off. She accused me of not caring about the wedding."

"That's pretty rough."

"She's probably right," he conceded. "I mean, I'm not having second thoughts or anything. But a big, giant wedding? Ugh. Flower arrangements. Center-pieces. Guest lists. Seating charts. Goody bags? I don't know what I pictured. I guess I just wanted to wake up one morning already married."

He looked glum. And I wondered how many of the grooms in this place felt exactly the same way.

"But I love her," he said, shrugging. "And if it's going to work, she says I need to recommit myself and prove I really love her. Especially after what I did."

"What you did?"

He looked sheepish. "Uh, yeah. I guess I kinda did something stupid."

I braced myself for whatever he was going to say next. Strip club addiction? Gambling addiction? Secret credit card? Secret girlfriend with a secret credit card?

"I applied for an art scholarship in Florence, and I got it."

"That's wonderful!" I swear it was out of my mouth before I realized I'd said it.

"That's what I thought, at first. I even found out I could get a sabbatical from work. Unpaid. But Mimi's right, I was being selfish. Besides, she says art's too risky for a family man. She says I'm lucky to have a stable job with good prospects. And she's right. I mean, there's no arguing with her logic."

"I dunno. I thought the point of having a partner was to encourage each other."

"She is encouraging me. She's just encouraging me to keep my current job."

He shook his head. "The funny thing is, Mimi is great at her job. She loves it. She lives for it. That's one of the things I love about her. I just want to feel the same way when I get up every morning."

"So maybe you have a little talk," I said. "Explain that to her."

"I did. Or tried to. At first, she thought I was kidding. When she realized I was serious, she got really pissed. Told me I wasn't thinking about us, I was only thinking about myself. And I guess I was. Being an artist has always been my dream. I guess it's a pipe dream. When I applied for the scholarship, I never thought I'd actually get it. But the last time I brought it up? Oh, man, that was definitely the last time I'll ever mention it. She cried and got all hysterical and said I just didn't love her enough. And it was over— we were over. I had to beg her to take me back. She only agreed if I promised to recommit, put her first, and prove my love."

He looked so pathetic. I'd just met the guy, and my heart was breaking.

"Why do you have to prove anything?" I asked.

He looked startled, as if the thought had never occurred to him.

We sat there in silence for a couple of beats. And when Dennis finally met my eyes, I swore I saw a light-bulb pop on over his head.

He stood up. His posture was straighter. His voice was stronger. "You're right. This is bullcrap. Mimi and I need to talk." And for the first time since I'd met him, the guy actually smiled. "Thanks for listening."

"Hey, it was nothing. Good luck."

Nick pulled up his chair. "There is a back door, but it's locked. Where's he going?"

"Date with destiny."

"Does she have a sister?"

Chapter 38

Ninety minutes later, I'd learned more about the history and importance of fine crystal, formal china, and "a place setting that bespeaks quality" than I would ever use in my lifetime. Even if Nick and Gabby turned my home into a teahouse and started serving scones on the front lawn.

The girls were eating it up. Like me, several had whipped out notebooks. Sophie had brought a laptop. The way they were sitting at attention, taking notes, and asking questions, I half expected there was going to be a final exam.

If there was, I was screwed. Even though I was actually getting paid for this, my eyes were glazing over.

The guys were, to a man, silent and slouched in their chairs. I swear I saw Mike nod off once.

When Cherry started winding up her spiel, I was already picturing myself racing Nick for the car.

"Now for the really fun part!" Cherry proclaimed.
What?

She went around the room and handed each couple—specifically each guy—an electronic pricing gun. "Now we get to pick out the goodies we want. Remember the guidance you've received here today. First, foundation. You want to pick the major pieces— things around which you can build a kitchen, a home, a lifestyle—that will coordinate and suit your lives together. Second, quality. Select items that will hold up and last for a long time. And, last but not least, functionality. You want things that will serve all of your needs now, and your potential needs into the future."

"I want to get the hell out of here while I still have a future," Nick hissed.

"Shush!" I said.

"Find one of the three computer stations located around the store and line up. My assistants will enter your information to establish your registry. Then they'll show you how to activate your gun. When you zap an item, it goes on your list. You can even indicate how many you'd like. This is especially important for the elements of your place setting."

"I wonder how many times I'd have to shoot myself with this thing to commit suicide," Nick whispered.

"Sssh! If you behave, we'll stop for ice cream on the way home."

He rolled his eyes.

"If one of you makes a mistake and zaps something that doesn't belong on your list"—Cherry paused for effect and the girls giggled—"just push this button and it's gone."

"You think that would work with her?" Nick hissed.

"OK, couples," Cherry said with a dramatic hand flourish, "get gifting!"

"I wanna get gone. I'm gonna wait in the car."

"Come on, *Jim*," I said through clenched teeth. "This is actually the fun part."

"Trust me, there is no fun part."

"Look, you take the gun. Zap everything you've ever wanted to outfit the kitchen of your dreams. Go crazy."

"What about foundation, quality, and functionality?

"What about Larry, Moe, and Curly? Go nuts. Have fun. Pick out the crap you want, and give me fifteen minutes to soak up some color for the story. Then we're out of here."

"Deal! I wonder if they have the Fryz-It. I've always wanted one of those. Have you seen the infomercials? You can dump in a raw turkey and an hour later, it's deep-fried and delicious."

"Have at it, chief."

After we created "our" registry, I followed around making notes while Nick outfitted the Vegas bachelor pad of his dreams. Martini glasses. Swizzle sticks. Three different kinds of coasters. He even managed to find a Plexiglas poker-chip caddy with chips. He zapped it five times.

When we got to the kitchen section, he really went into high gear. I lost track of him when I stopped to chat with Sandy and Phil and Sophie and Mike.

Nick found us a couple of minutes later. "They didn't have the Fryz-It, but they had something else that does pretty much the same thing. I zapped three of them."

"Man, that is awesome," Mike said, giving him a high five.

After the guys walked off together, Sophie pulled me aside. "Are you sure that's a good idea?" she asked. "You can't just let him run loose with that thing. What are you going to do with three deep-fat fryers?"

"No sweat. He can have them in the divorce."

After that, I'd had enough. But by the looks of it, I was going to have to pry that gun out of Nick's hand.

He zapped an industrial-size coffee urn, complete with trolley. ("One pot a day, and we'd be set," he said.) A stainless-steel barbecue grill. ("Charcoal's the only way to go.") And a Crock-Pot "for Baba."

I don't know who was happier to see him head for the door, me or Cherry.

"OK, so you had a decent time after all," I said, as I started the car.

"Yeah. Did you hear about the drawing? One lucky couple will win one of the items on their list. I don't know which I want more, the grill, the fryer, or the coffee urn. Can you picture Thanksgiving with a deep-fried turkey?"

I could. And I didn't have enough homeowner's insurance.

"Man, that Sophie's a piece of work," he said. "I feel sorry for Mike."

"Yeah, she liked you, though."

"I deduced that."

"What was your first clue? The sly looks? The hair flipping?"

"I guess it was when she slipped me her phone number."

OK, have to say, I didn't see that one coming.

"You're not gonna . . . ?"

"Oh hell, no. I love Gabby. Even if I'm not sure she

feels the same way. Besides, Mike's cool. We're going to the boat show next week."

"So it wasn't a totally wasted evening. Next stop, home."

"No way, José. I was promised ice cream."

Chapter 39

Trip's Corvette was in the driveway when we got home.

"Who wants ice cream?" Nick called out as he opened the door.

"We're in the kitchen," Trip answered.

I found him sitting at the table with his sleeves rolled up, tie loosened, and suit jacket hanging over the back of a chair.

"Baba made me dinner," he said happily.

Baba patted him on the back and beamed. "Two helpingsful," she said proudly.

Was it any wonder I loved the guy?

"I just wanted to stop by and catch up on what you learned in the hearing this morning, but Gabby explained that you two were out. So I thought I'd hang around until you got back."

"Cool. Grab your coat, and we can talk on the porch. Nick, you're in charge of dessert."

"Got it," Nick said.

"Thanks again, Baba," he said, kissing the top of her head. "That was great."

"Bah!" she said, grinning as she gave him another pat-pat-pat on the back.

"Thanks," I said, when we got to the porch. "Thanks for watching out for them. And thanks for not telling them."

He grinned. "You're welcome. Besides, I love Baba. Although I suspect she could more than hold her own against Margaret. Gabby, too, for that matter."

I lowered my voice. "Two helpings?"

"It wasn't that bad. Plus I missed lunch. And those rolls of Nick's are first-rate."

"I'll see if he can spare any of the cinnamon buns for you to take home. They melt in your mouth. He's gonna start selling the stuff to the bed-and-breakfast across the street."

"Gabby was telling me. So did you ever find out if the lord of the manor has a better half?"

"Nah. Turns out he's running the place with his father, Harkins. And he's not really 'Sir Ian.' That was just his dad's idea of marketing."

"Ah, so you've already met the parents," he said, steepling his fingers. "Ex-cell-ent. What's next in your evil plan?"

"Catch a killer, get my life back?"

"Fair enough. Any more ideas?"

"Margaret or Walters," I said.

"Which one?"

"Could be either. One was losing her husband and her lifestyle. The other was losing a company that his father founded. And from what I've been able to dig up, or the sheer lack of it, Walters lives for that job. I don't think he has much of a personal life. Or much of a life, period. I just don't understand why he teamed up with Coleman in the first place."

"I think he was blackmailed into it," Trip said.

"For real? Do you have proof?"

"No, just a gut feeling. But I've been asking around. Rumor has it, Walters Senior died of AIDS. Remember, this was back in 1987 when they were still calling it 'the gay plague.' There was a lot of fear, a lot of hysteria. And damn little compassion. People were terrified of it and terrified of anyone who had it. And it was pretty much a death sentence."

"Margaret was his nurse," I breathed.

"She had access to all his medical records. Written proof of what he really had."

"And if the true cause of death had gotten out, there would have been a huge scandal," I said. "Clients would have bolted. The firm would have tanked."

"So Benny made a deal with the devil to keep his father's secret and save the family business," Trip said. "But if that's what really went down, I'm surprised Benny didn't kill Coleman sooner."

"It was probably a pretty effective partnership for a while," I said. "Coleman had the chutzpah and the ambition. And he loved the spotlight. Walters had the education and the skill and knew all the D.C. power brokers. A perfect marriage."

"A marriage born in blackmail that may have ended in murder."

"Bottom line: both Margaret and Walters had a lot invested in C&W," I said. "And Coleman was about to break up their dysfunctional little family. So how do we find out if one of them killed him?"

* * *

After Trip left, with a care package of brioche rolls and a dozen cinnamon buns, Baba turned in early. Nick flipped on the backyard lights and took Lucy outside for a quick training session.

She understood "sit" and "come." But she was having trouble with "stay." And "no" just confused her.

That last one was kind of important to me, since everything in the house could be divided into two groups: things Lucy chewed a lot, and items she just hadn't gotten to yet.

Afterward, Nick scrubbed up, sequestered himself in the kitchen, and spent the rest of the night baking various kinds of cookies.

For my part, I worked on the bridal story. God knows, after this evening, I had enough material.

But the vibe between Gabby and Nick was weird. Strained. Except for a few extended bathroom breaks with her phone, Gabby stayed on the sofa with her laptop.

I wondered if I was just reading too much into it because I knew a little more about their situation. Or if the chill had anything to do with Nick spending the evening with a gaggle of "happily engaged" couples.

Either way, I could tell he was hurting. And I felt at least partly responsible.

When Nick and Gabby had first arrived, if they were in the same room, they'd be drawn together. Like magnets. As the days wore on, he was more often the one to approach her. But the outcome was usually the same.

Now he seemed to be keeping his distance. And so was she.

At 10:59, I flipped on the TV to catch the local news. I wanted to see what they said about C&W, if anything. Talk about "ripped from the headlines." Ripped-off was more like it. All three local stations basically repeated Billy Bob's story, word for word. All from live stand-ups. All from different spots in front of C&W's office building.

One more reason I was glad I'd skipped work.

My landline rang as soon as the weather guy appeared on the screen.

"God, these cinnamon things are great!"

"Our mom's recipe. But Nick does it better."

"The boy is seriously gifted."

"He had a lot of time on his hands in Arizona. And the oven was the one thing his roommate couldn't pawn."

I hollered in to Nick. "Trip likes your buns!"

"Damn right!" Nick hollered back.

"He says 'thanks,'" I said.

"Chaz is in the wind."

"For real?"

"Missing. Gone. MIA. Pulled a bunk. Flown the proverbial coop. The police have been trying to reach him all day to have a little sit-down. They can't find him."

"He's either covering his ass or he's dead," I said.

"Flip a coin. You sound heartbroken, by the way. This is your ex-boyfriend we're talking about."

"Mira's probably going to write that I buried him in the backyard."

"Did you?"

"No, but only because he'd poison the lawn. Do you think Mira has him stashed somewhere? He's her source."

"Or she could have just tipped him that the cops were coming to call."

"Wish someone had done that for me."

"Why? You wouldn't have run."

"No, but I'd have at least gotten dressed. They caught me in the pink bathrobe."

"With the flowered slippers?"

"Yeah," I admitted.

"Not a good look. Are you sure they weren't the fashion police?"

I ignored him. "I just can't see Chaz killing Coleman. There's nothing in it for him."

"That we know of."

"Chaz was Coleman's favorite flying monkey."

"Well, now he's flying solo," Trip said.

"If he didn't get his wings clipped," I countered. "Why do the cops want to talk to him?"

"Officially, just another round of reinterviewing the witnesses. Unofficially, Billy Bob found out that Chaz might have had a front-row seat to some of the stuff the state and the feds are both looking into."

"Be a witness now or a defendant later."

"Sounds like," Trip said. "Unless you just lie low for a while."

"The best decision is no decision. I can see that."

We were both quiet for a minute.

"If he really does know something, that turns up the heat on C&W," I said. "Which means that Chaz is in danger, whether he knows it or not. And as dim as he is, I'm guessing he knows it not."

"The dumb guy thinks he's playing it smart? You've got to love it. You think he'll try his hand at blackmail?"

"If he does, I don't think anyone's going to wait thirty-one years to get rid of him."

"Be great if you could find him," Trip said.

"Next time we clean C&W's suite, I'll give Chaz's office a little extra attention."

"When will you charwomen hit there next?"

"No telling," I said. "Lately, Gravois isn't sticking to the schedule. He's skipping all over the place."

"That's odd," he said.

"Yeah, just what I need. One more mystery to solve."

Chapter 40

I'd gotten spoiled.

For two days and one glorious night, I'd been so busy writing my freelance story, trying to puzzle out who killed my ex-boss, and thwarting C&W's plans to ruin my life, I'd forgotten all about my lousy night job.

Now it was five o'clock. Time to wake up and smell the lime cleaner.

Gabby was at the mall. Nick was sweating through his last few batches of cookies for Ian's garden party on Sunday. And Lucy was parked under the kitchen table.

"Bye-bye, baby," I said, peeking in at her. "Be a good girl. Don't eat too many goodies."

"And you," I said, pointing at Nick. "Don't feed her too much of that stuff. It's not good for her."

"Don't worry. I cut her off hours ago. But every time the oven buzzer goes off, she howls. Don't you, you nutty little dog?"

"That reminds me," I said, lowering my voice. "Where's Baba?"

"She was here a minute ago. And Baba's not nuts. She's just . . . determined."

"'Nutty' didn't remind me of her—it reminded me of Margaret. Who is major-league crackers. Keep an eye out, and don't let anybody go outside alone, OK?"

"If Margaret shows up, I'll make her eat the last batch of my butter cookies. Scorched those suckers good."

"Seriously, Nick, this woman is psycho. Keep the windows and doors closed and locked. Nobody goes outside unless you go with them. And if you see her, call the cops."

"Yes, Mom."

"That's just mean."

"You don't know the half of it," Nick said wiping his hands on a dish towel. "Annie called me this morning. They left Venice."

"They just got there."

"Mom said the place was old and smelled funny," he reported.

"Their hotel?"

"Venice. Annie said she had two choices: drop Mom in a canal, or decamp."

"How close was it?"

"Too many witnesses. They're in London."

"OK, you've got custody of Baba," I said. "Try not to burn the place down."

"I promise nothing. But if anything happens, I'm saving the baked goods first. After Baba and Lucy."

"At least you've got your priorities straight."

"Hey, you're the one who lost Baba," he said.

"I didn't lose her. I just misplaced her. She's little and stealthy."

"Like a ninja. Honestly, I'm more worried about Gabby. She was supposed to be home an hour ago."

"How are you guys doing?" I asked.

He sighed. "I don't know. Not great. I'm just trying to focus on this right now."

"I'll get out of your hair. I've got the cell, if you need me."

It didn't take me long to find Baba. She was sitting in the passenger seat of my car. With her purse in her lap and the seatbelt buckled. The seat was rolled halfway to the glove compartment, and her sneakers were planted firmly on the floor mat.

So how exactly do you extract a volatile Russian sprite from a gas-powered vehicle? I'm betting this is one job even those guys from *The Hurt Locker* wouldn't tackle.

She looked at me, smiled, then looked straight ahead. I had a fleeting fantasy about borrowing Nick's car. But Gabby had beaten me to it.

"Baba, I've got to go to work now."

"*Da,*" she said.

"I can't take you with me."

"*Da.*"

"Baba, I'm going undercover. Before I left my old job, I planted a listening device—a recorder. And I have to get it back. That's why I joined the cleaning crew. The people I work with, they don't know me. They don't even know my real name. And I'm really not going to be working this job much longer."

Hell, I didn't think I'd be working it this long.

"But I have to do this. I'll be with a group of people the whole time. This is the best way—the safest way—to get my recorder back. And I believe what's on that recorder will help me fight the lies my ex-co-workers are spreading about me."

"Is foolishness."

No argument there.

"My former boss's wife is nuts. Someone's been coming by the house and stealing the mail. I think it was her. Whoever it was has been using that information to hurt me. They're the ones who had the phone and the power cut off. And I found out they tried to give my house back to the bank."

Baba looked at me and her dark eyes went wide.

"Someone—a woman—called my mortgage lender and told them she was me. Told them she was out of work and couldn't afford the payments. She said she wanted to give the house back to the bank so that she wouldn't have to go through foreclosure."

"You are going to lose house?"

"No, I explained everything to the bank. And we put some passwords on the account, so she can't do it again. I've called everyone else I do business with— from my doctor to the insurance company—and done pretty much the same thing. I'm even picking up my mail at the post office. I'm pretty sure it's Margaret—my former boss's wife. But I don't have proof. And I don't know why she's doing it. All I know is that she's crazy, and she hates me. My last day at the P.R. firm, she slapped me across the face so hard I think Mom felt it in Europe."

"She hit you?"

"Yeah. And I think she's been coming by here. I'm safe where I'm going. Surrounded by people. But here? Nick's distracted. And God knows where Gabby is half the time."

"You need me to stay."

"Yeah."

Funny thing is, I started out trying to convince her I needed to go to work. Alone. But what came out of my mouth was the truth. I needed her here. I needed her safe. I needed Nick safe. And they'd be safer together.

She unbuckled the seatbelt. "I stay." She turned to me. "You have phone with you? Phone that works?"

"Yes, I'm taking my cell. I'll turn it on and keep it with me all night."

Even if it will reek of lime cleaner for the next fifty thousand years.

"You call me. Every hour. I wait by phone."

What she didn't say: if I didn't call, she'd have the cops, the FBI, and the National Guard descend on my office building. And she'd show up herself, armed with a flame-thrower.

She didn't have to say it. It was implied.

"I'll call. And I'll be back here by twelve thirty."

She patted my hand. "Be safe. We be safe, too."

Chapter 41

I must have been living right. When we got to the office park, Gravois announced we'd be cleaning floors eight, nine, and ten.

Then my life took a turn to the dark side. Again.

Out of the corner of my eye, I saw Maria and Olga exchange glances. Maria raised her hand, and Gravois barked at her.

"Yes? What?"

She threw me a sly look and coughed. "Olga and I should vacuum and polish. I'm not feeling well." She threw in another cough for good measure.

"Fine. Elia, you and Gabrielle clean bathrooms."

Olga snickered. Maria smirked. Elia just looked exhausted.

While Gravois went to move the van, Maria leaned in. "You were out sick again last night. And this is payday. What's it worth to you to get out of cleaning toilets tonight?"

What's it worth to you not to have someone kill you with a mop?

"Come now," Elia said, putting a hand on my arm. "We need to start."

"Wait a minute. What did you have in mind, Maria?" I asked.

"Half your pay. Both of you."

Elia looked at me and shook her head. "Too much for me. I need my money."

"Fine, hope you don't get too sick," Maria said, flouncing away.

Shit. I needed that digital recorder. God willing, this would be my last night. I didn't know how much longer I could stand the hours. And the way things were going, if I kept this job another week, I'd have to start bringing my whole family along with me.

"If you give in, she will never stop," Elia whispered. "You will be out of here soon. But I will be cleaning the bathrooms for the next four years."

She was right. And, even as tired as she was, she reminded me of a bust I'd once seen of Nefertiti. But I don't think Nefertiti ever manned a toilet scrubber.

"You're right. This is crap. Hey, Maria, I'm getting a hundred and forty-four bucks tonight. It's yours to split if you two do the toilets. Last offer, take it or leave it."

Elia shot me an angry look. Regal. But angry.

"*Spaciba*," Maria said grinning.

"*Nichevo*," I returned, digging the cell phone out of my pocket. "Hey, Elia, smile for the camera."

She turned, and I clicked her picture.

"What are you doing?" she said, exasperated.

"Again, with feeling!"

She glared at me and my phone. Nefertiti had come to life, and she was royally pissed.

Les Deux Gravois reappeared on the ramp. "All right, ladies," Mr. Gravois said, clapping his pudgy hands. "Time to clean.

For the next few hours, Elia said barely a word as we cleaned the offices on eight and nine. After my third call to Baba, she sank into a cubicle chair. "Who is it you are calling?"

"My grandma. She worries about me working nights."

"Is that why you took my picture?"

"No, that's for my sister, Annie."

"You want my picture for your sister?"

"She runs a modeling agency. She's always looking for new talent. Girls with exotic looks. Modeling's not easy. But it beats cleaning toilets. And it would give you the cash you need to cover college and med school."

"When you say 'modeling' . . . ?"

"Fashion modeling. The real thing. My sister is Anastasia. She has her own agency in Manhattan now."

Her eyes popped open. "Anastasia is your sister? You do not look like her."

"Tell me about it."

"I did not mean . . ."

"Hey, no skin off my nose. To be fair, you're not exactly seeing me at my best," I said, wiping my forehead on the sleeve of my black cardigan.

Elia smiled.

"You think she would hire me?"

"No idea. But it's worth a shot."

"How would it work?"

"If she likes the photos, you'd go to New York for an interview. It's a three-hour train ride. If she hired you, she'd find the jobs and send you. You could study on the train ride to New York, and she's got clients in D.C., too."

"I could work nights?"

"No, mostly during the day. But even just a few jobs a month would pay more than a year of cleaning offices. Even if you missed a class now and then, you'd still have a lot more time for college. And during the summer, you could work all week and really stockpile some cash."

She closed her eyes. "That would be wonderful."

"So you're not still mad?"

"I am too tired to be angry," she sighed. "And even if your sister does not hire me, just the idea is beautiful."

"Yeah, but I know how much you'd miss Maria and Olga."

"And whatever would Monsieur Gravois do without us?"

By the time we got to C&W's offices, it was 10:45. The good news: no one was around. The bad news: I was almost too tired to care.

I made a beeline for the conference room door. It was locked.

I looked down. No light coming from underneath. I knocked. No answer. I put my ear to the door. Silence.

Screw it. I wasn't wasting one more night of my life in this place. I rifled through a secretary's desk and nicked a paper clip.

I glanced over at Elia. She looked puzzled but kept vacuuming. I straightened the clip and pushed it into the tiny hole next to the door lock, wiggling it until I felt a "pop."

I grabbed the knob and twisted. It opened! I might not be in Gabby's league, but I felt triumphant. I flipped on the lights, rushed to the Wedgwood vase, and shoved my hand inside.

For all I knew, they'd replaced my recorder with a mousetrap. Or a snake.

I stretched and reached to the very bottom. "Yes!" Elia peeked in. "Shsssh!"

"It's here!" I whisper-shouted. "It's here! It's here! It's here!"

I checked the side of the recorder. The red light was out. The batteries were probably dead. No telling what, if anything, it had captured. And I was going to have to wait to find out.

Next I headed for Chaz's office like a woman on a mission. Which I was.

Chaz displays a lot of tchotchkes in his small space. A collection of NCAA shot glasses. His UVA diploma. A grip-and-grin with Donald Trump. A community service plaque from his college frat. Another grip-and-grin with George W. Bush. Chaz tells people he was "involved" in the 2004 reelection campaign. I happen to know it was taken at a local Barnes & Noble during the former president's book tour.

In another shot, Chaz—wearing a helmet and fatigues—gives a thumbs-up in front of a helicopter. The implication: home from a successful mission. The reality: ten-dollar chopper rides at a Maryland air show.

But that was Chaz. From "sun streaks" that magically appeared in his hair every three weeks to the deep, year-round tan, and that whiter-than-white shark smile, I always wondered: was there any "there" there? Or was he just an empty suit?

Whatever he is—or was—someone had cleaned his office.

I grabbed the trash can first. Empty.

All the pictures were still in place. Except for Bush and The Donald.

I went through his desk. I knew he kept a dopp kit at work. I'd seen him head to the bathroom to shave before evenings out with clients. And he was compulsive about brushing his glow-in-the-dark teeth after every meal.

But the kit was gone, too.

OK, Chaz was in the wind. And it looked like he'd left with supplies. Which meant he had probably gone voluntarily. So where would he go?

I moved the mouse, and his computer came to life. I clicked the Chrome icon and scrolled through his search history. The last three sites he'd visited were cabin rentals in the West Virginia mountains.

I picked up his phone and hit "redial."

"Thank you for calling Amtrak! For station locations and routes, press '1.' For special travel deals and prices, press '2.' If you would like to speak with an attendant, please press '0.'"

Jeez, Chaz, why not leave me a trail of bread crumbs while you're at it?

It was either a clever feint, or Chaz was just as witless as I'd always suspected. I copied down the names of the cabin-rental places and logged off. Clearly the cops hadn't been looking all that hard or they'd have him already. I'm guessing they viewed him more as an additional witness than a serious suspect.

It was almost 11. I grabbed my cell and dialed Trip.

"Hey, Bob Woodward, how's it hanging?" he said.

"I think Chaz is renting a cabin in West Virginia. He took the train, so he may have rented a car or caught some sort of shuttle."

"Do I want to know how you know?"

"My name is Anonymous Tipster."

"Ah, so you're a well-meaning public citizen who doesn't have an ax to grind."

"I vote, I give blood, and I love my dog."

"And bake apple pies in your spare time."

"When I'm not twirling a flaming baton in the Fourth of July parade."

"OK, I'd pay to see that." He dropped his voice. "Speaking of things I'd pay for, what are the chances you could get me a few more of those cinnamon rolls?"

"I might be able to hook you up. Want to know exactly where Chaz is?"

"In all honesty, right now I'd rather have the cinnamon rolls. I missed lunch again. But shoot."

"Try Blue Mountain Resorts, Shenandoah Retreats, and Joe's Cabin Rental."

"Joe's Cabin Rental? Joe really used a lot of imagination coming up with that one."

"Yeah, well my money's on Joe. He takes cash. And he's a lot cheaper than the first two. Plus, it was the last site Chaz visited on his computer."

"You do tend to find things in the last place you look."

"Oh, and I got the you-know-what."

"You're kidding."

"I know," I said. "After two weeks, it doesn't seem possible. The batteries are dead, so I'm guessing it's got something. I just don't know what."

"Sounds like Baba's cooking."

I looked at the desk clock: 11:03. "Oh, shit, I gotta go! I gotta call Baba!"

Before we left, I had one more dirty job: Walters' office.

Unlike Chaz, he was neat to the point of OCD. The room was sparse, the desk was clean, and everything was arranged at right angles.

I'd heard rumors that he bagged his own trash and carried it out with him. Looking around, I believed it.

Besides the blotter and the computer, there were only two things on the desk: a black-and-white wedding portrait that appeared to have been taken in the late 1950s. His parents, I figured. And, in a matching frame next to it, a color photo—an older, heavier version of the woman from the wedding shot.

I moved his mouse with a rubber-gloved hand. Password protected.

OK, OCD and paranoid. Time to go old school.

I yanked one desk drawer. Locked. Definitely someone with something to hide. But was it murder or just dirty dealing?

I grabbed the paperclip out of my pocket and popped the lock on the long, shallow drawer in the center of his desk. Neat as a pin. Post-it notes, push-pins, pens, and more paper clips. It looked like one of those display desks they set up in furniture stores.

I closed it and popped a small drawer to the right. Pads, pencils, and a giant bottle of aspirin—half empty. Or half full, depending on your perspective.

And I thought the guy only gave headaches. Who knew?

I pulled out the pad on top and grabbed a pencil. What the heck, it worked in the movies.

I lightly rubbed the side of the lead against the top sheet to see if I could raise an image. Like "Dear Diary, Today I killed Everett Coleman."

Or "To do: 1. Take bloody suit to cleaners. 2. Buy yogurt."

Instead, it revealed a number: 3045550122.

Ten digits. Too short for an account number. Most of the ones I'd seen were thirteen digits or more.

A phone number! Three-zero-four was the area code for West Virginia. I'd learned that in Chaz's office. I grabbed my cell and dialed Trip.

"Yeah," he said. Flat.

"Billy Bob around?" I asked.

"Left about twenty minutes ago," Trip said in a very businesslike tone. "Family emergency. He's going to visit some relatives in coal country. He wanted to be there by daybreak. But I'll tell him you asked after him."

"I think I have the direct number to Chaz's room," I whispered into the phone. "I found it in Walters' office."

"No, I'm beat. I don't think I can make it tonight. But give me the details, just in case I change my mind."

"Who's there—editorial higher-ups or the cops?"

"First things first. I'll finish up here, and then see how I feel."

"Gotcha," I said, firing off the number. Apparently our editors were on the warpath again, and I didn't have to be Sherlock Holmes to figure out that Billy Bob's stories were the reason why. "And may the Force be with you."

I shoved the phone in my pocket, along with the pencil rubbing. Then I oh-so-carefully replaced everything.

Next I sprang the larger, file-sized drawer underneath. No files. But what I found floored me.

One small, intricately carved wooden box. It was a handcrafted, one-of-a-kind item that Annie had brought back from Spain. It had lived in my desk during my tenure at C&W. And the last time I'd seen it, a few days before I was fired, it was holding a pair of silver filigree earrings she'd picked up on another trip. The box and the earrings had both been missing when I'd collected my stuff last week. I'd figured Amy had grabbed them.

I opened the box. Empty.

He also had a small bottle of Oscar. My perfume.

This wasn't my own bottle, specifically. But it was the scent I always wore. And, to my knowledge, I was the only one in the office who did.

Majorly creepy. What was Walters doing with my stuff?

With the phone in one pocket and the recorder in the other, I was seriously short on storage space. I grabbed the recorder and, with a little rearranging, managed to work it into my bra. I might look a little lumpy. But it was wedged in tight.

Thank God for the black smock.

I scooped up the box and slipped it into my jeans pocket. It was a present from my sister, and I was taking it home.

Elia stuck her head in the door. "Maria and Olga are coming. You must leave now."

I slammed all the desk drawers shut and dropped the telltale paper clip into my other pocket.

Walters was in for a hell of a surprise on Monday.

Chapter 42

By the time I got back to the office of Gravois & Co., I could barely keep my eyes open. I collected my weekly cash and—as per our agreement—passed it over to Maria and Olga. After the others left, I stayed behind to tell Les Deux Gravois that this was my last night.

"Humph!" said Madame Gravois, as she puffed on a cigarette.

"Two weeks' notice," said Mr. Gravois.

"No, this is it for me. It was a great job. Thanks for the opportunity." *To ruin my lungs. And by the way, just how long will it take to get the lime-cleaner smell out of my nose?*

"Have to give two weeks' notice," Gravois insisted. "We see you Monday, six o'clock."

"No, this is my last night. I'm giving notice."

"We treat you like family, and this is the thanks we get?" said Madame Gravois.

Family? Outside of a Grimm's fairy tale, who made family scrub toilets at midnight? With chemicals that were probably banned by the FDA, the USDA, and the ASPCA?

"I'm sorry, but I haven't been well. And the cleaning chemicals are aggravating my condition. So, as much as I'd love to work here for the rest of my life, I'm making this my last night. But again, thank you both for the opportunity, and good luck in all your future endeavors."

At that point, I'd pretty much burned through my allotted portion of polite. So I turned, quick-stepped to the door, and didn't look back.

I had a warm, happy glow. I was finally free. And I planned to sleep for a week.

The glow faded when I saw my Chevy.

All four tires were flat. Someone had carved a giant "X" onto the hood. And gouged the word "bitch" into one side of the car. And etched "slut" on the other.

Four years of college, a dozen years of professional writing, and I could come up with exactly one word. "Crap!"

I pulled out my cell phone and dialed 9-1-1. The cops had cleared me. Who was I to hold a grudge?

Once the emergency operator determined it was my tires that had been slashed and not me, she put me on hold. Phone to my ear, I wandered back to Gravois's storefront. He was locking up. She was sitting in their car, a new burgundy Cadillac, with the window down, puffing away into the cold fog.

"Someone slashed all four of my tires," I told her.

"Humph!" she said, before launching into a wet, hacking cough.

"I'm on the phone with the police, but they're going to be a while," I said to him. "Can I wait here with you or inside?"

Down the block, an alarm went off. Followed by what sounded like rapid-fire gunshots. Joined by more shots—-from a different gun. Gravois sprinted for the car. "Sorry!" he called. "Employees only."

"You said I was family. You don't leave family alone in the dark. It's cold out here."

"Rapidement, Étienne! Rapidement!"

"You will be fine. Safe neighborhood. Good people. Good-bye!" He hit the door locks, jammed the key in the ignition, threw the Caddie into reverse, then hit the gas.

So much for good old Uncle Étienne.

I gave up on the cops and dialed Trip.

"Hey, you'll never guess where I am."

"Dulles International, about to board a plane to a country with no extradition?"

"Close. Cold, dark parking lot in Arlington with four flat tires."

"Wow, somebody really likes you."

"Story of my life."

"You caught me just as I was heading home," he said. "Where exactly is this alleged parking lot?"

"I-395 to the Arlington exit. Left on Clovis. Then just follow the sound of the gunshots."

"Any place you can go 'til I get there?"

"Not if I want to live to see morning."

"Anybody wants your wallet or your car," Trip said, "you give 'em up and scream like a girl."

"Anybody coming after me doesn't want wheels or cash. I'm dressed like a cleaning lady, and my car has four flat tires. If somebody gets close, I'm gonna kick 'em in the nuts and run like hell."

"So how alone are you?" he asked.

"Well, there's some guy across the street pacing under a street light and screaming into a cell phone. Oh, shit."

"What?"

"He doesn't have a cell phone. He doesn't have a cell phone!"

"And I'm officially making the jump to hyperspace," Trip said. "If I get a ticket, you're paying the fine."

"As long as the court system takes baked goods and hot iPods, I'm all set."

"We've really got to get your life back on track."

"Yeah, I don't know what's worse," I said. "The fact that I've hit bottom. Or the sinking feeling that I'm not quite there yet."

Chapter 43

By the time Trip pulled up, I was standing by my car chatting with a patrol officer.

"Jeez, this is much nicer than your usual street corner," my best friend said. "You're really moving up in the world."

"This is Trip Cabot. Trip, this is Officer Sanchez. He took my report, and he's been keeping an eye out while I'm stuck here."

"Have you talked to her Baba yet?" Trip asked.

"That would be the elderly Russian female?"

Trip looked at me in astonishment. "You didn't!"

"It was the only way we could keep her from charging out here. I don't know who's behind this, but I'm pretty sure she and Nick are safer at home."

"I'm gonna roll," said Officer Sanchez. "You need anything, just dial 911. They'll get me back out here."

"Thanks," I said. "We should be OK. And good luck with the little one."

Sanchez gave a two-fingered salute.

"Little one?" Trip asked as we climbed into the Corvette, and he cranked the heat all the way up.

"He and his wife just had a baby," I explained. "Two months ago. Two months of colic, crying, and sleepless nights. Baba gave him a few suggestions that worked with my dad."

"Why do I get the feeling you'd have been just fine on your own?"

"Tell that to my car. Not only did someone slit all four tires, they engraved 'slut' and 'bitch' on the sides and carved an 'X' on the hood."

"'X' marks the spot," he said. "Sounds like some pent-up woman-rage. Especially the vocabulary. Margaret?"

"I'm thinking Margaret."

"But why?" he said. "You weren't sleeping with her husband."

"Or carrying his baby," I added.

"There's something we're not seeing."

"Yeah, and it's wearing my earrings and perfume."

"You've lost it," he said. "And you've lost me. I'm beat, and I could really use a cheeseburger. What happens if we're not here to do a personal meet-and-greet with your tow-truck driver?"

"You mean if I'm not here with my wallet open, ready to hand over all my available cash? He keeps driving, and we have to wait another two hours."

"I was afraid you were going to say that," Trip said wearily. "So do you have any actual cash on you?"

"No, I'm going to write him a bad check."

He rolled his eyes. "Why couldn't you get a flat in

front of a five-star restaurant? Or an all-night donut shop?"

"Don't tell me. Tell Margaret."

"OK, what's all this about your perfume and earrings?" he asked.

I told him what I'd found in Walters' desk.

"Holy cross-dressers, Batman. Maybe your friend Walters does have a personal life after all."

"And I'm his fashion muse? I don't think so. And Margaret seems to have a violent, irrational hatred of me. Cutting off my credit cards. Disconnecting my power and my phone. Eighty-sixing my health insurance. Probably savaging my car. Hell, Trip, someone tried to give my house back to the bank."

"If this was her tonight, she's getting a lot more violent," he said. "And a lot more hands-on."

"OK, so what if Walters is feeding that hatred? Pointing her in my direction?"

"Why?"

"I don't know. But I only found the earring box. What if he dropped the earrings somewhere private, where Margaret was sure to find them?"

"And sprayed around a little of 'your' perfume to complete the effect?" Trip said. "It's diabolical. But why?"

"How do you kill someone without leaving fingerprints?" I asked.

"With gloves. Preferably something stylish."

"Better than gloves," I said. "You incite someone else to do it for you."

"Especially if that person seems to be drinking more and losing her grip on reality," he concluded.

"Which means at this point Margaret could really believe I was schtupping her husband."

"And, based on the condition of your car, she's unraveling."

"How did she know I was here?" I asked. "This isn't exactly her kind of neighborhood."

"It's Friday night," Trip said. "She probably figured a big-time hoochie like you would have plans. She followed you."

My stomach dropped. "Do you know Baba planted herself in the car before I left? Insisted she was coming with me."

He smiled. "That sounds like her. The woman is spooky."

"But it means Margaret has seen my family. She's dangerous. This time it was only my car. Next time it could be Lucy, or Nick, or Baba."

"How'd you like another houseguest?"

"Are you serious? I don't even have a spare bed to offer."

"I can sleep on the sofa," Trip said. "No biggie."

"What about Tom?" I asked.

"Tom would need a bigger sofa," Trip said.

"You know what I mean."

"Tom's a good guy," he said. "He'll understand. And it's just for a night or two."

"Everybody says that when they show up at my door. And nobody's left yet."

"Despite the cramped quarters and zero-star cuisine. You could give lessons to Sir Bed-and-Breakfast."

"Oh, you should know," I warned. "Nick and Gabby have hit a rough patch."

"No live sex show in front of Baba. Check."

"No, I mean they're barely speaking. And she's spending a lot of time locked in the bathroom with her phone. Possibly talking business, possibly talking to her ex."

"Hey, if I wanted family tension, bad food, and homicidal maniacs, I'd have gone home for Christmas," Trip said.

"You did."

"Well, there you go. I'll fit right in. So when do we get to listen to that tape?"

"I figure as soon as we get home, and I can pop in some fresh batteries."

"Over a big plate of cinnamon buns?" he prompted.

"After a big bowl of Baba's stew."

"If you ever want to get a boyfriend," Trip said with a grin, "we're going to have to teach you to lie."

Chapter 44

When we finally arrived home, Trip was treated like a returning war hero. My reception was only slightly warmer than the Gravois' parking lot.

First, Baba hugged me. Then she glared, shook her head, and toddled off to the kitchen.

All I wanted was a very long, very hot shower.

After draining my water heater and nearly a full bottle of liquid soap in the shower, I pulled on my sweats and wandered into the kitchen.

Baba had plied Trip with bowls of stew and steaming mugs of hot coffee. Nick had slipped him a few brioche rolls to make it more palatable. And followed it up with warm cinnamon rolls and cold milk. Lucy was dozing at Trip's feet.

When I appeared, the happy chatter stopped.

Baba dished up another bowl of stew, set it in front of me with a loud "clunk," and immediately turned back to the stove.

Gabby's eyes went wide. I looked at Nick. He shrugged.

Trip inclined his head to Baba and nodded.

"I quit the night job," I said loudly, to no one in particular. "Tonight was my last night."

Baba turned and looked at me. There were tears in her eyes. I rushed over and gave her a full-body hug.

"I'm so sorry," I said. "So sorry. I didn't mean to worry you."

"Nichevo, nichevo," she said, gently patting me on the back.

"Hey, sob sisters," Nick called from behind us. "The food's getting cold."

"She's got some not-so-good news, too," Trip said.

"I'm broke?"

"Margaret," he prompted.

I sighed. "My ex-boss's wife, Margaret, seems to believe I was sleeping with her husband. Obviously, I wasn't. But she's been stealing the mail. And I'm pretty sure she was the one who attacked my car tonight."

"The problem is she's getting more violent," Trip cut in. "And more personal. And she's been by here more than once. We think she followed Alex from here to work tonight. The woman seems to be coming unhinged—which makes her dangerous."

"This is my worst nightmare," I said. "Because she hates me, you guys could be in danger, too."

"Hey, if this is your way of trying to kick us out, we're not leaving," Nick said.

"Damn straight, sugar," Gabby said.

Baba set her mouth in a grim, determined line.

"Then we need to stick together," I said. "Nobody goes off anywhere alone. Until this is over, we keep to groups of twos and threes. Trip's even agreed to stay over for a few nights, so we can have an extra pair of eyes."

"What about the cops?" Nick asked.

"I've talked to them," I said. "A couple of times. The problem is, I suspect it's Margaret, but I can't prove it. As far as the police are concerned, I've had some incidents of identity theft and an unrelated case of vandalism in a bad neighborhood twenty miles away. They won't even concede it's the same person."

"So we have to go with what we know and protect ourselves," said Trip.

Baba nodded. "Is true."

"So, do we, like, sleep in shifts, or what?" Gabby asked.

"To start, I think we just make sure the doors and windows are always locked and travel in groups," I said. "Trip's sleeping on the sofa, and all the bedrooms are full, so I don't think she's going to risk a full-on home invasion. She's more the type to try and take advantage of an opportunity."

"Then we don't give her any," Nick said.

"So where's that gorgeous car of yours?" Gabby asked Trip.

"Parked over at the B&B across the street," he said. "I'm brave, but I'm not crazy."

Chapter 45

Saturday morning my kitchen looked like the set of a zombie movie.

Grunting, bleary-eyed bodies shuffled back and forth across the kitchen to the coffeemaker.

The only ones who seemed immune to the effects of the late hours were Baba and Lucy, who both bounced up with the sun.

After we'd all drained two pots of caffeine, Trip volunteered to go out and bring back breakfast.

"Where's Baba?" I asked Nick, when I realized I hadn't seen her for a while.

"Out for a walk with Lucy," he said, yawning.

"You let her go out alone?"

"She's wearing combat boots, and she's armed with a frying pan the size of a garbage-can lid. She might scare the crap out of your neighbors, but she'll be fine. And what do you mean 'let her'? Like I could stop her?"

Trip patted me on the shoulder. "It's all right. I'll pick them both up on my way to Burger King. We'll be back in twenty minutes with food. Then we can listen to that recording of yours."

"I just hope it was worth two weeks of working nights. Hang on!" I ran into my bedroom and rooted through the dirty laundry bin until I came up with an old green blanket. I gave it the sniff test. It smelled like lasagna, but Lucy would probably appreciate that.

"Here," I said, tossing it to Trip. "So she doesn't shred your leather seats."

"That's no way to talk about our grandmother," Nick said.

Trip smelled the blanket and wrinkled his nose. "Spaghetti?"

"Lasagna."

"Don't even want to know."

"Hey, it was a rainy, B-movie Sunday. A double feature. *She Married a Stranger* and *Don't Forget to Scream.*

"Definitely two Oscar contenders," Trip said.

"Forgive her," Nick chimed in. "No cable, no TiVo, no satellite, no Xbox. I'm sorry, what *have* you got?" he said, turning to me.

"A life," I countered.

Nick grinned over his coffee mug. "Not from where I'm sitting."

Ninety minutes later, we were all as full as ticks. While Trip gathered up the remains of our fast-food feast, Baba prepped a batch of goulash on a back burner of the stove.

The rest of us clustered in the living room.

"What's in goulash?" Gabby whispered, pointing toward the kitchen.

"Beets, carrots, potatoes, onions, turnips," Nick said under his breath. "And some kind of meat."

"It sounds healthy," Gabby said. "And it should taste good."

"It should, but it won't," Nick said. "What I can't figure out is how everything comes out gray and slimy."

"I think that's the noodles," I said. "Apparently they kind of fall apart after they've been simmering for five hours."

"Noodles!" he said, snapping his fingers. "Of course!"

"There were noodles in that stuff?" Gabby asked.

"Yeah, and I swear I tasted peanut butter in the last batch," I said.

"You did," Nick said. "I saw it on the counter, but I didn't say anything."

"Why not?" Gabby asked.

"It's like a mob hit," I explained. "The less you know, the better off you are."

Trip and I migrated to the porch. It was bright and sunny. Just cool enough to wear a sweater. And I swear the air smelled like chocolate.

"I've got about fifteen hours on here," I said. "Where do you want to start?"

"The beginning? Call me crazy."

"Anyone ever mention that you editors are unnaturally wedded to routine?"

"Every day of my life," he replied. "Usually with words of a more colorful variety."

"That's why you get the big bucks."

"What I really need is a whip and a chair. Cordova and Whatley got into it again yesterday."

"How bad was it?" I asked. I'd had a ringside seat to their last bout—touched off when one accused the other of not taking their current investigative assignment "seriously enough."

"They're getting better. No stitches this time. An hour later, they were off to lunch together."

"Amazing."

"Admit it," Trip said, "you miss it."

"Parts of it. And it definitely beats cleaning bathrooms. Or flacking for P.R. weasels."

"Exactly what my college career counselor said. Word for word. Look, all I'm saying is, when all this is over, at least think about coming back."

I sighed. "I loved the job. And the people. But the pay was lousy. When I left for C&W, I really was selling my soul. The sad thing is, I'd probably still be there if they hadn't wanted my body to go with it. Soooo, the beginning it is . . ."

An hour later, we'd listened to the entire meeting I'd missed the day Walters and Margaret threw me out. And hadn't learned a single thing.

I got to hear Walters telling my former co-workers that I was "the prime suspect in Everett Coleman's murder."

"She's dangerous and likely desperate," he intoned from Olympus. "She's already tried to enter this office once illegally. If anyone sees her again, call security, then inform either myself or Margaret. We'll contact the authorities. In the meantime, until she's in custody, we ask that you all be careful and look out for yourselves."

The sound from Annie's recorder was so good, it even picked up Margaret's snuffling in the background.

I rolled my eyes. Trip grinned.

"So exactly when did you go back there again?" he asked.

"With the cleaning crew? That night."

"Vigilantes without the vigilance. Got to love it."

"Give 'em credit. I was wearing a disguise. Glasses and a headscarf."

"Clark Kent only needed glasses," he said.

"Clark Kent wasn't a redhead."

We fast-forwarded over a boring meeting about a budget for a new client. And another forty-five minutes for a lunch seminar on how to pitch new services to existing clients. Yawn.

"This is crap. I wanna hear about the audit and who got Coleman's accounts," I whined.

"Walters probably had those discussions in his office," Trip said. "With the door firmly closed."

"I don't know. One night when we were there cleaning, he was locked in the conference room. And he was still there when we left. But he was alone. So there wasn't any conversation to activate the recorder."

"Look, we knew this part of it was a crapshoot. Recording or no recording, you dug up all kinds of information by working that grubby job. And at this very minute, Billy Bob is tracking the wily Chaz through the hills of West Virginia."

"Will he bring him back tied to the hood of his car?"

"He may have mentioned something about a bungee cord and a tarp, but I try not to micromanage," Trip said. "Seriously, how does a guy named Lopez turn out to be such a total redneck?"

"You really want to know?"

"Suddenly, I get the feeling I might not. Proceed."

"Billy Bob's family is from Orlando," I said. "Real name's Lopes. They own some kind of big commercial farm. He learned Spanish growing up, from the migrant workers. And he traded the 's' for a 'z' when he discovered there was a premium on minority journalists."

"You're shitting me."

"Give the man credit. He never claims to be Hispanic. He just introduces himself, and people assume. Plus he speaks Spanish like a native."

"Sometimes I think you and I are the only ones who aren't working some kind of scam," Trip said. "And I'm not so sure about you."

"You leave my family out of this."

"Come on, we might as well hear the next installment of *The Dull and the Deadly*. Are you sure Coleman didn't just drop from sheer boredom?" He pressed "play."

"Hang on," I said, hitting "pause." "In the beginning, whoever started this had things under control. But lately, it's been unraveling. Chaz is MIA, and the Feds and the state guys are sniffing around. I'm betting it's spinning out of control."

"Just like your life."

"Exactly! So I say we play the tape backward."

"And see if there's a message from the Devil?"

"Not backward-backward," I said. "Start at the end. Roll back twenty or thirty minutes and play that segment. And keep going that way."

"Start at the end of the maze and work back," he said. "I like it."

I fiddled with the recorder, pressing one button, then another. I finally hit "play."

There was a sound, like paper shuffling. Then a knock.

"Benjamin." Jennifer Stiles' voice. Weird.

"Come in." Walters answered.

"Well, Benjamin, you certainly seem to be working hard." Jennifer again. And there was a taunting quality to her voice that I'd heard myself on a couple of occasions. This wasn't the angry mistress or the grieving girlfriend. This was the Jennifer who'd sashayed into C&W on her first day like she owned the place.

Trip and I exchanged glances.

"Do you need something?" Walters said. Flat. Dismissive.

"Actually, I have something for you," she said. There was a rustling sound.

"What's this?"

"It's really from Everett and me. A little something you're sure to appreciate."

If I didn't like her, I'd have said her tone was smug. And I didn't like her.

Trip and I were treated to the sound of ripping paper. Walters opening his mystery gift.

"What do you get for the partner you're pushing out of the company?" I whispered to Trip.

"I'm thinking some nice cuff links," Trip said.

"What in God's name is this?" Walters thundered.

"OK, whatever it is, I'm betting she won't be getting a thank-you note," Trip said.

"What is the meaning of this?' Walters yelled. "A white and blue stick?"

Oh, crap.

"It's a pregnancy test," Jennifer said smoothly. "My pregnancy test. Everett and I are expecting a baby."

"Everett's dead," Walters said.

"Damn," I said. "I really wish I had some popcorn for this."

"Hush!" Trip said.

"Everett's gone," Jennifer's voice continued. "But luckily for all of us, a part of him will live on. Through his child. Through his fiancée. And through his business."

"In case you've forgotten, Everett already has two children. And a wife."

"Divorcing. Unfortunately, it hadn't been a real marriage for years. And the children took him for granted. He was nothing but a walking checkbook to them."

"Were they engaged?" Trip mouthed.

I shook my head. "Spin."

More rustling. "Why on earth would you give this, this . . . thing . . . to me?" More scraping, followed by Jennifer's light, high laughter.

"It's all right, Benjamin. You can touch it. It's perfectly sanitary. Unless you think my 'girl cooties' will contaminate you." More laughter. "I gave it to you because this is a new beginning for this agency. A new partnership. And we're both going to make a lot of money together."

"My firm's going to make a lot of money. Period. You're going to be out of a job soon. And don't count on getting a recommendation from me or anyone connected with this company," he said slowly, pausing. "But I'm sure Margaret will be more than happy to help you arrange things so that you can have health insurance for your blessed event."

I could practically see the flinty squint on his face. And I knew from experience exactly what kind of "help" Margaret was going to offer.

"Oh, Benjamin," Jennifer said.

Uh-oh. Cue the video of sharp teeth going in for the kill.

"You're so charmingly quaint. Do you have any idea what happens if you fire a pregnant woman? Especially one who's carrying your late partner's baby? Not only will there be multiple investigations and a very expensive lawsuit, but there's all that juicy publicity. And, unlike you and poor, dear, Margaret, I'm very telegenic. Did I ever tell you that I got my degree in broadcasting?

"Everett was my fiancée, my soul mate," she continued. "Cut down in his prime. His drunken ex is delusional, possibly even dangerous. I'm just a brave young mother, grieving for the love of my life, and working to provide for our baby. And, of course, ready, willing, and able to testify all about the inner workings of this firm, no matter how much personal pain it brings me."

For the next thirty seconds, there was dead silence. Talk about your pregnant pauses.

"Of course, it doesn't have to go that way," Jennifer purred.

"Because whistle-blowers don't get rich?" Walters said.

"Believe me, Benjamin, I'm going to get very rich, whichever hand I play. I'm simply giving you the chance to be on the winning side of the table."

"How kind of you."

I elbowed Trip. "Told you we needed popcorn."

"Don't make me get the duct tape," Trip replied.

I stuck out my tongue.

"You see, I know about the key-man policy, Benjamin."

"And I suppose you want part of it."

"It's not a matter of wanting, Benjamin. A portion of it belongs to me. Under the terms of your business agreement, all of Everett's heirs are entitled to compensation for his half of the agency. That makes my baby and me significant stakeholders."

"No, that means your child is possibly an heir. If it's actually born. And if it passes a paternity test. And that's assuming Everett's family even consents to a DNA test, which I doubt."

"I can force it. Legally."

"Everett was cremated. Good luck getting DNA from ashes. Or maybe you want to ask Margaret for blood from her babies, so that you can try to cheat them out of their inheritance?" Walters' own laugh was short, dry, and mirthless.

"It doesn't matter what Margaret wants anymore. Everett's child is Everett's heir."

"I can promise you that will be one, long expensive legal battle. And with you out of work, I can't think there will be many attorneys willing to go up against us pro bono. Especially given the connections our firm has in this town. But let's assume that, in spite of those very long odds, you do manage to eke out a win. The most you'd get would be a pittance. Scraps. No control. And as managing partner, I'd move to have that money put in trust until your poor, unfortunate child turns twenty-one. Or perhaps twenty-five. Of course, I would see to it that I—or someone who answers to me—would be named trustee. You see, while I may be, how did you put it, 'charmingly quaint,' I do know a lot of very influential lawyers, bankers, and judges.

"So that little win will leave you with a mountain of legal bills, two decades of minimum-wage jobs, and absolutely nothing else," Walters continued evenly. "No one will even think of hiring you. I'll make sure of that. Especially after the stunt you and Everett attempted. Did you really think I didn't know about that? Your secret visits to the lawyers across town? Pushing me out of *my own business*? The agency *my father* founded? Did you think I wouldn't find out? That I'd let you walk off with my family's legacy?"

His hushed voice was like sandpaper. And he was relentless. "What have you done to earn it? You barely scraped out a degree from a second-rate school, and you know how to wiggle your ass. Congratulations. That may have worked wonders with my partner. But it's not going to cut it with me—or anyone else—ever again. I will promise you that. You see, the men in this town love to parade around with their arm candy. But if one of the little tramps tries to go public, she's out. Damaged goods. In D.C., reputation is everything.

"You think you're telegenic?" he mocked. "Not after the media gets the full rundown of every misstep you've ever made, from that married English professor you seduced in college to your little three-way in that Chicago hotel last year. There are color pictures of that one, I understand."

"I'm not ashamed of my past."

"That's fortunate. Because you're about to see it all again—in gory living color—every time you turn on the television, use a computer, or pick up a newspaper. And so will your parents, your neighbors, your boyfriends, and everyone you've ever met. You think the public is going to buy your little love story and eat you up? The media machine is going to rip you apart and grind you into hamburger. Your name will become shorthand for 'whore.' You'll be reduced to a punch line.

"Oh, I'm sorry," Walters continued, barely pausing. "I interrupted you. You were explaining how you're holding the winning hand. Please continue. Tell me how you're going to get 'very rich'?"

"Everett and I were in love."

"Oh, please. You were a side effect of his Viagra."

"He never needed Viagra with me. Not once."

"He was going through those little blue pills like they were breath mints. You forget, in this office, Margaret handles the insurance claims. His doctors tried to code it as something else. But she's dogged, our Margaret. A few phone calls to the right nurses, and she found out exactly what Everett was picking up every time he stopped by the pharmacy. And she knew she certainly wasn't receiving any of the benefits."

"I know what Everett had on you, Benjamin," Jennifer said, her voice shrill. "I want a full partnership. Fifty percent. Or I will tell the world. You think I'm going to be a joke? Wait until your secret gets out. You won't have a client left. So you better get used to sharing your precious agency with—what did you call me? 'Arm candy'? Because it beats having no agency at all."

"What is it?" Walters asked evenly.

"What is what?"

"What is it you think Everett had on me?"

"The truth," she screeched. "In black and white."

"What truth, Jennifer?"

"Do you think I'm kidding?"

"No, Jennifer, I think you're bluffing. And I'm calling you on it. So, what is this alleged secret? This horrible truth?"

"You won't like seeing your story in print, either, Benjamin," she said with the lilt back in her voice. "Maybe I'll just talk to that reporter who used to work here. I happen to know she's very interested in what goes on around this place. She's phoned me three times this week. I've been avoiding her calls, but perhaps I should invite her over for coffee. Decaf for me, of course."

"First rule of thumb in blackmail, my dear: don't ever bluff. Now get out of here."

"I don't care what you say. Everett was my fiancé. I'm carrying his child. And I will have a partnership in this firm, whether you like it or not. Here's what you need to know, Benjamin . . ."

"No," Walters interrupted, his rough voice barely above a whisper. "Here's what you need to know. You're a cheap little tart. You're not going to win in court. Or in the court of public opinion. Consider yourself on an extended leave of absence until further notice. I don't want to see you in this office. And I'm quite certain Margaret doesn't, either. You can show yourself out."

There was a shuffling sound, then ten seconds of silence followed by a familiar click: the conference room door closing.

I fast-forwarded. Nothing. "That's it. Show's over."

"Any way to tell when that scene was recorded?" Trip asked.

"Nope. But it's the last thing on the tape. Could have been last week. Could have been yesterday."

"Given that she mentioned the investigations and used you as a bargaining chip, I'm willing to bet it's recent," he said. "You didn't actually call her, did you?"

"Hell, no," I said. "She's your girlfriend. If I'd wanted a heart-to-heart, I'd have had you do it."

"I'm living in your house, sleeping on your sofa, *and* you're giving me orders," Trip said. "Did we inadvertently get married?"

"I can't even begin to process all of this," I said. "A confirmed pregnancy. And a second blackmail attempt."

"So Margaret knew that Coleman was cheating."

"If you believe Walters," I said.

"Do you?"

"If lying was college basketball, both of these two would be in the Final Four," I said. "You wanna know which one is telling the truth? Neither. You can't believe a word either one of them says."

"So what did we learn?" Trip said. "Or, more to the point, what have I got to show for the last hour and a half of my life?"

"Walters hates Jennifer. Jennifer hates Walters."

"Check."

"Jennifer tried to blackmail Walters," I said. "First with the pregnancy test, and later with the mystery information. Probably his father's AIDS diagnosis. But it sounds like Jennifer didn't really know about that. Could be she knew that Coleman blackmailed his way into C&W, but Coleman never bothered to share all the details."

"Check and check," he said. "And by the way, next time you do this, plant a camera, too. I would love to have seen the look on Walters' face when he opened his 'present.'"

"Worst surprise party ever."

"I don't think she killed him," Trip said.

"Yeah, Nick nailed that right from the beginning. She had too much to lose if he died. And too much to gain if he lived."

"But Walters might have. Or Margaret."

"Yes and yes," I said. "You want to know what—out of this whole conversation—I actually believe? I think the bit about Margaret and the Viagra is true. That definitely sounds like her. So I'm guessing she knew Coleman was having an affair. But when she went looking for the likely culprit, for some reason Walters pointed her in my direction."

"What if it wasn't Walters?" Trip theorized. "What if it was Coleman himself?"

"Why?"

"You know how you always said that the weasels at C&W employed misdirection about as often as other cubicle-dwellers used Microsoft Word?"

"Yeah," I said. "The old focus-on-this-don't-look-at-that routine."

"Coleman was afraid of his wife, yes?"

"Definitely yes," I said.

"And the last thing he wanted was for scary, controlling Mommy wife to find out about his tender young love and their plans for a new life together," Trip said. "So he threw her off the scent with a red herring."

"Which explains Margaret's attitude change toward me after a couple of weeks. I kept wondering what I'd done wrong. If I'd inadvertently snubbed her somehow."

"If you tried being nicer to her . . ." he started.

"I did. Like an idiot."

"That would have just made her madder," Trip said. "She'd have thought you two lovebirds were mocking her. All he'd have had to do was drop a few subtle hints. Nothing too obvious."

"Because if he wanted to really sell it, she'd have had to 'discover' it herself," I said. "So he left a trail of clues that led her to my door. Literally."

"And if he was totally fiendish . . ." Trip started.

"Which he was," I interrupted.

"When she confronted him, he would have confessed. Crocodile tears, phony remorse, the whole schmear."

"Then if he went missing for a few hours to visit

Jennifer or their lawyers, she would have just assumed I was working my wiles again."

"You minx, you," he said.

"And if Walters wanted to get rid of Coleman, he could have used that little charade to his advantage," I said.

"Hence the perfume and the missing earrings," Trip said. "It fits. But which one of them did it?"

"Flip a coin," I replied. "Either. Or neither. It could still be one of his happy ex-employees. Billy Bob getting any information there?"

"A dozen guys who are delighted that Coleman's dead but swear they didn't do it."

"Everett P. Coleman," I said. "To know him is to loathe him."

"Is that what they're etching on the headstone?"

"Hey, this is a guy who even screwed over his own kid," I said. "I mean, maybe he cut off college because Pat changed majors. Or maybe Coleman was just grabbing all the available cash to fund the next chapter of his own life." I paused. "You think Jennifer's in danger?"

"If she's blackmailing a killer, she's got the life expectancy of a jelly donut at a Weight Watchers meeting," Trip said. "I really hate the fact that she dragged your name back into this. But I keep flashing back to the first rule of reporting."

"Spell the names right?"

"OK, the second rule," he said.

"No preconceptions, and we go where the information takes us."

"And where is the information taking us?" he asked.

"To visit the blackmailing liar to find out about the double-dealing liar?"

"Very good," Trip said. "If you were Lucy, I'd give you a cookie."

"Jennifer doesn't know who did it, either," I said. "If she did, she'd have threatened Walters with it. Or she'd be using it against Margaret to get a share of the insurance money."

"She might know without knowing she knows," Trip countered. "Things she's seen and heard. But Walters was right about one thing: she was bluffing about knowing what Coleman had on him."

"No reason for Coleman to tell her," I said. "He wasn't planning to die. And otherwise, it's like sharing the secret of a magic trick. Coleman seems like a big man because he can make Walters jump through hoops. Loses a little of the luster if you know Margaret was the one who did the heavy lifting. And that the only reason Coleman married Margaret in the first place was so he could blackmail his way into the company."

"Remind me again why you wanted to work with these people?"

"Damned if I know."

"And how was it you finally wised up?"

"I was fired and frogmarched from the building."

"Please tell me you've learned something from all of this," Trip said.

"I promise if I ever sell my soul again, I'm holding out for a higher price."

"That's my girl."

Chapter 46

Ten minutes later, we were in Trip's car with the top down, soaking up the April sunshine and racing toward Jennifer's home.

According to Google and MapQuest, she lived in Georgetown, not far from Trip.

We decided we might have more luck if we just showed up. And I'd talked Nick out of a half-dozen chocolate cupcakes, which I figured should buy at least enough goodwill to get us in the door.

I've always loved Georgetown. I can't afford it myself. But that's part of the charm.

As much as I disliked Jennifer, I had to admit her neighborhood was gorgeous. Brick row houses lined the street, as they probably had for over 250 years. Gas-style electric lights dotted the block. And shutters and doors were painted Colonial-inspired shades of slate gray, forest green, burgundy, and black.

In this end of town, if you had to ask what anything cost—as I frequently did—you definitely couldn't make the mortgage.

"I'm thinking Everett might have been paying her

rent," I said, as Trip pulled into a spot a block down from Jennifer's townhouse.

"Yeah, I'm guessing this is where he would have moved after he took over C&W and ditched Margaret."

"Man, talk about feathering your nest. If Margaret ever finds this place, she's gonna go bananas."

"You may want to mention that to Jennifer," Trip said, as he took the cake box out of my hands, and we started up the block. "She may swim with the sharks, but she doesn't appear to recognize the risks."

"First rule of business: show no fear."

"Not showing it is fine. Not feeling it is nuts."

Jennifer's row house had dark green shutters with a door to match. I could see my reflection in the gleaming brass knocker.

I rapped three times and stepped back.

Half a minute later we were still standing there.

"I hear music," Trip said. He cupped one hand and leaned into the door. "Coming from inside. Sounds like U2."

"OK, so she's a nasty human being with excellent taste in music." I banged the knocker three more times. Loudly.

Two minutes later, we were still standing there. But from what we could hear through the door, Bono and the boys had launched into "I Still Haven't Found What I'm Looking For."

I went back down the steps and stood on the sidewalk, studying the house. All the drapes were drawn. But there was an alley between Jennifer's townhouse and the one next door.

I whistled to Trip and jerked my head toward the alley. He nodded and followed.

As we cut around the corner between the buildings, I felt a chill down my spine. Spring weather, I told myself.

We rounded the corner. The gate was open, and Jennifer's brick patio looked like it had been hit by a freak storm. A little café table lay on its side, next to two broken clay flowerpots. Potting soil and yellow tulips were crushed into the brick.

The French doors were closed. The drapes were drawn. But I could still hear the music.

"I don't like the look of this," Trip said quietly.

"Gust of wind, maybe?"

"Have to be a pretty strong gust. My money's on a tempest of the two-legged variety."

"Jennifer just lost her boyfriend and her job. Plus she's pregnant. Could she have had a bit of a temper tantrum?"

"Yeah, keep selling, I'm still not buying. As your hired muscle and self-appointed bodyguard, I think we should turn around, head for the car, and forget I ever suggested this little picnic."

"We came all the way back here. I'm at least going to knock. If it makes you feel better, pull out your cell phone. Worse comes to worst, we scream our heads off and call the cops."

"Anyone ever tell you you're boneheaded stubborn?" he said, juggling the cake box in one hand and producing an iPhone in the other.

"OK, except for the slight Virginia accent, you ound like my mother."

"As long as I don't sound like *my* mother."

I knocked sharply on the door. "Jennifer, we're on the patio! And we brought cupcakes!"

I looked at Trip. He rolled his eyes.

"Hey, if somebody showed up at my door with cupcakes, I'd at least come to the peephole," I said.

"If Freddy Krueger showed up at your door with cupcakes, you'd knock him down rushing the box."

"I have a healthy relationship with food."

"You're a cupcake whore," he said.

"They have something from all the major food groups. They're nature's perfect food."

"I'm pretty sure that's eggs."

"Yeah, but cupcakes have eggs in them," I said.

"If Jennifer is home, she's probably calling the cops right now. 'Hello, police? There's a deranged woman on my patio threatening me with diabetes.' So can we get the bleep out of here already? This place is giving me a serious case of the creeps."

I rapped on the door again. "Candy-gram!"

I tried peeking through the curtains but couldn't see a thing. So I slipped my hand inside my jacket pocket and used it as a glove to press down the door lever. It gave.

"What did you do, Lucy?"

"Hey, Ethel, it's open."

"What's with the jacket trick?"

"No fingerprints. If she gets mad and calls the cops, there's no physical proof we let ourselves in. It's her word against ours."

"B&E 101? The things they teach in J-schools these days."

"If the door's unlocked, it's not breaking. Just entering."

"Thanks, Ruth Bader Ginsburg. I'll be sure to remember that when Bruiser asks what I'm in for."

I pushed the door open with my foot and called in, "Jennifer! Hey, Jennifer, it's Trip and Alex."

"Oh sure, do something semi-illegal and suddenly I get top billing," Trip hissed.

"Well, she likes you," I whispered back.

"We thought you might be hungry," I shouted, stepping across the threshold. "So we brought you a little something!"

In that moment, I knew.

The room was a wreck. And the smell. Metallic. Jennifer wasn't upstairs calling the cops. Jennifer wasn't going to be calling anyone ever again.

I forced myself to look across the room. And that's when I saw her. Almost hidden behind one sofa, her forearm covering her head. Her long brown hair matted with blood.

"Oh. My. God," I breathed. "Oh, God. Oh, God. Oh, Trip! Oh, God."

My knees felt like jelly. For a split second, I thought they were going to buckle. I took a giant step back. Right into Trip. He clamped an arm around my shoulder.

"Come on, honey. Let's get out of here. We can't help her now. We'll call the cops from the car."

"This isn't right. This is so wrong. They can't get away with this."

"They won't. But we have to leave. It's not safe here. Come on."

I didn't want to look. Yet it seemed wrong to look away—like I was ignoring someone in pain or need.

"Oh, God, give me a sec." I forced my eyes to sweep the room. The place had been savaged.

A glass coffee table was completely shattered. What had probably been a tall bookcase was now nothing but shards of glass and a toppled teak frame. Books and sharp pieces of colored glass and pottery were strewn across the room.

A set of low, sleek black leather sofas had been slashed end to end, leaving traces of blood on the leather and exposed stuffing. Meaning someone had killed first, then used the same weapon to brutalize the sofas.

Finally, I brought my eyes full circle to Jennifer. That's when I saw it. Next to her elbow.

My stomach dropped.

One delicate, silver earring. My earring. One of the pair that belonged in the box I'd found in Walters' desk.

I took a step toward her. Trip moved his arm to block me. "What the hell are you doing?"

"Trip, that's my earring."

He craned his neck and squinted. "Next to her arm? Oh, shit. This just gets better and better." Still balancing the cake box in his other hand, he dropped the phone into his jacket pocket and fished around.

"Here, at least use this," he said, proffering a starched linen handkerchief. "It's monogrammed. So try not to get blood on it."

"Like you're ever going to use it again."

"I'm going to burn it as soon as we get back to your house. But I don't want to be arrested for murder before I can destroy evidence. See? I went to J-school, too."

I stood as far from Jennifer as humanly possible, leaned over, grabbed the earring with Trip's handkerchief, and stuffed the whole wad into my jeans pocket. Then I crossed myself.

"OK, not to be selfish, but do you see anything else that could in any way be linked to me?"

"Hey," he said. "Do you smell that?"

"I'm honestly trying not to."

"Not that," he said. "The perfume. Do you smell perfume?"

"Oscar."

"Oscar," he confirmed. "Did Jennifer wear it, too?"

"Un-uh," I said. "Opium. It was her trademark."

"Then it's official, sweetheart. Someone is definitely trying to pin this one on you."

Chapter 47

In the next fifteen minutes, neither of us said five words.

Thanks to Trip's knowledge of the neighborhood, we were able to hoof it two blocks up and double-back to the car.

"Do you think anyone saw us?" I asked, once we were headed for the highway.

"I hope not. Knowing Sweetie, she'll put my arrest photo on her next Christmas card."

"What do you think the police are going to do when they find out I tampered with evidence?"

"Technically, the murderer tampered with evidence by planting your earring," he said. "You just tidied up for the CSI guys."

"If anybody saw us, I'm going to jail," I said.

"You? What about me? I brought cupcakes to a crime scene."

"Spill your guts to the cops. At worst, you'll just be an accessory."

"And you know what they say, 'accessories are everything.'"

"Thank you," I said.

"For what?"

"If I had to find a body with anyone, I'm glad it was you."

"I wonder if Hallmark makes a card for that?"

"God, I hope not." I popped open the bakery box and inhaled the scent of frosting.

Trip looked over. "You can't possibly be hungry."

"Aromatherapy. I've got to get that metallic smell out of my nose. Besides, at this rate, I may never eat again. Or wear Oscar. God, Trip, I just keep seeing her. We knew her. With Coleman, it was almost theoretical. I knew he'd been killed. But I never actually saw the body. But seeing Jennifer. Like that. Whoever did that was evil. Just pure evil. And it had to be Walters."

He nodded, grim. "With the earring and the perfume, that'd be my guess. The problem is, we have no proof."

"Thanks to me. The same evidence that implicated him also pointed to me. And I took it."

"You did what you had to do," he said. "At this point, we're playing defense. And admittedly not great defense. I think we're going to have to move you and that traveling circus you call a family out to the Farm until the cops lock up someone besides us."

"Something's bugging me," I said.

"The fact that we just found a body? Or that the murderer is your ex-boss? Or that he's framing you?"

"Besides all that."

"At this point, if we have bigger worries, I'm not sure I want to hear them."

"Ripping the place apart like that. The love nest? That doesn't feel like Walters. That feels like Margaret."

"Yeah," he agreed. "And I can see her Hulking out like that. What I can't see is her then dusting off her hands, spraying around a little perfume and tossing an earring over her shoulder on the way out the door."

"Maybe her meds finally kicked in," I ventured. "Or her booze ran out."

"I'm beginning to wonder if C&W is home to more than one homicidal maniac. What the hell are they putting in that coffee?"

"Vodka and fistfuls of money."

"We hit the house," Trip said. "Tell everybody what happened, grab toothbrushes and the beast, and we can be at the Farm in thirty minutes. Once we're there, you can call Holloman, and see what we do."

"Fine." I grabbed my purse and dug through it for my phone. I dialed Nick.

No answer.

Trip took the I-66 on-ramp. "Red, it's going to be OK," he shouted over the wind.

"She mentioned me," I hollered back.

"What?"

"On the recording," I yelled. "When Jennifer was trying to blackmail Walters. She said I was investigating C&W. That I was looking into things there. She was right, even if she didn't know it. And now she's dead."

Trip steered the Corvette into the far left-hand lane and pressed the gas pedal to the floor.

Chapter 48

Nick's car was there when we pulled into my driveway.

"Hey, no fair jumping out until I come to a full stop," Trip hollered.

"Just need to do a quick head count and make sure everyone's OK," I said, running for the door.

But the house was quiet. Everyone was gone. So were Nick's platters of cupcakes, cookies, and scones. All that was left in the kitchen was the lingering scent of baked goods, mingling with the smell of the goulash still simmering on the back of the stove.

I ran from room to room.

Nothing. No one.

My heart dropped to my stomach.

"Red! Come quick!"

I ran toward the bathroom and Trip's voice.

He was bending over something crumpled on the floor. A motionless, auburn lump.

Lucy.

"Oh, my God!" I said. "What happened!"

"I walked in, and she tried to stand up and just collapsed," he said. "Her breathing's labored."

I looked into her liquid brown eyes and saw pain.

Trip gently stroked her side. Lucy flinched. She let out a low whine, then went quiet and her eyes fluttered shut.

"We've got to get her to a vet. Now. Where the hell is everybody?" I scooped her up and ran for the car.

When I hit the porch, Nick, Gabby, and Baba were coming up the walk.

"Lucy's hurt," I said. "Bad. We've got to get her to the vet. I don't even know where her vet is."

"Lucy? Baby? How's my little baby?" Nick crooned.

Lucy stirred and licked his hand, but didn't open her eyes. She let out another soft moan.

"I know where it is," Nick said. "Eighth and Poplar. We took her there for her puppy shots last week."

"Will they be open now?" Trip asked.

Nick nodded. "They have an animal ER that's twenty-four hours."

"Good man," Trip said. "You take Lucy, and I'll drive. We'll see just how fast that car of mine can fly. Alex, you load everybody into Nick's car and meet us there. Eighth and Poplar. No stops." He gave me a meaningful look.

Nick took Lucy from my arms, talking to her the whole time. "Come on, baby. Come to Daddy. Open your eyes. Look at Daddy. Time to rise and shine, little girl."

Lucy let out another low moan. She opened her eyes. Then closed them again. Her breathing was ragged.

Nick carried her to the Corvette, cradling her lik a dozen eggs wrapped in dynamite.

A half-minute later, Trip gunned the engine and they were gone.

"We were just out of the house for a few minutes," Gabby said. "We had to carry the stuff over to Sir Ian's place for the party. Nick puppy-proofed the bathroom and put her in there so she wouldn't get into trouble."

I ran into the house and turned off the stove, ran back out, and locked the front door. Gabby and Baba were already in the car. I climbed in the passenger side, and we were off.

At the first red light, I glanced into the backseat at Baba. She was kneading her hands, mouth in a grim line.

I reached around and gave her a quick pat. She nodded but didn't smile.

"Look, there's no easy way to say this . . ." I started.

"Sugar, she's going to be fine," Gabby interrupted, never taking her eyes off the road. "We have to think positive."

"Not that. When Trip and I were out, we went to visit Jennifer Stiles." To Baba, I said, "She's a woman who used to work at my old P.R. firm."

"The glamorous one who was boin . . . uh . . . involved with your boss?" Gabby asked.

"That's the one. And they weren't just involved. She was pregnant. She tried to blackmail the other partner, Walters, for a piece of the company. She was also threatening to help the state and federal regulators. And she was promising to talk to me, too."

"That girl wouldn't last a week in Las Vegas," Gabby said, shaking her head.

"She's dead."

"Nooo-ooo."

"Unfortunately, yes. When Trip and I showed up, we found her. It was pretty awful."

I slid my eyes over to the rear-view mirror and saw Baba quickly cross herself.

"Anyway, we all have to get the heck out of Dodge for a couple of days, until they catch whoever it is. Trip's family owns a place in Manassas. He's going to put us up. It's remote, they have their own security, and no one will think to look for us there."

"You really think that's necessary? I mean, you weren't threatening anybody. Or sleeping with anybody."

"We have Jennifer on tape saying I was calling her, trying to get an interview. And she was promising to spill everything to me. Whoever killed her might have wanted to shut her up. But they probably don't know she never talked to me. Which means I'm in danger. Which means anyone around me is in danger, too."

"Is that what happened to Lucy? Did someone poison her?"

"She was in a closed bathroom inside a locked house, so I don't think so."

Please, God, I hope not.

When the three of us hustled into the vet's office, Trip was sitting in the waiting room alone.

"They're examining her and running a few tests," he said. "Nick is with her."

Baba planted herself in the chair closest to the front entrance and fixed her gaze on the doors that led to the exam areas.

Gabby sank into the chair next to Trip. "It's funny. But Lucy just took to Nick right off. The first time she saw him, she acted like he was some long-lost relative. Wriggled into his lap and stayed there. I mean, I found her in an alley and brought her home. But Nick? The love of her life."

I had noticed that. It was one of the reasons I loved that crazy dog so much. She adored him.

Twenty minutes later Nick came out to the waiting room. His face was dry, but his eyes were red, and his lashes were still clumped together.

"They palpated her gut. There's a blockage. She's getting weaker by the minute, so they don't want to wait. They're operating now. She's so small." His voice broke, and Gabby wrapped her arms around him. Baba materialized silently beside us. Trip reached out and took my hand.

For the next two hours, we all clustered together, like a living worry knot.

When the vet finally came through the swinging doors, I tried to read her face. Concern. Exhaustion.

We gathered protectively around Nick.

"She made it through the surgery. And we got all of the obstruction. But she's very weak. She's a mixed breed, and she was in excellent health prior to this, so that's on her side. But she's still a puppy. Tonight's going to be critical. I wish I had better news."

"What was it?" Nick asked. "The blockage?"

"A sock."

"A sock?" Trip repeated.

"An athletic sock," the vet said, nodding. "She ate it. Probably sometime in the last twenty-four hours. She managed to swallow it, but the bigger pieces got lodged in her stomach and small intestine."

"She'd been quiet most of the day," Nick said. "She was curled up under the kitchen table. I was so wrapped up in the damn baking, I just thought she was dozing and enjoying the smell of food."

"Until it became acute, there wouldn't have been any symptoms to notice," the vet said. "Her appetite may have been a little off, but that's about it."

"Everyone always feeds her behind my back. I didn't think anything of it."

The vet smiled. "So she's a little moocher, huh?"

Nick nodded.

"You're welcome to stay with her tonight. I've noticed it seems to help when they know their people are around. I'll be here throughout to keep an eye on her."

We all nodded. The pup was small, but she belonged to a large pack.

"Definitely," Nick said. "Is she awake? Can I see her?"

"I'll take you back now. She's still out, but she ought to be coming around in the next ten minutes or so."

Gabby gave him a hug, and Baba patted his back.

"Tell her we're all here," I said.

Nick smiled. "I'll tell her." He gave a little wave and disappeared behind the swinging doors.

"Looks like the Farm will have to wait a day," I whispered to Trip.

"The idea was to get you all out of the house, to some place a crazed psycho killer wouldn't find you," he said. "I'm betting an animal E.R. definitely qualifies."

Chapter 49

Nobody slept much that night.

I stretched out over two chairs and caught about an hour. Baba nodded off sitting up, only to jerk awake when her head almost hit her own shoulder.

Gabby found the coffeepot in the break room and kept it going all night. For sheer acid, it gave the cop shop a run for its money.

And we all took turns with Lucy.

I read to her from the children's books I found in the lobby. Nick told her about the fun they were going to have when she came home. Trip read her restaurant reviews from the paper—putting special emphasis on the meatier words, like "filet mignon" and "roasted pork." Baba spoke softly to her in Russian.

Through it all, the pup dozed.

And Gabby more than lived up to her name. She marched into the recovery room armed with an *Us* magazine from the back of Nick's car. When I walked in, she was going off-the-cuff about who was dating who in Hollywood.

"Run out of magazine?"

"Hell, that thing is two weeks old. Half those couples have split by now."

"You gotta keep the little dog current."

"Your brother named her, you know."

I shook my head.

"I was still calling her 'Puppy.' The first time he saw her, he started calling her 'Lucy.' I asked him why. He said, 'She's a crazy redhead, and she's into everything.' Then he did his silly Desi Arnaz voice, 'Heeey, Loo-cy?' She just went nuts and started licking his face."

I smiled and looked over at the sleeping russet form. Her little pink belly, shaved from the surgery, made her look even more vulnerable. I stroked her back.

Gabby lowered her voice. "The truth is, I love how much she loves him."

"I know," I said. "Me, too."

I opened my eyes and got up to stretch, just as Nick walked through the big double doors with a smile on his face. He looked around the waiting room at everybody sleeping in chairs and shook his head.

"You gotta see this," he whispered to me. "Come on."

We walked into the recovery room. Lucy was curled up in her little doggie bed. "Rowr. Rowr, rowr. Ruh-urowr!"

"She's awake!"

"She's awake. And the doc says she's doing great. If she keeps it up and the X-rays look good, we can take her home tonight."

"Oh my God, that's fantastic! You hear that, Lucy?" I said stroking her. "You get to come home!"

"And you'll get to wear one of those little satellite dish collars," Nick said in a high, happy voice. "Won't you? Won't you?"

"Rowr."

"Oh, poor little baby," I said. "She's probably starving. When can she start eating again?"

"She'll get some liquid stuff for breakfast. Later today, some solid food. If she passes the poop test, she can come home."

Suddenly it dawned on me. Lucy couldn't go home. None of us could.

I filled Nick in on what had happened to Jennifer, and Trip's plan to take us all to the Farm. Give Nick credit, after everything he'd been through, he didn't bat an eye.

"I don't want to take Lucy that far from her vet. If anything happens, we've got to be able to get back here, quick."

"It's in the middle of horse country," I said. "They've got to have some good vets. I'll talk to Trip and Dr. Scott."

"What are you going to tell her? That we're running from a slasher, or that we're running from the law?"

"I was going to say we're having work done at the house and have to stay with friends for a few days."

"Yeah, I'd go with that," he said, yawning.

"How much sleep did you get last night?" I asked.

"Pretty much none," he said. "Hey, did you know Baba can sleep with her eyes open? It's really freaky."

"Yeah, she gets it from you. You do the same thing when you're really tired."

"I do not."

"Ever since you were a kid," I said. "Between you and Baba catnapping in chairs, it looked like *The Walking Dead* out there. I'm telling you, that alone kept me awake."

"Oh, please," he said. "Little Miss I-Don't-Snore. Every time *you* nodded off, it was like being on a flight path to Reagan National."

"Ruff. Rrrr. Rowr. Phfft. Ha-ruff."

"See? She agrees with me," Nick said, ruffling the top of her head. "Hell, I don't care where we go as long as we have a vet nearby, and the pup can take it easy for a few days. And I can get some sleep."

"Just leave everything to Trip and me. The place is great. It's like a hotel. You'll love it. It'll be a mini-vacation."

"All the comforts of home without the crazed killers. Sounds good to me."

Chapter 50

If anyone had predicted I'd start blubbering over the sight of a dog pooping, I'd have thought they were nuts.

Honestly, I blame the sleep deprivation.

Ever the party dog, Lucy slept most of the morning. Later that afternoon, when she took a short walk across the backyard of the vet clinic, she had more eyes on her than Oprah at a red-carpet event.

Lucy being Lucy, she darted behind a flowering green bush to do her thing. Then she doubled back and put her nose to one of the white blooms.

That's when I lost it. Tears soaked my face, and I cried silently until my body shook. All the fear and tension of the past twenty-four hours flooded out.

Trip put his arm around my shoulders. "You're going to have to use your sleeve this time, Thelma. I'm fresh out of hankies."

I giggled and hiccuped. Then I took a couple of deep breaths. Out in the yard, Nick flashed a double thumbs-up to the crowd.

"Heard anything about Jennifer?" I asked Trip, once I'd regained control of my voice.

"Yeah, Billy Bob is really pissed off he was out of town for that one. But once he stopped swearing at me, he made a few calls. Seems the cops want to talk with one Mrs. Everett Coleman, but she's missing."

"Like Chaz?"

"Chaz is no longer missing," he said. "Chaz is staying at a five-star resort in West Virginia, courtesy of Billy Bob's company Amex card."

"Nice step up from a camping cabin. Is he talking?"

"According to Billy Bob, he's got diarrhea of the mouth. I think he's afraid if he stops spilling, Billy Bob will turn him over to the cops. Which is about right."

"Anything useful?"

"Remains to be seen," Trip said. "Right now, a lot of first-person stories and hearsay. Don't know how much of it is legit. We know he was feeding Mira a load of crap. But he claims your friend Walters is calling the shots."

"But the police want to talk to Margaret, not Walters."

"Yup. She's officially 'a person of interest.'"

"Cop-speak for 'suspect,'" I said. "So where is she?"

"Housekeeper says she's at a spa. When the cops tried to find out which spa, she claimed she didn't know and lapsed into German."

"Margaret's on the lam," I concluded.

"Sounds like. And Walters is playing it cool. Has one lawyer handling press calls, while another communicates with the cops."

"And?"

"They interviewed him," Trip said. "Briefly. Were

in and out of his office in fifteen minutes. Either they don't think he's involved or, more likely, they don't have enough evidence yet to sweat him on the murder."

"Because they don't know Jennifer was trying to blackmail him."

"It's your recording," he said. "What do you want to do?"

"Get everyone to the Farm. Talk to Holloman. Have him take me and the recording to the cops. After making a copy for Billy Bob, of course. God, it kills me that I have to hand this story off to someone else."

"So don't," Trip said. "Write a first-person, insider's account. If we don't buy it, sell it to the competition. Or *Washington* magazine. You're the one with the inside track. You actually knew these people. You worked there every day. You saw how the place operated. And you're the one who fought back. Bottom line: you get to choose. Not the cutthroats at C&W. Not the bigwigs at the paper. You."

"You really want to get me blubbering again, don't you?"

"Yeah, I figured I'd snap a blackmail shot with my cell phone," he said. "We can run it with your story."

"It would still be better than that one Mira used. Where did she get it?"

"Better question: where is Mira?"

"West Virginia? Jail? Disney World?"

"Don't know," Trip said. "She's also disappeared. The cops wanted to chat with her about some of the things she allegedly 'uncovered,'" he said, using giant air quotes. "First, she spouted the usual First Amendment defense. Then she vanished. Supposedly, nobody from her paper has heard from her. I say 'supposedly' because she could be chasing down leads. Or she could be shacked up somewhere with her billionaire wunderkind. Or maybe she really is gone."

"That's weird," I said. "As rabid as Mira is, it's not like her to disappear in the middle of a story. Could she be tracking Margaret?"

"Could be. But at the wake, she seemed more intent on nailing you. And after her column, she has a vested interest in proving you're the guilty party. Ethical and unbiased, she's not."

"Well, Chaz was missing, but we found him," I said.

"Temporarily," Trip said. "Billy Bob's threatening to disappear him again if I leave them alone much longer."

"Chaz has that effect on people. So Margaret and Mira are missing."

"And Jennifer's dead."

"And I can't go home."

"That pretty much sums it up," Trip said. "It might be a good time to start folding up the Big Top and get the circus wagons heading to the Farm."

"Have I said 'thank you' yet?"

"You don't have to thank me," he said. "You just have to help me keep Baba out of the kitchen."

Chapter 51

Later, I ducked into Lucy's recovery room. The pup was snoozing, and Nick was watching her small chest go up and down.

"Trip and I are gonna take the girls back to the house and pack a few things. Anything special you need?"

"Just grab my shaving kit, a pair of jeans, and a couple of T-shirts," Nick said. "I can hit a Walmart for anything else."

"Got it. Where's Gabby?"

"She needed to catch some shut-eye," he said. "She's taking a nap in the car."

When I got back to Nick's Hyundai, Baba was already strapped into the passenger seat and Gabby was dead asleep in the back. Apparently, I was driving.

"I'll follow in my car," Trip said. "Take it easy. Keep me in sight, and don't lose me."

"Yes, Mom."

You'd think it would be easy to keep track of a big, shiny red sports car. But by the time we were back in my neighborhood, Trip's Corvette was nowhere to be seen. I was hoping he'd somehow passed us.

Just as I rounded the corner to my street, Gabby popped up in the backseat.

"Oh, thank God," she drawled, looking pained. "Sugar, I gotta use your little girl's room. The sooner the better."

"Almost there. How many pots of that coffee did you drink?"

"I lost count. People kept drinking it, so I kept making it," she said, bouncing on the seat as I pulled into the driveway.

I sometimes got an odd prickling sensation down the back of my neck when the animal-instinct part of my brain was trying to tell me something. It was the same feeling I'd had right before Trip and I found Jennifer.

And I felt it now.

Everything around my house looked normal. But something was different. Off. And after a night with almost zero sleep, I couldn't even begin to guess what it was.

So I checked the rear-view mirror and threw the car into reverse. Still no Trip.

"Sugar, I don't mean to be pushy, but you're moving in the wrong direction. And I'm kind of desperate here."

"Slight change of plans. How'd you like to use a lovely Victorian powder room?"

"Is it close by?" she said, squirming in the seat.

"Virtually right across the street."

"Fine by me, honey. Right now I'd settle for a milk carton."

Cars lined half the street, and more were doubled

up in Ian's driveway. The garden party! We'd been so worried about Lucy, I'd totally forgotten about it.

I wasn't exactly dressed for a genteel tea. I was wearing the same T-shirt, jeans, and Windbreaker I'd inadvertently worn to a crime scene. And slept in.

But I also didn't want to go home right now. At least, not until Trip showed up and we could storm the place together. Or sneak over and secretly scope it out.

Where the hell was he?

Thanks to Gabby's purse, I was at least wearing makeup. And one of the vet techs had managed to find us brand-new toothbrushes. Mine was purple with a gold doggy bone embossed on the handle.

I figured if I could find a space on the curb near Ian's house, Trip might realize we were over there and not at my place.

Baba had nodded off on the drive home and was snoring softly in the passenger seat. In the back, Gabby had traded bouncing for rocking.

"Look, sugar, there!" she said, pointing frantically.

A parking spot—right smack in front of Ian's rambling home. Vacant only because it was also right smack in front of a fire hydrant.

"We'll get a ticket. Or Nick will."

"Honey, I'll come right back out and move it. I swear, I won't be long."

I gave up and angled the car into the spot. If the cops showed up, maybe they could escort me home and figure out what was going on at my place. And find Trip.

Where was he? And why wasn't he here already?

The second I was out of the car, Gabby threw the driver's seat forward and scrambled out.

I got back in and put a gentle hand on Baba's shoulder. "We're here."

She blinked and looked out the window. *"Schtow?"*

"Something's weird at my place. I don't know what, exactly. And Trip's not here yet. So we're going to wait at Ian's. Gabby's in there already, using the bathroom."

"Da, hadasho," she said, patting my knee. With that, she unbuckled the seatbelt, clutched her large black purse to her chest with both hands, and climbed out of the car.

Harkins answered the door, outfitted in a black suit, gray silk vest, and matching tie. With white gloves. His face lit up when he saw us.

"Good afternoon, ladies, and welcome!" he said, stepping back to open the door with a flourish. "Sir Ian will be so pleased that you've come. He will be with you presently. In the meantime, we have canapés and pastries on the back lawn, along with several varieties of tea and a bit of bubbly. Allow me to escort you." He dropped his voice to barely above a whisper. "I believe your brother's fiancée is indisposed but will join you shortly."

We must have been the last to arrive. While the house was virtually deserted inside, there was noise and music coming from the backyard. Harkins threw open the French doors to the patio.

The party was in full, noisy swing. The neighbors would have complained. But most of them were here already. A string quartet was set up just off the patio. Guests were milling about on the lawn, animatedly chatting, laughing, toasting, and eating. And it was quite the crowd.

If Ian wanted publicity, it looked like he was going to get it. I spotted two girls from the lifestyle section of my former paper, along with the main travel writer. And there was an equally strong contingent from the *Sentinel.* I prayed Mira Myles really was missing. If not, chances were she was here, too.

In the far corner of the yard, I spied Lydia Stewart. Decked out in a fuchsia sheath dress, heels, and a white fascinator with a huge pink flower, she'd gone for full-on Ascot regalia. I also recognized the two guys in suits next to her—one was a freshman congressman, the other a longtime state official.

I looked back at the closed patio doors behind me. The drapes were drawn. But the glass was so clean, I could see my reflection. I had to hand it to Ian, the place looked great.

That's when it hit me. Closed drapes.

When we'd dropped everything to run Lucy to the vet yesterday, it was a sunny Saturday afternoon. While the windows were locked, the plantation blinds in the living room had been open. And we'd left in such a rush that all I did was turn off the stove and lock the front door.

But when we'd pulled into the driveway a few minutes ago, the blinds were closed tight.

Someone was—or had been—in my house. And Trip was headed there now. I had to warn him.

I pulled out my phone. But it was dead. Again.

Guess that's what happens when you leave it on for two days straight.

"Baba, Trip still isn't here. I'm going to duck into

the kitchen and try to call him. Why don't you have a cup of tea and try some of Nick's goodies? Gabby should be out here in a minute, and we can reconnoiter."

She fixed me with a dubious expression—a cross between disbelief and alarm. I honestly didn't know what she was going to do next. But she gripped the straps of her big black purse and marched over to one of the tea tables. So far, so good.

With Baba safely surrounded by VIPs, and Gabby locked in the powder room, I needed to get to a phone and find out what was keeping Trip. And thanks to my tour of the house last week, I knew Ian had a landline in the kitchen.

Out of the corner of my eye, I thought I saw a familiar silhouette. And those beer-garden braids. I planted my feet and scanned the yard. Ian was nowhere in sight. Harkins was shuttling a silver tray of tea and cakes to the outdoor tables.

A night of no sleep and I was jumping at shadows.

I took a deep breath and turned to go inside. And saw her reflection looming in the glass.

Margaret.

"Well, hello, Alexandra. Not exactly dressed for a party, are we?"

She was clad in a shapeless black silk thing that, on anyone else, would have been dubbed a "little black dress." Not so little on Margaret. But, with the right accessories, it could take her from mourning visits to afternoon tea to poisoning her enemies over an elegant dinner. She was, literally, dressed to kill.

Drink in hand, she sauntered to the far side of the yard and joined a group of couples chatting amiably.

Numbly, I watched her, a thousand questions in my head. She looked over and gave me a friendly wave.

I felt an icy current down my spine.

My first instinct was to collect Baba and Gabby and run. But something told me we'd be safer here, in a crowd, than if we went off alone. I looked over and saw Baba on the opposite side of the yard. Harkins was pouring her a glass of champagne.

I took another deep breath. We were OK for now.

Still, I needed reinforcements. If Margaret really was a "person of interest" to the cops, I certainly didn't mind letting them know where she was.

Ian's kitchen looked like it belonged in a hotel. Or an old English castle. Everything was restaurant-sized and spotless. Trays of food and tea were laid out with hospital precision. And there wasn't a soul around.

But the phone was exactly where I remembered it: on the wall next to a large farm-style sink. I was praying that Trip was OK. And that he hadn't drained his phone like I had.

"You filthy little slut!"

Oh, shit.

Chapter 52

I whirled around and saw Margaret filling the doorway.

"You think you can steal my husband, destroy our lives, and go swanning around like nothing ever happened? You lured him away and ruined him with your dirty sex tricks! You're nothing but a common little street tramp!"

Her accessory of choice: the most chilling smile I'd ever seen. And the way her eyes glittered told me that she and reality had parted company a long time ago.

Then there was the knife. With a long serrated blade. She held it in her right hand almost absentmindedly. Making little jabbing motions to emphasize her points as she spoke.

I searched the counters for anything I could use as a weapon.

Nada.

Offering nothing more threatening than butter cookies, the food trays were too far away. With an advancing Margaret in between.

Unfortunately, the Victorians liked their servants the way they liked their children: seen but not heard. The kitchen was tucked away on the far end of a very empty house. With a loud party in full swing out in the yard, not to mention the live music off the patio, I could scream my head off and no one would ever hear me. At least, not in time.

I opted for my strong suit: running my mouth.

Fighting every instinct, I took a step forward. Toward her. If I kept calm and kept talking, I might be able to distract Margaret long enough to make a break for the door.

"There was never anything even remotely romantic between Everett and me. I never touched him. And I certainly never slept with him. I worked for the firm. He was my boss. That was it."

"You are such a little liar," she said, her dark little piggy eyes shimmering. When she pronounced the word "liar," her grin turned into a growl. "I *know* what you did. He *told* me what you did. Every. Filthy. Thing."

Jab, jab, jab, the knife punctuated as she approached.

"How you ambushed him, late one night at the office. How you pounced when he was tired. After he'd been drinking. How you plied him with more alcohol and worked your charms—your whore's tricks," she snarled, waving the knife like an extension of her big, beefy hand.

She was way too comfortable with that blade. Too practiced.

I remembered Jennifer. Was this the last thing she ever saw?

"He *tried* to break it off. He *promised* to break it off.

But, noooo. No, you just kept luring him back," she spat, pushing forward—body-blocking me. Effectively pinning me against the sink. "You cheap little skank."

I took a deep breath—my last?—and positioned myself nonchalantly against the sink. Body language: Two girls chatting. No biggie.

Behind my back, my hands groped around for something—anything—I could use to fight my way to the door. And there wasn't a blasted thing.

Damn that neat-freak Ian!

"Margaret, your husband was sleeping with Jennifer Stiles, not me," I said calmly, fighting to keep my voice even. "He lied to you. And he used me as a decoy. He manipulated both of us. He was never the least bit interested in me. And if he'd tried anything, I'd have sued him. And C&W. I couldn't stand the guy. I didn't even like working for him."

Man, was that ever true.

"Liar! All you little tramps know how to do is lie and throw yourselves at rich, powerful men. You're nothing. All of you! Worthless little whores!"

Uh-oh. Margaret's slow burn was morphing into a full-on inferno.

I faked left, dodged right, and grabbed the only loose object remotely near the sink: a bottle of dish soap.

She snatched my hair and yanked my head toward her.

I squeezed the soap bottle for all I was worth.

And the stream hit its mark.

"Aaarr-rrrrgggg," she roared.

But while she dropped the knife to wipe her eyes with one massive paw, she tightened the grip on my hair with the other—jerking my head from side to side like a rag doll.

"Help me! Somebody help me!" I screeched.

I kicked her solidly in the knee. She howled again, but hung onto my hair—and clocked my head against the counter. Hard.

Everything started to swim. I fought to stay conscious.

Dammit! No! She can't get away with this! She can't win!

I head-butted her in the gut, throwing all my weight behind the push, and let out a howl of my own. Because it hurt. A lot.

Suddenly, we were rolling around on the floor. I couldn't see the knife. But I could see she didn't have it.

I landed a strong punch on her nose. It spurted blood.

Margaret snarled, smiled, and grabbed another fistful of my hair.

She jerked it around and rolled on top of me, her huge hands around my throat.

Her big, round face looked like a Halloween pumpkin with tiny gleaming slits for eyes and that horrible slash of a grin. A jack o'lantern that reeked of scotch.

I clutched at her hands around my neck, struggling to pry loose a finger. If I could break just one, I could end the death grip on my throat. I bent one back, gave it a quick, hard jerk, and heard a crack. And a bellow of rage.

But instead of easing, the living vise seemed to tighten. And the smile deepened.

Pain made her stronger.

I kept pulling at the hands. At the same time, I kicked out, hoping to free one of my legs and get some leverage. But my torso was pinned under her weight, and my running shoes weren't getting any traction.

My head throbbed. I saw spots. Everything was fading.

No! No! No!

I struggled like a fish that didn't want to go into the boat.

Suddenly, the unholy pressure was gone. And I could breathe. Sweet, cool air.

I scrambled to my knees.

Margaret was laid out across the kitchen floor like a corpse. Baba was standing there in front of me— feet planted in a batter's stance, hands wrapped around a small cast-iron skillet. I'm guessing that's what she'd been toting in the big black purse.

"Oh my God," I gasped, rubbing my throat. "Oh my God. Baba, are you OK?"

"Da," she said, never taking her eyes off Margaret.

For her part, Margaret wasn't moving. I couldn't even tell if she was breathing. I reached up, grabbed a silver spoon off a tea service on the counter, and shoved it under her broken nose.

It fogged.

"She's alive," I rasped.

"I hit again," Baba said, raising the frying pan.

"No, no! We want her alive," I hissed. My throat was so strained, I couldn't get any volume. My words came out barely above a whisper. "She'll go to jail fo life. She's killed two people. Come on, we've got to call the cops."

My head was pounding. My arms and legs were limp. Even my hair hurt. But I was alive.

I wrapped my arms around Baba and hugged her. "Thank you for saving me," I croaked.

A tear slid down her cheek.

Just then Ian appeared in the doorway with a gaggle of guests. "And this is the kitchen, where all . . ."

In that split second, the group took in the whole grisly scene. Me, disheveled. Baba, gripping the frying pan. And Margaret passed out cold on the floor.

When my gaze met Ian's, I swear those blue eyes twinkled.

"Ladies and gentlemen, I'm afraid you've discovered our little secret. We are currently in rehearsals for our first murder mystery weekend, which will take place in just a few weeks. It will feature thrills, chills, and a ripping good mystery. Along with five unforgettable gourmet meals. All-inclusive, of course.

"Well," he said, looking at me knowingly, "we'll get out of your way, and leave you to it."

"Wow, the big lady is really good," I heard one woman say as they trooped out. "She didn't even flinch when we walked in."

"A total pro," Ian responded, lightly. "She'd never break character."

A few minutes later, Harkins appeared. "Ian thought you might be able to use some assistance," he said quietly.

"That's Margaret Coleman," I rasped, pointing. "She's killed two people and tried to strangle me just now. I'd be dead if Baba hadn't knocked her out with a frying pan."

Harkins bent down and put two fingers to the side of Margaret's neck, checking for a pulse. He nodded and stood.

"We had best summon the local constabulary," he pronounced, reaching for the phone.

Gabby came barreling through the kitchen door and skidded to a stop when she saw Margaret.

"Holy shit!"

"She tried to kill me," I wheezed. "Baba knocked her out. She's alive but unconscious. Harkins is calling the cops. And if anyone asks, this is a rehearsal for a murder mystery weekend this place is hosting in a couple of weeks."

Baba nodded.

"What's wrong with your voice?"

"Margaret was strangling me when Baba bopped her."

Baba crossed herself.

"Frying pan?" Gabby asked, looking Margaret up and down.

"Yup. Cast-iron."

"That'll do it," she said, nodding. "Should we bury it before the cops get here?"

I was hoping she meant the frying pan.

"It was self-defense," I said.

"OK, but if you change your mind, we can always stash it under the mulch in the yard."

Obviously, Margaret had no idea what she was getting into when she picked a fight with my family.

"You might want to tell them to send a second

Gabby said. "That gray guy from the cocktail party just arrived, too."

"Walters? Walters is here?"

Gabby nodded. "I saw him walk in when I was moving Nicky's car. And I swear it looked like he was coming from your place."

I needed to think. My head was clanging. And just like that, it hit me. I saw the game from Walters' side of the board. He and Margaret weren't working together. He was using Margaret as a weapon to get rid of his enemies. And blaming it on me.

But Margaret was on that enemy list herself. She had inherited Everett's half of the business and didn't want to sell. She was also the one who had betrayed Walters' father in the first place.

I was just a loose end.

So I'm guessing that when Margaret unleashed her rage this time, there weren't supposed to be any survivors. Margaret would kill me, or I would kill Margaret. Then Walters would step in and eliminate the winner. And make it look like we'd dispatched each other. Wife vs. "mistress" in a bloody battle to the death. Intrepid Margaret defending home and hearth against the amoral sexpot reporter.

Yeah, he could definitely sell that.

Walters was bloodless. I couldn't see him stabbing, strangling, or swinging any proverbial "blunt instruments." Remote and calculating, the man wasn't out to get his hands dirty. He'd distance himself.

But that final death—Margaret's or mine—had to like the result of our "heated confrontation."

one solution I could think of fit both scenarios.

And if Walters was here, it meant he was tying up loose ends.

Like me.

"Gabby, I need a really big favor."

"Sure thing, sugar. Just name it."

Chapter 53

Minutes later, Gabby was back in the kitchen. And making a face.

"Now what, sugar?"

"The cops are on their way," I said. "But we need to make sure Walters stays put. Got anything sharp in that purse of yours? A metal nail file? A pocketknife?"

"I have a switchblade. Will that do?"

"Uh, you carry a switchblade in your purse?" I asked.

"Sugar, you're the one asking for something sharp. Besides, a girl's got to be prepared."

"You're right. A switchblade would be perfect."

With Gabby's version of "feminine protection" in my jacket pocket, I walked out the front door and scanned the street for Walters' car. A sleek, silver Rolls-Royce Phantom.

No luck.

Chances were, he and Margaret had arrived at my place well before the party. Before it looked like a new car dealer had taken over the block. And Walters have needed to park somewhere convenient, but not too obvious. Which probably meant down the block from my house or on a nearby side street.

I headed down the sidewalk and crossed the street to my house. The plantation shutters were still closed tight. So just how long had they been camped out in there? A few minutes? Or did I need to start charging them rent, too?

I got to the end of my block and looked both ways. And spotted a likely contender.

I strolled around the corner to the front of the car. Bingo. A Rolls-Royce Phantom. In silver.

From the back, I wouldn't have recognized it. But from the front, the grille and hood ornament were unmistakable. Plus there was the powder blue parking sticker from the "executive" section of the lot at work. Offering valet service, detailing, and reserved parking for a hefty premium, it was the only place Coleman or Walters ever put their pricey wheels.

I popped open the blade and slashed Walters' front left tire. It made a "whoosh." Then I sliced the back one, walked around the car, and cut the other two. The Rolls looked like it was sinking into the street.

Carefully, I closed the blade, shoved it in my pocket, and jogged back toward my house.

My head started hammering and I slowed to a walk. If I ever got out of this alive, I was due for some serious R&R. And maybe a brain scan.

As I passed my house, it was all I could do not to head for the front door. I could smell the pine stra from the sidewalk. The red tulips along my walkw were budding. I glanced wistfully at my cozy li bungalow.

Would I ever be able to just go home?

As I crossed the street to Ian's, Baba and Gabby were waiting on the curb.

"Is Walters still here?" I asked, relieved I was getting some volume back—even if I didn't sound like myself.

"Yup," Gabby said. "The police are on the way. And the missus is still passed out in the kitchen. Hasn't budged."

Baba quickly crossed herself again.

"Did you find his car, sugar?"

"Yeah, on the next side street up from my house. If he tries to make a quick getaway, he's got four flat tires."

I gingerly handed Gabby her switchblade.

"Honey, he's going to know it was you," she said, dropping it into her pink leather tote.

"That's the plan. I want him to know he's trapped, and I want him to know it was me. We've taken away his means of escape. The cops are coming. And I'm betting his and Margaret's fingerprints are all over my place. Plus, they probably broke a window or a door to get in. Let him try to explain that one."

Gabby grinned and shook her head. Baba smiled.

"Can you guys stay here and flag down the cops? I'm going to check on Walters and Margaret."

"You got it, sugar."

Baba wrinkled her brow.

"I'll be fine. I just want to make sure everyone is ere they should be."

he looked doubtful.

promise."

ba squinted and gave me a stoic look. It was as

close as I was going to get to assent. I took it and ran. Metaphorically speaking.

Gabby wasn't kidding about Margaret. When I got back to the kitchen, she was exactly where we'd left her. But I could see her chest going up and down. So, hopefully she'd be nice and well-rested for jail.

"Well, Miss Vlodnachek, I must say you're looking remarkably chipper."

Walters.

If I lived long enough, I was definitely hanging a bell on that kitchen door.

"Wow, I didn't know you cared," I said, turning. "You really should have seen me ten minutes ago, after my tussle with Margaret. I looked like hell and felt worse."

"Yes," he said, pursing his lips, and barely glancing at the large form on the floor. "She does seem to be falling down on the job lately. And she had been so effective."

"You might want to tell her that alcohol isn't a food group."

He shook his head. "I'm afraid we've reached an impasse."

"So just how long were you two camped out at my house? "

Walters started. "You couldn't possibly . . ."

"Next time you try to ambush someone, don't close their blinds."

He paled.

Then we heard sirens. It sounded like the boys in blue had rounded the corner and were tearing u the street. And if the noise was any indication, they brought plenty of company.

"Window or doorframe?" I asked.

"Excuse me?"

"How did you get into my house?" I asked convivially. "Window? Or doorframe?"

He smiled. "Well, that doesn't really matter now, does it?" With a steely look, he reached into his coat pocket dramatically.

Suddenly, his expression changed. He fumbled around and produced a silver object. Confusion and panic spread across his face like a rash.

"That's the lid to a butter dish," I said helpfully. "My future sister-in-law swapped it for your gun about ten minutes ago. Right before I slashed all four tires on that pretty silver Rolls you parked around the block from my house."

Chapter 54

I spent the next half hour in Ian's "solarium," repeating my statement to a string of cops and detectives.

Billy Bob had called it. The detectives already had a pretty good idea who was behind Everett's murder. And Jennifer's.

Margaret, Walters, and the coven at C&W may have been holding me out as a suspect, but to the cops I was nothing but a red herring.

When I finally joined Baba and Gabby out front, I noticed that Ian's garden party had dissolved. But a few neighborhood stalwarts were holding court on the lawn, drinks in hand, enjoying the show.

And Lydia Stewart was giving me the evil eye.

Behind me, Harkins cleared his throat. I didn't even know he'd been standing there.

"I shall now return to the house, Miss," he said, with a little bow. "Thank you all for a very *lively* afternoon."

I put an arm around Baba's shoulders, and the three of us—Gabby, Baba, and I—strolled down the lawn and jaywalked across the street to my yard.

The reporters had dropped all pretense and were pointing cell phone cameras at the back of the squad car, shouting questions, and trying to get shots of Walters, as he slouched down in the seat.

I heard more sirens. Lots of them. Thirty seconds later, two cop cars and an ambulance came to a screeching halt in the middle of the street halfway between my house and Ian's.

And a shiny red Corvette jumped the curb and fishtailed into my driveway.

Trip leapt out looking stressed and totally disheveled. "Are you OK? Is everybody OK? I got here as fast as I could. What the devil's going on?"

"Everybody's fine," I said, in my new Lauren Bacall voice. "Walters is handcuffed in the back of that police cruiser, getting his fifteen minutes of fame. And Margaret's off to the hospital." I waved at the two EMTs pouring a limp, languid Mrs. Coleman into the back of an ambulance.

I'd been in the kitchen when they first tried to get her onto the gurney. She bit, kicked, and hit anyone who got close. I'd left as one of the EMTs was loading a very large needle.

In her natural habitat, they'd have had to use a tranquilizer gun.

Trip took it all in—glancing at Walters, then Margaret, over to Baba and Gabby, and back at me. "I had a front-row seat to a multi-car fender-bender, and the cops pulled me over as a witness. What happened?"

Baba took his arm and patted him on the back reassuringly. "*Nichevo, nichevo.* Is good. Is all good."

I kissed Trip on the cheek. "We caught the bad guys. And I've got my life back."

Chapter 55

Crime scene or not, it was great to be home.

After the police let us back into my house, Trip returned to the vet clinic to wait for Nick and Lucy, while Baba settled in for a well-earned nap.

Gabby was strangely quiet. I thought it might have had something to do with the squadron of police officers who'd commandeered the block.

Turns out I was wrong. Again.

"Sugar, I don't know how to say this, but I'm going home," she started.

"We are home," I said. "Finally." For a while there, I didn't think it was ever going to happen.

Gabby looked almost sad. Or as sad as I'd ever seen her. "Not here, sugar. *My* home. In Vegas. With Rick." She plopped down on the sofa.

I thought I must have heard her wrong. "Rick? Who's Rick?"

"He's kind of my boyfriend."

"Kind of?"

"We'd been together for three years," Gabby said.

"I thought he was the love of my life. But he's married to his job."

I sat down next to her. "What's he do?" I asked, expecting her to say he was a doctor or an engineer. Or a mobster.

"He's a professional wrestler."

"Wrestler?"

"His professional name is 'Rodeo Rick Steed,'" she said proudly. "But that's just his stage name. His real name is Richard Stumpelfig."

"Yeah, I'd stick with 'Rick Steed.'"

"It's a really competitive field," Gabby said. "Once he was picked up for the pro circuit, that was all he ever thought about. Every minute of the day. If he wasn't at the gym, or the tanning booth, or rehearsals, or doing promotions, he was working. I felt like he was taking me for granted. But in the last few weeks we've been talking. Really talking. About us. About our future."

That explained the marathon phone sessions in the bathroom.

Gabby dug into the very bottom of the giant pink purse and produced a worn paperback. Some kind of self-help tome. From between its pages, she slipped out a picture.

Mr. Photo Strip.

Only in this one, he was dressed as a cowboy. Or a male stripper's idea of a cowboy. He wore aviator frames, tight jeans, cowboy boots, and a lasso strapped to one slim hip. A brown suede vest didn't do much to hide what looked like about six and a half feet of tanned, rippling muscles. His jaw reminded me of a granite boulder dusted with a five o'clock shadow.

Gabby touched the photo like a talisman and grinned.

I knew the answer before I even asked the question. "Are you sure?"

She nodded her glossy blond hair. A thin line of black roots told me it was probably her own. "I was crazy about Nicky. But Rick—he's my true love. My soul mate. I want to be with him. I want to have his babies."

I tried to picture their offspring. All I got was a vision of little bleached-blond, aviators-sporting tots with deep spray-tans running around with lassos.

This is going to kill Nick.

Weirdly, I was going to miss her, too. I had plenty of honest, trustworthy friends who'd totally ghosted during my recent travails. But Gabby had been right there, helping out, every dreadful step of the way. With a smile on her face and a bouncy attitude to match. My never-quite-in-law, sometimes outlaw houseguest might have been a thief and a bit of a grifter, but she had a big heart.

She really was the most likable girl Nick ever dated. If I'd had to share a house for two weeks with the surly Avril Lavigne fanatic, one of us would have "disappeared."

Coin flip as to which one.

"I've already got my plane ticket," she said. "And I've called a cab. If I pack my stuff into a couple of cartons, can you just drop them off at the shipping store?"

After everything we'd been through together, how could I refuse? Although it was a toss-up whose name I'd sign when I delivered those boxes.

I sighed. "If you change your mind, or you ever need anything, you call me."

"You got it, sister girl," Gabby said, hugging me.

"What do I tell you-know-who?"

"I'll stop by the vet's before I blow town," she said. "He already kind of knows. Both of us suspected this was just temporary. He's a great guy. And if it wasn't for him, Rick and I wouldn't have finally come to our senses. Nicky's going to find someone, and she's going to be sensational. He deserves that."

"He does."

"And you, keep your eye on that English stud muffin. He's cute. And he's hot for you. Trust me, I know hot."

Turns out she might have been right about that, too.

Chapter 56

After Gabby left for the airport—and while Baba was still napping—I dialed Annie's cell. I wanted to share the good news that my long ordeal was finally over. Though hers, I suspected, was still ongoing.

Annie answered on the first ring. "Elia's gorgeous. I've already signed her."

"That's fantastic!"

"Hey, I'm the one who's impressed. You've got a good eye for talent. I may just have to put you on the payroll."

"No objections here. By the way, I wanted to let you know that that other little situation's been resolved."

"Is that Alexandra?" Mom called from the background. "Tell her London does smell much better than Venice."

"Glad to hear it," Annie said to me, pausing. "Is everything, um, the way you want it?"

At this point, she might as well have been speaking in Morse code. Or pig Latin.

"Total vindication. Cleared my name, and the real killers are cooling their heels in jail. Pending their very public trials."

"Aces!"

"But the crowds are hell," Mom continued in the distance. "And the prices? Nothing short of highway robbery."

"Mom sends her love," Annie said.

"So I hear. Better you than me."

"Don't laugh," my sister said, dropping her voice. "As soon as she clears customs next week, she's your problem."

A few minutes after I hung up, there was a firm knock on the door.

I flinched. At this point, it was a reflex. And sheer exhaustion.

Trip and Nick were still at the vet's with Lucy. And Baba was making up for lost sleep.

I checked the peephole. Ian.

After crashing his sedate Victorian garden party with cops, criminals, sirens, bodies, EMTs, and gurneys, I figured we'd go back to polite-neighbors-from-a-safe-distance status.

So what was he doing on my front porch?

I took a deep breath and opened the door.

"Hullo again," he said cheerily. And that's when I noticed he was hefting a big, stainless-steel Dutch oven. And Harkins was coming up the walkway bearing a large casserole dish.

"Thought you might not be up to cooking tonight," Ian said. "So we whipped up a little something to feed the army. Beef bourguignon with some nice Duchess potatoes. All you have to do is heat and serve."

My three favorite words. And it smelled delicious. Rich and meaty. I was also pretty sure it didn't have peanut butter in it. Or liquified noodles.

"Ian, I just want to apologize," I stammered. "About this afternoon . . ."

"No need. You caught the villains. Everyone survived. And it certainly didn't hurt the B&B. Five groups want to book afternoon tea. And we're already sold out for our first murder mystery weekend."

"You're kidding."

He grinned. As he handed off the pot, our fingers brushed, and I felt that strange, happy tingling in my stomach.

"But if you're still feeling slightly guilty," he added, leaning in and lowering his voice. "I may ask for your help with plotting the mystery. That body in the kitchen was a nice touch."

Chapter 57

Over the next week, I called, visited, and pestered every source I had, piecing together the last details of Coleman's murder. The real story. Not the Mira Myles melodrama.

I even played the guilt card with a couple of the cops who'd used me as a red herring.

It was surprisingly effective.

And I had to hand it to Walters. His plan was elegant, brilliant, and totally Machiavellian. Thank God it failed anyway.

Something "seemed off" from the beginning, according to one of the detectives. Especially after they learned about the audit and the missing money. Once they started pumping Billy Bob for information on me (big surprise: leaks go both ways), they realized that the stories they were getting from C&W were just that. Although they didn't mind using that fiction for cover.

I should have been angry. But I was just relieved.

The sky looked bluer. The sun felt warmer. Even Baba's goulash tasted better.

Though that could have been because I finally cleared the lime cleaner out of my sinuses.

I took Trip's advice and sold my story—a first-person account of the implosion of Coleman & Walters—to *The Washington Tribune,* my former newspaper. They're planning to run it as a three-part series under the headline: "When Good Companies Go Bad."

It's not an insider exposé of the P.R. industry. But it is a pretty good snapshot of what happens when one company and its executives go totally off the rails.

I even managed to snag a decent price: five thousand dollars.

That only took two solid days of negotiating and a "special dispensation" from the managing editor. "But don't tell anyone, because we can't do this again," he pronounced confidentially.

I felt like saying the same thing when he offered me my old job back. At my old salary. I suspect he just wanted to get my exclusive without having to pay extra for it.

Trip showed up at the house that evening with a bottle of champagne.

"Damn, this is the good stuff!" I said, hefting the bottle as he rummaged through the cupboards.

"Yup," he said, pulling out a jelly jar and a couple of wineglasses. "Uh, do you have any champagne flutes?"

"Sure, left over from the last time I hosted a reception for the Queen."

"What about New Year's Eve?"

"Plastic from the party store."

"Just like the champagne you served," he said. "As I recall, it tasted more like shampoo."

"Hey, I splurged twenty-five bucks. I wanted to have really good luck this year."

"Clearly that worked."

"So how much was this stuff?" I said, studying the French label as he set two wineglasses on the counter.

"It's not what you spend, it's what you get for the money," he said, grabbing a tea towel in one hand and carefully taking the bottle with the other.

"You stole it from Tom, didn't you?"

"Right out from under his very nose," Trip said, popping the cork. "After he recommended the brand and vintage, of course. I told him we were going to toast to your freelance success."

I was truly moved. Especially since Trip had been lobbying hard for me to rejoin the paper.

And I'd been seriously tempted. Even with the puny salary. But I decided to keep freelancing for a while. No paid health insurance. No paid vacation. No regular income.

Also no meetings, no bosses, and no corporate intrigue.

For once, I was setting my own schedule and calling my own shots. It was scary, but I liked it.

"To fame and fortune," Trip said, lifting one glass and handing me the other.

"To staying out of jail and making the mortgage," I countered, and we clinked.

"Oooooh, this stuff is seriously good," I said.

"That it is. Although you can't use the leftovers for paint stripper, like you did with your last bottle."

"I didn't use it to strip paint. I used it to wash windows. Besides, I don't think there's going to be any left over."

"Got that right."

"Let's take this party outside. I'll snag a practice batch of Nick's chocolate chip cookies."

"Best offer I've had all day," Trip said. "Speaking of which, where's the rest of the Vlodnachek clan?"

"PetSmart. Nick needed a few things for Lucy, and Baba's riding shotgun."

"Not literally, I hope."

"All the cast-iron pans are present and accounted for," I said. "But she did mention something about wanting to make sure the dog treats are 'best quality.' Her words."

On the front porch, we sipped in silence for a few minutes, savoring the warm spring evening. There was a gentle breeze, and I could smell ozone. Rain was coming.

"I still can't believe Jennifer faked a pregnancy," Trip said, refilling both our glasses.

"I don't think it started out that way. I heard her in the office bathroom right after Coleman died. She really did believe she was pregnant. And Coleman's death left her in the lurch. So she devised her own plan. Then, when she found out it was a false alarm, she decided to bluff."

"She underestimated Walters," he said quietly.

"They both did."

"Fortunately for us, his strategy was upended by a puppy and a sock," Trip said.

"And Margaret. Walters tried to contain her here. She was supposed to stay put until I arrived home. But when she saw me going to Ian's party she had to follow. And Walters couldn't stop her. But give the man credit, he devised a detailed plan. You know the cops discovered that while they were camped out here, Walters even called Margaret's house a couple of times from my landline. To bolster his story that I 'lured' her to my home."

"You've got to be the only person I know under forty who still has a landline."

"It's classic tech," I said.

"It's one step above two tin cans and a string," he said.

"It's the centerpiece of my new home office. Which is mere steps from Nick's new home business. You'll never guess what he's calling it."

"House of Carbs?"

"Baba's Bakery."

"No!" Trip said.

"Yup."

"Your Baba doesn't bake," he said. "She doesn't even cook. Not well, anyway."

"And no one ever has to discover that. Nick even wants to use her face on the marketing."

"He's got marketing?"

"OK, he's *talking* about using her face on the marketing," I admitted.

"And she's all right with that?"

"Thrilled. Literally can't stop smiling."

"To new beginnings," Trip said, clinking my glass.

Chapter 58

The Sunday that part one of my series ran, Baba hit the kitchen at dawn. And for once, it was cause for celebration.

Because she was making the one thing she really could cook: potato pancakes.

She spent hours grating potatoes and onions by hand. No food processor for her. According to Baba, if you didn't risk your knuckles, they weren't real potato pancakes.

I tried to help on several occasions. It always ended the same way: a pile of wasted potatoes for her, and half a box of Band-Aids for me. So now I mostly just kept her company.

As a result, I've picked up a few things. About her, about our family, about life. Like the time Baba admitted she cried when she first saw the Statue of Liberty. But not for the reasons you'd think.

Baba was twelve when she traveled to this country alone. She never talked about what came before.

She'd been ill for most of the voyage, so she was on the deck when they entered New York Harbor. She had no idea where she was going or even if they'd let her off the ship. She was sick, exhausted, and terrified she'd be sent back.

Then she saw The Lady.

A crew member had loaned Baba his binoculars. What astonished her was the face: Lady Liberty looked just like her mother.

At that moment, a lost child knew she was home. That everything would be all right. And that her own mother was still watching over her.

The chance to hear that story? Worth a few scraped fingers.

Our breakfast was one for the books. Nick scrambled some eggs, and we gorged until we were ready to pop. I was relieved to see that he finally had an appetite—for the first time since Gabby had left.

Baba even made an onion-free batch of potato pancakes for Lucy. Still navigating the satellite-dish collar after her surgery, the pup was so excited running for her bowl, she clipped the doorway and went spinning across the kitchen like a car on ice.

"It's official, she's definitely a Vlodnachek," Nick said, ruffling the fur on her back, as she buried her face in her dish.

"Yeah, but I think she inherited your table manners," I said.

"She knows a good thing when she sees it," Nick said.

Baba beamed.

After breakfast, she wiped down the stove from top to bottom, went into the bedroom, and reappeared in her traveling clothes.

"Are you sure?" I asked, hoping she'd reconsider.

"*Da*. Is time. Must pay bills. Clean house."

Nick, Lucy, and I drove her back to Baltimore. When we got back, the house was quiet and empty. Hollow.

Nick leashed up Lucy for a long walk, and I settled in to put the finishing touches on my bridal story.

With the editor's blessing, I was writing it as a humorous look at the "bridal industrial complex" from a non-bride's point of view. It turned out great, and I was really psyched.

Shortly after Nick left, I saw the message light blinking on my landline. Two missed calls.

Trip can knock my old-school phone all he likes. It doesn't need juice, and works no matter what the weather. Thanks to a couple of batteries, I even have caller ID.

Which came in handy when every bill collector in town was calling.

I hit "speaker" and pressed "1." My mother's voice filled the room.

"A murder suspect? And fired? And you didn't think to tell me? Your own mother? I had to find out from some week-old newspaper on the plane. A newspaper! I'll be at baggage claim at Dulles in two hours. You can tell me all about it then. Starting with why you felt the need to keep this from me, when clearly the rest of the world knows all about it. Was your sister in on this too? Did she know the whole time? Anastasia Vlodnachek, I have a bone to pick with you . . ." Then—mercifully—a dial tone.

I checked my watch. I still had ninety minutes to get to the airport. Or maybe Florida.

The second message clicked on. Annie's voice. "Alex, it's me. I'm calling you from the airplane bathroom.

We just landed in New York. Just a heads-up: She knows. Repeat: The feline has exited the sack. I kept her in the dark as long as I could. And let me tell you, it wasn't easy. That woman has the attention span of a mosquito. Whenever we had a couple of minutes' downtime, she wanted to check email or read online news sites. So I had to keep her entertained. Constantly. I feel like I haven't stopped moving for three weeks straight. There isn't a gallery, museum, cathedral, or coffee shop in London, Paris, Venice, or Rome that I haven't been in at least once this trip. That's probably why I fell asleep on the flight home. Big mistake. Somehow she got her hands on a local paper. And she is royally pissed. Anyway, the good news is you don't have to face her alone. I've juggled my schedule so I can spend a couple of days in D.C. I booked into this darling little B&B. It's right in your neighborhood. Fun! We'll be at baggage claim in two hours. See you then!"

My stomach clenched. It felt like I'd swallowed a fistful of pebbles.

Not only was Mom going to read me the riot act, but once Ian saw Annie, he'd forget I even existed. No more lighthearted flirting. No more pop-in visits. Or gifts of flowers and food.

On the bright side, no more scones. Which made me wonder: How big an engagement rock would he buy her?

Just as the message finished, my cell rang. I held my breath and checked caller ID. Trip.

"Quick, turn on Channel 2," he said.

"Hello to you, too."

"Channel 2, Channel 2," Trip chanted.

I hit the remote and was treated to a vibrating, bird's-eye view of an upmarket shopping center. Cookie-cutter familiar, it could have been anywhere in the continental U.S.

"What am I looking at?"

"High-end home store in Arlington—someplace called Inside & Out," Trip said. "From Chopper 2. The SWAT team's on its way."

"The SWAT team?"

"Yeah," he said. "Apparently, some bride went bat-shit. Walked into the china section and started pulling plates off the shelves and smashing them, screaming something about shattered dreams. By the time they realized she was just getting warmed up, she'd taken out a couple racks of stemware, too. When the store manager tried to grab her, she waved a broken brandy decanter and told him to—and I quote—'back the hell off.' That's when he evacuated the store and called the cops.

"Billy Bob's on his way over there, and the photog's already in place. If he gets the shot, that's tomorrow's metro front. Maybe even the front page."

"The front page?"

"Slow news day," he said. "P.S. Your story is getting some good play. The wire services picked it up."

"Woo-hoo! Makes me double-glad I held out for a living wage."

We both went quiet as the video switched to a stand-up shot in the parking lot. A local reporter announced that the police department's crisis nego-tiator and S.W.A.T. team had both arrived on the scene, and that the negotiator was going in.

"Hate to be that guy," Trip said.

"Or the ex."

"Know when to hold 'em, know when to fold 'em," he said. "If the groom is smart, he'll blow town for a while."

For five long minutes, the news crew rehashed what they knew and mused on what they didn't. Short version: The groom dumped the bride and hopped a flight to Europe.

"See, I told you," Trip said. "A smart man leaves town."

"Shshsh!"

"Kimberly, did police say why the belligerent bride selected this particular store?" a puffy, middle-aged anchor asked the sleek, twentysomething blonde at the scene.

"Well, Mark, apparently this was one of several stores where she and her intended were supposed to register for wedding gifts. But then her groom had other ideas."

"Sounds like the makings of a bad break-up, Kimberly," the anchor said, chuckling.

"That it does, Mark," Kimberly responded with a blinding smile. "They say breaking up is hard to do. But this bride is taking it to a whole new level."

"And what about the price tag?" the anchor inquired. "Any estimates on the damage, so far?"

"Well, clearly they won't have an exact figure until . . ."

"Behind you, Kimberly! It looks like something's happening!"

Suddenly, the camera zoomed in on the store's front door. A cop marched out with a petite brunette in gray sweats, hands cuffed behind her back. Her hair was disheveled, and she kept her chin down. When she finally looked up, she fixed the TV cameraman with a look of such raw fury that I'm surprised the camera didn't burst into flames. Even the news photographers took a collective step back. And I'd have recognized those bangs anywhere.

"Mira Myles!" Trip and I said in unison.

"Couldn't have happened to a nicer girl," Trip said. "I guess Denny Stafford finally came to his senses."

Denny. *Dennis?*

Mira Myles. *Mimi?*

Hopped a flight to Europe. *To study art in Florence? Well, what do you know?*

"Hey Trip," I said, bouncing on the sofa. "Have I got a story for you."

ACKNOWLEDGMENTS

A very grateful shout-out to several people without whom this book would not be in your hands (or on your reader) right now: Erin Niumata, of Folio Literary Management, is a champion—one agent in a million. Her guidance and advice on shaping the story was pivotal. Alicia Condon, at Kensington Publishing, is the best editor (and audience) a writer could want. And artist Michelle Grant created a wonderful cover that invites readers to pick up the book.

A very big thank-you to all!

Read on for a sneak preview of

Seeing Red

the next Alex Vlodnachek adventure.

Alex and her crazy family are in more
hot water, as they tangle with spies
art thieves, nasty business rivals—and a baby.
When the same health inspector who
shuttered Nick's bakery turns up dead
in the B&B's basement and a "reproduction"
of a missing Renoir appears in its library,
Alex and Nick begin to suspect that Ian Sterling
is much more than a simple hotel owner . . .

It all started when I walked into the kitchen and found the baby.

Just after sunrise and still bleary-eyed, I made straight for the stainless-steel coffeepot that lives on the counter near the sink. I'd been up 'til two finishing a freelance story that was due this morning. And in a few hours, I was off to meet another editor about a temporary gig that would (hopefully) pay the bills for the next six weeks. I was drained but happy.

That's when I saw it. Resting on the kitchen table. Ensconced in one of those plastic car-seat things, like a mollusk in its shell. I flipped on the kitchen light, blinked hard, and looked again.

Still there.

"Holy crap!"

The butcher-block counter was solid. I touched the coffeepot, which was cold. I smelled chocolate and butter—the scent of freshly baked chocolate chip cookies. And I was surrounded by stainless-steel cooling racks holding dozens of the cookies my younger brother, Nick, had spent most of the night baking for a client. So this wasn't another weird stress-dream.

I grabbed a cookie, then cautiously took a step closer. The downy blue blanket tucked around it—him?—moved rhythmically, rapidly, up and down. Between the blanket and his white knit cap, only the circle of a little pink face was exposed, along with two small, balled-up fists resting near his chin. Like a miniature pugilist. His eyes were closed tight.

I scanned the table. No note. No clues. Nada.

I looked under the table: nothing but Lucy's water dish.

Nearby, the kitchen door was locked and double-bolted.

I walked into the living room eating the cookie as I went. The front door was also locked and double-bolted.

I padded to Nick's door and knocked.

Silence.

I knocked harder.

"Go away!"

"You left something on the kitchen table."

"Yeah, cookies. Go away!"

I could hear the click of Lucy's nails on the hard-wood floors. Then rustling near the door. "Rowr? Rowwwrrr! Rowr!"

"I meant the other thing," I called through the door. "The baby."

"Gotta sleep! Go away!"

"Rowr! Rowr!" Lucy chimed in, scratching at the door.

"Nick, this is an emergency!" I yelled, pounding on the door. "Get up! Now!"

"Is the house on fire?"

"Yes!"

Two minutes later, the three of us—Nick, Lucy, and I—stood in the kitchen eyeing our little intruder.

"So you really didn't put him there?" I asked quietly.

"Un-uh," he said, smoothing down a bad case of blond bed-head with his left hand. "I mean, the cookies are mine, but that's it."

Reflexively, I brushed the telltale crumbs off my pink bathrobe. "The doors are all locked and bolted from the inside. I checked."

"Anybody else have a key?" he asked.

Nick was living with me temporarily. After a sudden career change and relocation from Arizona by way of Vegas. Followed by an even more sudden engagement that had recently crashed and burned.

That was about the same time I'd launched my new freelance career. Which sounded a lot better on LinkedIn than saying I'd been accused of murder and fired.

We Vlodnacheks had kinda had a rough couple of months. But, hey, we land on our feet. I was already getting steady assignments and making enough to keep the bills paid. Provided I didn't develop any expensive habits, like cable TV or eating out.

And Nick's new venture, a bakery he ran from our kitchen, was growing like kudzu. His hours were as bad as mine, but his clients were a lot quicker with the paychecks.

"Two keys: yours and mine," I answered. "You didn't happen to hand any out, did you? Mom? Annie? Brandon the Burnout? That cute girl at the Yogurt Hut?"

"No way. This is my sanctum sanctorum. My Fortress of Solitude. My . . ."

"Got it, no extra keys," I said. With any luck, his ex–business partner, Brandon, was at least 2,000 miles away. And after what happened with Gabby, his ex-fiancée, Nick was still nursing a broken heart. Despite the best efforts of a large chunk of suburban D.C.'s female population.

"What about Trip?" he asked, meaning my best friend and former news editor, Chase Wentworth Cabot III. "Trip" to his friends.

"Uh, no. And besides, Trip doesn't go around playing stork and dropping off babies in the middle of the night."

"Are you sure? 'Cause what I'm seeing would indicate otherwise."

"Trust me, you couldn't get him to deliver a newspaper at this hour, much less a baby."

"So where'd it come from?" Nick asked.

"Didn't Mom and Dad have that talk with you?"

"OK, we know where it came *from*. But how did it end up here?"

"He," I corrected. "He's wearing blue. That means he's a boy."

"You want to test that hypothesis?" Nick challenged.

"Not really," I admitted. "I'd rather figure out why he's here. And how he got in."

We'd had a break-in four weeks ago. My ex-boss. Head of the PR firm that wooed me away from a twelve-year stint at the newspaper, then fired me after three months. And tried to frame me for murder. Long story. But after the dust settled, I'd beefed up security and had the old doors, door frames, and deadbolts professionally replaced with top-of-the-line gear. It was exorbitantly expensive. And the insurance company only paid part of the bill. But I slept great.

When I had the time.

"Man, you are the only person I know so tapped out that crooks are now breaking in to leave stuff," Nick said.

"Should we call the cops?" I asked.

"I don't think he's got a record. Plus, I'm pretty sure they don't make handcuffs that small."

"Yeah, but he'd have the world's cutest mug shot," I said, studying the tiny sleeping stranger, who suddenly puckered his mouth and made suckling motions. "Seriously, somebody's got to be missing him."

"Somebody actually thought he'd be better off here," Nick countered.

That stopped us both cold.

"So we should find out who he is and what's going on, before we return him," I said, thinking out loud.

"And in the meantime, we—and whoever left him here—will know he's safe," Nick said.

"If we don't get arrested for kidnapping. Why do I think that's the same thing you said when you guys found Lucy?"

Hearing her name, Lucy looked up expectantly. Nick grabbed a bone-shaped treat out of the big mason jar on the counter and offered it to her. She dropped to the floor and held it delicately between her two front paws, crunching contentedly.

"She'd been abandoned, " he said softly, wiping his hand on his pajama bottoms. "She was foraging out of trash cans in an alley. This little guy was left warm and dry in a safe place."

"A locked kitchen that smells like cookies?"

"Works for me," he said, grabbing two Toll House cookies from a nearby rack and tossing one at me.

"He must be loved," I said between bites. "Not only did they beat out those deadbolts to get him in here, but that car seat looks expensive. And he's got that rosy, healthy, chubby-baby thing going."

"So if his family left him here, we're not kidnapping him," Nick reasoned. "We're just babysitting."

"Some babysitter I am. I'm eating cookies for breakfast."

Connect with Us

Visit us online at
KensingtonBooks.com
to read more from your favorite authors, see books
by series, view reading group guides, and more.

Join us on social media

for sneak peeks, chances to win books and prize packs,
and to share your thoughts with other readers.

facebook.com/kensingtonpublishing
twitter.com/kensingtonbooks

Tell us what you think!

To share your thoughts, submit a review,
or sign up for our eNewsletters, please visit:
KensingtonBooks.com/TellUs.